Robert Ludlum, a

War, was born in

Hills, New Jersey and educated in Connecticut.

A former actor and theatrical producer, at forty he decided to change careers and try his hand at writing. The rest is history – a reputation for immediate bestsellers, publication in 28 countries and 32 languages, and sales of 195 million copies worldwide.

Robert Ludlum lives in Florida with his wife Mary, a former actress and his first critic. They have three children.

BY THE SAME AUTHOR

The Scarlatti Inheritance
The Osterman Weekend
The Matlock Paper
The Rhinemann Exchange
The Gemini Contenders
The Chancellor Manuscript
The Holcroft Covenant
The Bourne Identity
The Matarese Circle
The Parsifal Mosaic
The Aquitaine Progression
The Bourne Supremacy
The Icarus Agenda
Trevayne
The Bourne Ultimatum
The Road to Omaha
The Scorpio Illusion
The Apocalypse Watch

ROBERT LUDLUM

THE ROAD TO GANDOLFO

THE OSTERMAN WEEKEND

HarperCollins*Publishers*

This omnibus edition published in 1999 by
HarperCollins*Publishers*
77-85 Fulham Palace Road,
Hammersmith, London W6 8JB

ISBN 0 261 67220 7

Printed and bound in Great Britain by
Caledonian International Book Manufacturing Ltd, Glasgow

For John Patrick

A distinguished writer, an honoured man, a good friend. Whose idea this was.
With affection

A large part of this story took
place a while back. And quite a bit of
it tomorrow.
Such is the poetic licence of
Liturgical Drama.

A WORD FROM THE AUTHOR

The Road to Gandolfo is one of those rare if insane accidents that can happen to a writer perhaps once or twice in his lifetime. Through divine or demonic providence a concept is presented that fuels the fires of his imagination. He is convinced it is truly a *staggering* premise which will serve as the spine of a truly *staggering* tale. Visions of one powerful scene after another parade across his inner screen, each exploding with drama and meaning and . . . well, damn it, they're just plain *staggering!*

Out come reams of paper. The typewriter is dusted and pencils are sharpened; doors are closed and heady music is played to drown out the sounds of man and nature beyond the cell of staggering creation. Fury takes over. The premise which will be the spinal thunderbolt of an incredible tale begins to take on substance as characters emerge with faces and bodies, personalities and conflicts. The plot surges forward, complex gears mesh and strip and make a hell of a lot of noise – drowning out the work of true masters like that Mozart fellow and what's-his-name Handel.

But suddenly something is wrong. I mean *wrong!*

The author is giggling. He can't *stop* giggling.

That's horrible! Staggering premises should be accorded awed respect . . . heaven knows not chuckles!

But try as he may the poor fool telling the tale is trapped, bombarded by a fugue of voices all repeating an old *ars antigua* phrase: *You've-got-to-be-kidding*.

Poor fool looks to his muses. Why are they winking? Is that *The Messiah* he's hearing or is it *Mairzy-Dotes*? What happened to the staggering thunderbolt? Why is it spiraling out of whack in a clear blue sky, hiccuping its way to a diminished . . .*giggle?*

Poor fool is bewildered; he gives up. Or rather, he gives in because by now he's having a lot of fun. After all, it *was* the time of Watergate, and nobody could invent *that* scenario! I mean it simply wouldn't play in Peoria. At that point-in-time, that is.

So poor fool plunges along, enjoying himself immensely, vaguely wondering who will sign the commitment papers, figuring his wife will stop them because the oaf does the dishes now and then and makes a damn good martini.

The *oeuvre* is finally presented and, most gratefully for poor fool, the closeted sound of laughter is heard. Followed by screams of revolt and threats of beyond-salvage termination with extreme-prejudice.

'Not under *your* name!'

Time mandates change, and change is cleansing.

Now it's under my name, and I hope you enjoy it. I *did* have a lot of fun.

Robert Ludlum

Connecticut Shore, 1982

PART ONE

Behind each corporation must be the singular force, or motive, that sets it apart from any other corporate structure and gives it its particular identity.

Shepherd's Laws of Economics:
Book XXXII, Chapter 12

PROLOGUE

The crowds gathered in St Peter's Square. Thousands upon thousands of the faithful waited in hushed anticipation for the pontiff to emerge on the balcony and raise his hands in benediction. The fasting and the prayers were over; the Feast of San Gennaro would be ushered in with the pealing of the twilight Angelus echoing throughout the Vatican. And the bells would be heard throughout all Rome, heralding merriment and good feeling. The blessing of Pope Francesco the First would be the signal to begin.

There would be dancing in the streets, and torches and candlelight and music and wine. In the Piazza Navonna, the Trevi, even sections of the Palatine, long tables were heaped with pasta and fruit and all manner of home-produced pastries. For had not this pontiff, the beloved Francesco, given the lesson? Open your hearts and your cupboards to your neighbour. And his to you. Let all men high and low understand that we are one family. In these times of hardship and chaos and high prices, what better way to overcome but to enter into the spirit of the Lord and truly show love for thy neighbour?

For a few days let rancours subside and divisions be healed. Let the word go forth that all men are brothers, all women sisters; and all together brothers and sisters and very much each other's keepers. For but a few days let charity and grace and concern rule the hearts of everyone, sharing the sweet and the sad, for there is no evil that can withstand the force of good.

Embrace, raise the wine; show laughter and tears and accept one another in expressions of love. Let the world see there is no shame in the exultation of the spirit. And once having touched, having heard the voices of brother and sister, carry forth the sweet memories beyond the Feast of San Gennaro, and let life be guided by the principles of Christian benevolence. The earth can be a better place; it is up to the living to make it so. That was the lesson of Francesco I.

A hush fell over the tens of thousands in St Peter's Square. Any second now the figure of the beloved *Papa* would walk with strength and dignity and great love on to the balcony and raise his hands in benediction. And for the Angelus to begin.

Within the high-ceilinged Vatican chambers above the square, cardinals, monsignors, and priests talked among themselves in groups, their eyes continuously straying to the figure of the pontiff seated in the corner. The room was resplendent with vivid colours: scarlets, purples, immaculate whites. Robes and cassocks and head pieces – symbols of the highest offices in the Church – swayed and were turned, giving the illusion of a constantly moving fresco.

And in the corner, seated in a wing chair of ivory and blue velvet, was the Vicar of Christ, Pope Francesco I. He was a plain man of wide girth, and the strong yet gentle features of a *campagnuolo*, a man of the earth. Standing beside him was his personal secretary, a young Black priest from America, from the archdiocese of New York. It was like Francesco to have such a papal aide.

The two were talking quietly, the pontiff turning his enormous head, his huge, soft brown eyes looking up at the young priest in serene composure.

'*Mannaggi'!*' whispered Francesco, his large peasant hand covering his lips. 'This is crazy! The entire city will be drunk for a week! Everyone will be making love in the streets. Are you sure we have it right?'

'I double-checked. Do you want to argue with him?' replied the Black, bending down in tranquil solicitousness.

'My God, no! He was always the smartest one in the villages!'

A cardinal approached the pontiff's chair and leaned

forward. 'Holy Father, it is time. The multitudes await you,' he said softly.

'Who —? Yes, of course. In a minute, my good friend.'

The cardinal smiled under his enormous hat; his eyes were filled with adoration. Francesco always called him his good friend. 'Thank you, your Holiness.' The cardinal backed away.

The Vicar of Christ began humming. Then words emerged. *'Che gelida ... manina ... a rigido esanime ... ah, la, la-laa – tra-la la, la-laaa ...'*

'What are you *doing*?' The young papal aide from the archdiocese of New York, Harlem district, was visibly upset.

'Rodolfo's aria. Ah, that Puccini! It helps me to sing when I am nervous.'

'Well, cut it out, man! Or pick a Gregorian chant. At least a litany.'

'I don't know any. Your Italian's getting better, but it's still not so good.'

'I'm trying, brother. You're not the easiest to learn with. Come on, now. Let's go. Out to the balcony.'

'Don't push! I go. Let's see, I raise the hand, then up and down and right to left —'

'Left to right!' whispered the priest harshly. 'Don't you listen? If we're going on with this honkey charade, for God's sake learn the fundamentals!'

'I thought if I was standing, giving – not taking – I should reverse it.'

'Don't mess. Just do what's natural.'

'Then I sing.'

'Not that natural! Come on.'

'All right, all *right*.' The pontiff rose from his chair and smiled benignly at all in the room. He turned once again to his aide and spoke softly so that none could hear. 'In case anyone should ask, which one is San Gennaro?'

'Nobody will ask. If someone does, use your standard reply.'

'Ah, yes. "Study the scriptures, my son." You know, this is all crazy!'

'Walk slowly and stand up straight. And smile, for God's sake! You're *happy*.'

'I'm *miserable*, you African!'

Pope Francesco I, Vicar of Christ, walked through the enormous doors out on to the balcony to be greeted by a thunderous roar that shook the very foundations of St Peter's. Thousands upon thousands of the faithful raised their voices in the exultation of the spirit.

'Il Papa! Il Papa! Il Papa!'

And as the Holy Father walked out into the myriad reflections of the orange sun setting in the west, there were many in the chambers who heard the muted strains of the chant emerging from the holy lips. Each believed it had to be some obscure early musical work, unknown to all but the most scholarly. For such was the knowledge of the *erudito*, Pope Francesco.

'Che ... gelida ... manina ... a rigido esanimeee ... ah, la, la-laaa ... tra-la, la, la ... la-la-laaa ...'

CHAPTER ONE

'That son of a bitch!' Brigadier General Arnold Symington brought the paperweight down on the thick layer of glass on his Pentagon desk. The glass shattered; fragments shot through the air in all directions. *'He couldn't!'*

'He did, sir,' replied the frightened lieutenant, shielding his eyes from the office shrapnel. 'The Chinese are very upset. The premier himself dictated the complaint to the diplomatic mission. They're running editorials in the *Red Star* and broadcasting them over Radio Peking.'

'How the hell *can* they?' Symington removed a piece of glass from his little finger. 'What the hell are they saying? "We interrupt this programme to announce that the American military representative, General MacKenzie Hawkins, *shot the balls* off a ten-foot jade statue in Son Tai Square"? - Bullshit! Peking wouldn't allow that; it's too goddamned undignified.'

'They're phrasing it a bit differently, sir. They say he destroyed an historic monument of precious stone in the Forbidden City. They say it's as though someone blew up the Lincoln Memorial.'

'It's a different kind of statue! Lincoln's got clothes on; his balls don't show! It's not the same!'

'Nevertheless, the White House thinks the parallel is justified, sir. The President wants Hawkins removed. More than removed, actually; he wants him cashiered. Court-martial and all. Publicly.'

'Oh, for Christ's sake, that's out of the question.' Symington leaned back in his chair and breathed deeply, trying to control himself. He reached out for the report on his desk. 'We'll transfer him. With a reprimand. We'll send transcripts of the - censure, we'll call it a censure - to Peking.'

'That's not strong enough, sir. The State Department made it clear. The President concurs. We have trade agreements pending —'

'For Christ's sake, Lieutenant!' interrupted the brigadier. 'Will someone tell that spinning top in the Oval Office that he can't have it on all points of the compass! Mac Hawkins was *selected*. From twenty-seven candidates. I remember exactly what the President said. Exactly. "That mother's *perfect*!" That's what he said.'

'That's inoperative now, sir. He feels the trade agreements take precedence over prior considerations.' The lieutenant was beginning to perspire.

'You bastards kill me,' said Symington, lowering his voice ominously. 'You really frost my apricots. How do you figure to do that? Make it "inoperative", I mean. Hawkins may be a sharp pain in your diplomatic ass right now, but that doesn't wash away what *was operative*. He was a fucking teenage hero at the Battle of the Bulge *and* West Point football; *and* if they gave medals for what he did in Southeast Asia, even Mac Hawkins isn't strong enough to wear all that hardware! He makes John Wayne look like a pansy! He's *real*; that's why that Oval Yo-yo picked him!'

'I really think the office of the presidency - regardless of what he may think of the man - as commander in chief he —'

'*Horse-shit!*' The brigadier general roared again, separating the words in equal emphasis, giving the crudity of his oath the sound of a military cadence. 'I'm simply explaining to you - in the strongest terms I know - that you don't publicly court-martial a MacKenzie Hawkins to satisfy a Peking complaint, no matter how many goddamned trade agreements are floating around. Do you know *why*, Lieutenant?'

The young officer replied softly, sure of his accuracy. 'Because he would make an issue of it. Publicly.'

'*Bing-go.*' Symington's comment sprang out in a high-pitched monotone. 'The Hawkinses of this country have a constituency, Lieutenant. That's precisely *why* our commander in chief picked him! He's a political palliative. And if you don't think Mac Hawkins knows it, well – you didn't have to recruit him. I did.'

'We are prepared for that reaction, General.' The lieutenant's words were barely audible.

The brigadier leaned forward, careful not to put his elbows in the shattered glass. 'I didn't get that.'

'The State Department anticipated a hard-line counterthrust. Therefore we must institute an aggressive counterreaction *to* that thrust. The White House regrets the necessity but at this point in time recognizes the crisis quotient.'

'That's what I thought I was going to get.' Symington's words were less audible than the lieutenant's. 'Spell it out. How are you going to ream him?'

The lieutenant hesitated. 'Forgive me, sir, but the object is not to – ream General Hawkins. We are in a provocatively delicate position. The People's Republic demands satisfaction. Rightly so; it was a crude, vulgar act on General Hawkins's part. Yet he refuses to make a public apology.'

Symington looked at the report still in his right hand. 'Does it say why in here?'

'General Hawkins claims it was a trap. His statement's on page three.'

The brigadier flipped to the page and read. The lieutenant drew out a handkerchief and blotted his chin. Symington put down the report carefully on the shattered glass and looked up.

'If what Mac says is true, it *was* a trap. Broadcast *his* side of the story.'

'He has no side, General. He was drunk.'

'Mac says *drugged*. Not drunk, Lieutenant.'

'They were drinking, sir.'

'And he was drugged. I'd guess Hawkins would know the difference. I've seen him sweat sour mash.'

'He does not deny the charge, however.'

'He denies the responsibility of his actions. Hawkins was the finest intelligence strategist in Indochina. He's drugged couriers and pouch men in Cambodia, Laos, both Vietnams, and probably across the Manchurian borders. He knows the goddamned difference.'

'I'm afraid his knowing it doesn't *make* any difference, sir. The crisis quotient demands our acceding to Peking's wishes. The trade agreements are paramount. Frankly, sir, we need gas.'

'Jesus! I figured that was one thing you *had*.'

The lieutenant replaced the handkerchief in his pocket and smiled wanly. 'The levity is called for, I realize that. However, we have just ten days to bring everything into focus; to make our inputs and come up with a positive print.'

Symington stared at the young officer; his expression that of a grown man about to cry. 'What does that mean?'

'It's a harsh thing to say, but General Hawkins has placed his own interests above those of his duty. We'll have to make an example. For everybody's sake.'

'An example? For wanting the truth out?'

'There's a higher duty, General.'

'I know,' said the brigadier wearily. 'To the – trade agreements. To the gas.'

'Quite frankly, yes. There are times when symbols have to be traded off for pragmatic objectives. Team players understand.'

'All right. But Mac won't lie down and play busted symbol for you. So what's the – *input*?'

'The inspector general,' said the lieutenant, as an obnoxious student might, holding up a severed tapeworm in Biology I. 'We're running an in-depth data trace on him. We know he was involved in questionable activities in Indochina. We have reason to believe he violated international codes of conduct.'

'You bet your ass he did! He was one of the best!'

'There's no statute on those codes. The IG specialists have caseloads going back much further than General Hawkins's *ex-officio* activities.' The lieutenant smiled. It was a genuine smile; he was a happy person.

'So you're going to hang him with clandestine operations that half the joint chiefs and most of the CIA know would bring him a truckload of citations – if they could talk about them. You bastards kill me.' Symington nodded his head, agreeing with himself.

'Perhaps you could save us time, General. Can you provide us with some specifics?'

'Oh, no! You want to crucify the son of a bitch, you build your own cross!'

'You do understand the situation, don't you, sir?'

The brigadier moved his chair back and kicked fragments of glass from under his feet. 'I'll tell you something,' he said. 'I haven't understood anything since nineteen forty-five.' He glared at the young officer. 'I know you're with Sixteen-hundred, but are you regular army?'

'No, sir. Reserve status, temporary assignment. I'm on a leave of absence from Y, J, and B. To put out fires before they burn up the flagpoles, as it were.'

'Y, J, and B. I don't know that division.'

'Not a division, sir. Youngblood, Jakel, and Blowe, Los Angeles. We're the top ad agency on the Coast.'

General Arnold Symington's face slowly took on the expression of a distressed basset hound. 'The uniform looks real nice, Lieutenant.' The brigadier paused, then shook his head. 'Nineteen forty-five,' he said.

Major Sam Devereaux, field investigator for the Office of the Inspector General, looked across the room at the calendar on his wall. He got up from the chair behind his desk, walked over to it, and Xed the day's date. One month and three days and he would be a civilian again.

Not that he was ever a soldier. Not really; certainly not spiritually. He was a military accident. A fracture compounded by a huge mistake that resulted in an extension of his tour of service. It had been a simple choice of alternatives: Re-enlistment or Leavenworth.

Sam was a lawyer, a damn fine attorney specializing in criminal law. Years ago he had held a series of Selective Service deferments. Through Harvard College and Harvard Law School; then two years of postgraduate specialization and clerking; finally into the fourteenth month of practice with the prestigious Boston law firm of Aaron Pinkus Associates.

The army had faded into a vaguely disagreeable shadow across his life; he had forgotten about the long series of deferments.

The United States Army, however, did not forget.

During one of those logistic crunches that episodically grip the military, the Pentagon discovered it had a sudden dearth of lawyers. The Department of Military Justice was in a bind - hundreds of courts-martial on bases all over the globe were suspended for lack of judge advocates and defence attorneys. The stockades were crowded. So the Pentagon scoured the long-forgotten series of deferments and scores of young unattached, childless lawyers - obtainable meat - were sent unrefusable invitations in which was explained the meaning of the word 'deferment' as opposed to the word 'annulment'.

That was the accident. Devereaux's mistake came later. Much later. Seven thousand miles away on the converging borders of Laos, Burma, and Thailand.

The Golden Triangle.

Devereaux - for reasons known only to God and military logistics - never saw a court-martial, much less tried one. He was assigned to the Legal Investigations Division of the Office of the Investigator General and sent to Saigon to see what laws were being violated.

There were so many, there was no way to count. And since drugs took precedence over the black market - there were simply too many American entrepreneurs in the latter - his inquiries took him to the Golden Triangle where one-fifth of the world's narcotics were being funnelled out, courtesy of powerful men in Saigon, Washington, Vientiane, and Hong Kong.

Sam was conscientious. He didn't like drug peddlers and he threw the investigatory books at them, careful to make sure his briefs to Saigon were transmitted operationally within the confused chain of command.

No report signatures. Just names and violations. After all, he could get shot or knifed – at least, ostracized for such behaviour. It was an education in covert activities.

His trophies included seven ARVN generals, thirty-one representatives in Thieu's congress, twelve US Army colonels – light and full – three brigadiers, and fifty-eight assorted majors, captains, lieutenants, and master sergeants. Added to these were five congressmen, four senators, a member of the President's cabinet, eleven corporation executives with American companies overseas – six of which already had enough trouble in the area of campaign contributions – and a square-jawed Baptist minister with a large national following.

To the best of Sam's knowledge, one second lieutenant and two master sergeants were indicted. The rest were – 'pending'.

So Sam Devereaux committed his mistake. He was so incensed that the wheels of South-east Asian justice spun off the tracks at the first hint of influence that he decided to trap a very big fish in the corruption net and make an example. He chose a major general in Bangkok. A man named Heseltine Brokemichael. Major General Heseltine Brokemichael, West Point '43.

Sam had the evidence, mounds of it. Through a series of elaborate entrapments in which he himself acted as the 'connection', a participant who could swear under oath to the general's malfeasance, he built his case thoroughly. There could not possibly be two General Brokemichaels, and Sam was an avenging angel of a prosecutor, circling in for his kill.

But there were. Two. Two major generals named Brokemichael – one Heseltine, one Ethelred! Apparently cousins. And the one in Bangkok – Heseltine – was not the one in Vientiane – Ethelred. The Vientiane Brokemichael was the felon. Not his cousin. Further, the Brokemichael in Bangkok was more an avenger than Sam. He believed *he* was gathering evidence on a corrupt IG investigator. And he was. Devereaux had violated most of the international contraband laws and *all* of the United States government's.

Sam was arrested by the MPs, thrown into a maximum security cell, and told he could look forward to the better part of his lifetime in Leavenworth.

Fortunately, a superior officer in the inspector general's command, who did not really understand a sense of justice that made Sam commit so many crimes, but did understand Sam's legal and investigatory contributions to the cause of the inspector general, came to Sam's aid. Devereaux had actually filed more evidentiary material than any other legal officer in South-east Asia; his work in the field made up for a great deal of inactivity in Washington.

So the superior officer allowed a little unofficial plea bargaining in Sam's case. If Sam would accept disciplinary action at the hands of a furious Major General Heseltine Brokemichael in Bangkok, constituting a six-month loss of pay – no criminal charges would be brought. There was just one more condition: to continue his work for the inspector general's office for an additional two years beyond the expiration of his army commitment. By that time, reasoned the superior officer, the mess in Indochina would be turned over to those messing, and the IG caseloads reduced or conveniently buried.

Re-enlistment or Leavenworth.

So Major Sam Devereaux, patriotic citizen-soldier, extended his tour of duty. And the mess in Indochina was in no way lessened, but indeed turned over to the participants, and Devereaux was transferred back to Washington, D.C.

One month and three days to go, he mused, as he looked out his office window and watched the MPs at the guardhouse check the automobiles driving out. It was after five; he had to catch a plane at Dulles in two hours. He had packed that morning and brought his suitcase to the office.

The four years were coming to an end. Two plus two. The

time spent, he reflected, might be resented, but it had not been wasted. The abyss of corruption that was South-east Asia reached into the hierarchical corridors of Washington. The inhabitants of these corridors knew who he was; he had more offers from prestigious law firms than he could reply to, much less consider. And he did not want to consider them; he disapproved of them. Just as he disapproved of the current investigation on his desk.

The manipulators were at it again. This time it was the thorough discrediting of a career officer named Hawkins. Lieutenant General MacKenzie Hawkins.

At first Sam had been stunned. MacKenzie Hawkins was an original. A legend. The stuff of which cults were born. Cults slightly to the political right of Attila the Hun.

Hawkins's place in the military firmament was secure. Bantam Books published his biography – serialization and *Reader's Digest* rights had been sold before a word was on paper. Hollywood gave obscene amounts of money to film his life story. And the anti-militarists made him an object of fascist-hatred.

The biography was not overly successful because the subject was not overly cooperative. Apparently there were certain personal idiosyncrasies that did not enhance the image, four wives paramount among them. The motion picture was less than triumphant insofar as it comprised endless battle scenes with little or no hint of the man other than an actor squinting through the battle dust, yelling to his men in a peculiar lisp to 'get those Godless ... [Roar of cannon] ... who would tear down Old Glory! At 'em, boys!'

Hollywood, too, had discovered the four wives and certain other peculiarities of the studio's on-the-set technical adviser. MacKenzie Hawkins went through starlets three at a time and had intercourse with the producer's wife in the producer's swimming pool while the producer watched in fury from the living room window.

He did not stop the picture, however. For Christ's sake, it was costing damn near *six mill*!

These misfired endeavours might have caused another

man to fade, if only from embarrassment, but not so Mac Hawkins. In private, among his peers, he ridiculed those responsible and regaled his associates with stories of Manhattan and Hollywood.

He was sent to the war college with a new specialization: intelligence, clandestine operations. His peers felt a little more secure with the charismatic Hawkins consigned to covert activities. And the colonel became a brigadier and absorbed all there was to learn of his new speciality. He spent two years grinding away, studying every phase of intelligence work until the instructors had no more to instruct him.

So he was sent to Saigon where the escalating hostilities had blossomed into a full-scale war. And in Vietnam – both Vietnams, and Laos, and Cambodia, and Thailand, and Burma – Hawkins corrupted the corruptors and the ideologues alike. Reports of his behind-the-lines and across-the-neutral-borders activities made 'protective reaction' seem like a logical strategy. So unorthodox, so blatantly criminal were his methods of operation that G-2, Saigon, found itself denying his existence. After all, there were limits. Even for clandestine activities.

If *America First* was a maxim – and it was – Hawkins saw no reason why it should not apply to the filthy world of covert operations.

And for Hawkins, America *was* first. Ir-re-fucking-gardless!

So Sam Devereaux thought it was all a little sad that such a man was about to be knocked out of the box by the manipulators who got to where they were by draping the flag so gloriously and generously around themselves. Hawkins was now an offending lion in the diplomatic arena and had to be eliminated in the cause of double-think. The men who should have been upholding the general's point of honour were doing their best to sink him fast – in ten days, to be precise.

Normally Sam would have taken pleasure out of building a case against a messianic ass like Hawkins; and regardless of his feelings to the contrary, he would build a case against him. It was his last file for the inspector general's office, and he was not going to risk another two-year alternative. But he was still sad. The Hawk, as he was known – misguided fanatic as he might be – deserved better than what he was getting.

Perhaps, thought Sam, his depression was brought about by the last 'operative' instruction from the White House: find something in the morals area Hawkins can't deny. Check to see if he was ever in the care of a psychiatrist.

A psychiatrist! Jesus! They *never* learned.

In the meantime, Sam had dispatched a team of IG investigators to Saigon to see if they could dig up a few negative specifics. And he was off to Dulles airport to catch a plane to Los Angeles.

All of Hawkins's ex-wives lived within a radius of thirty miles of each other, from Malibu to Beverly Hills. They'd be better than any psychiatrist. Christ! A psychiatrist!

At 1600 Pennsylvania Avenue, Washington, D.C. they were all novacained above the shoulders.

CHAPTER TWO

'My name is Lin Shoo,' said the uniformed Communist softly, slant-eyeing the large, dishevelled American soldier who sat in a leather chair, holding a glass of whisky in one hand and a well-chewed cigar in the other. 'I am commander of the People's Police, Peking. And you are under house arrest at this moment. There is no point in being abusive, these are merely formalities.'

'Formalities for what?' MacKenzie Hawkins shouted from his armchair – the only occidental piece of furniture in the oriental house. He put his heavy boot on a black lacquered table and flung his hand over the leather back, the lighted cigar dangerously close to a silk screen room divider. 'There aren't any goddamned formalities except through the diplomatic mission. Go down there and make your complaints. You'll probably have to get in line.'

Hawkins chuckled and drank from his glass.

'You have chosen to reside outside the mission,' continued the Chinese named Lin Shoo, his eyes darting between the cigar and the screen. 'Therefore you are not technically within United States territory. So you are subject to the disciplines of the People's Police. However, we know you will not go anywhere, General. That is why I say it is a formality.'

'What have you got out there?' Hawkins waved his cigar towards the thin, rectangular windows.

'There are two patrols on each side of your residence. Eight in all.'

'That's a big fucking guard detail for someone who's not going anywhere.'

'Small liberties. Photographically, two is more desirable

than one and three is menacing.'

'You taking liberties?' Hawkins drew on his cigar and again rested his hand over the back of the leather chair. The lighted butt was no more than an inch from the silk.

'The Ministry of Education has done so, yes. You will admit, General, your place of isolation is most pleasant, is it not? This is a lovely house on a lovely hill. So very peaceful, and with a fine view.' Lin Shoo walked around the chair and unobtrusively moved the panel of the silk screen away from Hawkins's cigar. It was too late; the heat of the butt had caused a small circular burn in the fabric.

'It's a high-rent district,' replied Hawkins. 'Somebody in this people's paradise, where nobody owns anything but everyone owns everything, is making a fast buck. Four hundred of 'em every month.'

'You were fortunate to find it. Property can be purchased by collectives. A collective is not private ownership.' The police officer walked to the narrow opening that led to the single sleeping room of the house. It was dark; where sunlight should have been streaming through the wide window there was a blanket nailed across the frame into the thin surrounding wall. On the floor a number of mats had been piled one on top of another; wrappings from American candy bars were scattered about and there was a distinct odour of whisky.

'Why the photographs?'

The Chinese turned from the unpleasant sight. 'To show the world that we are treating you better than you treated us. This house is not a tiger cage in Saigon, nor is it a dungeon in the shark-infested waters of Holcotaz.'

'Alcatraz. The Indians got it.'

'I beg your pardon?'

'Nothing. You're making a big splash with this thing, aren't you?'

Lin Shoo was silent for a moment; it was the pause before profundity. 'Should someone – who has for years publicly denounced the deeply felt objectives of your beloved motherland – dynamite your Lin-Kolon Memorial inside your Washington Square within your state of Columbia, the robed barbarians on your Court of Supreme Justice would, no doubt, have executed him by now.' The Chinese smiled and smoothed the tunic of his Mao uniform. 'We do not behave in such primitive ways. All life is precious. Even a diseased dog, such as you.'

'And you gooks never denounced anybody, is that it?'

'Our leaders reveal only truth. That is common knowledge throughout the world; the lessons of the infallible chairman. Truth is not denunciation, General. It is merely truth. All knowing.'

'Like my state of Columbia,' muttered Hawkins, removing his foot from the lacquered table. 'Why the hell did you pick me out? A lot of people have done a lot of goddamned denouncing. Why am I so special?'

'Because they are not so famous. Or infamous, if you will—. Although I did enjoy the film of your life. Very artistic; a poem of violence.'

'You saw that, huh?'

'Privately. Certain portions were extracted. Those showing the actor portraying you murdering our heroic youth. Very savage, General.' The Communist circled the black lacquered table and smiled again. 'Yes, you are an infamous man. And now you have insulted us by destroying a revered monument —'

'Come off it. I don't even know what happened. I was drugged and you goddamned well know it. I was with your General Lu Sin. With *his* broads, in *his* house.'

'You must give us our honour back again, General Hawkins. Can't you see that?' Lin Shoo spoke quietly, as though Hawkins had not interrupted. 'It would be a simple matter for you to render an apology. A ceremony has been planned. With a small contingent of the press in attendance. We have written out the words for you.'

'Oh, boy!' Hawkins sprang out of the chair, towering over the policeman. 'We're back to that again! How many times do I have to tell you bastards? *Americans don't crawl!* In any goddamned ceremony, with or without the goddamned

press! Read that straight, you puke-skinned dwarf!'

'Do not upset yourself. You place far too much emphasis on a mere ceremonial function; you place everyone - *all of us* - in most difficult positions. A small ceremony; so little, so simple —'

'Not to me it isn't! I represent the armed forces of the United States and nothing's little or simple to us! We don't trip easy, buddy boy; we march straight to the drums!'

'I beg your pardon?'

Hawkins shrugged, a touch bewildered by his own words. 'Never mind. The answer's no. You may scare the lace-pants boys down at the mission, but you don't shake me.'

'*They* appealed to you because they were instructed to do so. Certainly that must have occurred to you.'

'Double bullshit!' Hawkins walked around to the fireplace, drank from his glass and placed it on the mantel next to a brightly coloured box. 'Those fags were cooking up something with that group of queens at State. Wait'll the White House - wait'll the *Pentagon* reads *my* report. Oh, boy! You bowlegged runts will hightail it to the mountains and then we'll blow *them* up!' Hawkins grinned, his eyes bright.

'You are so abusive,' said Lin Shoo quietly, shaking his head sadly. He picked up the brightly coloured box next to the general's glass. 'Tsing Taow firecrackers. The finest made in the world. So loud, so bright with white light when they go *bang*, *bang*, *bang*. Very lovely to watch and to hear.'

'Yeah,' agreed Hawkins, slightly confused by the change of subject. 'Lu Sin gave 'em to me. We shot off a motherload the other night. Before the fucker drugged me.'

'Very beautiful, General Hawkins. They are a fine gift.'

'Christ knows he owed me *something*.'

'But do you not see?' continued the police officer. 'They sound like - explosives. Look like - detonating ammunition, but they are neither. They are only show. Semblances of something else. Real in themselves but only an *illusion* of *another* reality. Not dangerous at all.'

'So?'

'That is precisely what you are being asked to give. The semblance, not the reality. You have only to *pretend.* In a short, simple ceremony with but a few words that *you* know are only an illusion. Not dangerous at all. And very polite.'

'Wrong-o!' roared Hawkins. 'Everybody knows what a firecracker is; *nobody'll* know I'm pretending.'

'Between the two of us, I must differ. It is nothing more than diplomatic ritual. Everyone will understand, take my word for it.'

'Yeah? How the hell do you know that? You're a Peking cop, not a Kissing-ass.'

The Communist fingered the box of firecrackers and sighed audibly. 'I apologize for the minor deception, General. I am not with the People's Police. I am second vice-prefect for the Ministry of Education. I am here to make an appeal to you. An appeal to your reason. However, the rest is quite true. You *are* under house arrest, and the patrols outside *are* policemen.'

'I'll be goddamned! They sent me a lace-pants.' Hawkins grinned again. 'You boys are worried, real worried, aren't you?'

The Communist sighed once more. 'Yes. The idiots who started this thing have been shipped to mining collectives in Outer Mongolia. It was lunacy; although I'll grant them you were a temptation, General Hawkins. Have you any *idea* the volumes of scurrilous attacks you've made on every Marxist, Socialist, and, forgive me, even vaguely democratically oriented nation on the face of this earth? The worst examples I should say *best* examples of demagoguery!'

'A lot of that crap was written by the people who paid me to speak,' said Hawkins, a bit reflectively. And then he quickly added, 'Not that I didn't believe it! Goddamn, I *believe*!'

'You're impossible!' Lin Shoo stamped his foot as a child might. 'You're as insane as Lu Sin and his band of growling paper lions! May they all crack many rocks and fornicate with Mongolian sheep! You are simply impossible!'

Hawkins stared at the Communist - both at the furious

expression on his face and the brightly coloured box of firecrackers in his hand. He had made a decision and both of them knew it.

'I'm also something else, slant eyes,' said the lieutenant general, approaching Lin Shoo.

'No! *No!* No *violence*, you idiot —' It was too late for the Communist to scream. Hawkins grabbed the cloth of his tunic, pulled him swiftly off his feet and chopped Lin Shoo beneath the mandible.

The vice-prefect of the Ministry of Education slumped instantly into unconsciousness.

Hawkins grabbed the box of firecrackers out of Lin Shoo's hand and raced around the lacquered table into the sleeping quarters. He grabbed the blanket nailed across the window, folded back a tiny section on the edge and looked outside at the rear of the house. There were the two policemen chatting calmly, their rifles at their sides. Beyond them was the sloping hill that led down to the village.

Hawkins released the blanket and ran back into the main room, dropping immediately to his hands and knees and scrambling obstacle-style towards the front door. He stood up and silently opened it a crack. The two flanking policemen were about forty feet away and were as relaxed as the troops in the rear. What's more, they were looking down the descending road, their attention *not* on the house.

MacKenzie took the brightly coloured box of firecrackers from under his arm, ripped off the lightweight paper and shook out the connecting strings of cylinders. He wound two separate strands together, twisted both fuses into one, and removed his World War II Zippo from his pocket.

He stopped; he sucked his breath, angry with himself. Then, holding the strands of firecrackers at his side, he walked casually past the windows into the bedroom and removed his holster and cartridge belt from another nail in the thin wall. He strapped the apparatus around his waist, removed the Colt .45 and checked the magazine. Satisfied, he shoved the weapon into its leather casing as he walked out of the bedroom. He circled the armchair in front of the Han

Shu mantel, stepped over the immobile Lin Shoo, and returned to the front door.

He ignited the Zippo, and held the flame beneath the twisted fuse, then opened the door and threw the entwined strands on to the grass beyond the porch.

Closing and bolting the door softly and swiftly, Hawkins dragged a small red lacquered chest from the foyer and forced it against the thick, carved panel. Then he raced into the sleeping quarters and pulled back a small section of the window blanket and waited.

The explosions were even louder than he remembered; made so, he guessed, from the combined strands bursting against one another.

The guards at the rear of the house were jolted out of their lethargy; their weapons collided in midair as each whipped his off the ground. Rifles in waist-firing position, the two men raced towards the front of the house.

The moment they were out of sight, Hawkins yanked down the blanket, crashed his foot into the thin strips of wood and thinner panes of glass, shattering the entire window. He leaped through on to the grass and started running towards the fields and the sloping hill.

CHAPTER THREE

At the base of the hill was the main dirt road that circled the village. Like spokes from a wheel, numerous offshoots headed directly into the small marketplace, in the centre of the town. A semi-paved thoroughfare branched outward tangentially from the circling road and connected with a paved highway about four miles to the east. The American diplomatic mission was twelve miles down that highway within Peking proper.

What he needed was a vehicle, preferably an automobile, but automobiles were practically non-existent outside the highest official circles. The People's Police had automobiles, of course; it had crossed his mind to double back around the hill to find Lin Shoo's, but that was too risky. Even if he found it and stole it, it would be a marked vehicle.

Hawkins circled the village, keeping to the high ground above the road. They would be coming after him. He could stay in the hills indefinitely; that didn't bother him. He had bivouacked underground in the mountains of Cong-Sol and Lai Tai in Cambodia for months at a time; he could live in the forests better than most animals. Goddamn, he was a *pro*!

But it was also pointless. He had to get to the mission and let the Free World know what kind of enemy it was sucking up to. Enough was enough, goddamn it! They could send out radio messages, barricade the whole complex, and fight it out until the offshore carriers sent in air strikes to pinpoint pulverize, even if it meant blowing up half of Peking. Then the copters could come in and get them out.

Of course, the civilians would shit in their pants, but he would control them. Teach the fancy pants how to fight. *Fight! Not talk!*

MacKenzie stopped his fantasizing. Below to the right, coming around the bend in the road a quarter of a mile away was a lone motorcycle. On it was a *shee-san* police official, a kind of Chinese state trooper. The answer to a prayer!

Hawkins rose from the tall grass and started scrambling down the hill. In less than a minute he was at the edge of the dirt border. The bike was still around the curve out of sight, but he heard it coming closer. He threw himself down in the dirt in the middle of the road, drawing his legs up to appear smaller than he was, and lay perfectly still.

The motorcycle's engine roared as the driver came around the curve, then sputtered as it skidded to a stop. The *shee-san* got off the bike and whipped out the kick-stand. Hawkins could hear and feel the quick footsteps as the trooper approached.

The *shee-san* bent over him and touched his shoulder, recoiling at the recognition of the American uniform. Mac moved. The *shee-san* shrieked.

Five minutes later Hawkins had stretched the *shee-san*'s tunic and pants over his rolled-up trousers and shirt. He slipped the trooper's goggles over his eyes and put on the ludicrously tiny visor hat, using the chin strap to hold it in place, a cloth pimple sitting on the crew-cut, greyish black hair. Fortunately for his sense of well-being, he had a cigar. He chewed the end to its desired juiciness and lighted up.

He was ready to ride.

The diplomatic attaché ran into the director's office without saying a word to the secretary or even knocking at the door. The director was threading his teeth with dental floss.

'Excuse me, sir. I've just received the instructions from Washington! I knew you'd have to read them!'

The director of the diplomatic mission, Peking, reached for the cable and read it. His eyes widened and his mouth opened in astonishment. A long strand of dental floss, caught in his teeth, extended down to the desk.

*

He saw the road-block cutting off his entry on to the Peking highway. It was about three quarters of a mile down the semi-paved thoroughfare; a single *shee-san* patrol car and a line of troopers stretching across the road was all he could distinguish through the fogged-up goggles.

As he drew nearer, he could see that the guards were shouting to each other. One trooper stepped in front of the line and began waving his rifle in the air – hysterically – back and forth, a signal for the approaching rider to stop.

There was only one thing for it, thought Hawkins. If you're going to buy a goddamned grave, buy it *big*! Go out with all weapons on repeat-fire, blazing barrels of thunder and lightning; go out with the screams of the Commie bastards ringing in your ears!

Goddamn! He couldn't see for the fucking dust, and his goddamn *foot* kept slipping off the tiny fucking gas pedal.

He slapped his hand to his holster and pulled out the .45.

He couldn't focus worth shit, but by *Christ*, he could squeeze the trigger! He did so repeatedly.

To his astonishment the *shee-san* did not fire back; instead they dived into the mounds of dirt and sand, screaming like hysterical piglets, scampering into and over the mounds of dirt burying their asses from the fire-power of his single .45 weapon.

Goddamn! *Disgraceful!*

Unless his goggles were playing tricks with the dirt and cigar smoke and the onrushing blurs, even the trooper in front – an officer, by Christ; he had to be – even *he* didn't have the balls to fight back.

An *officer*!

MacKenzie kept the bike at top-throttle and exhausted the clip of the .45. He careened up and over a mound of dirt and sand and cascaded on to a sloping hill of grass. As the bike was in midair he glimpsed the blurs of screaming heads beneath him and wished to hell he had more ammo. He twisted the handlebars violently so he could angle down and zoom diagonally back towards the road.

Goddamn! He hit the surface again! He'd broken through the barricade! He was barrel-assing on to the Peking highway!

The flat concrete was a joy. The spinning wheels of the motorcycle hummed; the wind rushed against his face – clear, intoxicating blasts of clean, dustless air which forced the smoke of his cigar into whirling pockets around his ears. Even the goggles were clear now.

He took the next nine miles like a star-spangled meteor through an unknowing Chincom sky. Another mile and he would turn into the northern side streets of Peking. Goddamn! He was going to make it! And then, by Christ, the Commie bastards would find out what an American counter-strike was!

He raced the bike through the crowded streets and careened off the kerb at the entrance to Glorious Flower Square, the final stretch of the mission which stood at the end of the small plaza, fronting the street in alabaster, Oriental splendour. There were, as usual, crowds of Pekingers and out-of-towners milling about, waiting to catch glimpses of the strange, huge pink people that came and went through the white steel doors inside the medium-sized compound.

It wasn't much of a compound at that; there was no brick wall or high metal fence surrounding the mission. Only a thin latticework of decorative wood, lacquered against the elements, enclosing the clipped grass lawn that fronted the steps.

The protection was in the windows and doors: iron grillework and steel.

MacKenzie revved the bike's engine to maximum, figuring the noise would part the throngs of onlookers.

It did.

The Chinese scattered as he raced down the street.

And Hawkins damn near fell off the bike's saddle at what he saw in front of him; what – in a sense – was rushing towards him at goddamn near fifty miles an hour on that short stretch of pavement in Glorious Flower Square.

There were *three sets of wooden barricades* - elongated horses - in front of the closed latticework gate! Each horizontal plank was a foot or so above the other, forming a receding escalator wall of thick boards backed up by the delicate, filigreed fence.

Standing in a line at port-arms were a dozen or so soldiers, flanked by two officers, all staring straight ahead. At him.

This is it, thought MacKenzie, nothing left but the gesture, the motion - the act itself.

Total defiance!

Goddamn! If he only had some ammo left!

He crouched and headed the bike right into the centre of the barricade; he twisted the bar accelerator to the maximum and pressed the foot choke all the way down.

The speedometer's needle wavered in a violence of its own as it quivered and shot up swiftly towards the end of the dial; man and machine burst through the air corridor like a strange, huge bullet of flesh and steel.

Amid the screams of the hysterical crowds and the scattering of the panicked soldiers, Hawkins yanked the handlebars furiously back and slapped the weight of his body against the rear of the saddle. The front wheel rose off the ground like an abstract, spinning phoenix - followed by a mad extension of tail and rider - and crashed into the upper section of the barricade.

There was a thunderous shattering of wood and latticework as MacKenzie Hawkins shot up, into - and through - the tiers of obstructions, a maniacally effective human cannonball that dragged the rest of the weapon with him.

The bike plummeted down into the path of washed pebbles that led to the steps of the mission. As it did so, MacKenzie was hurled forward, somersaulting over the bars, rolling on the tiny stones until he thudded into the base of the short flight of steps to the white steel door, the cigar still gripped between his teeth.

Any second now the Chincoms would regroup, the fusillade would begin, and the sharp chops of icelike pain would commence, giving him, perhaps, only seconds before oblivion came.

But the firing did not begin. Only louder and louder screaming from the crowds and the soldiers. Oriental heads peered over the mass of wreckage, above the shattered planks, in front of the smashed latticework. Most of the soldiers who had thrown themselves on the ground were now on their hands and knees.

Yet no one fired a weapon. Then MacKenzie understood: he was, technically, within US territory. If he was shot inside the compound it might be construed as an execution on American soil. It could become an international incident. *Goddamn!* He was protected by lacepants fol-de-rol! Diplomatic niceties were keeping him alive!

He scrambled to his feet, ran up the steps to the white steel door and began punching the bell and pounding his hand on the metal panel.

There was no response.

He banged louder and kept his free hand on the bell. He yelled to those inside and after what seemed like minutes, the single rectangular slot in the door was opened.

A pair of wide, frightened eyes peered out.

'For Christ's sake, it's *Hawkins*!' roared MacKenzie, putting his screaming mouth inches in front of the panicked set of eyes. 'Open the goddamned door, you son of a bitch! What the hell are you doing?'

The eyes blinked, but the door did not open.

Hawkins yelled again, and again the eyes blinked. After several seconds the eyes were replaced by trembling lips.

'No one's home, sir,' came the quivering, unbelievable words.

'*What?!*'

'Sorry, General.'

The shaking lips were now replaced by the rapid slamming of metal. The slot was closed.

MacKenzie stood there in temporary shock. Then he started pounding once again and yelling again and punching the bell buttons so hard the Bakelite cracked.

Nothing.

He looked back at the crowds and the soldiers, and became aware of the screams and grins and wave after wave of giggles.

Hawkins jumped down the set of steps and began running across the lawn in front of the building. All the windows were not only shut, but the iron inner shutters had been closed behind the grillework. The whole goddamn mission was sealed tight, an enormous white, rectangular clam.

He raced around the side. It was the same everywhere: closed windows, iron shutters, grillework.

He rounded the back lawn and ran to the large rear entrance. He began pounding the door and yelling louder than he thought he had ever yelled in his life.

Finally the slot opened and another set of eyes appeared – less frightened than those in front but nevertheless wide and disturbed.

'Open this fucking door, goddamn it!'

Once more lips appeared, and now MacKenzie could see the grey moustache. It was the ambassador.

'Get away from here, Hawkins,' said the deep, anglicized voice, cultivated in the Eastern Establishment. 'You're just not operative!'

And the slot was closed.

MacKenzie stood there immobilized. Time and space fused into nothingness. He was vaguely aware that the crowds and the soldiers had moved around the latticework fence at the sides and the rear of the mission.

Without really thinking, he backed away from the entrance and looked up at the outside wall of the building and at the roof.

He could do it, using the grillework of the windows. He jumped to the first window and climbed up the grillework until he reached the next protrusion of crisscrossing bars.

In several minutes he had scaled the side of the building and pulled himself over the edge of the sloping tiled roof.

He trudged up to the apex and looked around.

The flagpole was centred in the grass on the lawn to the left of the gravel path. The gently waving cloth of Old Glory undulated in the breeze in isolated splendour.

Lieutenant General MacKenzie Hawkins tested the wind and then unzipped his fly.

CHAPTER FOUR

Devereaux smiled at the doorman of the Beverly Hills Hotel, then walked around the huge automobile to the driver's side, tipped the parking attendant, and climbed in behind the wheel, the glare of the sunlight bouncing off the hood. It was all so Southern California: doormen, parking attendants, silent tips, oversized cars, and blinding sunlight.

As was the telephone conversation he had held two hours ago with the first Mrs MacKenzie Hawkins.

He had decided to begin logically, piecing together a progressive disintegration of the man. Surely a pattern would emerge; it would be easier to document this contemporary version of the Rake's Progress if he started with the subject's introduction to the really corrupt world: soft silks and money as opposed to mere killing, torture, and West Point arrogance.

Regina Sommerville Hawkins was that introduction. According to the data banks, Regina was Virginia Hunt Country, spoiled-rich out of Foxcroft and Finch. She had set her cotillion bonnet for the trophy called Hawkins in 1947, when the celebrated youthful warrior of the Bulge had further impressed the nation with dazzling feats on the gridiron. Since Daddy Sommerville owned most of Virginia Beach, and Ginny was an authentic Southern belle - money *and* magnolia, not just the fragrance - the match was easily arranged. The heroic up-from-the-ranks West Pointer was met, overwhelmed, and temporarily subdued by the lilting drawl, large breasts, and indigenous conveniences of this soft but persistent daughter of the Confederacy.

Daddy knew a lot of people in Washington, so, combined with Hawkins's own talents and track record, Regina expected to be a general's wife within six months. A year at best.

In Washington. Or Newport News. Or New York. Or perhaps lovely Hawaii. With servants and uniforms and dances and more servants and ...

However, Hawkins was peculiar, and Daddy did not know *that* many people who could curb his odd behaviour. The Hawk did not want the la-de-da life of Washington, Newport News, or New York. He wanted to be with his troops. And there was a congressional on his sheet; requests were not denied lightly. Regina found herself in out-of-the-way army camps where her husband furiously trained disinterested draftees for a war that wasn't. So she decided to shed her trophy. Daddy did know enough people to make that easy. Hawkins was transferred to West Germany and Regina's doctors made it clear she could not take the climate. The distance between them just made it feasible to call the whole thing quietly off.

Now, nearly thirty years later, Regina Sommerville Hawkins Clark Madison Greenberg was living in a suburb of Los Angeles called Tarzana with her fourth husband, Emmanuel Greenberg, motion picture producer. On the phone two hours ago she had said to Sam Devereaux:

'Listen, lover, you want to talk about Mac? I'll get the girls together. We usually meet on Thursdays, but what the hell is a day?'

So Sam wrote down the directions to Tarzana and was now on his way in a rented car to Regina's manse. The car radio played *Muddied Waters*, which seemed appropriate.

He found the driveway of the Greenberg residence and entered it, ascending, he was sure, the final crest of the hills. Halfway into the property was an iron gate, operated electrically; it swung open as he approached.

He parked in front of a four-car garage. On the flat asphalt surface there were two Cadillacs, a Silver Cloud Rolls and, in rather obvious counterpoint, a Maserati. Two uniformed chauffeurs were talking idly, leaning against the Rolls. Sam got out of the car with his attaché case and closed the door.

'I'm Mrs Greenberg's broker,' he said the chauffeurs.

'This is the *place*, man,' laughed the younger chauffeur. 'Merrill, Lynch, and The Girls. That's what they ought to call it.'

'Maybe they will some day. Is that the path to the door?' Sam gestured towards a flagstone walk that seemed to disappear into a short forest of California fern and miniature orange trees.

'Yes, sir,' said the older, dignified chauffeur, as if it were important to cut short the younger man's informality. 'To the right. You'll see it.'

Sam walked down the path to the front door. He had never seen a pink door before, but if he had to see one, he knew it would be in Southern California. He pushed the doorbell and heard the chimes ring out the opening notes of the *Love Story* theme. He wondered if Regina knew the ending.

The door opened and she stood in the foyer, dressed in tight-fitting shorts and an equally tight, translucent shirt that made her huge breasts burst forward in an absolutely challenging fashion.

Though in her forties, Regina was dark haired, tanned, unlined, and lovely, and she carried her frontage with the assurance of youth.

'You're the m*ay*jor?' she asked, the rank emerging in the low, slow, flat *A* of the Hunt Country.

'Major Sam Devereaux,' he confirmed. It was silly to state the name so formally but his attention was on her two titanic challenges.

'Come on in. I reckon you figured we'd all take offence at a uniform.'

'Something like that, I guess.' Devereaux smiled foolishly, forced his eyes away from the shirt and walked into the foyer.

The foyer was short; the entrance to a huge sunken living room, the far wall of which was nothing but glass. Beyond the glass was a kidney-shaped pool surrounded by a terrace of Italian tile, bordered by an ornate iron fence overlooking the valley.

All this he noticed after, say, fifteen seconds. The first quarter minute was taken up observing three additional pairs of breasts.

Each pair was magnificent in its individual style. Full and Round. Narrow and Pointed. Sloping yet Argumentative.

They belonged in turn to Madge, Lillian, and Anne; Regina Greenberg made the introductions swiftly and pleasantly. And Sam automatically related the breasts - the girls - to the data in his attaché case.

Lillian was number three. Palo Alto, California.

Madge was number two. Tuckahoe, New York.

Ann was number four. Detroit, Michigan.

A nice cross-section of America.

Regina - Ginny - was obviously the oldest, not so much in appearance as in authority. For in truth, all the girls were in that vague age range between middle thirties and the next decade - a span Southern California was expert in obscuring. And each was attractive and commanding in a way slightly different from the others. And each was dressed in sexy Southern California: casual but minutely engineered for that effect.

MacKenzie Hawkins was a man whose tastes and abilities were to be envied.

The courtesies were got over with rapidly, courteously. Sam was offered a drink, which he dared not refuse in this company, and seated in a sunken bean bag from which it was impossible to rise. He managed to place the attaché case at his side, but immediately realized that the contortions required to reach over, pick it up, and open it on his lap would tax Plastic Man, so he hoped it would not be necessary.

'Well, here we all are,' drawled Regina Greenberg. 'Hawkins's Harem, as it were. What does the Pentagon want? Testimonials?'

'There's one we'll all give without reservation,' said Lillian brightly.

'Enthusiastically,' said Madge.

'Oooh,' said Anne.

'Yes, well. The general's abilities are enormous,' stammered Sam. 'I mean – well, I didn't expect to meet you all at once. Together. In a group.'

'Oh, we're a real sorority, Major.' Madge, Round and Full, sat in a bean bag next to Sam and reached over, touching his arm. 'Ginny told you. Hawkins's —'

'Yes, I understood,' said Devereaux, swiftly interrupting.

'Talk to one of us about Mac, you talk to all of us,' added Lillian – Narrow and Pointed – from across the room in a particularly mellifluous voice.

'That's right,' cooed Anne – Sloping yet Argumentative – standing outrageously in front of the centre pane of glass on the swimming pool wall.

'In the event we don't have a quorum, I act as spokeswoman,' drawled Regina Greenberg from a jaguar-skin couch against the right wall. 'That's because I was there first and have seniority.'

'Not necessarily in years, dear,' said Madge. 'We won't let you malign yourself.'

'It's difficult to know how to begin,' said Sam, who, nevertheless, plunged into the difficulty. He touched first, gently, on the abstract hardships of dealing with a highly individualistic personality. He slowly, gently explained that MacKenzie Hawkins had involved his government in a most delicate situation for which a solution had to be found. And although said government was filled with undeniable and undying gratitude for General Hawkins's extraordinary contributions, it was often necessary to study a man's background to help him – and his government – resolve delicate situations. Frequently the partially negative led to the positive, if only to balance and accentuate the affirmative.

'So you want to screw him,' recapped Regina Greenberg. 'It had to happen, didn't it, girls?'

There was a chorus of yesses and uh-huhs.

Sam knew better than to offer a flat denial; there was more intelligence – or perception – in that room than might have been evident at first. 'Why do you say that?' he asked Ginny.

'*Gaw*d, *Mayjor!*' replied Titanic. 'Mac's been on a collision course with the high-brass pricky-shits for years! He sees through their manure piles. That's why they like it when those Northern liberals make him out a joke. But Mac's no joke!'

'Nobody thinks he's funny right now, Mrs Greenberg. Let me assure you.'

'What's Mac done?' The question was put defensively by Anne, still silhouetted splendidly at the window.

'He defaced —' Sam stopped; bad choice of word. 'He destroyed a national monument belonging to a government we're trying to maintain a détente with. Like our Lincoln Memorial.'

'Was he drunk?' asked Lillian, eyes and narrow frontage levelled at Sam; two sets of sharp artillery.

'He says he wasn't.'

'Then he wasn't,' stated Madge positively from the bean bag beside him.

'Mac can drink a whole battalion under a mess hall slop shoot.' Ginny Greenberg's drawl was punctuated by her affirmatively nodding head. 'But he never, *never* plays the whisky game to the disadvantage of that uniform.'

'He wouldn't put it into words, Major,' said Lillian, 'but it was a stronger rule than any oath he ever took.'

'For two reasons,' added Ginny. 'He surely didn't want to disgrace his rank, but just as important, he didn't like for the pricky-shits to laugh at him because of booze.'

'So you see,' stated Madge in the bean bag, 'Mac didn't do what they said he did to the Lincoln Memorial. He just wouldn't.'

Sam looked back and forth at the girls. Not one of these ex-Mrs Hawkinses was going to help him; none would utter a negative word about the man.

Why?

He struggled like hell to get out of the bean bag and tried to assume the stance of a cross-examining attorney. A very soft, gentle attorney. He paced slowly in front of the massive window. Anne went to the bean bag.

'Naturally,' he began, smiling, 'these circumstances, this group here, evoke several questions. Not that you're under any obligation to answer, but frankly, speaking personally, I don't understand. Let me explain —'

'Let *me answer*,' interrupted Regina. 'You can't figure out why Hawkins's Harem protects its namesake. Right?'

'Right.'

'As spokeswoman,' continued Ginny, receiving nods of assent from the others, 'I'll be brief and to the point. Mac Hawkins is one great guy – in bed and out, and don't snicker at the bed because most marriages haven't got it. You can't live with the son of a bitch, but that's not his fault.

'Mac gave us something we'll never forget because it's with us every day. He taught us to break our moulds. Sounds simple, doesn't it? "Break your mould." But, lover, it sets you *free*. "You're your own goddamned inventory," he used to say. "There's nothing you *have* to do and nothing you *can't* do; use your inventory and work like hell."

'Now, I don't think that all of us believe that's holy writ. But by gawd, he made each one of us try a lot harder. He set us free before it was chic and we haven't done badly. So, you see, there's not one of us – if Mac came knocking at the door – who wouldn't accommodate him. You dig?'

'I dig,' replied Sam quietly.

The telephone rang. Regina reached behind the couch to the French phone on the marble table. She turned to Sam. 'It's for you.'

Sam looked a bit startled. 'I left your number with the hotel but I didn't expect ...' He walked to the table and took the phone.

'He *what*?!' Blood drained from Sam's face. He listened again. 'Jesus! He *didn't*!' And then in the weariness of aftershock: 'Yes, sir. I can see he most certainly did ... I'll go back to the hotel and await instructions. Unless you'd rather turn this over to someone else; my tour is up in a month, sir. I see. Five days at the outside, sir.'

He hung up and turned to Hawkins's Harem. Those four

magnificent pairs of mammaries that both invited and defied description.

'We're not going to need you, ladies. Although Mac Hawkins may.'

'I'm your only contact with Sixteen-hundred, Major,' said the young lieutenant as he paced – somewhat childishly, thought Sam – the plush Beverly Hills Hotel room. 'You can refer to me as Lodestone. No names, please.'

'Lieutenant Lodestone, Sixteen-hundred. Has a nice ring to it,' said Devereaux, pouring himself another bourbon.

'I'd go easy on the alcohol.'

'Why don't you go to China instead? Of *me*, that is.'

'You do have a long, long flight.'

'Not if *you* make it, I don't.'

'In a way, I wish I could. Do you realize there are seven hundred million potential consumers over there? I'd really like to get a see-you shot of that market.'

'A who?'

'Close-up look. A real peek-see.'

'Ohh. *C-U*. Not see-you —'

'What an opportunity!' The lieutenant stood by the hotel window, his hands clasped behind his back. *Caveat consumer*.

'Then *go*, for Christ's sake! In thirty-two days I've got a permit to get out of this Disneyland and I don't want to trade my uniform in for a Chinese smock!'

'I'm afraid I can't, sir. Sixteen-hundred needs pro-PR now. All the other slambangs are gone. Some are turning out a crackerjack house organ at Dannemora ... Damn!' The lieutenant turned from the window and walked to the writing-desk where there were half a dozen photographs, five by seven. 'It's all here, Major. All you need. They're a little hazy, but they show Brand X, all right! He certainly can't deny it now.'

Sam looked at the blurred but definable telephotos from Peking. 'He almost reached, didn't he?'

'Disgraceful!' The lieutenant winced as he studied the

photographs. 'There's nothing left to be said.'

'Except that he almost made it.' Sam crossed to an armchair and sat down with his bourbon. The lieutenant followed him.

'Your head IG investigator in Saigon will fly his reports directly to you in Tokyo. Take them with you to Peking. They've got a lot of real dirt.' The young officer smiled his genuine smile. 'Just in case you need some final stickum for the coffin.'

'Gee, you're a nice kid. Ever meet your father?' Sam drank a great deal of his bourbon.

'You mustn't personalize it, Major. It's an objective operation and we have the input. It's all part of the —'

'Don't say again —'

'... game plan.' Lodestone swallowed the words. 'Sorry. And anyway, if you do personalize it, what more do you want? The man's a maniac. A dangerous egotistical madman who's interfering violently with peaceful pursuits.'

'I'm a lawyer, Lieutenant, not an avenging angel. Your maniac made several contributions to other – game plans. He's got a lot of people in his corner. I met with eight –*four* – this afternoon.' Sam looked at his glass; where did the bourbon go?

'Not any more, he doesn't,' said the officer flatly.

'He doesn't what?'

'Whatever constituency he had will disappear.'

'Constituency? He's a politician?' Sam decided he needed another drink. He couldn't follow this Buster Brown any longer. So why not get really drunk?

'He *peed* on the Stars and Stripes! That's a Peoria no-no!'

'Did he really reach?'

'We're sending you to China,' continued Lodestone, overlooking the question, 'in the fastest way possible. Phantom jet aircraft over the northern route, stops in Juneau and the Aleutians, into Tokyo. From there a supply carrier to Peking. I've brought all the papers you need from Washington.'

Devereaux mumbled into his bourbon. 'I don't like moo

goo gai pan and I hate egg rolls ...'

'May I suggest you get some rest, sir? It's almost twenty-three hundred and we have to leave for the airbase at oh four hundred. You take off at dawn.'

'Wish I'd said that, Lodestone. Nice ring to it. Five hours. And you're down the hall but not *in here*.'

'Sir?' The young man cocked his head.

'I'm going to give you an order. Go away. I don't want to see you until you come to sew in my name tags.'

'What?'

'Get the hell out of here.' And then Sam remembered and his eyes – though slightly glazed – were laughing. 'You know what you are, Lieutenant? You're a pricky-shit. A real, honest-to-God pricky-shit. Now I know what it means!'

Four hours ... He wondered.

It was worth a try. But first he needed another drink.

He poured it and walked to the writing-desk and laughed at the Peking telephotos. The son of a bitch had flair, no question about it. But he was not at the desk to look at the photographs; he opened the drawer and took out his notebook. He turned the pages and did his best to focus on his own handwriting. He walked to the telephone by the bed, dialled nine, and then the number on the page.

'Hello?' The voice was magnolia-soft and Sam could actually smell the oleander blossoms.

'Mrs Greenberg? This is Sam Devereaux —'

'Well, how're *you*?' Regina's greeting was positively enthusiastic; there was no attempt to conceal her pleasure that the caller was a man. 'We were all wondering which one you'd call. I'm really flattered, M*ay*jor! I mean, actually, I'm the elder stateswoman. I'm really touched.'

Her husband was probably out, thought Sam through the bourbon, warmed by the memory of her challenging, translucent shirt.

'That's very kind of you. You see, in a little while I'm going to go on a long, long trip. Over oceans and mountains and more oceans and islands and ...' *Jesus!* He hadn't figured out how to put it; he hadn't really been sure he could dial her number. Goddamn bourbon fantasies! 'Well, it's sheecrit - *secret*. Very covert. But I'm going to talk to your - namesake?'

'Of *cawsse*, lover! And naturally, you didn't get half a chaynce to ask all those important government questions. I understand, I *really do*.'

'Well, several items came up, one in particular —'

'It usually does. I do believe I should do all I can to help the government in its delicate situation. You're at the Beverly Hills?'

'Yes, ma'm. Room eight twenty.'

'Wait a sec.' She put her hand over the receiver, but Sam could hear her calling out. *'Manny!* There's a national emergency. I have to go to town.'

CHAPTER FIVE

'Major! Major Devereaux! Your phone is off the hook. That's a no-no.'

An incessant, ridiculously loud knocking accompanied Lodestone's nasal screams.

'What the gawd-almighty hell is *that*?' asked Regina Greenberg, nudging Sam under the covers. 'It sounds like an unoiled piston.'

Devereaux opened his eyes into the visual abyss of a hangover. 'That, dear patron saint of Tarzana, is the voice of the evil people. They surface when the earth churns.'

'Do you know what time it is? Call the hotel police, for heaven's sake.'

'No,' said Sam, reluctantly getting out of bed. 'Because if I do, that gentleman will call the joint chiefs of staff. I think they're scared to death of him. They're merely professional killers; he's in advertising.'

And before Devereaux could really focus, hands had dressed him, cars had driven him, men had yelled at him, and he was strapped into an Air Force Phantom jet.

They all smiled. Everyone in China smiled. With their lips more than their eyes, thought Sam.

He was met at the Peking airfield by an American diplomatic vehicle, escorted by two flanking Chinese army cars and eight Chinese army officers. All smiling; even the vehicles.

The two nervous Americans that came with the diplomatic car were attachés. They were anxious to get back to the mission; neither was comfortable around the Chinese troops.

Nor did either attaché care to discuss very much of anything except the weather, which was dull and overcast. Whenever Sam brought up the subject of MacKenzie Hawkins - and why not? he had relieved himself on *their* roof - their mouths became taut and they shook their heads in short, lateral jerks and pointed their fingers below the windows at various areas of the automobile. And laughed at nothing.

Finally Devereaux realized they were convinced that the diplomatic car was bugged. So Sam laughed, too. At nothing.

If the automobile *was* fitted with electronic surveillance, and if someone *was* listening, thought Devereaux, that person was probably conjuring up a picture of three adult males passing dirty comics back and forth.

And if the ride from the airfield seemed strange to Sam, his half-hour meeting with the ambassador at the diplomatic mission in Glorious Flower Square was ludicrous.

He was ushered into the building by his cackling escorts, greeted solemnly by a group of serious-faced Americans who had gathered in the hallway like onlookers in a zoological laboratory - unsure of their safety but fascinated by the new animal brought in for observation - and propelled quickly down a corridor to a large door that was obviously the entrance to the ambassador's office. Once inside, the ambassador greeted him with a rapid handshake, simultaneously raising a finger over his slightly quivering moustache. One of the escorts removed a small metal device about the size of a pack of cigarettes and began waving it around the windows as though blessing the panes of glass. The ambassador watched the man.

'I can't be sure,' whispered the attaché.

'Why not?' asked the diplomat.

'The needle moved a touch, but it could be the loudspeakers in the square.'

'Damn! We have to get more sophisticated scanners. Scramble a memo to Washington.' The ambassador took Sam's elbow, leading him back to the door. 'Come with me, General.'

'I'm a major.'

'That's nice.'

The ambassador propelled Sam out of the office, across the corridor to another door, which he opened, and then preceded Devereaux down a steep flight of stone steps into a large basement. There was a single light bulb on the wall; the ambassador snapped it on and led Sam past a number of wooden crates to another door in the barely visible wall. It was heavy and the diplomat had to put his foot against the surrounding cement in order to pull it open.

Inside was a long-out-of-use, walk-in refrigerator, now serving as a wine cellar.

The ambassador entered and struck a match. On one of the racks was a candle, half burned down. The ambassador held the flame to the wick, and the light swelled flickeringly against the walls and the racks. The wine was not the best, observed Devereaux silently.

The ambassador reached out and yanked Sam into the centre of the small enclosure and then pulled the heavy door almost shut, but not completely.

His lean, aristocratic features accentuated by the wavering flame of the candle, the ambassador smiled apologetically.

'We may strike you as a touch paranoid, but it's not the case at all, I can assure you.'

'Oh, no, sir. This is very cosy. And quiet.'

Sam tried to return the ambassador's smile. And for the next thirty minutes he received his last instructions from his government. It was an appropriate place to get them: deep underground, the surrounding earth inhabited by worms that never saw the light of day.

Armed with his briefcase and no courage whatsover, Devereaux walked out the mission's white steel door, to be greeted by a Chinese officer who waved at him from the foot of the path. Sam saw for the first time the evidence of wreckage - large splinters of wood, several angle irons lying about on the lawn.

The officer stood outside the border of the property and

grinned a flat grin. 'My name is Lin Shoo, Major Deveroxx. I will escort you to Lieutenant General Hawkins. My car, should you please.'

Sam climbed into the back seat of the army staff vehicle and settled back, his case on his lap. As opposed to the nervous Americans, Lin Shoo was not at all inhibited about talking. The subject quickly became MacKenzie Hawkins.

'A highly volatile individual, Major Deveroxx,' said the Chinese, shaking his head. 'He is possessed by dragons.'

'Has anyone tried reasoning with him?'

'I, myself. With great and charming persuasion.'

'But not with great or charming success, I gather.'

'What can I tell you? He assaulted me. It wasn't proper at all.'

'And you want a full-scale trial because of *that*? The ambassador said you were adamant. A trial or a lot of hazzerai.'

'Hazzerai?'

'It means trouble. It's Jewish.'

'You don't look Jewish ...'

'What about this trial?' interrupted Sam. 'Are the charges centred on assault?'

'Oh, no. That would not be philosophically consistent. We expect to suffer *physically*. Through struggle and suffering there is strength.' Lin Shoo smiled; Devereaux didn't know why. 'The general will be tried for crimes against the motherland.'

'An extension of the original charge,' said Sam, making a quiet statement.

'Far more complex, however,' replied Lin Shoo, his smile fading into resigned depression. 'Wilful destruction of national shrines - not unlike your Lincoln Memorials. He escaped once, you know. With a stolen truck he ran into the statuary on Son Tai Square. He is now charged with defacement of venerated artistic craftsmanship - the statuary he ran into was sculptured after the designs of the chairman's wife. And there can be no counter-argument concerning drugs for this. He was seen by too many diplomatic people. He made great sums of noise in Son Tai.'

'He'll claim extentuating circumstances.' No harm in testing, thought Devereaux.

'As with assault, there is no such thing.'

'I see.' Sam didn't but there was no point in pursuing it. 'What could he draw?'

'How so? Draw? The sculpture?'

'Prison. What sort of prison sentence? How long?'

'Roughly four thousand, seven hundred and fifty years.'

'*What?* You might as well execute him!'

'Life is precious to the sons and daughters of the motherland. Every living thing is capable of contribution. Even a vicious criminal like your maniac imperialist general. He could have many productive years in Mongolia.'

'Now just hold on!' Devereaux changed his position abruptly to look Lin Shoo full in the face. He could not be sure, but he thought he heard a metallic click from the front seat. Not unlike the springing of a pistol's safety catch.

He decided not to think about it. It was better that way. He returned his attention to Lin Shoo.

'That's *crazy*! You know that's just plain dumb! What the hell are you talking about? Four thousand - *Mongolia*?' Devereaux's attaché case fell out of his lap; he heard - again - the metallic click. 'I mean, let's be reasonable ...' Devereaux's words drifted off nervously. He picked up the leather case.

'These are the legitimate penalties for the crimes,' said Lin Shoo. 'No foreign government has the right to interfere with the internal discipline of its host nation. It is inconceivable. However, in this particular case, perhaps, it is not entirely unreasonable.'

Sam paused before speaking; he watched the scowl on Lin Shoo's face return slightly, ever so slightly, to its previous polite, unhumorous smile. 'Do I detect the beginnings of an out-of-court settlement?'

'How so? Out of court?'

'A compromise. Do we talk about a compromise?'

Lin Shoo now allowed the scowl to float away. His smile

came as close to being genial as Devereaux could imagine. 'Please, yes. A compromise would be enlightening. There is strength, also, in enlightenment.'

'And maybe a little less than four thousand years in Mongolia - in the compromise?'

'Fraught with possibilities. Should you succeed where others have not. After all, it is to our natural advantage to reach a compromise.'

'I hope you know how right you are. Hawkins is a national hero.'

'So was your Speero Agaroo, Major. Your President said so himself.'

'What can you offer? Dispense with the trial?'

Lin Shoo dropped his smile, too suddenly for comfort, thought Sam.

'We cannot do that. The trial has been announced. Too many people in the international community know of it.'

'You want to save face, or do you want to sell gas?' Devereaux sat back; the Chinese officer did want a compromise.

'A little of both is a compromise, is it not?'

'What's your little? In the event I can get Hawkins to be reasonable.'

'A reduction of the sentence would be one consideration.' Lin Shoo's smile returned.

'From four thousand to twenty-five hundred years?' asked Devereaux. 'You're all heart. Let's start with probation; I'll concede acquittal.'

'How so? Probation?'

'I'll explain later; you'll like it. Give me some real incentive to work on Hawkins.' Sam fingered the top of his attaché case, tapping his nails on the leather. It was a silly thing that usually split adversaries' concentration and sometimes produced a hasty concession.

'A Chinese trial takes many forms. Long, ornate, and quite ritualistic. Or very short, swift, and devoid of excess. Three months or three hours. I can, perhaps, bring about the latter —'

'That *and* probation, I'll buy,' said Sam quickly. 'That's incentive enough to make me want to work real hard. You've got a deal.'

'This probation. You will have to define more legalistically.'

'Basically, you not only save face and sell gas, but you can show how tough you are and *still* be heroes in the world press. All at the same time. What could be better than that?

Lin Shoo smiled. Devereaux wondered briefly if there wasn't more understanding beyond that smile than the Chinese cared to show. Then he dismissed the thought; Lin Shoo distracted him by asking a question and answering it before Sam could speak.

'What could be better than that? Having General Hawkins out of China. Yes, *that* would be better.'

'What a coincidence. Because that's one insignificant part of probation.'

'Really?' Lin Shoo looked straight ahead.

'You, I can handle,' said Sam, almost reflectively. 'I've still got to worry about Brand X.'

CHAPTER SIX

The cell could be seen clearly through a single pane of unidirectional glass embedded in the heavy steel door. There was a western-style bed, a writing desk, recessed overhead lights, both a desk lamp and bedside light, and a large rug on the floor. There was an open door on the right wall that led to a small bathroom, and a horizontal clothes rack on the left. The room was no more than ten by twelve feet, but all things considered, far grander than Sam had visualized.

The only thing missing was MacKenzie Hawkins.

'You see,' said Lin Shoo, 'how considerate we are; how well appointed are the general's accommodations?'

'I'm impressed,' replied Devereaux. 'Except I don't see the general.'

'Oh, he is there.' The Chinese smiled and spoke softly. 'He has his little games. He hears the footsteps and conceals himself on either side of the door. Twice the guards were alarmed and made ill-considered entrances. Fortunately, there were several to overcome the general's strength. Now all the shifts are alerted. His meals are delivered through a slot.'

'He's still trying. ...' Sam chuckled. 'He's something.'

'He is many things,' added Lin Shoo enigmatically as he approached a webbed circle beneath the unidirectional glass and pushed a red button. 'General Hawkins? Please, General, show yourself. It is your good and gracious friend, Lin Shoo. I know you are beside the door, General.'

'Up your ass, slant eyes!'

Lin Shoo released the button momentarily and turned to Devereaux. 'He is not always the essence of courtesy.' The Chinese returned to the speaker and pushed the button again. 'Please, General, I have a countryman of yours with me. A representative of your government. From the armed forces of your nation —'

'You better check her goddamned purse! Maybe up her skirt! Her lipstick might be a bomb!' came the shout from the unseen general officer.

Lin Shoo turned back to Devereaux in bewilderment. Sam gently moved the Chinese out of the way, pushed the button himself, and yelled into the speaker.

'Get off it, you chicken fucker! You're a goddamn bruise on my prick! Show that hairy ass you call a face or I'll open the slop-shoot and drop in that fucking lipstick! I'll *frag* you, you miserable son of a bitch! – Incidentally, Regina Greenberg says hello.'

The immense head of MacKenzie Hawkins slowly appeared in the pane of unidirectional glass. It emerged from the side, huge, crew-cut, leather-lined. Mac's expression was one of utter consternation. A half-chewed cigar was gripped between his teeth, beneath wide, blood-shot eyes that betrayed disbelieving curiosity.

'How so? What do you say?' Lin Shoo's controlled lips were parted in astonishment.

'It's a highly classified military code,' said Devereaux. 'We only employ it under extreme conditions.'

'I will not pursue the matter; it would not be courteous. If you flip the lever on the side of the glass, General Hawkins will see you. When you feel comfortable, I shall admit you. However, I will remain outside, please.'

Sam pushed the small handle on the side of the glass; there was a click. The large, squinting face reacted with instant hostility. Devereaux had the feeling that Hawkins was observing something very obscene but unimportant: Sam, the military accident.

Devereaux nodded to Lin Shoo. The Chinese reached out with both hands, as if to pull with one and push with the other, and unlatched the door. The heavy steel panel opened; Sam walked in.

To an enormous fist that came rushing towards him, on a

direct collision course with his left eye. The impact came; the room, the world, the galaxy spun out of orbit into the shimmering of a hundred thousand splotches of white light.

Sam felt the wet cloth over his face before he felt the pain in his head, especially his eye, and he thought that was strange. He reached up, pulled the cloth away and blinked. All he saw at first was a white ceiling. The centre light hurt his head, especially his left eye. He realized he was on a bed, so he rolled over and everything came back to him.

Hawkins was at the writing desk, papers and photographs scattered about the top. The general was reading from a sheaf of stapled papers.

Devereaux did not have to move his painful head farther to know that his opened attaché case was somewhere near the general. Nevertheless, he did so and saw it at Hawkins's feet. Open and upside down. Empty. The contents in front of the general.

Sam cleared his throat. He could not think of anything else to do. Hawkins turned; his expression was not pleasant. Somehow absent was that welcoming, manly bond of recognition between comrades at arms.

'You little pricky-shits have been busy, haven't you?'

Painfully, Devereaux swung his legs over the side of the bed and touched his left eye. He touched it gently, mainly because he could barely see out of it. 'I may be a shit, General, but I'm not so little, as one day I hope to prove to you. Christ, I hurt.'

'*You* want to prove something' - Hawkins gestured at the papers and allowed himself the inkling of a cynical grin 'to *me*? With what you *know* about me? You've got moxie, boy. I'll say that for you.'

'That phrase is about as antediluvian as you are,' muttered Sam as he stood up. Unsteadily. 'You enjoying the reading material?'

'It's some goddamned record! They'll probably want to make another movie about me.'

'Leavenworth Productions. Film processed in the prison

laundry. You *are* a bona fide fruitcake.' Devereaux pointed to a blanket draped over the door covering the pane of unidirectional glass. 'Is that smart?' He gestured at the blanket.

'It's not dumb. It confuses them. The oriental mind has two very pronounced pressure points: confusion and embarrassment.' Hawkins's eyes were level.

The statement startled Sam. Perhaps it was Hawkins's choice of words, or maybe the quiet intelligence behind the voice. Whatever it was, it was unexpected. 'I mean it's a little useless; the room is bugged. Bugged, hell! All they have to do is push a red button and they can hear everything we say.'

'Wrong, soldier,' replied the general as he got out of the chair. 'If you *are* a soldier and not a goddamn lace-pants. Come here.' Hawkins walked over to the blanket and folded back, first, a corner on the right, then the opposite section of the cloth on the left. In both small areas were barely visible holes in the wall, now very visible with wet toilet paper shoved into the centres. Hawkins dropped the two sections of the blanket and then pointed to six additional plugs of wet toilet tissue - two on each wall, upper and lower - and grinned his leather-lined grin. 'I've gone over this fucking cell palm-spread by palm-spread. I've blocked out each mike; there aren't any others. Naturally, I didn't touch 'em before. See how careful the goddamn monkeys were? Even got one right over the pillow in case I talked in my sleep. That was the toughest to spot.'

Grudgingly, Sam nodded his approval. And then he thought of the obvious. 'If you *have* plugged every one, they'll race in here and move us. You should realize that.'

'You should think better. Electronic surveillance in close areas is wired terminally into a single unit. First, they'll figure they've got a short in the unit circuit, which will take 'em an hour to trace - if they don't have to break down the walls and can do it with sensors - and that'll confuse 'em. Then, if they rule out a short, they'll guess *I* plugged 'em and that'll embarrass 'em. Confusion and embarrassment; the pressure points. It'll take 'em another hour to figure how to get us somewhere else without admitting error. We've got at least two hours. So you better do some pretty fine explaining in that time.'

Devereaux had the distinct feeling that he had better be capable of some pretty fine explaining. Hawkins was a wily pro and Sam did not relish any confrontation. Certainly not physical or, he was beginning to suspect, mental.

'Don't you want to hear about Regina Greenberg?'

'I've read your notes. You've got lousy handwriting.'

'I'm a lawyer; all lawyers have lousy handwriting. It's part of the bar exam. Also I didn't intend to have them typed up.'

'I should hope not,' said Hawkins. 'You've also got a dirty mind.'

'You've got terrific taste.'

'I don't discuss former wives.'

'They've discussed *you*,' countered Sam.

'I know the girls. You didn't get anything you could use. Not from the girls, you didn't. Anything else you got is none of my business.'

'Do I detect a moral position?'

'In my own crude way. I got a little class, boy.' Hawkins pointed to the desk; his arm, hand, and extended finger all were very steady. 'Now, start explaining that stuff.'

'What's there to explain? You've read it, you say. Do I have to tell you that it represents an airtight case of *persona non grata* on one side, and a large embarrassment for the other? If I do, I just have.' Devereaux touched his eye; it hurt like hell, so he sat down again on the bed.

'That stuff in Indochina,' growled Hawkins, walking to the desk and picking up the stapled pages, 'it's written up like I was working for the fucking gooks!'

'I wouldn't go that far. It raises certain questions as to your methods of operation —'

'That's going *that* far, boy!' interrupted the general. 'I was either working for 'em or working with *both* sides, or just pocketing half the pouch money in Southeast Asia! *Or* I was so *dumb* I didn't know what I was doing at all!'

'Ahh!' sang Sam in a lilting, false tremolo. 'Now we are

beginning to understand, said Alice to Cock Robin. A military, really military, man with two Congressional Medals of Honour is a dubious bet for traitor. But all that combat, all those banging noises and that scurrying behind the lines and capture and torture and primitive means of brutal survival – the cumulative effect of all *that* would certainly flip out said hero right into laughing land. Very sad, but the human psyche can take only so much.'

'Horseshit!' roared Hawkins. 'My head's screwed on a hell of a lot tighter than those fuckers who asked for all this crap!'

'Two points for the general,' said Devereaux, holding up his fingers in the *V* sign. 'I hereby state for the record that the general's head is screwed better than anyone at Sixteen-hundred. And, I might add, so is the general.'

'What does that mean, boy?'

'Oh, come on, Hawkins. You're finished! How and why it happened, I don't know. I just know that you got in the way at a rotten time; you made too much noise and you are *expendable*! Not only expendable, but a goddamned pawn that Sixteen-hundred's giving up loud and clear. You're even an *example*!'

'Horseshit, again! Wait'll the Pentagon gets wind of this!'

'They've – *it's* – already got its nostrils full. The brass noses are colliding with each other, running to the deodorant factories. You don't exist, General! Except maybe as a wayward memory.' Sam got up from the bed. The pain in the eye was spreading throughout his head again.

'You can't sell that and I won't buy it,' said Hawkins defensively, his voice indicating a slightly diminished confidence. 'I've got friends. I've got a career sheet that reads like a recruiting poster. Goddamn it, soldier, I'm a general officer who came up from the ranks – from the fucking mud in Belgium! They won't treat me this way!'

'I'm not a soldier. I'm a lawyer and I'm telling you you've been treated – with several layers of forget-me gas. Those telephotos from your buddies in Peking sealed the whole ball of wax. You've bubbled over.'

'They've got to prove it!'

'They've got that, too. I was given it in a pitch-black wine cellar about an hour ago. By a psychotic holding a candle. A very solid citizen. They've got you.'

Hawkins squinted his eyes and removed the chewed, unlit cigar from his mouth. 'How?'

'"Medical records." That's the hard evidence. Psychiatric and physical. "Stress collapse" is only the beginning. The Defence Department will issue a statement that says, in essence, you were purposely placed in ambivalent situations so they could ascertain the development. "Schizoid progression," I think it's called. Conflicting objectives like the Indochina stuff. Also those pictures of you pissing on the mission's roof have a very complicated psychiatric explanation.'

'I've got a *better* one. I was goddamned angry! Wait'll I give my version.'

'You won't get a chance to tell it. If the game plan becomes an issue, the President plans to go on the air, praise your past, show your current medical records – with heartbreaking reluctance, of course – and ask the country to pray for you.'

'Couldn't happen.' The general shook his head confidentially. '*No* one believes a president anymore.'

'Maybe not, but he's got the buttons. Not his own, maybe, but enough others. You'll be strapped down in a Nike silo, if he says so.' Sam saw that there was a metal mirror in the small cubicle that housed the toilet. He walked towards the door.

'But why should he *do* it? Why would anyone *let* him do it?' Hawkins's cigar was held limply in his hand.

Devereaux looked at the size and hue of the shiner over his left eye. 'Because we need gas,' he replied.

'Huh?' Hawkins dropped his cigar on the rug. Obviously without thinking, he stepped on it, grinding it into the surface. 'Gas?'

'It's too complicated. Never mind.' Sam pressed the sensitive flesh around his eye with his fingers. He hadn't had a mouse in over fifteen years; he wondered how long it would take for the swelling to recede. 'Just accept the situation for what it is and make the best deal you can. You haven't got much choice.'

'You mean I'm supposed to lie down and *take* it?'

Devereaux walked out of the toilet, stopped and sighed. 'I'd say the immediate objective was to keep you from lying down in Mongolia. For some four thousand-plus years. If you cooperate, maybe I can pull it off.'

'Out of China?'

'Yes.'

'How much cooperation? With the gooks *and* Washington?' Hawkins's squint was very pronounced.

'A lot. All the way down the pike.'

'Out of the army?'

'No point in staying. Is there, really?'

'Goddamn!'

'I agree. But where does it get you? There's a big world out of that uniform. Enjoy it.'

Hawkins crossed back to the desk in angry silence. He picked up one of the photographs, shrugged and dropped it. He reached into his pocket for a fresh cigar. 'Goddamn, boy, you're not thinking again. You're a lawyer, maybe, but like you say, you're no soldier. A field commander sucks in a hostile patrol, he doesn't feed it, he cuts it down. Nobody's going to let me enjoy. They'll put me in that Nike silo you mentioned. To keep me from talking.'

Devereaux exhaled a long breath through his lips. 'It's just possible I can build a shield acceptable to all parties. After you went down the pike over *here*. Full confession, public apology, the works.'

'Goddamn!'

'Mongolia, General ...'

Hawkins bit into the cigar; the bullet between his teeth, thought Sam.

'What's a "shield"?'

'Off the top of my head, I figure a letter to the secretary of the army, accompanied by a tape of your reading it – verified by voice print. In the letter, *and* the tape, you state that in moments of complete lucidity you're aware of your illness – et cetera, et cetera.'

Hawkins stared at Devereaux. 'You're out of your mind!'

'There are a lot of Nike silos in the Dakotas.'

'Jesus!'

'It's not as bad as it sounds. The letter and the tape will be buried in the Pentagon. Used only if you publicly make waves. Both to be returned, say, in five years. How about it?'

Hawkins reached into his pocket for a book of matches. He struck one and a cloud of pungent smoke nearly fogged out his face; but his voice was clear behind it. 'Down this Chinese pike of yours, there's no talk about that psychiatric bullshit. No one tries to make me out a nut.'

'Hell, no. Nothing like that. Simple fatigue.' Devereaux paced back and forth in the small enclosure as he so often did in conference rooms, weaving the fabric of defence. 'A little booze, maybe; that's sympathetic, even kind of cute when the client's a ballsy type.' Sam stopped, clarifying his thoughts. 'The Chinese would prefer an ideological approach; it'd soften them up. You saw the light. They've been generous to you, nice to you. The People's regime is dandy. *And* tolerant. You didn't realize that. You're really sorry for all those nasty things you've said for a quarter of a century.'

'Goddamn! You make me *bleed*, boy!' With a technique that escaped Sam, Hawkins actually chewed on his cigar as he roared. And then he removed it and lowered his voice. 'I know, I know —. The silos or Mongolia. *Jesus!*'

Devereaux watched the man – painfully. He took several steps towards him and spoke softly. 'You've been squeezed, General. By righteous pieces of plastic; nobody knows that better than I do. I've read your file and I agree with maybe one-fiftieth of what you stand for; in many ways I think you're a menace. But one thing you're not is a manipulator. And you're no joke. Remember what you told the girls? You said everyone's his own inventory. That says a lot to me. So let me help you. I'm no soldier, but I'm a damned good lawyer.'

Hawkins turned away. In embarrassment, thought Sam.

When the words came, there was a defencelessness about them that made him wince.

'Don't know why I'm so concerned about what anybody says - or why I don't settle for a silo *or* Mongolia. Goddamn, boy, I've spent thirty-some years in this man's army. You take off the uniform - no matter what you put me into - I'm as naked as a plucked duck. I only *know* the army; I don't know anything else, not trained for anything when you come right down to it. Never spent any time with the technological - except little stuff in G-two, things like that. Don't know anything about fancy doings like "negotiations". All I know how to do is fuck up and trap pouch thieves - those Indochina reports are right about that: I outsmarted the KGU, the CIA, the ARVN, and even the sellouts on the Saigon general staff. But that's different. I can handle personnel, I suppose. But they always gave me the misfits, the stockade products; if they'd been civilians they wouldn't be allowed on the streets. I was always good with them. I could control those devious bastards; I could put myself in their slimy shoes and *use* 'em, *use* their goddamned angling. But there's nothing I can do on the outside.'

'That doesn't sound like the man who said everyone's his own inventory. You're better than that.'

Hawkins turned and faced Sam. He spoke slowly, reflectively. 'Shit, boy. You know what? The only goddamned thing I'm trained for is to be a crook, maybe. And I'd probably fuck that up because I don't give that much of a damn about money.'

'You look for challenges. Talented people always do. Money's a by-product; usually the challenge there is in the amounts, what they represent, not what they can purchase.'

'I guess so.' Hawkins took a deep breath and stretched; his resignation was coming into focus for him, thought Devereaux. He walked past Sam aimlessly, humming the opening notes of *Mairzy-Doats*. Devereaux knew from long experience with clients to let the moment subside, allow the client time to fully accept the decision.

'Wait a minute, boy. *Wait* a minute .' Hawkins took the

cigar out of his mouth and levelled his eyes with Sam. 'Everybody wants my cooperation. The Chinks, those assholes in Washington - probably a dozen gas conglomerates. I mean they not only *want* it, they *need* it. So much so they'll fake records, build a case —. That ball of wax got out of *control* —'

'Now hold on. What we're faced with —'

'No, *you* hold on, boy! I'm not going to give you a hard time. I'll make you a better deal than you thought possible.' Hawkins shoved the cigar between his teeth, his eyes alive, his voice thoughtful yet intense. 'I'll do exactly - *say* exactly, whatever you bastards want me to say and do. Word for word, gesture for gesture. I'll kiss every butt on Son Tai Square, if you want. But *I* want two things. Out of China *and* the army - they go together. And one thing more: three days in the G-two files back in D.C. Just my *own*, nobody else's. What the hell, I wrote *up* the goddamned things! A last look at my contributions, all the guards you want. I'll be making my final evaluations and additions. Standard procedure for discharging intelligence officers. How about it?'

Sam hesitated. 'I don't know. That stuff's classified —'

'Not to the officer who filed it! Clandestine Operations, Regulation seven seven five, Statute of Amendments. Actually, he's *required* to make his final evaluations.'

'Are you *sure*?'

'Never more sure of anything in my life, boy.'

'Well, if it's standard —'

'I just gave you the regulation! It's military bible, boy!'

'Then I can't see any obstacles —'

'I want it in writing. In exchange for that letter and tape that certifies me so fatigued I eat lizard shit. In fact, *I'll* make the ultimatum: D.C. ussues me a written order to comply with CO Reg seven seven five upon my return to the States, or I'll opt for all the silos in Mongolia! I've still got a lot of supporters back home. They may be a little squirrelly, but they're also goddamned noisy.'

MacKenzie Hawkins chuckled; his cigar was a mangled pulp of itself. It was Sam's turn to squint.

'What are you thinking of?'

'Not a hell of a lot, boy. You just reminded me of something. Everyone *is* his own inventory. The sum of his parts. There may *be* a big goddamned world out there. And a challenge or two.'

PART TWO

This closely held corporation — that is, the company whose investors are few, regardless of capitalization — must have at its financial core men of generous heart and stout courage, who will infuse the structure with their dedication and sense of purpose.

Shepherd's Laws of Economics:
Book CVI, Chapter 38

CHAPTER SEVEN

The People's trial went brilliantly for all concerned. MacKenzie Hawkins was the image of converted, reformed hostility; he was a manly pussycat, playing his role to perfection. On his arrival at Travis Air Force Base in California, he emerged from the plane a stoic figure and spoke clearly into the cameras, and at the crowds of press and lunatic fringers; charming the media and defusing the screeching superpatriots.

He stated simply that there came a time when old soldiers – even youngish old soldiers – should step aside gracefully; times changed and values with them. What was perfidy a decade ago was, perhaps, a proper course of action today. The military man, the military *mind* was not equipped – nor should it be trained – for great international issues. It was enough that the military man, a simple warrior in his nation's legions – *sic ... ibid ... in gloria transit ...* MacKenzie Hawkins – adhere to the eternal truths as he saw them.

It was all very refreshing.

It was all very heartfelt.

It was all bullshit.

And Mac Hawkins was superb.

It was remarked that the man in the Oval Office watched from deep down in a sunken armchair with his pet 150-pound dog, Python, protectively on his lap. He laughed and clapped his hands over Python's fur and stamped his feet and giggled and had a wonderful time. His family skipped in and laughed and clapped their hands and giggled and stamped their feet just like daddy. They weren't sure why daddy was so happy, but it was the best fun they'd had since daddy shot that awful little spaniel in the stomach.

Sam Devereaux watched the transformation of MacKenzie Hawkins from roaring bear to passive possum with dubious awe. The Hawk had turned into a soft-bellied mushy-beak, and what was basically lacking was the motive. Not that Sam discounted the spectre of imprisonment - Mongolia *or* Leavenworth - but once Hawkins had agreed to the plea of guilty, the public apology, the *letter* and gratuitous photographs of his bowed head during the hundred-year sentence of probation, he could have merely resumed his military bearing and let whatever storms rage that might. Instead, he went to extremes to still any controversy. It seemed as though he really wanted to fade away (terrible phrase, thought Devereaux).

Naturally, it crossed Sam's mind that Hawkins's behaviour was somehow related to Washington's quid pro quo regarding the G-2 files - the CO Regulation 775, and MacKenzie's access to them. If so, it was an unnecessary effort on the general's part; three intelligence services had looked over the files and found nothing to compromise national security. By and large the entries concerned old-hat Saigon conspiracies, some ancient European network speculations, and a slew of conjectures, rumours, and unsubstantiated allegations - dipsy-doodle nonsense.

If Hawkins honestly believed he could make a compromising dollar - and for what other purpose would he insist on CO 775? - from these out-of-date, unconfirmed recordings, there was no harm in it. What with inflation, the reduced pension he would receive, and the overall untouchability of his status, things were going to be rough enough. So nobody much cared what he did with his old files. Besides, if there was any resulting embarrassment there was also *the letter*.

'Goddamn, it's good to talk to you again, young fella.' MacKenzie's voice was loud and enthusiastic over the telephone, causing Sam to jerk the instrument away from his ear. The gesture was part audio-input, part raw fear of association.

Devereaux had left the Hawk over two weeks ago in California, just after the press conference at Travis. Sam had flown back to Washington, his discharge barely three days off, and he had spent the time wrapping up any and all desk matters that might conceivably – even *barely* conceivably stand in the way of that glorious hour.

Hawkins wasn't a desk matter, but his mere presence was an abstract threat. On general principles.

'Hello, Mac,' said Sam cautiously. They had dispensed with the military titles at the beginning of the Peking trial. 'You in Washington?'

'Where else, boy? Tomorrow I trek over to G-two for my seven seven five. Didn't you know?'

'I've been pretty busy. There's been a lot to close out here. No reason for anyone to tell me about your seven seven five.'

'I think there is,' replied the Hawk. 'You're escorting me. I thought you knew that.'

There was a sudden, huge lump in the middle of Devereaux's stomach. He absently opened his desk drawer and reached for the Maalox as he spoke. '*Escorting* you? Why do you need an escort? Don't you know the address? I'll give you the address, Mac, I've got it right here. Don't go away. *Sergeant!* Get me the address of G-two Archives! Move your *ass*, Sergeant!'

'Hold on, Sam,' came the soothing words of MacKenzie Hawkins. 'It's just military procedure, that's all. Nothing to get uptight over. Anyway, I *know* the address; you should, too, boy and that's a fact.'

'I don't *want* to escort you. I'm a *lousy* escort! I said good-bye to you in California.'

'You can say hello again over dinner. How about it?'

Devereaux breathed deeply. He swallowed the Maalox and waved away the WAC who was his sergeant-secretary. 'Mac, I'm sorry, but I *do* have a number of things to finish up. Maybe at the end of the week; anytime actually – the day after tomorrow. At sixteen hundred hours to be precise.'

'Well, Sam, I thought we ought to go over the G-two routine for tomorrow morning. I mean you *have* to be there, son. It's in the orders. We wouldn't want anything fucked up over there, would we? *Jesus!* They wouldn't let either one of us out then.'

'Where do you want to have dinner?' asked Devereaux. He grimaced. The Maalox bottle was empty.

You're escorting me. I thought you knew that ... It's in the orders. We wouldn't want anything fucked up over there, would we?

No, we certainly would not. Devereaux shook his head. A couple in the next booth were staring at him. He stopped and grinned foolishly; the couple whispered to each other and looked away. Their reaction was clear: You never knew who was being sentenced next.

A tall man came through the curtained arch across the room. It was Sam's turn to stare. In awe.

It was the Hawk. He was sure of it. But the tall man threading his way politely through the crowded room bore little resemblance to the dishevelled, cigar-chewing MacKenzie Hawkins who had squinted at him through the glass of a Peking cell. And even less to the close-cropped Hawkins who stood ramrod straight at all times and took each step as though marching to the tune of a thousand pipers - against a strong wind.

To begin with there was the Van Dyke beard. Granted it was new, but the definition was clear and exceedingly well groomed. As was the hair; it was not only growing out, but it had been shaped by tonsorial hands so that the grey swept over the ears in waves. Very, very distinguished. And the eyes - well, one could not really see the eyes because they were covered by tinted, tortoiseshell glasses, a very light tint that was more academic, or diplomatic, than mysterious.

And the man's walk. Good God! Hawkins's ramrod military posture had been replaced by a tasteful, goddamn it, *elegant grace*. There was a softness about the whole bearing, a kind of casual glide that was more Palm Beach than Fort Benning.

'I saw you watching me,' said the Hawk as he slid into the booth. 'Not bad, eh, boy? Not one of those pricky-shits stopped me. How about that?'

'I'm astonished,' answered Sam.

'You shouldn't be, son. First thing you learn in infiltration is adaptability. Not just terrain, but a good-sized accent on local customs and behaviour. It's a form of psycho-war.'

'What the hell are you talking about?'

'Behind the lines, Sam. This is enemy territory, don't you know that?'

By the time Mac Hawkins had elegantly spooned his iced vichyssoise he had reached the heart - the core the bombshell of his reason for dinner with Sam. It was explosively capsuled in a single name.

Heseltine Brokemichael. Late Major General of Command, Bangkok. Currently in limbo, Washington, D.C.

'Yes, Sam, old Brokey was with me in Korea and points east and south. Damn fine officer; a little hot-headed, but then he always had to contend with that stupid bastard cousin of his. What's that idiotic name of his? Ethelred? Can you imagine? *Two* Brokemichaels in the same goddamned army, both with freak names!'

'I'm not hungry any more,' said Devereaux quietly. The Hawk continued.

'Yes, sir, you really laid the heavy mortar on Brokey's career. He couldn't get another star on his collar if he bought all the astrologers in the Pentagon. You see, they can never be *sure*; one of the goddamned Brokemichaels is a crook, but, of course, you never proved that, either.'

'They wouldn't let me!' Devereaux's whisper carried farther than he cared to think about. The couple in the next booth stared again. Sam grinned again. 'I had the evidence; I built the case. They made me drop it!'

'And a good man was cut down just when the joint chiefs were looking kindly on him. I tell you, it's a pity.'

'Get off it, Mac. I had that bastard cold -'

'The wrong bastard, boy. And even then you committed serious crimes to get your so-called evidence.'

'I took a calculated risk because I was damned angry. I paid for it with two years of my life in that cockadoodle uniform. And that's *it*. I want out.'

'That's too bad. I mean, I'm sorry to hear you say that because you may have to spend a little more time over at IG if I —'

'*Hold it!*' interrupted Devereaux in a whisper that bordered a roar. 'I'm out the day after tomorrow! Nothing, *nothing's* going to change that!'

'I certainly hope not. Let me finish. You *may* have to spend time if I can't talk old Brokey out of this crazy idea of his. You see, those charges against you in Bangkok weren't actually dropped; they were sort of suspended because of the complicated circumstances, and what with all those peace freaks screaming against the military. Now, Brokey doesn't hold anything against you, Sam, but he'd really like to clarify his own status, you can understand that. He figures that if he resurrects those charges, you can dig up the files and get the *right* Brokemichael – you'd *have* to or be on a rock pile – and he'd have the JCS smiling nicely on him, just like they used to. Wouldn't take more than, say, six or seven months. A year at the outside – *maybe* eighteen months if the trial was a long one, but you'd both get what you want —'

'I want *out*! That's *all* I want!' Sam wrung his napkin so tightly it squeaked. 'I *paid* for my moral indignation. It's *past*.'

'Past for you, boy. Not old Brokey.'

'The facts are *there*. I made a goddamned apology; it's in writing. The day after tomorrow, after sixteen hundred hours, I'll dictate a statement – to a civilian secretary – recapping the whole thing in one-syllable words. I will *not* reopen that case!'

'You will if old Brokey pulls out a certain Bangkok file and issues a directive for your arrest. He *is* a general officer, Sam. Even though he may have pulled duty cleaning out the fucking high-brass latrines, for all I know.'

Hawkins had pursed his lips, tsking, and shaking his head slowly; the wide, innocent eyes behind the tinted glasses, conveyed anything but innocence.

'All right, Mac. Game time is over. You said, *if* you couldn't talk Brokemichael out of this nonsense. *Can* you talk him out of it?'

'Either talk him out of it, or remove him from the scene for a couple of days. Yes, I can do one or the other. Once you've got that discharge, boy, Brokey'd have a hell of a time convincing anyone to go after you. That paper's sort of a statute of limitations, you know. But I don't have to tell *you* that.'

'No, you don't. Just tell me what rotten thing you want from me.'

The Hawk removed his tinted glasses and, elegantly, wiped the non-prescription lenses as though he were polishing jade. 'Well, as a matter of fact, I've been giving a lot of thought to my immediate future. And I think there's a place for you, but I'm not sure.'

'Don't ever be. Next week I'll be back at my desk in Boston with Aaron Pinkus Associates, the best law firm in the Bay State.'

'Well, you could take an extra few weeks. Say a month, couldn't you? *Jesus*, boy, it's been four years; what's another month?'

'Aaron Pinkus will one day be on the Supreme Court. Every day with him is an education and I'm not giving up thirty years of paid education. What do you mean, you think there's a place for me? Doing what?'

'I may need an attorney. I think you're the best I ever met.'

'I'm probably the only one you've ever met —'

'But you've got a few weak spots, young fella,' interrupted Hawkins, replacing his tinted glasses. 'I'm sorry to say that, but it's a fact. So I don't know whether to hire you or not. I have to ponder some more about you.'

'In the meantime, you'll keep Brokemichael out of the picture?'

'And you'll give some consideration to acting as my

attorney? Just for a couple of weeks? You see, I've got a little money saved up —'

'I know exactly how much money you've got,' broke in Devereaux sympathetically. 'I *had* to. You want advice for investments?'

'Sort of —'

'Then without qualification I'll help you. I mean that.' Sam did. After a lifetime of devotion, risk, and service, Mac had managed to amass a sum total of fifty-odd thousand dollars. No other assets whatsoever. No houses, real estate, stocks. Nothing. That and a reduced pension was all he had for the rest of his life. 'And if I can't give you the advice I think you should have, I'll find someone else who can.'

'That's mighty touching, son.'

Was there a hint of a glistening tear in this tough old-line officer's eyes? It was difficult to tell with the tinted glasses.

'It's the least I can do. It may sound corny, but it's the least any taxpayer can do for you. You've given a lot, and you've been shafted by the plastic men. I know that.'

'Well, boy,' said Hawkins, inhaling deeply, heroically, 'everyone does what he has to do in this world. At a given moment of time — *Ouch!* This goddamn faggot suit is tighter than a Memorial Day uniform.' The Hawk pulled out a folded, faded magazine from his breast pocket. The pages showing were dog-eared and marked with red pencil.

'What's that?' asked Devereaux.

'Oh, some Chincom propaganda the slants left in my cell. It's the standard Commie crap, misspelled English and all. This is an article that's supposed to show the kind of injustice that's widespread in organized religion. This here Catholic pope has a first cousin – kind of like the Brokemichaels in a way, except they don't have the same names – but they look alike. Actually they're identical, except that this pope's cousin grows a beard to hide the likeness.'

'I don't understand. Where's the injustice?'

'This cousin is a small-time singer in a minor opera company and half the time he's out of work. The Chincoms make the obvious comparison. The singer sings his heart out for the people's culture and starves half to death, while his pope cousin eats like a guinea gourmet and steals from the poor.'

'It interested you so much you marked it up?'

'Hell, no, boy. I just picked out the inaccuracies to show this priest friend of mine. It may surprise you, but I've been doing a little studying about things I haven't thought much about before. God, and the church, and things like that —. Don't you laugh, now.'

Devereaux smiled gently. 'I'd never laugh at a thing like that. I don't think it's anything to laugh at. A man's religious thoughts are not only his constitutional right, but often his very real sustenance.'

'That's a mighty nice way to phrase it. Real deep, Sam. By the way, just one thing about this Brokemichael business. Tomorrow morning at G-two. Keep your fucking mouth shut and do as I say.'

Hawkins was waiting under the canopy when Sam pulled up to the kerb in front of the hotel. He held what looked like a very expensive briefcase in one hand, opened the car door with his other and slid in. There was a broad grin on his face.

'*Goddamn!* It's a beautiful morning!'

It was not. It was cold and wet and the skies promised a heavy rain.

'Your barometer's a little off.'

'Nonsense! The day - like age - depends on how you feel, boy. And I feel just grand!' Hawkins smoothed the lapels of his tweed suit, adjusted the deep red paisley tie over the modish striped shirt, and ran his fingers delicately over the hair above his ears.

'Glad you're in such good spirits,' said Sam, starting up the car and entering the flow of traffic. 'I don't want to dampen them but you can't take a briefcase with you. You can't remove any papers. Nothing leaves the G-two offices.'

Hawkins laughed. He pulled out a cigar from his shirt pocket. 'Oh, don't worry your legal head about details,' he said, snipping off the end of the cigar with a sterling silver clipper. 'I've taken care of all that.'

'There's nothing to take care of! I'm responsible for you and I've got twenty-four hours to keep my nose clean.' Devereaux took his hostility out on the horn; the sound was returned in good measure by the surrounding vehicles.

'*Jesus*, you're in a foul temper. You just keep your eyes on the high ground, don't concern yourself with the flanks.'

'God*damn* it, doesn't anybody speak English anymore? What goddamned flanks? What does *that* mean?'

'It means what I said last night.' MacKenzie spoke as he lighted his cigar. 'Do as I say and don't make waves. By the way, would you like to know the name of the fella in charge of the G-two archives? Well, no reason for you to know, but he's a bright son of a bitch, a real genius. Didn't know what I was doing for the service when I got him out of that prison camp west of Hanoi a few years back. He's a Pointer, too. Can you beat that? Class of forty-seven. Same as me. Goddamn! The coincidences in this world —'

'*No!* ... No, Mac! *No!* No, no *no*! You can't! I won't let you!' Sam attacked the horn again. Viciously hammering on it. At a crippled old lady who was having a difficult time crossing the intersection. The poor, trembling thing sank her head farther into her quivering shoulders.

'Regulation seven seven five makes it clear that a legal escort is just that. An escort. Not an observer. He takes the clandestine operations officer to and from the place of examination, but he's not permitted inside the room. I guess there're a lot of dishonest lawyers, Sam.' MacKenzie took a long, savouring intake of cigar smoke.

'There's *another* thing that's not allowed in that room, you son of a bitch!' Devereaux slammed his hand in fury on the rim of the horn once more. The crippled old lady was now splayed out in the middle of the street. 'And that's a *briefcase*!'

'It is, if the officer is making his final contributions. *Nobody* can see those but the ranking archivist of G-two. It's classified material.'

'There's nothing *in* there!' yelled Sam, pointing at his briefcase.

'How do you know? It's locked.'

Upon entering the offices of army intelligence, Hawkins was escorted quietly, professionally, to the specific room selected for his 775, by two flanking military police. Sam took up the rear. It seemed to Devereaux as formal an exercise as an execution, except that Mac was loose and slightly slouched in his modish tweed suit, not ramrod at all. But once the four of them were inside the room, Hawkins straightened up and replaced his warm civilian tones with the harsh bark of a leather-lined general officer. He ordered the MPs to take Sam into the next room and summon their superior. The MP captains saluted, took Devereaux by the elbows silently into the adjacent room, slammed the door, locked it, checked the corridor, and walked in Wehrmacht unison out into the hallway. They locked that door, too.

He had a vague feeling of *déjà vu*; then he remembered. He'd watched a late night movie on television several weeks ago. *Seven Days in May*. He walked to the single window and looked out. And down. Through the bars. It was four storeys to the street. G-2 wasn't taking any chances with legal escorts from the inspector general's office, he thought.

There was the sound of voices from the next room. And then overly masculine laughter accompanied by eruptions of profanity. Old comrades-in-arms recalling the good old days when everyone got his ass shot off, except the generals. Sam sat down in a chair and picked up a dog-eared, worn-out copy of *Let's Stamp Out V.D. in G-2*, and read.

His reading – which was actually rather fascinating – was suddenly interrupted by the steady repetition of another sound from the examination room.

Therump-chump. Therump-chump. Therump-chump.

Devereaux swallowed several times, annoyed with himself for leaving his antacid tablets in the car. The sound he was hearing could not be confused with any other sound in his frame of reference, no matter how hard he tried. It was a Xerox machine.

Why would an examination room for the processing of eyes-only classified files have a Xerox machine?

On the other hand, why wouldn't it?

The first question was infinitely more logical. A Xerox machine was a contradiction - in spirit and in fact - to the purpose of Regulation 775.

Sam went back to his reading, unable to keep his mind even on the pictures.

An hour and twenty minutes later the *therump-chumping* stopped. Several minutes after that a metallic crack of a lock was heard and the door of the examination room was opened. MacKenzie emerged carrying his expensive briefcase, now bulging and strapped together with shining steel G-2 bands, and a foot-long steel chain dangling from the crossbar.

'What the hell is that?' asked Devereaux from the chair, apprehensively and not at all kindly.

'Nothing,' replied the Hawk casually. 'Just some Fleet-Pac-Com-Sat transfer files.'

'And what the hell is that?'

'*Major,*' continued MacKenzie, raising his voice, standing suddenly very erect. 'I present Brigadier General Beryzfickoosh! *Atten ... hut!*'

Devereaux shot up from the chair and snapped his hand in salute as a barrel-chested officer with twelve rows of ribbons, an eye patch and, Sam swore, a fright wig on his head, walked swiftly into the room. The salute was returned with a vibrating flourish; the officer then extended a large, muscular hand.

'Hear you're up for discharge, Major,' said the general gruffly.

'Yes, sir,' answered Devereaux, gripping the outstretched hand.

At which instant Hawkins slapped the briefcase chain over Sam's wrist, securing the triple combination lock between the links, and barked, 'First transfer completed, General!'

'*Confirmed*, sir!' shot back the general, still holding Devereaux's hand in an iron grip, his one eye staring at Sam. 'Fleet-Pac-Com-Sat is now in your custody, Major! Prepare for second transfer!'

'For what, General?'

'Say!' The general released Sam's hand. 'Aren't you the legal prick who shafted old Brokey Brokemichael?'

Devereaux's stomach was suddenly in agony; perspiration formed instantly on his forehead, as the heavy briefcase pulled him halfway to the floor. 'There are two sides to that story, sir.'

'Goddamned right!' shouted the general. 'Brokey's and some shit-ass noncombatant's who *should* be on a stockade rock pile!'

'Now, just a minute, General —'

'*What*, soldier? You being *insubordinate*?'

'No, sir. Not at *all*, sir. I would just like to point out —'

'Point *out*!? You point your ass in the direction of that door and secure the transfer of Fleet-Pac-Com-Sat, or I'll point you right into a court-martial! For insubordination *and* incompetence!'

'Yes, sir! Right away, sir!' Sam tried to salute but the chain and the briefcase were too heavy, so he made a rapid about-face and headed for the door, which was miraculously opened by the two MP captains.

The formalities at the entrance desk were over with quickly. The steel G-2 bands securing the briefcase were some kind of symbol of authority. Devereaux signed the checkout book and the miniature camera silently took his photograph.

Out on the street, Sam turned to the Hawk. 'That guy's crazy! Another ten seconds he would have thrown me into solitary! For *what*?'

'Old Brokey's got a lot of friends,' said MacKenzie. 'Here, I'll drive.'

'Thanks.' Devereaux reached awkwardly into his pocket and gave Hawkins the keys, his hand still trembling. They walked to the parking lot and got in the car.

Fifteen minutes later, in the middle of a Washington traffic jam, Sam's nerves began to calm down. His panic at being faced with a weird, apoplectic general screwing up his discharge at the last minute was fading. But that concern was being inexorably replaced with another very genuine fear. Brought about partially by the Hawk's silence.

'Mac, now that this pile of fleet-kumquats is in my custody, what the hell am I supposed to do with them? Where's this second transfer taking place?'

'Don't you know?'

'Of course not.'

'The general thinks you do.'

'Well, I *don't*!'

'You want to go back and ask him, Sam? Personally, I don't recommend it. Not with the way he feels about you. *Jesus!* He might dig up all kinds of very serious violations. And you just got your picture taken. One thing always leads to another, you know what I mean? Like the domino theory. Your trial could last for a year or two.'

'*What the hell's in here, Hawkins?* Don't bullshit me! What *is it*?'

'Sorry, Sam. I'm afraid I can't discuss it. You understand, boy. It's classified.'

Sam sat forward on the couch, his arm stretched out over the coffee table. MacKenzie manipulated the hacksaw back and forth over the chain.

'Once I get this goddamned chain off, we can work on the lock,' said Mac comfortingly. 'It would be easier with a small blowtorch.'

'Not on *my* arteries, you son of a bitch! And thanks for not telling me you didn't have the combination.'

'Now, don't worry, I'll have it off in ten or fifteen minutes. The steel's a touch harder than I figured.'

An hour and fourteen minutes later the last links were severed, leaving one dangling chain and a triple combination lock around Devereaux's wrist.

'I've got to get in touch with my office,' Sam said. 'They'll expect me to check in.'

'No, they won't. You're with me. Covering my seven seven five. That's what the agreement states. One day minimum, three days maximum.'

'But we're not there.'

'We went to lunch ...' MacKenzie cleared this throat.

'I should still telephone —'

'*Goddamn*, you've no faith in me at *all*! Why the hell do you think I waited until this morning before going to G-two? You've got one day left and *I* account for your time. You can't get in trouble if you're not *there*.'

'Of course not. No trouble – just a firing squad.'

'Nonsense.' Hawkins got up from the floor, carrying the freed briefcase to the hotel writing desk. 'You're safer with me. I know those IG close-outs. You think you're winding everything up and some pricky-shit waltzes in and tells you you're not going anywhere until some brief is completed.'

Devereaux looked over at the general, now snapping the G-2 bands and opening the expensive briefcase. There was logic in Mac's madness. There *was* sure to be some ball-breaking file or other that a confused superior did not care to have left in his lap. A memorandum could be misplaced – or not read. A confrontation, even a discussion, between legal officers could not be overlooked. Hawkins definitely had a point: Sam was safer away from the office.

MacKenzie removed several hundred Xeroxed pages and put them on the desk beside the briefcase. Devereaux pointed to them and spoke cautiously, 'That's all *your* seven seven five?'

'Well, not exactly. A lot of it's open stuff that's never been closed out.'

Sam was suddenly more uncomfortable than he had been for the past three hours. 'Wait a minute. You said back at G-two that it was just raw material on people you'd run across.'

'Of people *other* people ran across. I added that, son, I really did. You were just so upset you didn't listen.'

'Oh, Christ! You removed raw files on subjects that weren't *yours*?'

'No, Sam,' replied the Hawk as he squared off some pages. '*You* did. It says so right at the security desk. Your signature.'

Devereaux sank back in the couch. 'You devious son of a bitch.'

'That kind of says it,' agreed Hawkins sadly. 'There were times in the field – operating way the hell behind the lines, of course – when I wondered how I could bring myself to do the things I did. But then the answer was always the same. I was trained to survive, boy. And survive I do.' The Hawk now had four piles of Xeroxes neatly to the left of the briefcase on the desk. He tapped his fingers over them as if playing a piano and then looked over at Sam pensively. 'I think you're going to do real fine. You *will* accept the temporary appointment as my attorney, won't you? It won't be for long.'

'And it's a little more complicated than investments, isn't it?' Devereaux remained well back in the couch.

'A mite, I suspect.'

'And if I refuse I don't even have to worry about Brokemichael. He's minor. Now there's a small matter of removing classified files from G-two. No statute of limitations on that little caper.'

'Don't imagine there is.'

'What do you want me to do?'

'Work up some contracts. Pretty simple stuff, I should think. I'm forming a company. A corporation, I guess you'd call it.'

Sam inhaled deeply. 'That's really kind of amusing, if it weren't so sad. Purpose and intent notwithstanding, there's a not-so-minor item called capitalization required when you form a corporation. I know your finances. I hate to disabuse you but you're not exactly in the corporate assets league.'

'No faith, that's your trouble. I expect you'll change.'

'And what does that cryptic remark mean?'

'It means I've got the assets figured out to the dollar, that's what it means.' Hawkins planted his fingers over the Xeroxes in an elongated press. As if he had found the Lost Chord.

'What assets?'

'Forty million dollars.'

'*What!*' In his stunned disbelief, Sam leaped up from the couch. The dangling steel chain followed swiftly and, in a howling instant of pain, the bottom links whipped across his eye.

His left eye.

The room went around and around.

CHAPTER EIGHT

Devereaux ripped open the envelope the instant he closed the hotel door. He pulled out the rectangular slip of heavy paper and stared at it.

It was a cashier's cheque made out to his name. The amount was for ten thousand dollars.

It was absurd.

Everything was absurd; nothing made any sense at all.

He had been a civilian for exactly one week. There had been no hitches regarding his discharge; no Brokemichael surfaced, and no last-minute problems developed in the office because he had not gone to the office until an hour before his formal separation from the army. And when he arrived he not only had a patch over his left eye, but a thick bandage around his right wrist. From burns.

He had moved out of his apartment, sent his belongings to Boston, but did not follow them because a devious son of a bitch named MacKenzie Hawkins stated that he needed 'his attorney' in New York. Therefore Sam had a two-room suite at the Drake Hotel on Park Avenue, reserved and paid for. The suite was leased for a month; Hawkins thought it would be enough time.

For what? Mackenzie was not yet ready to 'spell it out'. However, Sam was not to worry; everything was 'on the expense account'.

Whose expense account?

The corporation's.

What corporation?

The one Sam would soon be forming.

Absurd!

Forty million dollars' worth of delusions that screamed for a frontal lobotomy.

And now a cashier's cheque for ten thousand dollars. Free and clear and no receipt required.

Ridiculous! Hawkins could not afford it. Besides, he had gone too far. People did not send other people (especially lawyers) ten thousand dollars without some kind of explanation. It simply was not healthy.

Sam walked over to the hotel telephone, checked the confusing litany on the pull-out tab beneath the instrument, and placed a call to MacKenzie.

'Goddamn, boy! That's no way to behave! I mean, you might at least say thank you.'

'What the hell for? Accessory to theft? Where did you get ten thousand dollars?'

'Right out of the bank?'

'Your savings?'

'That's right. Didn't steal from anyone but myself.'

'But why?'

There was a slight pause in Washington. 'You used the word, son. I believe you called it a retainer.'

There was a second pause. In New York. 'I think I said I was the only lawyer I knew who had a retainer based in the sort of blackmail that could march me in front of a firing squad.'

'That's what you said. And I wanted to correct that impression. I want you to know I value your services. I surely wouldn't want you to think I didn't appreciate you.'

'Cut it out! You can't afford it and I haven't done anything.'

'Well, boy, I believe I'm in a better position to judge what I can afford. And you *did* do something. You got me out of China some four thousand years before my parole was due.'

'That's different. I mean –'

'And tomorrow's going to be your first day of work,' interrupted the Hawk. 'Not much, but a beginning.'

There was now a long pause in New York. 'Before you say

anything, you should understand that as a member of the bar, I subscribe to a canon of ethics that is very specific. I'll do nothing to jeopardize my standing as an attorney.'

Hawkins replied loudly, with no pause whatsoever, 'I should hope not! Goddamn, boy, I don't want any slippery shyster in *my* corporation. Wouldn't look good on the stationery —'

'*Mac!*' roared Devereaux in exasperation. 'You didn't have stationery printed?'

'No. I just said that. But it's a hell of an idea.'

Sam did his best to control himself. 'Please. *Please.* There's a law firm in Boston and a very nice man who'll be on the Supreme Court someday who expects me back in a couple of weeks. He wouldn't look kindly on my being employed by - somebody else during my leave. And you said my work for you would be finished in three or four weeks. So no stationery.'

'All right,' agreed Hawkins sadly.

'Now, what's on for tomorrow? I'll charge you by the day and deduct it from the ten thousand and return the rest at the end of the month. From Boston.'

'Oh, don't worry about that.'

'I *do* worry. I should also tell you that I'm not licensed to practise in the state of New York. I may have to pay outside attorney's fees; depending upon what you want done. I gather it involves filing for this corporation of yours.' Devereaux lit a cigarette. He was happy to see that his hands were not shaking.

'Not yet. We'll get to that in a couple of days. Tomorrow I want you to check out a man named Dellacroce. Angelo Dellacroce. He lives in Scarsdale. He's got several companies in New York.'

'What do you mean "check out"?'

'Well, I undestand he's had business problems. I'd like to know how serious they are. Or were. Sort of find out what his current state of well-being is.'

'"Well-being"?'

'Yeah. In the sense of his being around and not in jail, or anything like that.'

Devereaux paused, then spoke calmly, as if explaining to a child. 'I'm a lawyer, not a private investigator. Lawyers only do what you're talking about on television.'

Again MacKenzie Hawkins replied quickly. 'I can't believe that. If somebody wants to become part of a corporation, the attorney for the company should find out if the fellow's on the up-and-up, shouldn't he?'

'Well, it would depend on the degree of participation, I suppose.'

'It's considerable.'

'You mean this Angelo Dellacroce has expressed interest?'

'In a way, yes. But I wouldn't want him to think I was being rude by making inquiries, if you know what I mean.'

Devereaux noticed that his hand now trembled slightly. It was a bad sign; better than a pained stomach but still bad. 'I've got that strange feeling again. You're not telling me things you should tell me.'

'All in good time. Can you do what I ask?'

'Well, there's a firm here in the city that my office uses used to use, anyway. Probably still does. They might be able to help.'

'That's fine. You see them. But don't forget, Sam, we've got a lawyer-client relationship. That's like a doctor or a priest or a good whore; my name doesn't get mentioned.'

'I could do without the last reference,' said Devereaux.

Damn it. His stomach growled. He hung up.

'*Angelo Dellacroce!*' Jesse Barton, senior partner, son-of-founder, Barton, Barton, and Whistlewhite, laughed. 'Sam you've been away too long!'

'*That* bad?'

'Let's put it this way. If our mutual Boston friend and your erstwhile employer – I *assume* he's still your employer Aaron Pinkus, thought you were seriously considering Dellacroce for some kind of money deal, he'd call your mother.'

'That bad?'

'I'm not kidding. Aaron would question your sanity and

personally remove your name from the office door.' Barton leaned forward. 'Dellacroce is Cosa Nostra with a capital Mafia. He's so high in the charity rackets the cardinal invites him to the Alfred E. Smith dinner every year. And naturally, he's untouchable. He drives district attorneys and prosecutors right out of their gourds. They can't get him, but not for lack of trying.'

'Then Aaron mustn't learn of my very innocent inquiry,' replied Sam in confidence.

'Your indiscretion is safe with me. Incidentally, is it an indiscretion? This party of yours, is he really that naïve?'

Sam's stomach began to answer for him. He spoke rapidly to cover the sound. 'In my judgement, yes. I'm paying back a debt, Jesse. My client saved my ass in Indochina.'

'I see.'

'So he's important to me,' continued Sam. 'And according to you he's naïve. About this Dellacroce.'

'Don't take my word for it,' said Barton, reaching for his telephone. 'Miss Dempsey, get me Phil Jensen downtown, please.' Jesse replaced the receiver. 'Jensen's second in command at the prosecutor's office. Federal district, not municipal. Dellacroce's been a target over there ever since Phil joined; that was damn near three years ago. Jensen gave up an easy sixty thou' to go after the evil people.'

'Commendable.'

'Bullshit. He wants to be a senator or better. That's where the real money is —' The telephone rang. Barton picked it up. 'Thank you ... Hello, Phil? Jesse, I've got an old friend here; he's been away for a few years. He was asking me about Angelo Dellacroce —'

The explosion on the other end of the line reverberated throughout the office. Jesse winced. 'No, for Christ's sake, he's not involved with him. Do you think I'm crazy? ... I told you he's been away; out of the country, as a matter of fact.' Jesse listened for a moment and looked over at Sam. 'Were you in northern Italy? ... Where, Phil? ... Around Milan?'

Devereaux shook his head. Barton continued, one ear at the telephone, his words directed at Sam.

'Or Marseilles? ... Or Ankara? ... What about Rashid?'
Devereaux kept shaking his head.

'*Algiers?* ... Were you in Algiers? ... No, Phil, you're way off. This is very straight. I wouldn't be calling you if it was anything else, now would I? ... Simple investment stuff, very legitimate. ... Yes, I know, Phil. ... Phil says those bastards will own Disneyland next. ... Come on, Phil, that's not kosher; he'll simply walk away from him. I just wanted to confirm Dellacroce's status. ... Okay. All right. I've got it. Thanks.'

Barton replaced the phone and leaned back. 'There you are.'

'I touched a raw nerve.'

'The rawest. Dellacroce not only skipped free of an airtight indictment last week, but because of a grand jury leak, the prosecutor's office has to issue a public apology. How does that grab you?'

'I'm glad I'm not Jensen.'

'Jensen's not. His office will lay off Dellacroce for a couple of months then ring him in again. Won't do them any good; Dellacroce's got his ass in butter. He slides in and out of courtrooms.'

'But my client should stay away.' Devereaux did not ask a question.

'Several continents,' replied Barton. 'Clothes don't make the man; his investors do. Ask anyone from Biscayne to San Clemente.'

'Well, goddamn, isn't that interesting? You just can't tell anymore, can you?'

'Stay clear of him,' said Devereaux, shifting the hotel phone and reaching for the glass of bourbon on the other side of the desk. 'He's bad news and you don't want him near you.'

'I see what you mean –'

'I'd rather you said "Yes, Sam, I'll stay away from Angelo Dellacroce." That's what I'd like to hear you say.'

'See what you mean.'

'You're not listening. When you pay a lawyer a retainer

you listen to him. Now, repeat after me: "I will not go near —"'

'I know you've had a hard day, but you might put your mind to the next order of business. Just sort of think about it.'

'I'm still thinking about Angelo Dellacroce.'

'That part's finished with —'

'Glad to hear it.'

'– for the time being. Now, I want you to begin roughing out a kind of standard corporation agreement. A real legal document that has blanks for people putting in money.'

'People like Dellacroce?' Devereaux's voice made clear his position.

'*Goddamn*, forget about that guinea bastard!'

'From what I know about him I think you should refer to him as the Roman-blood-royal. But I'd rather you never referred to him again. What kind of corporation? If you want it filed in New York, I'll have to bring in another attorney. I told you that.'

'*No, sir, boy!*' Hawkins shouted the words. 'I don't want anyone else involved! Just you!'

'I made it very clear: I'm not licensed to practise here. I can't file in the state of New York.'

'Who said anything about filing? I just want the papers.'

Sam was numb. He was not sure what he was supposed to say; what he could say: 'Do you mean to tell me you retained me for ten thousand dollars to prepare legal papers you are not going to execute – strike that – *file*?'

'Didn't say I wouldn't sometime. I'm just not going to worry about it now.'

'Then why get a lawyer until you need one? And why the hell am I in New York?'

'Because I don't want you in Washington. For your own good. And when a man raises money for a corporation, he's got to have real legal-looking documents to give for it. I reversed the order of your questions.'

'I'm glad you told me. I won't pursue either one. What kind of corporation?'

'A regular one.'

'There's no such thing. Every company is different.'

'The kind where profits are shared. Among investors.'

'In that they're all the same. Or should be.'

'That's the kind I want. No monkey business.'

'Wait a minute.' Devereaux put down the phone and crossed to the chair where he'd left his attaché case. From it he took out a yellow legal pad and two pencils and returned to the desk. 'I'll need the specifics. I'm going to ask you some questions so I can rough out this not-to-be-filed, unexecuted legal document.'

'Go ahead, boy.'

'What's the title? The corporate name.'

'I thought about that. What do you think of the Shepherd Company?'

'Not a hell of a lot. I don't know what it means. Not that it makes any difference. Call it anything you like.'

'I like the Shepherd Company.'

'Fine.' Sam wrote out the words. 'What's the address?'

'United Nations.'

Devereaux looked at the telephone. 'What?'

'The address. Whatever the United Nations building is.'

'Why?'

'It's ... symbolic.'

'You can't use a symbolic address.'

'Why not?'

'I forgot. You're not filing. All right. The depository?'

'Who?'

'The bank. Where the corporate funds will be deposited.'

'Leave that blank. A couple of lines. There'll be several banks.'

Sam's pencil involuntarily stopped. He forced it onward. 'What's the purpose of the company?'

There was a pause in Washington. 'Give me some legal-sounding choices.'

Now a longer pause in New York. Devereaux's pencil really objected. 'Let's start with "intent".'

'Obviously, to make money.'

'How?'
'By having something people will pay for.'
'Manufacturing? Production of merchandise?'
'No, not really.'
'Marketing?'
'That's nearer. Keep going.'
'Where?'
'Some more words,' replied Hawkins.
'I'm not a corporate attorney but if I remember the books, a company's purpose - its motive for profit - is in one form or another of production, manufacturing, marketing, acquisition, services —'
'Hold it! That one.'
'Services?'
'That's good, but I mean the one before that.'
Sam exhaled. 'Acquisition?'
'That's it. Acquisition.'
'Acquiring at one price, disposing at a second, higher price. You're in brokerage?'
'That's very good, Sam. That's really using the old noodle.'
Devereaux pushed the pencil against its inanimate will and wrote on the pad. 'If you're a broker, there's got to be a product. Services or real estate or merchandise —'
'Of a deeply religious nature,' interrupted MacKenzie, his voice low and solemn.
'What is?'
'The product.'
Sam inhaled; it was a long breath. When he exhaled it was with a hum. 'Are you saying that you are forming a company to broker the acquisition of religious merchandise?'
'That'll do,' answered Hawkins simply.
'Artifacts?'
'That's even better.'
'For Christ's sake, *what* is?'
'"Broker the acquisition of religious artifacts." Goddamn, boy. Perfect!'

*

Devereaux borrowed the standard New York State forms for a limited partnership agreement from Barton. It was a relatively simple matter to transcribe his notes into the partnership forms and have the hotel stenographer re-type the pages as though they had been dictated. Things were looking up, thought Sam as he scrutinized the finished product, replete with its blank lines for investors, depositories, amounts; and the inane description of 'brokering the acquisition of religious artifacts'.

But it looked as legal as a chapter in Blackstone. Yes, Sam mused as he balanced the envelope containing the gobbledygook he was about to mail to MacKenzie Hawkins. Things *were* looking up. He'd be back in Boston with Aaron Pinkus Associates in a few days; his 'legal' work for the Hawk was finished. Altogether it had taken him nine days, some three weeks short of the month Mac had figured.

He had agreed to stay at the Drake a day or two longer, giving Mac sufficient opportunity to approve of his labours. There was no question that approval would come, and it did.

'My word, Sam, that's a mighty impressive looking document,' said the Hawk over the telephone from Washington. 'I'm downright amazed you were able to write it all up so quickly.'

'There are certain guidelines to follow; it wasn't that difficult.'

'You're too modest, young fella.'

'I'm anxious, that's what I am. Anxious to get back to Boston —'

'I can certainly understand that,' broke in Hawkins without the commensurate affirmative that would have curtailed the sudden, growing pain in Devereaux's stomach.

'*Listen*, Mac —'

'I see you made me president of the company. You didn't tell me that.'

'There were no other names. I asked you about the corporate officers and you said leave the lines blank.'

'What are those titles *secretary* and *treasurer*? Are they important?'

'Not if you're not filing.'

'Suppose someday I decided to?'

'The standard procedure is to combine the two. Most states require a minimum of two general partners for a limited partnership agreement.'

'But I could have more if I wanted to, couldn't I?'

'Certainly.'

'I just wanted to know what's right, Sam. Not important. It's never going to be filed. Just passes the time.'

Devereaux thought he detected a note of melancholy in Hawkins's voice. Was Mac beginning to come to grips with his own fantasies? Did he begin to understand that his irrational foray into corporate legalities was simple compensation for the absence of command decision? Sam began to relax. He actually felt sorry for this old warhorse. *Passes the time* was a euphemism for *filling up the days*. 'I'm sure it does, General.'

'Why, Sam, you haven't called me general in weeks.'

'Sorry. A slip.'

'I'll be in touch with you tomorrow, boy. You've worked hard. Have a little fun tonight. Remember, it's on the expense account.'

'As to that ten thou'. It's very generous of you but I don't want it. I don't need it. I'll deduct whatever legal expenses - stenographer, supplies, that kind of thing - and return the rest. Then there's an investment counsellor I know in Washington —'

Devereaux stopped. He realized that the click on the other end of the line had terminated the conversation.

There was no point in not having a good time. He had spent enough weekends in New York to know where the action was: the singles' bars on Third Avenue.

Sam was spectacularly successful. His catch was a nubile young thing who had come out of Omaha, Nebraska - the county seat of Henry Fonda and Marlon Brando - to scale the Broadway heights. She was terribly impressed with a lawyer who did a lot of work for Metro-Goldwyn-Warner-

Brothers when he wasn't handling contracts for *Dirty Sally* and *Masterpiece Theatre*.

Sam was impressed, too. All during the night, throughout most of the next morning, well into the following afternoon and (with time out for food and limited discussion) into the next evening.

It was 9.27 when the telephone rang; 9.29 when the nubile young thing spoke sleepily. 'Sam, the phone's on my side.'

'You're very observant.'

'Shall I get it?' she asked.

'Since it's on your side, I'd say yes.'

'You're sure?'

Sam opened his eyes. The girl had raised herself and was stretching; the sheet had fallen away. 'Make it quick,' Devereaux said.

'If you're sure.'

'I have no wife and my mother doesn't know where I am and Aaron Pinkus wouldn't be mad. Get the phone, talk fast, and hang up.'

The girl reached for the instrument; Sam reached for the girl.

'There's a man with a raspy voice who wants to talk to you. He says his name is Angelo Dellacroce.' She handed Sam the receiver.

'Hey, *you*!' The words spat from the telephone. 'You Samuel Deverooze, sec'atary-treasurer of this Shepherd Company?'

CHAPTER NINE

Former Lieutenant General MacKenzie Hawkins, twice awarded the nation's highest honour for extraordinary heroism beyond the call of duty in deadly combat against the enemy, cowered like a frightened boy at the sight of former Major Sam Devereaux, military accident.

Hawkins could see Sam getting out of the taxi at the entrance of the North Hampton Golf Club. The brass lamps on top of the stone posts flanking the drive were the only source of light; it was a cold, cloudy night and no moon could be seen. The lamps, however, gave sufficient illumination to reveal the anguished expression on Devereaux's face.

Sam was furious, MacKenzie realized that. But, he thought to himself, he had not actually lied. Not really. He never told Devereaux he *wouldn't* approach Angelo Dellacroce. Only that he had no reason to do so when Sam pressed him on the point. At that moment. Not *later*.

The secretary-treasurer title was something else. It looked terrific on the partnership agreement: *Samuel Devereaux, Esq., Counsellor-at-law, Suite 4-F, Drake Hotel, New York*, right above the line reserved for the second most important office in the Shepherd Company. It was for Devereaux's own good; he'd understand that soon enough. But at the moment Samuel Devereaux, Esq., was mad as a caged bull fenced off from heifers in heat.

The Hawk had agreed to Dellacroce's rendezvous because it suited him. The Italian was so concerned about surveillance he had insisted on meeting Mac in the middle of the fairway on hole six at the North Hampton Golf Club between the hours of midnight and one in the morning. But if

Hawkins had objected and changed the location to the Bell Telephone Company, Dellacroce would have capitulated.

For Dellacroce had no choice. Mac had a folder on the Mafioso that would have guaranteed a jail sentence worthy of a court in the People's Republic.

Still, a meeting at night in terrain surrounded by thick woods and streams and small lakes appealed to Hawkins. He was at home in such territory. It wasn't Cambodia or Laos, but he could sort of keep his hand in, as it were.

He flew up from Washington in the afternooon and with false identification rented a car and drove out to North Hampton. As soon as it was dark, he circled the golf club and parked at the west perimeter. Dellacroce had told him that the club was closed for the evening and the night watchman would be replaced by one of his men.

Which meant, of course, that Dellacroce would double the patrols everywhere, especially around the area of fairway six.

His pockets stuffed with coils of thin rope and rolls of three-inch adhesive, Hawkins employed an old Ho Chi-minh tactic that had served him well in the past. He began his commando assault at the farthest point inside the hostile area and worked his way towards the front.

At 2300 the enemy patrols started to man their emplacements within the North Hampton Golf Club. There were nine (a few more than Mac had anticipated) spaced out in the rough by the edge of the woods on both sides of fairway six, the line of relay extending back to the clubhouse and the driveway.

One by one, Hawkins immobilized eight patrols; he removed all weapons, bound them, taped their faces - all facial muscles, not just the mouths - and rendered them unconscious with *kai-sai* chops at the base of the skull. Then he worked his way back to the ninth patrol who manned the entrance.

He saved for this man a strategy that was particularly effective against the Pathet Lao. For the guard had to be able to talk.

The man was exceedingly cooperative. Especially after Mac had sliced his trousers from crotch to cuff.

At ten minutes to midnight, Dellacroce's huge black limousine drove swiftly through the gates and up to the wide, pillared porch. In the darkness the ninth patrol, riveted to a pillar, spoke.

'Everything's fine, Mr Dellacroce. All the boys are spread good, like you said.'

The man's voice was a bit high and a little strained, but Hawkins figured rightly that Dellacroce had other things on his mind.

'Okay. Real good,' was the raspy reply as Dellacroce got out of the automobile, flanked by two heavyset bodyguards who walked like gorillas with their hands in their fur. 'Rocco, you stay here with Augie. You, Fingers, you come with me. And, Meat, you get the fuckin' car back in the lot outta sight.'

Before Dellacroce and Fingers had rounded the corner of the building, the ninth patrol was *kai-sai*ed out of commission. By the time Dellacroce and Fingers had disappeared across the lawn, Rocco had joined Augie in peaceful oblivion.

The gentleman named Meat was Hawkins's next dispatchee. It took nearly five minutes, but only because Meat was an experienced combat man. He did not park the limousine at the edge of the lot; instead, he had pulled to a stop in the centre. It was good positioning, thought Mac. Meat could observe all his flanks unencumbered by visual shadings or sightline obstructions. Meat was good.

But not good enough.

MacKenzie scrambled diagonally out of the parking area, over the first tee, and left through the rough towards fairway six. Since Dellacroce had made it clear he would be alone, Hawkins knew that Fingers would be hiding in the darkness, no doubt at the edge of the woods, and if he had a brain in his head, across the fairway on the east side for a superior line of fire.

But Fingers did not have much savvy. He remained in the

west rough, prone in the underbush, eliminating any rear flank observation.

Goddamn, thought MacKenzie, it was not much fun taking an asshole like Fingers.

Nevertheless, he took him. Silently. In eleven seconds.

Leaving Angelo Dellacroce alone in the middle of fairway six, the lighted end of a cigar protruding from his fat mouth, his squat body sagging at ease, his plump hands clasped behind his back as though waiting to be served a plate of linguini in a slow trattoria.

Three minutes later Devereaux's taxi was heard on the deserted back road fronting the golf club, and MacKenzie waited behind the pillar.

As Sam walked haltingly up the drive, Hawkins decided not to tell him about the immobilized patrols. It would only worry the ex-major; better to let him think Dellacroce was true to his word: he was alone on fairway six.

'God*damn!* Hello, Sam!'

Devereaux threw himself to the ground, hugging the gravel for dear life. And then he looked up; MacKenzie took out a small but powerful pencil light from his pocket and flicked it on.

The ex-major was certainly angry. His face was kind of pinched and puffed, as if it might explode right out of his skin.

'You unprincipled son of a bitch!' Sam whispered, fury and fear intermeshed. 'You lowlife! You're the most devious, despicable form of subhuman that ever lived! What the hell have you done, you *bastard*?'

'Now, now, that's no way to talk. Come on, get up; you look silly down there all splayed out ...' MacKenzie reached for Devereaux's hand.

'*Don't touch me*, you slug worm! Fucking Mongolian sheep is too *good* for you! I should have let Lin Shoo pry out your fingernails, one by one, for four thousand fucking years! Don't *touch* me!' Sam staggered to his feet.

'Look, Major –'

'Don't call me that! I don't own a serial number and I don't want to be addressed *ever* by anything *remotely* military! I'm a lawyer, but I'm not *your* goddamned lawyer! Where the hell are we? How many "torpedoes" have us covered with guns?'

MacKenzie grinned. 'There's nobody, boy. Just Dellacroce standing out on the fairway like a nice uncle at a backyard pasta party.'

'I don't believe you! Do you know what that gorilla told me on the phone when I said I wouldn't come out here? That goddamned hood told me my health would take a sudden turn for the worse! That's what he told me!'

'Oh, don't pay any attention to that sort of thing. Those fat slobs always talk tough.'

'Horseshit!' Devereaux peered into the darkness. 'That maniac said if I was late he'd send a basket of fruit to the hospital – *tomorrow*! And if I tried to leave town, some goon called Meat would find me before the week was up!'

The Hawk shook his head. 'Meat's pretty good, but I think you could take him. I'd put my money on you, boy.'

'I don't *want* to take him – or *any*body! And don't put any money on *me*! You're never going to see me again! I just wanted to get this over with. I want to meet this Dellacroce; tell him the whole thing's a crazy mistake! I had some typing done for you, and that's all!'

'Now listen to me, son. You're over-reacting. There's nothing to worry about at all.' Hawkins started walking across the lawn. Devereaux kept pace, his head snapping in the direction of every noise. 'Mr Dellacroce will be exceedingly cooperative. And there'll be no more tough talk, you'll see.'

'What was that?' There was a squishing sound.

'Relax, will you? I think you stepped on some dog turd. Do me a favour. Don't start explaining anything until I talk with Dellacroce, okay? It won't take me more than three or four minutes.'

'*No!* Absolutely *no*! I don't care to have a promising legal career cut short in the middle of a fairway at some Cosa Nostra golf course! These people don't play games! They use bullets, and chains, and heavy cement! And rivers! What was *that*?' There was a fluttering of wings in the dark trees.

'We alarmed a bird. Let's put it this way. If you just keep your mouth shut until I'm finished, I'll pay you another ten thousand. Free and clear. How about that?'

'You're a lunatic! No, again. Because I can't spend it displacing roots in a Boston cemetery! You could offer ten million; the answer's still no!'

'That's not out of the question —'

'For Christ's sake, have yourself committed before somebody else does!'

'Then I'm afraid I'll have to put it this way. You either shut up until my business with Mr Dellacroce is finished, or tomorrow morning I call the FBI and tell them there's an ex-major walking around peddling raw-file intelligence documents he illegally removed from the G-two archives.'

'Oh, no you don't! Because I'll tell the truth. I'll tell them how you blackmailed me, then conned me, then blackmailed me again. You'd get a lighter prison sentence in Peking!'

'It surely does get complicated, doesn't it? I mean you'd be reopening the Brokemichael business. How would it look? A man violates the espionage laws because he doesn't like spending a little extra time in the service of his country. In a cushy job, not even combat. Pretty weak blackmail, I'd say.'

'You *unprincipled* —'

'I know, I know,' said the Hawk wearily. 'You keep repeating yourself. What you've got to understand is that it doesn't make a whole lot of difference to me. As you said, I've been shafted. How much more shafting can they do?'

Hawkins kept walking. Devereaux followed reluctantly, his eyes darting everywhere, his nerves obviously frayed; a series of whispered squeaks emerged from his throat until he found the words. 'Have you no decency, sir? No sense of compassion? No love of your fellowman within your heart?'

'I surely do,' said the Hawk. They cut across the third tee on to fairway six. 'Now keep that eloquent tongue of yours inactive for a while. If you don't like the way things go, then speak your piece. Can I be fairer than that?'

The overcast sky was thinning out; intermittently the moon shone through. And a hundred yards ahead they could see the squat figure of Angelo Dellacroce his hands still clasped behind his back, the lighted stub of a cigar in his mouth.

'He must have ashes all over his front,' said Hawkins quietly. Then louder, 'Mr Dellacroce?'

There was a grunt from the obese body in front of them. MacKenzie flicked on his pencil light and held it over his own head, spilling the light on his longish steel-grey hair, throwing shadows down across his precisely barbered Van Dyke.

'You're making us a target!' whispered Sam.

'Who's going to shoot?'

They approached the Italian; Mac extended his hand. Dellacroce made no move to accept it. Hawkins spoke quietly. 'Even when I accepted gook surrenders I got a handshake. Sort of separates us from the animals.'

Reluctantly Dellacroce pulled his hand from behind his back and the two shook. 'I ain't no gook and this ain't no surrender,' said the raspy voice.

'Course it isn't,' answered MacKenzie brightly. 'It's the beginning of a profitable association. By the way, this is my attorney and good friend, Sam Devereaux —'

'*Mac!*'

'Shut up and shake hands,' said Hawkins *sotto voce*. 'Goddamn, boys. I said shake *hands*!'

With even greater reluctance, the two hands inched towards each other, touched briefly and separated as though the owners feared infection.

'That's better,' said the Hawk enthusiastically. 'Now we can talk.'

And MacKenzie did. He started by listing the illegal activities - both foreign and domestic - of Angelo Dellacroce. It took him two minutes.

'Now, Mr Dellacroce, the reason the authorities can't catch up with you is that they don't have access to a single financial clearinghouse that ties in specifically with all these here sundry enterprises. I realize it will sound strange to you, sir, but I believe I have that access. There's a bank in Geneva, Switzerland; the first three numbers of the account happen to be seven, one, five. In this account is something over sixty-two million dollars —'

'*Basta! Basta!*'

'– and the deposits were made directly from such locales as I've suggested. Now I guess you've studied the new Swiss laws relative to such accounts. They're tricky because fraud in one country may not constitute fraud in Geneva. But goddamn, would you believe there's now a way for Interpol to subpoena the records of those accounts? All the international police have to do is submit a copy of a payment – to a specific account – that's been made by a convicted narcotics dealer. And it surely is wondrous good fortune on my part to have in my possession Xeroxed copies of quite a few such payments —'

'*Basta!* You shut up!' Dellacroce roared. '*Fingers! Manny! Carlo! Dino!* Get out here! *Now!*'

There were only the sounds of the night in reply.

'There's no one there. At least no one that can hear you,' said the Hawk softly.

'*What? — Fingers! Figlio della prostituta!* Get out here!'

Nothing.

'Now, you and I, Mr Dellacroce, will step away from my friend and attorney, here, so we can talk real private-like.' MacKenzie touched the Italian's arm, which was instantly yanked away.

'*Meat! Augie! Rocco!* You hear me, boys? Get out here!'

'They're sleeping, too, sir,' said Hawkins kindly. 'They won't wake up for a couple of hours.'

Dellacroce whipped his head towards Mac. 'You got cops here? How many cops you got?' The questions overlapped.

'Nobody. Just me and my good friend and attorney – '

'How many? Alone you couldn't!'

'Alone, I did,' answered the Hawk.

'My best boys!'

'I'd hate like hell to see your support troops.' MacKenzie chuckled. 'Now it's time for our private talk.'

The Hawk led Dellacroce thirty feet away. He talked quietly for exactly four minutes and thirty seconds.

At which point a rasping, ear-splitting scream shattered the stillness of fairway six.

'*Mannnnaaagggiii*'!'

And Angelo Dellacroce fainted right there on the manicured grass.

MacKenzie bent over the man and gently slapped him back into consciousness.

They talked once more with the Hawk holding the obese Italian's neck as though he were a medical corpsman.

The scream came again.

'*Mannnnaaaaggggiii*'!'

And Dellacroce fainted again.

So the Hawk revived him again.

And they talked for two minutes more.

'*Mannnnaaaaggggiiii!*'

This time MacKenzie lowered the man's head on the grass of fairway six and got up. The moon had broken through the night clouds, revealing a stunned Sam staring at the sight of the fallen Dellacroce. This was it, thought the Hawk, as he walked slowly towards Devereaux. There was no point in procrastinating any longer. Sam would have to be told. There was no other way.

'Well, Sam,' began Mac with quiet confidence in the intermittent moonlight on fairway six, 'it's a pretty good start. Mr Dellacroce was eager to subscribe to the full amount reserved for him. The Shepherd Company has its first ten million dollars.'

Devereaux's knees buckled. The Hawk rushed forward and caught him before he hit the ground. The ground was not hard but MacKenzie wanted Sam to know he cared; it was always a good idea to let one's superior-adjutant know the commander was concerned for his well-being. 'God-damn, son, you've got to stop this kind of thing! You're behaving no better than Mr Dellacroce! Now that's just not proper; you're cut from a finer tunic!'

Sam's eyes were swimming around and around in the moonlight on fairway six. The words that emerged from his trembling lips were by and large incoherent, but several phrases were repeated often enough to be understood. 'Secretary-treasurer! – Oh, my God, I'm a *sec'atary-treasurer*! Ten million dollars' worth of cement! I'm in ten million dollars' worth of shit! I'll be sunk in concrete pyjamas! I'm *dead*!'

'Now, now, stop your wailin'. You're a big lawyer, fella; you shouldn't act like this.'

'I should never have met you, you squirrelly bastard! That's the only *shouldn't* of my life! Oh, my God! That killer passed out!'

'So did you. Almost. I caught you —'

'*Shhh!* Let's get out of here! I'll send him a letter – I'll get some Bellevue stationery – I'll certify you a fucking lunatic! It was all a lousy joke!'

'Oh, Mr Dellacroce knows better than that, boy!' Hawkins patted Devereaux's cheek with his right hand while, with his left, he kept an iron grip on the base of Sam's skull, inhibiting any movement above the waist. 'Dellacroce's a very religious man, most of these Italian fellas are; doesn't make any difference what they do for a living. That's separate. He knows I told him the truth.'

'What the hell are you talking about? What's religion got to do with anything? Get the fuck off my neck!'

'Religion helps a man recognize the truth. He may not like it; his *religion* may not like it, or even admit it is the truth, but because he's contemplated, the religious man can separate what's real from what's horseshit. You follow me?'

'Not for a goddamned second! My neck hurts!'

'Sorry, I'll ease up, but it's time we talk.' MacKenzie removed his hand. Instantly Devereaux bolted, but the Hawk merely rolled with him, pinning him back to the earth. 'I said we've got to *talk*, boy. You're a reasonable person; you can see the logic in that.'

'The problem,' whispered Sam, straining on the ground,

'is that you're *not* reasonable *or* logical! Do you know what you've done? Guys like that —' He gestured with his head; somehow, he could not use his hands. 'They freeze people for welching on their bookies! They think nothing about paying for the biggest funeral in town - for a *paisan* who held out on a skim! I *know*. I'm from *Boston*.'

'You're over-reacting again. Mr Dellacroce won't do anything like that. He knows where he stands - which is roughly in twenty feet of lye if he doesn't behave. That account in Geneva. He stole from his own people.'

Grudgingly, suspiciously, Devereaux stared at Mac in the moonlight. 'You're sure of that?'

'It was all in the G-two files. Trouble was nobody put it together. I don't think they wanted to; Dellacroce's crowd are big Pentagon supporters, what with government contracts and union affiliations —. Now, will you listen to me?'

With a reluctance born of fear, but with an assent formed in necessity, Sam nodded. The Hawk helped him up and the two men walked into the rough off fairway six. There was a large oak tree whose leaves filtered the moonlight. Sam sat down against the trunk; Mac fell to one knee in front of him, the line officer clarifying orders at a fire base.

'Remember a couple of weeks ago my telling you how I was looking into things I hadn't thought much about before? God and the church and things like that.'

'I remember saying I wouldn't laugh —' Devereaux's reply was flat, wary. A monotone.

'That was very thoughtful, boy. Well, I *was* doing some thinking, but not quite in the way you maybe considered. You and I know that ninety-nine per cent of all Commie propaganda is horseshit; everybody knows that. Ours is only say, fifty to sixty per cent, so we're way ahead on that score. But that one per cent of the Bolshie feedback got me to wondering. About this Catholic situation. Not what people *believe*, that's their business. But how the organization operates. And it seemed to me that these Vatican fellows got such a good thing going they should spread a little more around. I mean, they got investments, son. When the stock market goes up a couple of points anywhere in the world, they make zillions.'

'And if it goes down, they lose zillions.'

'Not so! The brokers get 'em out in time or they get canned from the Knights of Malta. It's part of the arrangement. And they can't get their pictures taken with the pope.'

'That *is* horseshit.'

'If it is, why do all the Catholic brokers on Wall Street have all those initials after their names. You know of any college degrees that start with the letter *K*? Malta, Columbus, Lourdes. And the saints! *Jesus!* Knights of Assisi, Knights of Peter, Matthew – it goes on for pages. It's kind of a social order. The more a fellow on the stock exchange does for the Vatican, the better the *K* after his name. And Wall Street's only one example. It's the same all over the place.'

'I think you've been reading some pretty strange books. The *Ku Klux Klanner*, maybe. Nineteen twenty edition.'

'Hell, no, I don't cotton to that shit. A man's got a right to believe anything he likes. I'm only talking about the financial part. Then there's real estate. Do you know the sort of real estate the Vatican boys have? I swear they pick up rent from the Ginza to the Gaza strips and most places in between. They own *the* prime properties in New York, Chicago, Hartford, Detroit – 'most every place where the micks, the wops, the Polacks and all those kind of people migrated. They always do it the same way. They go in early – before all the ethnics get settled – and buy up land and build a big church. Naturally, all these Ellis Islanders are nervous being in a strange place and all, so *they* build their houses near the church. In a generation or so the kids are lawyers and dentists and own automobile dealerships. So what do they do? They move out to the suburbs and go to work where they once lived, which is now the centre of *town*, the *business* district. And the church property skyrockets! It's a regular pattern, boy!'

'I'm trying to find something negative here and I can't.'

said Sam, staring in the shadows at the excited Hawkins. 'What's wrong with the pattern?'

'I didn't say it was wrong. I said it made for one hell of a centralized portfolio.'

'"Centralized portfolio"? You've got a new vocabulary.'

'Like you said, I've been reading. And not such strange books as you might think. You see, Sam, the product these Vatican boys manufacture – that's not meant disrespectfully, only in a business sense – doesn't change. It may have to adjust a mite now and then, take a tuck here or a nip there, but the basic merchandise stays the same. That reduces a major cost factor and allows for a continuous profit figure with no chance of negative entry —'

'"Negative entry"?'

'That's an accounting term.'

'I know it's an accounting term. How do *you* know – don't tell me. Your reading material.'

'Maggie's drawers, son.'

'What?'

'Never mind. You're on target, that's all. Now, you take an economic situation where the stock exchanges and the real estate markets hold firm, and that means you got the banks, because you control both money *and* land. Prime economic resources. And you add to that a product that requires minimum assembly alterations with maximum purchase growth – hell, boy, it's a worldwide *gold mine*.'

'You have been reading. But if you're right, why's there so much hassle over the parochial schools and *their* costs?'

'That's services, Sam. That's an entirely different entry column. I'm talking about basic portfolios, not annual operating expenditures; they fluctuate with economic conditions. Anyway, it's mostly blackmail.'

'That's succinct. They wouldn't like you in Boston.'

The Hawk shifted his weight and spoke a little more softly, but with no loss of emphasis. 'You mentioned before about something wrong. Well, I don't like to mention it because it only applies to the pricky-shit high brass and not the troops, but there is something that's got a bit of sting to it.'

'*You* found a *moral* position?'

'Morality and economics should be more related than they have been; everybody knows that. You take this political thing. Nobody's traded fire power with the Reds any better'n I have. God*damn*, nobody's going to bury me! But it strikes me that these Catholic boys in the Vatican – and that means all the powerful dioceses – use the Bolshie excuse a mite too freely to oppose just about everything that could make things better for the peasant slobs scratching a life out of very tough ground.'

Devereaux eyed Hawkins sceptically. 'That position's a little dated. A great many changes are taking place in the Church. This new pope is opening a lot of windows. Like John the Twenty-third did.'

'Not quick enough, Sam. What the Vatican brass needs is a good shake-up in command. Something to jolt their *be*robed asses out of their lethargy.'

'You can't change a two-thousand-year pattern overnight —'

'Oh, I understand that,' interrupted the Hawk. 'And I'm glad you brought up this new pope. This Francesco. Because he's a very popular fellow. Even those who hate his guts – for doing what he's doing – know he's the biggest asset they've got in the whole damn church – that's not meant in a religious sense, of course. I don't take positions that way.'

'What positions? What sense?'

'This Francesco,' continued Mac, overlooking Devereaux's questions, 'is more than just the pope, which is enough to begin with. He's a beloved individual, you know what I'm driving at?'

'I wish you wouldn't say that.'

'He's the sort of person every man jack of a Catholic would really sacrifice for, you see what I mean?'

'I don't like that phrase, either.'

The Hawk changed knees rapidly; it was good to redistribute weight as often as possible when in an immobile position. 'Do you know the estimated total communicant membership of the Catholic Church?'

'The *what?*'

'How many Catholics there are in the world? Never mind. I'll tell you. Four hundred million. Now, taking the median figure of one American dollar – setting a specific date for the rate of exchange; some giving more, most less – that comes to *four hundred million dollars*.'

'What does?'

'The projected gross.'

'What projected gross?'

'Of the Shepherd Company's business services. This here "brokering the acquisition of religious artifacts". It's a clear ratio of ten to one in terms of capitalization, but naturally the profit ratio, as opposed to the gross figure, will be affected by the necessary outlay for equipment and support personnel.'

'What the hell are you babbling about?!'

'We're going to kidnap the pope, Sam.'

'*Whaaat!*'

'I've got a trunkful of books, boy. I've really been studying the tactical problems and I think I've got 'em licked. You see, there's this place called Chiesa di San Tommaso di Villanova in Gandolfo – pardon my lousy Italian – and the route from the Vatican is over a kind of country thoroughfare called the Via Appia Antica. It's the road to this here Gandolfo – Castel Gandolfo, they call it. These Italians, they never use one word when they can use two.'

'*Whaaat?!*'

'Now, don't go over-reacting. You'll wake up Dellacroce.'

'*Whaaat?*'

'But first we have to corral the remaining capitalization. There's thirty million more coming. I believe I've almost narrowed down the three investors, but I've still got some refining to do.' The Hawk clapped his hand over Devereaux's open mouth. 'Now, don't start that again. You keep repeating yourself.'

Devereaux's eyes bulged above MacKenzie's spread hand, but the rest of his body was frozen. Sort of a form of comatose shock, thought Hawkins. He'd seen a lot of that kind of thing when raw recruits got their first taste of a fire fight. At least Sam wasn't screaming. Or struggling. He was just plain still and kind of cold. The Hawk continued; he had only a few words left to say. The in-depth command analyses would come later. In a way he was glad Devereaux's over-reaction was so extreme. In his enthusiasm he had nearly given Sam some tactical information he was not sure he wanted Devereaux to have.

'I didn't choose you lightly. No superior-adjutant is an easy choice for a commander to make, for in many ways the SA is an extension of himself. You got it on *merit*, boy. I don't say you're ideal, you've got deficiencies. I've told you that. But, goddamn, your assets out-point your liabilities. I say that as an honest friend as well as a superior officer.

'Now, there'll be certain executive orders that you'll be asked to carry out, not always knowing precisely why they're vital. You'll just have to accept them. Command is a lonely responsibility; there's not always the time to share the reasons for one's decisions. Ask any frontline officer who sends a battalion into fire. But you'll do splendidly. I just know you will. And if by any chance you're tempted to question the orders of your superior officer, or feel that you cannot in conscience implement them, I think you should know that our investor, Angelo Dellacroce, believes that you alone, as the attorney and secretary-treasurer of the Shepherd Company, compiled that list of his illegal activities and furnished me with them. I believe that's why he didn't care to shake hands with you. Coupled with your G-two espionage violations, I'd say your position was somewhat untenable. But if I were you and had my druthers, I'd choose to fight the government treason charges rather than our investor, Mr Dellacroce. I think that Mafia bastard would cut your balls off, grind 'em up in a blender, and serve 'em as a fancy pâté at your funeral. Like you said earlier, it'd probably be an expensive funeral.'

There was no point in the Hawk holding his hand over his superior-adjutant's mouth any longer. Sam had *merfed* and *gleefed* in a spasm of panic and passed out cold.

The moonlight, filtering through the leaves of the large, sturdy oak in the rough off fairway six, cut shafts of yellow and white across Sam's young, peaceful, unmistakably strong features.

Goddamn, thought MacKenzie, the boy's going to be fine! He just needed a little time to absorb the facts. Of course, if a person didn't know any better, he'd think the son of a bitch was dead.

CHAPTER TEN

Sam Devereaux sank despondently into the hotel chair and wished he were dead.

Well, not really, but it certainly would solve a lot of problems. Of course, it was entirely possible that the state of his demise might come about whether he desired it or not. Which brought his eyes back to the insane, unfiled but filled-out limited partnership agreement between the Shepherd Company, MacKenzie Hawkins, President, and the North Hampton Corporation, Mrs Angelo Dellacroce, President; Depository: the Great Bank of Geneva, Switzerland. He held the legal document in his hand and wondered absently where his fingernails had gone.

Prominently on the first page, directly under the title of president and above the line reserved for the secretary-treasurer, was his name.

Mr Samuel Devereaux, Counsellor-at-law, Suite 4-F, The Drake Hotel, New York City.

He speculated for a moment whether he could alter the Drake's registry and then abandoned the idea. What was the point? On one flank (*flank?*) was the United States government with very specific espionage laws, and on the other was Angelo Dellacroce and his guards-of-honour with their white ties on white shirts and dark glasses and black suits and very *un*specific methods of dealing with the likes of 'squeals' such as S. Devereaux, counsellor-at-law.

Sam wondered what Aaron Pinkus would do. Then he realized what Aaron would do and abandoned that thought, too.

Pinkus would sit *Shiva* for him.

He got out of the chair and wandered aimlessly through

the hotel suite. What the hell *was* he going to do? What in God's name *could* he do? His gaze fell on the unsigned, typewritten note on the desk.

Copies of this limited partnership agreement have been sent by messenger to MacKenzie Hawkins, Esquire, President, the Shepherd Company, c/o The Watergate Hotel, Wash. D.C. Instructions cabled: Great Bank of Geneva. Funds transfer awaits presence Sec.-Treas., Shep. Co., Samuel Devereaux in Geneva.

He had been *cabled – internationally*.

In some marble banking hall in Switzerland, a powerful broker of international finance had no doubt already listed him as the bona fide overseer of the transfer of ten million dollars into an account of a nonfiled but very much existing company named Shepherd.

That's what he was going to do whether he liked it or not. It was Geneva, or a lifetime of cracking rocks at Leavenworth, *or* Dellacroce justice – feet-in-cement style.

Kidnap the pope!

My God! That's what the crazy bastard said. He was going to *kidnap the pope*!

All of Mac's other insanities paled by any stretch of comparison! World War Three might be more acceptable! A simple war would be so much – well, simpler. Borders were defined, objectives properly obscured, ideologies flexible. A war was duck soup compared to 400 million hysterical Catholics; and heads of state moaning and groaning their obsequious platitudes, blaming every conceivable inimical faction, extremist or not (secretly glad to be rid of the meddling nuisance in the Vatican) and ....

My God! World War Three could be a very logical consequence of Hawkins's act!

And with that realization Sam knew what he had to do. He had to stop MacKenzie. But he could not stop him if he were in a maximum security cell in Leavenworth: who would believe him? And he certainly could not stop him if he were at the bottom of one of the deeper sections of the Hudson River, probably upstate, courtesy of Angelo Dellacroce; who would hear him?

No, the only way he could push the Hawk's insanity out of the realm of reality was to find out how the hell MacKenzie intended to pull off his papal score. The most foolish thing here would be to assume he couldn't do it. The Hawk was no joke; anyone who thought he was need only look at a few of Mac's accomplishments – including four extraordinary ex-wives who adored him, and a little matter of an initial capitalization of ten million dollars, to say nothing of military exploits spanning three decades and the same number of wars.

What the Hawk was bringing to the profession of crime were all the strategic resources, the finely honed discipline, and the leadership of an experienced general officer. MacKenzie was starting at the top; no graduate of the lineup he, but instead, a full-fledged criminal commander who had already outsacked a Mafia don in his own backyard.

The son of a bitch had flair. Christ! He had the balls of King Kong smashing the concrete off the Empire State Building as he climbed up the sides.

Kidnap the pope!

Who the hell would believe it?

Samuel Devereaux believed it, that's who believed it. What was left was for S. Devereaux, counsellor-at-law, to figure out how to stop it. And stay both alive and outside prison walls so doing. A vague idea was coming into focus, but it was still too blurred to make sense. Yet there was a core of possibility within the outlines.

'Don't be too confident,' said Sam out loud. 'You're dealing with a living, legal, spinal meningitis!'

But it *was* possible. He could pretend to go along with MacKenzie (always with great reluctance; to act otherwise would be out of character), gather in the diseased money and, at the last moment, convene the investors and blow the whole operation out of the sky. And to save his hide, there'd be a lot of 'in the case of my sudden demise, my own attorneys are instructed to publicly reveal . . .' any number of things.

Including the translation of the Shepherd Company's 'brokering of religious artifacts'.

Who would believe it?

'Stop that!' Sam grabbed his wrist, startled by the sound of his own voice. He was further startled by the sound of the telephone. He raced to it like a man facing execution rushing to hear what the governor had to say.

'Goddamn! This must be the attorney *and* secretary *and* treasurer of the Shepherd Company! With assets over ten million dollars! How does that strike you?'

'It's a leading question. I'll not indulge.'

'You know something, boy? You must be a pistol of a lawyer!'

'Are you sure you want to talk over the telephone?' asked Devereaux. 'It's been given a pretty good FCC rating lately.'

'Oh, that's all right. We won't say anything we shouldn't. At least, *I* won't, and I hope to hell you know better. I just wanted to tell you that the additional copies of the partnership agreement are downstairs waiting for you. I sent them up last night with an old master sergeant I used to know —'

'Good *God*, you had *duplicates* made? You damn fool! Those copy places usually keep a set! If they're photostats there'll be negatives!'

'Not where I was. Right down here in the Watergate lobby there's a big machine. You put in a quarter for each page — *Jesus!* You should have seen the crowds gather! They're a little jumpy around here, aren't they? But nobody saw anything. It was kind of weird. Everybody staring; nobody saying anything. Except two guys from the *Washington Post* who came running in from the street —'

'All right!' interrupted Devereaux. 'The copies are downstairs. What the hell am I supposed to do with them?'

'Put 'em in your fancy briefcase, the one I gave you. Take 'em to Geneva. You won't need 'em in Switzerland, of course, but there may be one or two other stops on the way back. Namely, London; that's pretty definite. You'll be at the

Savoy for a day or two. Airline tickets and everything will be at the hotel in Geneva. When you're in London a gentleman named Danforth will call you. You'll know what to do.'

'That's a dirty pool. I won't know what to do; I don't know what I'm *doing*! You can't just put me in this crazy situation and not tell me anything. I'm carrying documents! My *name* is on them! I'm involved with the transfer of ten million dollars!'

'Now, calm down,' said the Hawk with gentle firmness. 'Remember what I told you: There'll be times when, as my adjutant, you'll be asked to carry out orders —'

'*Bullshit!*' roared Sam. 'What am I supposed to *say* to people?'

'Well, what's bullshit to one man may be sugar-coated wheat to another. If anyone presses you, you're just helping an old soldier who's quietly raising a few dollars to spread religious brotherhood.'

'That's absurd,' said Devereaux.

'That's the Shepherd Company,' said the Hawk.

MacKenzie lifted up five specific pages from the Xeroxed G-2 files scattered over the hotel bed and took them to the desk across the room. He sat down, picked up a red crayon, and proceeded to mark each copy on the top left border. One to five.

Goddamn! It was the sequence he had been looking for, the pattern he knew was there because a man can't resist going back to his first method of fortune building if the circumstances appear right. And because time minimizes the problems and pressures a person felt decades ago, especially if the profits remain.

The covert intelligence out of Hanoi three years ago had been confusing but authentic. Authentic, that is, on the bottom line; everything else was distorted.

An Englishman was making a killing by brokering hardware and ammunition to North Vietnam.

No big deal; London did not frown on trade to the Commie bloc, although there were specific regulations as to war machinery. But it was a period during that screwed up, half-assed conflict when the boys in Hanoi *and* Moscow *and* Peking were running slow on the production lines. Money could be made in large bundles by anyone who could divert combat supplies into North Vietnamese ports.

One Lord Sidney Danforth had done just that.

Buying in the United States, West Germany, and France, he sailed under Chilean flag ostensibly for ports in the new African countries. Except the ships did not go anywhere near Africa. They altered their courses in international Pacific waters, sped north, refuelled in the Russian out-islands, and headed south to Haiphong as regulation-bound trading vessels.

G-2 could never prove Danforth's involvement because the Communist payments were made directly to the Chilean companies and Danforth stayed well out of sight. And Washington was not about to provoke an incident. Danforth was a powerful Englishman with a lot of clout in the Foreign Office. Nam wasn't worth it.

What had intrigued MacKenzie, however, were the two keys: Chilean flag and African ports. They were covers that had been used before. Thirty years ago. During World War II.

It was common knowledge in intelligence circles that certain South American companies with outside financing had fed war machinery to the Axis at enormous profit during the early forties. In those hectic wartime days the shipping destinations were always Capetown and Port Elizabeth because the manifest records in those harbours were chaotic at best, but usually non-existent. Scores of ships that were supposed to dock in South Africa altered courses in the southern Atlantic waters and headed into the Mediterranean. To Italy, generally.

Was it possible that one Lord Sidney Danforth had imitated his own operations of three decades past?

It was one thing to chisel a few million out of South-east Asia in the seventies, something else again to make a fortune out of the holocaust that tested the courage of the British

Lion. A man could get his name taken off the Buckingham Palace guest list pretty quickly for something like that.

It was time for the Hawk to have a transatlantic talk with Lord Sidney Danforth, seventy-two-year-old knighted paragon of British industry. And just about the wealthiest man in England.

Goddamn! The Shepherd Company was attracting some of the most interesting investors.

CHAPTER ELEVEN

The Strand was crowded. It was shortly past five o'clock; the legion of office workers were heading home.

Sam had arrived at Heathrow Airport on the 3.40 flight from Geneva and had wasted no time getting to the relaxed comfort of a Savoy suite. He needed it. Geneva had been a nightmare.

He had realized that for any future record, he had to convey a very specific ignorance as to the objectives of the Shepherd Company, cloaking this lack of knowledge in profound respect for the unnamed principals involved; especially the president, who was motivated by deeply religious convictions.

The Geneva bankers, were, at first, impressed by his humility. My God, ten million United States dollars and the overseeing lawyer only smiled and spoke convivial banalities, demurring when pressed for identities, nodding soulfully about religious brotherhood when the staggering amount was brought up. So they asked him out to lunch, where there were a lot of winks and drinks and offers of bedroom gymnastics of an incredible variety. This was, after all, Switzerland; a buck was a buck and this hard-nosed approach was not to be confused with yodelling and edelweiss and Heidi in her pinafores. Gradually, thought Devereaux, as the lunches evolved into dinners, the Geneva bankers thought he was either the dumbest attorney ever to practise before the American bar or the most implausibly secretive middleman ever to cross their borders.

He kept up the charade for three days and nights, leaving behind a half-dozen confused Swiss burgomasters, tearfully frustrated over unrequited confidences and terribly sick to their stomachs after too much industrial lubricant. And the strain on Sam was unbearable. He had reached the point where he could not concentrate on anything but his own rigid, blank smile and the necessary quiet control of his fears. He was so preoccupied with himself that when the vice-president of the Great Bank of Geneva saw him off at the airport, Devereaux just smiled and said 'Thank you' when the banker threw up over his raincoat.

In his anxiety to get the hell out of Geneva, he had left his shaving kit behind, which explained why he was now on The Strand looking for a drugstore. He walked south for a block and a half, opposite the Hippodrome, and went into the Strand Chemists. His purchases made, he headed back to the hotel, anticipating a long, warm bath, a shave, and a good dinner at the Savoy Grill.

'Major Devereaux!' The voice was enthusiastic, American, and feminine. It came from a taxi which stopped in Savoy Court.

It was Sloping yet Argumentative, the fourth Mrs MacKenzie Hawkins, the lovely lady named Anne. She hurled herself at Sam, encircling his neck with her arms, pressing her cheek and various other parts against him.

Instantly she withdrew and rather awkwardly composed herself. 'I'm awfully sorry. Gosh, that was real *forward* of me. Please forgive me. It was just so *terrific* to see a familiar face.'

'Nothing to apologize for,' said Sam, remembering that Sloping yet Argumentative had appeared to him as the most naïve, as well as the youngest, of the four wives. She had *oohed* a lot, if he recalled correctly. 'Are you staying at the Savoy?'

'Yes. I got in last night. I've never been to England before, so I spent the whole day just walking *everywhere*. Gosh, my feet are yelling at me.' She parted her very expensive suede coat and frowned at the lovely legs very much in evidence below her short skirt.

'Well, let's get you off them quickly. Into the bar, I mean.'

'I can't *tell* you! It's so *marvy* to see someone you know!'

'Are you here by yourself?' asked Devereaux.

'Oh yes, Don, he's my husband – now – is so darned busy with his marinas and restaurants and all those other things that he just said to me last week in LA, he said, "Annie, honey, why don't you get your pretty little ass out of the way for a while? This is going to be a heavy month." Well, I thought of Mexico and Palm Springs and all the usual places, and then I figured, damn! Annie, you've never been to London. So off I flew.' She nodded brightly to the Savoy doorman and continued as Sam gestured her through the entrance into the lobby. 'Don thought I was crazy. I mean, who do I know in England? But I think that was part of it, you know? I wanted to go someplace where there weren't all the usual faces. Somewhere really different.'

'I hope I didn't spoil it.'

'How?'

'Well, you said I was a familiar face —'

'Oh, my, no! I said familiar, but I didn't mean *familiar*. I mean, one little short afternoon at Ginny's isn't *that* kind of familiar.'

'I see what you mean. The lounge is right up those stairs.' Sam nodded towards the steps on the left that led to the Savoy's American Bar. But Anne stopped, still holding on to his arm.

'Major,' she began haltingly, 'my feet are still screaming and my neck is sore from looking up and my shoulder's aching from this darned purse strap. I'd really love to spend a little time straightening myself out.'

'Oh, sure,' replied Devereaux. 'I'm being thoughtless. And stupid. As a matter of fact I was going to do some, er, straightening out myself. I left my shaving gear in Switzerland.' He held up the bag from the Strand Chemists.

'Well, then, that's *marvy*!'

'I'll call you in about an hour —'

'Why do that? Have you seen the size of those johnnies upstairs? Wow! They're bigger than some of Don's ladies' rooms. In his restaurants, I mean. There's plenty of room. And those big, groovy towels. I swear they're terry cloth sheets!' She squeezed his arm and smiled ingenuously.

'Well, it *is* a solution —'

'The only one. Come on, we'll get some drinks from room service and *really* relax.' They started for the elevator.

'It's very kind of you —'

'Kind, hell! Ginny told us you called. She positively *lorded* it over us. Now it's my turn. You were in Geneva?'

Sam stopped. 'I said Switzerland —'

'Isn't that Geneva?'

Anne's suite was also on the Thames side, also on the sixth floor, and conveniently no more than fifty feet down the corridor from his.

Switzerland. Isn't that Geneva? Several thoughts crossed Devereaux's mind, but he was entirely too exhausted to dwell on them. And, for the first time in days, entirely too relaxed to let them interfere.

The rooms were very like his own. High ceilings with real mouldings; marvellous old furniture - polished, functional - desks and tables and pictures and chairs and a sofa that would do credit to Parke-Bernet; mantel clocks and lamps that were neither nailed down nor with embedded plastic cards proclaiming ownership; tall casement windows, flanked by regal drapes, that looked out on the river with the lights of small boats, the buildings beyond, and especially Waterloo Bridge.

He was in the sitting room, on the pillowhead sofa, with his shoes off and a tall drink in his hand. The London Philharmonic was on BBC1, playing a Vivaldi concerto, and the warmth from a heater filled the room with a splendid comfort. Good things came to the deserving, thought Sam.

Anne came out of the bathroom and stopped in the frame of the doorway. Devereaux's glass was suddenly checked on its way to his lips. She was dressed - if that was the word - in a translucent sheath that at once left little to, yet completely provoked, the imagination. Her Sloping yet Argumentative breasts swelled to blushing points beneath the soft, single layer of fabric; her long, light-brown hair fell casually and sensually over her shoulders, framing her extraordinary endowments. Her tapered legs were outlined under the sheath.

Without saying a word, she raised her hand and beckoned him with her finger. He rose from the sofa and followed.

Inside the huge, tiled bathroom, the enormous Savoy tub was filled with steaming water; several thousand bubbles gave off the scent of roses and wet springtime. Anne reached up and removed his tie, and then his shirt, and then unstrapped his buckle, unzipped his trousers and lowered them to the floor. He kicked them free himself.

She placed her hands on both sides of his waist and pulled down his shorts, kneeling as she did so.

He sat on the edge of the warm tub while she pulled off his socks; and she held his left arm as he slid over the side, his body disappearing under the steaming white bubbles.

She stood up, undid a yellow bow at her neck, and the sheath fell to the floor on top of the thick white rug.

She was utterly magnificent.

And she got into the tub with Sam.

'Do you want to go down to dinner?' asked the girl from beneath the covers.

'Sure,' replied Devereaux from under same.

'Do you know we slept for over three hours? It's nearly nine-thirty.' She stretched; Sam watched. 'After we eat, let's go to one of those pubs.'

'If you like,' said Devereaux, still watching her, his head on the pillow. She was sitting up now, the sheet had fallen to her waist. Sloping yet Argumentative were challenging all they surveyed.

'Gosh,' Anne spoke softly, a touch awkwardly, as she turned and looked down at Sam, who could barely see her face. 'I'm being real forward again.'

'Friendly's a better word. I'm friendly, too.'

'You know what I mean.' She bent over him and kissed him on both eyes. 'You may have other plans; things you have to do or something.'

'Things I want to do,' interrupted Devereaux warmly. 'All plans are completely flexible, subject only to whim and pleasure.'

'That sounds sexy as hell.'

'I feel sexy as hell.'

'Thank you.'

'Thank *you*.' Sam reached above and beyond her soft, lovely back and pulled the sheet over them.

Ten minutes later (it was either ten minutes or several hours, thought Devereaux) they made the decision: They really did need food, preceded, of course, by short, smoky drams of iced whisky, which they had in the sitting room, on the pillowed couch, under two soft, enormous bath towels.

'I think the word is "sybaritic".' Sam adjusted the terry cloth over his lap. BBC1 was now playing a Noel Coward medley and the smoke from their cigarettes drifted into the sprays of warm orange light from the fireplace. Only two lamps were turned on; the room was dreamed of in a thousand ballads.

'Sybaritic has a selfish meaning,' said the girl. 'We share; that's not selfish.'

Sam looked at her. Hawkins's fourth wife was no idiot. How in hell did he do it? Had he done it? 'The way we share, it's sybaritic, believe me.'

'If you want me to,' she answered, smiling and putting her glass down on the coffee table.

'Its not important. Why don't we dress and go eat?'

'All right. I'll just be a few seconds.' She saw his questioning expression. 'No, I will. I don't dawdle for hours. Mac once said —' She stopped, embarrassed.

'It's okay,' he said gently. 'I'd really like to hear.'

'Well, he once said that if you try to change the outside too much, you can't help but mix up the inside. And you shouldn't do that unless there's a goddamned good reason. Or if you really don't like yourself.' She swung her legs out from under her and rose from the couch, holding the towel around her body. 'One, I don't see any reason; and two, I kind of like me. Mac taught me that, too. I like *us*.'

'So do I,' said Devereaux. 'When you're finished, we'll go down to my room and I'll change.

'Good. I'll button your shirt and tie your tie.' She grinned and dashed through the foyer door into the bedroom. Devereaux got up naked, throwing the long towel over his shoulder, and went to the side table where the bar was set up in a silver tray. He poured a small quantity of Scotch and thought about Mac Hawkins's bathroom philosophy.

Change the outside too much – you mix up the inside.

It wasn't bad, all things considered.

The tiny white light shone between the red and green bulbs on the small panel beside Devereaux's door. Sam and the girl saw it simultaneously as they walked down the corridor and approached his suite. It was the sign that a message was at the front desk for the guest. Devereaux swore under his breath.

Goddamn it! Geneva had not been erased *that* quickly. Or so completely, either. The least Hawkins could do was to let him get a decent night's sleep!

'One of those lights was on for me this afternoon,' said Anne. 'I came back to change my shoes and found it; it means you have a phone call.'

'Or a message.'

'Mine was a call. From Don in Santa Monica. I finally got him back; you know, it was only eight o'clock in the morning in California.'

'Nice of him to get up and phone.'

'Not so. My husband owns two things in Santa Monica: a restaurant and a girl. The restaurant's not open at eight in the morning; forgive my bitchiness. I think Don just wanted to make sure I was really seven thousand miles away.' Anne smiled up at him naïvely. He was not sure how to respond, all things considered.

'Seems like a lot of trouble for, well, for checking up.' Sam snapped on the light switch in his foyer. Beyond, the sitting room lamps were on, as he had left them five hours ago.

'My husband suffers from a mental illness peculiar to cheap strayers. As a lawyer, I'm sure you're familiar with it.

He's paranoid about getting caught. Not morally, you understand; when he's juiced up, he flaunts *that* part. Just financially; he's scared to death some court will make him pay big if I opt for out.'

They walked into his sitting room; he wanted to say something but, again, all things considered he was not sure what it should be. He chose the safest. 'I think the man's out of his mind.'

'You're sweet, but you didn't have to say it. On the other hand, I suppose it's the safest thing you *could* say —'

'Let's find another subject,' he interrupted quickly, indicating the couch and the coffee table with the Savoy-supplied newspapers on it. 'Sit down and I'll be with you in a minute. I haven't forgotten: You button the shirt and tie the tie.' Sam started for the bedroom door.

'Aren't you going to call the desk?'

'It can *wait*,' he answered from the bedroom. 'I have no intention of letting anything interfere with a quiet dinner. Or for that matter, showing you a pub or two, if they're still open when we're finished.'

'You really should find out who's trying to reach you. It could be important.'

'*You're* important,' shouted Sam, removing a tan double-knit suit from the awkward hangar in his suitcase.

'It could be something vital,' said the girl from the sitting room.

'*You're vital*,' he replied, selecting a red-striped shirt from the next layer of clothes.

'I can't *ever* not answer a phone, or check for messages, or call back even a name I never heard of; that's being *too* casual.'

'You're not a lawyer. Ever tried to get a lawyer the day after you've hired him? His secretary is trained to lie with the conviction of Aimee Semple McPherson.'

'Why?' Anne was now standing in the bedroom doorway.

'Well, he's got your money; he's scrounging around for another fee. What the hell, your case probably entails an exchange of letters with the opposing attorney, other explanations notwithstanding. He doesn't want complications.'

Anne approached him as he slipped on the red-striped shirt. She nonchalantly began buttoning it. 'You're a very cool Clyde. Here you are in strange country —'

'Not so strange,' he broke in smiling. 'I've been here before. I'm your tour guide, remember?'

'I mean, you've just come from Geneva where you obviously had a bad time —'

'Not so bad. I survived.'

'- and now someone is desperately trying to find you —'

'What's desperate? I don't know anybody so desperate.'

'For Christ's sake!' The girl yanked his collar as she fastened it. 'Things like this make me nervous!'

'Why?'

'I feel responsible!'

'You shouldn't.' Devereaux was fascinated. Anne was very serious. He wondered ...

And the telephone rang.

'Hello?'

'Mr Samuel Devereaux?' asked the precise voice of a male Britisher.

'Yes, this is Sam Devereaux.'

'I've been waiting for your call —'

'I just got in,' interrupted Sam. 'I haven't checked my messages yet. Who is this?'

'At the moment, merely a telephone number.'

Devereaux paused, annoyed. 'Then I should tell you, you would have waited all night. I don't return calls to telephone numbers.'

'Come, sir,' was the agitated reply. 'You're not expecting any other caller of consequence.'

'That's a little presumptuous, I think —'

'Think whatever you like, sir! I'm in a great hurry and quite put out with you. Now, where do you wish to meet?'

'I don't know that I want to. Fuck off, Basil, or whatever the hell your name is.'

The pause was now on the other end of the line. Sam could

hear heavy breathing. In seconds the telephone number spoke. 'For God's sake, have pity on an old man. I've done you no harm.'

Sam was suddenly touched. The voice had cracked slightly; the man was desperate. He remembered Hawkins's last conversation. 'Are you —'

'No *names, please*!'

'All right. No names. Are you recognizable?'

'Extremely. I thought you knew that.'

'I didn't. So we meet someplace out of the way.'

'Very much so. I thought you knew that, too.'

'Stop saying that!' Devereaux was as much annoyed with Hawkins as he was with the Englishman on the telephone. 'Then you'd better choose it, unless you want to come to the Savoy.'

'Impossible! That's kind of you. I have several apartment buildings in Belgravia. One's the Hampton Arms; do you know it?'

'I can find it.'

'Good. I'll be there. Flat four seven. It will take me an hour to get into London.'

'Don't hurry. I don't want to meet in an hour.'

'Oh? At what time then?'

'When do the pubs close these days?'

'Midnight. A little over an hour.'

'Shit!'

'I beg your pardon?'

'I'll see you at one o'clock.'

'Very well. The Hampton security will be alerted. Remember, no names. Just flat four seven.'

'Four seven.'

'And, Devereaux. Bring the papers.'

'What papers?'

'The pause was longer now, the English breathing heavier. 'That goddamned agreement, you *ass*.'

The girl not only accepted the fact that their dinner would be short and that he had to leave the hotel, but she seemed positively elated.

Sam was wondering less and less. The *why* escaped him, but the *what* was becoming clearer. He agreed to have a nightcap with her when he returned. The hour was unimportant, Anne said; she gave him a key.

The taxi stopped at the kerb in front of the Hampton Arms. At Sam's mention of flat four seven, he was led by a doorman in a series of swift, secretive movements that took him through service doors, a short back staircase, a freight elevator, and the delivery entrance of the flat.

An ominous looking man with a north country accent asked for identification and then led Sam through a pantry, a large living room, a hallway, and finally to a small dimly lit library where a rather ugly little old man sat in the shadows by the window. The door closed. Devereaux stood, adjusting his eyes to the light and the unattractive ancient in the armchair.

'Mr Devereaux – naturally,' said the wrinkled old man.

'Yes. You must be the Danforth Hawkins spoke of.'

'Lord Sidney Danforth.' The ugly little person spat out the ugly words, then suddenly his voice was syrup. 'I don't know how your employer pieced together what he did, nor do I for a moment admit *anything*; it's all so preposterous. And so long ago. Nevertheless, I am a good man, a charitable man. Quite a *wonderful* man. Give me the damned papers!'

'What?'

'The agreement, you insufferable bastard!'

Stunned, Sam reached into his breast pocket where he had a folded copy of the Shepherd Company's limited partnership. He crossed to the ugly little person and gave it to him. Danforth swung out a portable desk panel from somewhere at the side of the armchair and snapped on a bright worklight at the top of the board. He grabbed the papers and started scanning them.

'Fine!' said Danforth, wheezing, flipping over the pages. 'They say absolutely *nothing*!' The little Britisher reached for a pen and began filling in the black lines. When he had finished, he refolded the papers and handed them distastefully to Devereaux. 'Now, get out! I am a marvellous man, a magnanimous provider; a humble multi-millionaire whom everyone adores. I have richly deserved the extraordinary honours heaped upon my person. Everybody knows that. And nobody. I repeat, *nobody* could conceivably associate me with such madness! I am only - spreading brotherhood do you understand me? *Brotherhood*, I say!'

'I don't understand anything,' said Sam.

'Neither do I,' replied Danforth. 'The transfer will be made in the Cayman Islands. The bank is listed and the ten million will be shifted within forty-eight hours. Then I'm through with you!'

'The Cayman Islands?'

'They're in the Caribbean, you ass.'

CHAPTER TWELVE

He could see the tiny white light shining fifty feet down the Savoy corridor. He did not have to get any closer to know it was the door to his rooms; avoiding it was a second, very good reason to let himself into Annie's suite.

'If that's not you, Sam I've got problems,' she called from the bedroom.

'It's me. All your problems are happy ones.'

'I like those kind.'

Devereaux walked into the large bedroom with the windows overlooking the river. Anne was sitting up, reading a brightly coloured paperback by the light of the table lamp. 'What's that?' he asked. 'It looks impressive.'

'A marvellous history of Henry the Eighth's wives. I got it at the Tower this morning. That man was a monster!'

'Not really. A lot of his troubles were geopolitical.'

'In his crotch they were!'

'That's more historically sound than you may think. How about a drink?'

'You've got to make a phone call first. I promised; first thing you did when you got back.'

The girl turned a page calmly. Sam was not only astonished, he was curious. 'What did you say?'

'MacKenzie called. All the way from Washington.' She turned another page.

'MacKenzie?' Devereaux could not help himself; he roared. 'Just - *MacKenzie called*! You're sitting there like you heard from room service and tell me MacKenzie called. How do *you* know he called? Did he call *you*?'

'Really, Sam, stop being so uptight.' Cold as ice, she

turned another goddamned page. 'It's not as though I didn't know him. I mean, after all —'

'Oh, no! Spare me the odious comparisons! I just want to know about this extraordinary coincidence that has you seven thousand miles from home taking a telephone call from an ex-husband who's calling *me* – three thousand miles from New York.'

'If you'll calm down, I'll tell you. If you won't, I'm just going to keep on reading.'

Devereaux thought about how much he wanted a drink, but he suppressed his anger and spoke quietly. 'I'm calm and I would very much like to have you speak. Please speak.'

Anne put the book down on her lap and looked up at him. 'To begin with, Mac was every bit as uptight as you are when I got on the line.'

'How *did* you get on the line?'

'Because I was worried.'

'That's why, not how.'

'If you recall, and I think you will if you try real hard, you left me at the table downstairs. You were running late and I insisted. I told you I'd sign the check and go upstairs. Am I right so far?'

'I owe you for dinner. Go on.'

'A nice young man in white tie and tails came to the table and said there was an urgent transatlantic call for you. Are they always so dressed up?'

'It's a Savoy custom. What did you say?'

'That you wouldn't be back until very late; I wasn't sure of the time. He seemed upset so I asked him if I could help. He said the caller was a General Hawkins from Washington, and I think the rank and the city made him nervous. Mac always does that; it gets better telephone service. So I told him not to worry about a thing. I'd talk to the old fart. He liked that.' Anne returned to her book. 'Now, go call him. The number's on the desk in the other room. It's also on the desk in your place and also downstairs. I'm very flattered that you got it here first.'

It *was* possible, Sam reflected. Unlikely but within the scope of possibility, as certain radio waves indicated the possibility of additional civilizations in galactic space. 'What did Hawkins say? How was he uptight?'

'Oh, just that I was *here*, I suppose,' said the girl, reluctantly taking her eyes off the page. 'He started swearing and yelling and giving orders. I said, "Mac," I said, "go wash your mouth out with brown soap!" I always used to tell him that. I mean he uses language we stayed away from in Belle Isle. Anyway, he calmed down and started to laugh.' Anne's eyes drifted upward, at nothing. She was remembering, thought Sam, and those memories were not cold ones. 'He asked me if I'd got rid of the fancy gigolo waiter yet – that's what he calls Don – and if not, *why* not. And how you were such a nice fellow. You know, Mac thinks a great deal of you. Anyhow, it is very important that you call him back. I said it'd be awfully late; maybe not until three in the morning. But he said that was all right; it would only be ten o'clock in Washington.'

'Can't it wait until morning?'

'No. Mac was very emphatic. He said if you thought about putting it off I should tell you it had something to do with an Italian gentleman who was asking for you.'

'Did he add that he was in the undertaking business?'

'No. But I think you should call him. If you want privacy, you can use the phone in the other room.'

'Goddamn, boy! Isn't it a real small world! There you are halfway across the globe and who do you run into but little old Annie. Not that she's old, you understand —'

'I understand,' interrupted Sam, 'that you've got greetings for me from Dellacroce. What did you tell your deeply religious friend now? That I crucified Jesus?'

'Hell, no. That was just a little psych-prod, in case you were reluctant to return my call. I haven't even talked to Dellacroce. I don't think he's in favour of any further communications. Does that make you feel better?'

Devereaux lit a cigarette. It helped cover the slight pain

that was developing in his stomach. 'I'll tell you the truth, Mac. It simply makes me nervous that you called me at all. It makes me feel that you are about to say something that will not bring me any closer to Boston, or my mother, or my real employer, Aaron Pinkus; that's the way your psych-prod makes me feel.'

There was a long series of audible tsks from MacKenzie Hawkins in Washington. 'You are a very suspicious person. It must be the lawyer in you. How did everything go with Danforth?'

'He's a madman. He blows out hot and cold like a psycho. He also signed the papers; he's in for ten million for reasons I can't possibly imagine. The bank's in the Cayman Islands, which is, I assume, the reason for your telephone call.'

'You mean you think I'd ask you to go to the Caymans?'

'It crossed my mind.'

'I wouldn't do that. The Caymans aren't any fun. Just dinky little hot spots with lots of banks and pricky-shit bankers. They're trying to make the place into another Switzerland. ... No, I'll fly down there myself and take care of it. And you've got another ten thousand added to your account. Thought you'd like to know that.'

'*Mac!*' Devereaux's stomach experienced a sharp, stinging sensation. 'You can't *do* that!'

'It's easy, boy. You just make the cashier's cheque out for deposit only.'

'That's not what I mean! You have no *right* putting money into my account!'

'The bank didn't argue —'

'The bank wouldn't argue! *I* argue! I *am* arguing! Christ, don't you understand? It means you're paying me!'

'One-tenth of one per cent? Goddamn, boy, I'm cheating you!'

'I don't *want* to be paid! I don't want anything to *do* with any money from you! That makes me an *accessory*!'

'I don't know anything about that, but it's surely not right for one person to call upon the time and the talents of another person and not pay him for it.' Hawkins's voice had the ring of a quiet evangelist.

'Oh, shut up, you son of a bitch,' said Devereaux, recognizing the inevitability of defeat. 'Outside of Danforth, why did you call?'

'Well, now that you mention it, there's a fellow in West Berlin I'd like you to talk with.'

'Wait. Don't tell me,' interrupted Sam wearily. 'The airline tickets and the hotel reservations will be at the Savoy desk before I can say kippered herring.'

'By morning, anyway.'

'Okay, Mac, I know when I'm hung.' He was getting in deeper. Somehow, some way, some time, Sam thought, he would have to climb out.

MacKenzie wrote out the figure numerically.

$20,000,000.00

Then he wrote it in words:

Twenty million dollars.

Strange, but it had no real effect on him. It was merely a means, not an end in itself. Although it had occurred to him that he could easily call it an economic day, wrap it up, and retire to the south of France. Certainly, neither Dellacroce nor Danforth would sue. Not bloody likely. But that wasn't what it was all about; the money was both a conveyance and a by-product. And in its way, a legitimate form of punishment. The two marks deserved their losses.

But time was running short and he could not allow himself to get sidetracked. Summer was only a few months away; there was an enormous amount of work to do. The selection and training of the support personnel would be time-consuming. The leasing and stocking of the manoeuvre site would be difficult, especially the covert purchasing of equipment. The manoeuvres themselves would take a number of weeks. All told, there was a great deal to accomplish in a short time. Because of this it was a natural temptation to veer from the initial strategy and go with less than the full capitalization, but it would be wrong. That's for sure. He had set the figure of forty million not merely for the numerical symmetry to the four hundred million (although it certainly looked proper on the limited partnership agreement, in the blank lines he had filled out), but because forty million took care of *everything*, including last-extremity contingencies.

Otherwise known as quick-witted evacuation of the fire base.

It would have to be forty million. He was just about ready for his third investor.

Heinrich Koenig, Berlin.

Herr Koenig had not been easy. Whereas Sidney Danforth had overworked his modus operandi in Chile, and whereas Angelo Dellacroce had been just plain sloppy with regard to his Mediterranean payments and entirely too ostentatious in his manner of living, Heinrich Koenig had made no obvious errors, and lived the quiet life of a country squire in a peaceful rural town twenty-odd miles from Berlin.

But twenty-two years ago Koenig had played an enormously dangerous game brilliantly. A game that not only netted him a fortune but also ensured the capitalization and ultimate success of his various business enterprises.

During the height of the Cold War, Koenig was a double agent-cum-blackmailer. He began by secretly informing on single agents to both sides, then extorting cash - financed through opposing intelligence channels - from those seeking protection from exposure. Soon he was issued exclusive international, nontariff 'franchises' for his new companies from scores of countries dependent upon the economic goodwill of both giant factions. Finally, with the grace of Mephistopheles, he forced Washington, London, Berlin, Bonn, and Moscow into declaring his companies *outside* the regulatory legalities that governed other industries. Koenig accomplished this by explaining to each that he would inform the others of its past activities.

And then, to the profound relief of many governments, Koenig retired. He had built his empire on the trampled bodies - deceased and paralysed - of half the bureaucratic and industrial population of Europe and America. He had remained untouchable because of the very real terror of chain reaction-reprisal. What bureaucrat, what undersecretary, what minister or statesman (indeed, what head of a government) would allow access to the horrors of Pandora's box? So, in retirement, Koenig remained as safe as during his halcyon days of furious activity.

Fear was Koenig's clout. But there was no fear or clout if a man didn't give a good goddamn about reaction or reprisals - governmental, industrial, or international.

And naturally this was Hawkins's weapon.

For there was an international army of victims who would quick-march for the kill if they thought they could do so with impunity, if everyone realized his past sins were known to everybody else. Complete disclosure was Mac's threat.

Koenig would certainly see the logic of this approach; it was the absence of it that had guaranteed his fortunes. He surely could foretell the effects of several hundred lengthy cablegrams sent simultaneously to several hundred inhabitants of the corridors of power throughout the world. Oh, yes! Koenig would be convinced, the instant a barrage of names, dates, and activities was rattled off to him.

MacKenzie picked up the raw-file Xeroxes from the bed, keeping the piles in sequence, and carried them to the coffee table in front of the couch. He sat down and with the red crayon he began circling two or three items on each page.

Things were going beautifully. It was all a question of making a realistic appraisal of one's capabilities and the logistics available to complement those abilities. Simple inventory. He picked up the Xeroxes, moved to the desk, and arranged the papers properly in front of the telephone. He was ready to calmly, dispassionately recite a record of international duplicity that would cause Genghis Khan to blush.

Heinrich Koenig would part with ten million dollars.

His eyes rimmed with black circles of exhaustion, Devereaux went through customs at Berlin's Tempelhof

Airport, fully prepared to have his forehead stamped by the officiously barking neo-Nazi who inspected his papers and luggage. Christ, he thought, give a German a rubber stamp and he went wild.

At one point he stared in amazement at the contents of his own suitcase. Everything was folded neatly and arranged tidily as though packed by Bergdorf Goodman, and he simply did not pack suitcases that way. Then through the fog of dislocation, he remembered that Anne had taken care of everything. She not only had packed for him, she had also accompanied him to the cashier's desk and helped him settle his bill.

She had done all this, reflected Sam, because he was not in condition to do much for himself. The insanity of his predicament had led him into a battle with a bottle of Scotch. He lost. The only thing he did remember to do was to airmail the goddamned limited partnership agreement to Hawkins.

Berlin's Kempinsky Hotel was a Teutonic version of New York's old Sherry-Netherland with a slightly harsher interior; the overstuffed lobby chairs seemed cast more in concrete than leather. Still, it screamed money, polished dark wood, and terribly proper clerks Sam knew hated his weak, democratically oriented, and inferior guts.

The front desk dispensed with him efficiently and swiftly. He was escorted by a disagreeable, ageing SS Oberführer who treated his suitcase as though it contained bagels and lox. Once inside the suite (it was enormous; Mac Hawkins did send him first class) the Oberführer snapped up the shades in the various rooms with the authority of a man used to issuing commands to a firing squad. Devereaux, fearing for his life, grossly overtipped him, saw him to the door as if he were a visiting diplomat and bid him a gracious *auf Wiedersehen*!

He opened his suitcase. Anne had possessed the foresight to wrap a full bottle of Scotch in a Savoy towel. If there was ever time to ingest the indigestible, it was now. Not much; just enough to get the motor running.

There was a knock on the door. Sam was so startled he coughed a mouthful of whisky over the bed. He corked the bottle and furiously looked for a place to hide it.

Under the pillow! Covered by the bedspread! He stopped. What was he doing? What the hell was the matter with him? What was *happening* to him? *Goddamn you, MacKenzie Hawkins!*

He took a deep breath, and calmly placed the bottle on the dresser top. He took another deep breath, opened the door, and promptly, involuntarily, expelled every bit of air in his lungs.

Standing in the door frame was the blonde Aphrodite from Palo Alto, California, catalogued in his memory as Narrow and Pointed. The third Mrs MacKenzie Hawkins. Lillian.

'I knew it was you! I said to the man at the desk that it *had* to be you!'

Sam was not sure why he had catalogued Lillian as Narrow and Pointed. 'Narrow' did the lady an injustice. Perhaps it was a relative adjective, subject to the immediate visual comparison to the other six.

Devereaux was thinking these absurd thoughts and - he was aware - staring like a twelve-year-old at his first *Artists and Models* magazine, while Lillian sat across from him, explaining that she had flown into Berlin three days ago to attend a two-week course in gourmet cooking.

Of course, it was unbelievable. After all, he was a skilled attorney. He had analysed scores of crime-ridden mentalities, stripping away the layers of fraud from sophisticated deceivers on all levels of the social jungle. In spite of his drained mind and body, he was not a man to be conned easily and he would let the third Mrs MacKenzie Hawkins know that - in *spades*! He stared at her harder, then mentally shrugged. What the hell!

'So there we are, Sam. I may call you Sam, mayn't I? It's amazing what an interest in really fine cooking can lead to.'

'But entirely plausible, Lillian! That's what makes

coincidences truly – well, coincidental!' Sam laughed quasi-hysterically, doing his best to control his eyes. He was simply too exhausted to be successful; he just gave up and let his eyes roam freely.

'And I can't think of a better way to see Berlin. If we're lucky, we can find an indoor tennis court! I hear the hotel has a swimming pool; perhaps a gymnasium —' Lillian stopped and Devereaux felt deprived; in his spent condition he was enjoying the soft, breathless, aural massage. 'I may be taking far too much for granted. Are you travelling alone?'

He knew he shouldn't. He *shouldn't*.

'More alone than I've ever been in my life.'

'Well, we certainly can't have that. If you don't mind my saying so, you look dreadfully tired. I think you've been working half to death. You really need someone to look after you.'

'I am only a warm shadow of my substance. ...'

'You poor lamb. Come over here and let me rub your shoulder blades. It does wonders, it really, really does.'

'I am a wasted vestige. I am filled with vacuum and molten lead. ...'

'You're exhausted, my lamb. That's the good boy; stretch out and put your head on Lilly's lap. Oh my, your temples are so warm. And your neck muscles are much too tense. There, that's better; doesn't it feel better?'

It did. He could feel her nimble fingers unbutton his shirt and the gentle hands moving about his chest, caressing his flesh with the touch of angels. What the hell. He opened his eyes, his sight was filled with the unbearable loveliness of two magnificent breasts inches above his face.

'Do you like hot tubs filled with lots of soap bubbles that smell like roses and springtime?' he whispered.

'Not actually,' she whispered back. 'I'm partial to warm showers. Straight up, as it were.'

Sam smiled.

CHAPTER THIRTEEN

The fragrance permeated the air around him; he did not need to open his eyes to know its source.

If he was able to reconstruct the previous evening with any accuracy – and the quiescence below his waist convinced him that he could – they had spent most of the night in the Kempinsky shower.

Sam opened his eyes. Lillian was beside him, sitting up against the pillows with a pair of horn-rimmed glasses perched on her lovely upturned nose. She was reading from an enormous piece of frayed cardboard, the white sheet covering her chest but not for an instant obscuring the shafts beneath.

'Hello,' he said quietly.

'Good morning!' She looked down at him and positively beamed. 'Do you know what time it is?'

The blonde creature *was* a healthy type, he considered. It must be all that California surfboarding, or perhaps MacKenzie Hawkins had taught her to do pushups. 'My watch is under the covers with my wrist. I do not know what time it is.'

'It's twenty after ten. You slept for eleven hours. How do you feel?'

'Are you telling me we went to bed – I was asleep – by eleven thirty last night?'

'You could be heard at the Brandenburg Gate. I kept shoving you to stop your snoring. You were positively operatic. How's your head?'

'Fairly secure, as a matter of fact. I wonder why?'

'All that steam. And exercise. Actually, you weren't capable of drinking a great deal. I think your bloodstream went into revolt.' Lillian picked up a pencil from the bedside table and lightly checked the menu.

'You smell terrific,' he said after several moments of looking up at her, remembering the sightlines from her lap and the touches of angels over his chest.

'So do you, lamb,' she replied, smiling, removing her glasses, and gazing down at Sam. 'Do you know, you have a very acceptable body?'

'It has its points.'

'I mean you have a fundamentally sound physique, moderately well proportioned and coordinated. It's really a pity you've let it disintegrate.' She tapped her glasses against her chin like a doctor studying postoperative conditions.

'Well, I wouldn't go so far as to say disintegrate. I played lacrosse once. I was pretty good.'

'I'm sure you were, well over a decade ago. Now look here —' Lilly put down her glasses and peeled the blankets away from Devereaux's chest. 'See here. And *here* and here and *here*! Absolutely no tone whatsoever. Muscle pockets that've had no discernible use for years! And *here*.'

'Ouch!'

'Your latissimi dorsi are positively non-*existent*. When was the last time you exercised?'

'Last night. In the shower.'

'That aspect of your condition cannot be debated. But it's a minor part of the whole being —'

'Not to me it isn't!'

' relative to the muscular network. Your body is a temple; don't let it crumble and decay with misuse and neglect. Spruce it up! Give it a chance to stretch and breathe and be useful; that's what it's meant for. Look at MacKenzie —'

'I object! I don't want to look at MacKenzie!'

'I'm speaking clinically.'

'I knew it,' mumbled Devereaux in defeat. 'I can't escape him. I'm possessed.'

'Do you realize that Mac is well over *fifty*? And take his body. It's taut. It's a coiled spring toned to perfection ...'

Lilly's eyes drifted up at nothing. As Anne's had done at

the Savoy. She was remembering, as Anne had remembered – and those memories were not cold.

'Well, for God's sake,' said Sam. 'Hawkins spent his whole life in the army. Running and jumping and killing and torturing. He had to stay in shape so he could stay alive. He had no choice.'

'You're wrong. Mac understands the meaning of full capacity, experiencing the total potential. He once said to me – well, never mind, it's unimportant.' The girl removed her hand from Devereaux's chest and reached for her glasses.

'No, please.' The bedroom in the Kempinsky might have been a bedroom in the Savoy. But the wives were not interchangeable; they were very individual. 'I'd like to hear what Mac said.'

Lilly held her glasses in both hands, fingering the stems pensively. '" Your body should be a realistic extension of your mind, pushed to its limit but not abused."'

'I liked the "change the outside, mix up the inside" better —'

'What?'

'Something else he said. Maybe I don't understand; the intellectual and the physical are poles apart. I might imagine I could fly off the Eiffel Tower, but I'd better not try it.'

'Because that wouldn't be realistic; it would be abusive. But you might train yourself to scale down it in record time. *That* would be the realistic, *physical* extension of your imagination. And it's important to attempt it.'

'Scale down the Eiffel Tower?'

'If flying off is a serious consideration.'

'It's not. If I follow this pseudoscholastic doggerel, you're saying that if you think about doing something you should actually translate it as much as possible into physical terms.'

'Yes. The main thing is not to remain inert.' Lilly waved her arms in emphasis; the sheet plummeted down.

Unbearably lovely, thought Devereaux. But at the moment untouchable; the girl was in debate.

'This is either far more complicated or much simpler than it sounds,' he said.

'It's more complicated, believe me,' she answered. 'The subtlety is in the obviousness.'

'You believe in this challenge concept, don't you?' Sam said. 'I mean it's fundamentally the necessary satisfaction of meeting the challenge, isn't it?'

'Yes, I suppose it is. For its own sake; to try to reach out for what you can imagine. To test your potential.'

'And you believe that.' There was no question implied.

'Yes, I do. Why?'

'Because at this moment my imagination is working so hard I can't stand it. I feel the necessity of physical expression; to test my potential. Within reasonable limits, of course.' He rose from his base camp until he sat facing her, their eyes level. He reached out and took her glasses, folded them, and dropped them over the side of the bed. He held out his hand and she gave him the menu.

Lillian's eyes were bright, her lips parted in a half smile. 'I was wondering when you were going to ask.'

And then the Nazi telephone rang.

The voice on the other end of the line belonged to a man brought up in his formative years watching all those war movies from Warner Brothers. Every syllable dripped evil.

'Ve do not - vill not - cannot shpeak on der telephone.'

'Go across the street and open a window. We'll shout,' replied Devereaux irritably.

'Der time ist der essence! You vill go down to der lobby, to der fart chair in front of der vindow, on der richt of der hentrance! Under der arm carry a folded copy of *Der Spiegel*. Und you vill be crossing der legs every twenty seconds.'

'I'm sitting down?'

'You vould look foolish crossing der legs standing up, mein Herr.'

'Suppose someone's sitting in the chair?'

The pause conveyed both anger and confusion. There followed a short, strange sound that gave rise to the image of a small pig squealing in frustration. 'Remove him!'was the reply that followed the squeal.

'That's silly.'

'You vill do as I say! Dere is no time to argue! You vill be contacted. Fifteen minutes.'

'Hey, wait a minute! I just got up. I haven't had breakfast; I've got to shave —'

'Fourteen minutes, mein Herr!'

'I'm hungry!'

The connection was broken by a loud click on the line. 'To hell with him,' said Devereaux, turning back in anticipation to the extraordinary Lillian.

But Lillian was not where she should have been. Instead, she was standing on the other side of the bed in Sam's bathrobe.

'To coin a phrase, my darling, we were saved by the bell. You have things to do, and I really must get ready for class.'

'Class?'

'Die erstklassige Strudelschule,' said Lilly. 'Less expert but probably more fun than the Cordon Bleu in Paris. It starts at noon. We're over in the Leipziger Strasse; that's past Unter den Linden. I really should hurry.'

'What about - *us*? And breakfast and - don't you shower in the morning?'

Lilian laughed; it was a nice, genuine laugh. '*Die Schule* day is finished by three-thirty. I'll meet you back here.'

'What's your room number?'

'Five eleven.'

'I'm five nine.'

'I know. Isn't that marvellous.'

'Or something ...'

The confusion in the Kempinsky lobby was absurd. 'Der fart chair in front of der vindow' *was* occupied by an elderly gentleman whose close-cropped, bejowled head kept nodding down into the folds of neck flesh as he dozed. On his lap, unfortunately, was a folded copy of *Der Spiegel*.

The elderly man was, at first, annoyed, then furious at the

two men who flanked his chair and told him in no uncertain terms to get up and come with them. Twice Sam tried to intercede, explaining as best he could that he, too, had a folded copy of *Der Spiegel*. It did no good; the troopers were interested only in the gentleman sitting in the huge armchair. Finally, Devereaux stood directly in front of the two contacts and every twenty seconds, crossed and uncrossed his legs.

At which point the bell captain came up to Sam and in perfectly good, loud English gave him the directions to the men's room.

Whereupon a large woman with a striking resemblance to Dick Butkus approached the trio around the armchair and began hitting the two Gestapo men with both a hatbox and an extremely large, black leather handbag.

There was only one thing for it, thought Devereaux. He grabbed one of the contacts around the neck and pulled him away from the fire zone.

'You crazy son of a bitch! *I'm* the one! You're from Koenig, aren't you?'

Thirty seconds later Devereaux was propelled out of the Kempinsky entrance and into a nearby alley.

Halfway down the alley, taking up most of the space between the buildings, was an enormous open truck with a canvas tarpaulin stretched across the rear rigging poles. Under the tarpaulin, from deck to canvas, were hundreds of crates piled on top of one another, filled with thousands (it seemed like thousands) of screeching chickens.

There was a narrow corridor in the centre of the van between the crates. It led to the rear window of the cab. In front of the window were two tiny stools.

'Hey, come on! This is ridiculous! It's goddamn it, it's unsanitary!'

His escorts nodded Germanically and smiled Germanically, and Germanically heaved Sam up into the tiny corridor and shoved him down the eighteen-inch passageway towards the stools.

All around him sharp beaks pecked at his person. The

noonday sun was completely blanketed out by the heavy canvas tarpaulin above. The odour of chickenshit was unbearable.

They drove for nearly an hour into the countryside, stopping every now and then to be looked over by cooperative East German soldiers who waved them on, pocketing *Deutschmarks* as they did so.

They entered a large farming complex. Cattle were grazing in the fields, silos and barns could be seen, barely, through the opening of the tiny passageway between the crates and the flying feathers at the rear of the truck.

Finally they stopped. Escort number one grinned his Germanic grin and led Sam into the sunlight.

He was marched into a large barn that reeked of cattle urine and fresh manure. He was led – Germanically – down a crisscross series of turns through the stinking building until they came to an empty stall. A row of blue ribbons denoted the residence of a prize steer.

Inside, sitting on a milking stool, surrounded by piles of bullshit, was the heavyset man Sam knew was Heinrich Koenig.

He did not get up; he sat there and stared at Devereaux. In his tiny eyes, surrounded by folds of blemished flesh, were thunderbolts.

'So. . . .' Koenig remained immobile, drawing out the word disdainfully, waving the escorts away.

'So?' replied Sam, his voice cracking slightly, aware of the wet chicken droppings on his back.

'You are the representative from this monster, General Hawkins?' Koenig pronounced the word 'general' with a hard Germanic *G*.

'I'd like to clear that up, if I may,' said Devereaux with false laughter. 'Actually, I'm just a slight acquaintance, barely know the man. I'm a low profile attorney from Boston; actually not much more than a law clerk. I work for a little Jewish man named Pinkus. You wouldn't like him. My mother lives in Quincy and through the strangest coincidence —'

'Enough!' A very loud fart could be heard in the vicinity of the milking stool. 'You are the contact, the intermediary, with this devil from hell!'

'Well, as to that, I would have to debate the legal association; said association subject to the clarification of intent with regard to foreknowledge. I don't believe —'

'You are a jackal, a hyena! But such dogs bark loudly if the meat is sufficient. Tell me. This Hawkins. He is a Gehlen operation, *nein*?'

'A who?'

'*Gehlen!*'

Devereaux remembered. Gehlen was the master spy of the Third Reich who bought and sold for all factions after the war. It would not do for Koenig to think there was any connection between Hawkins and Gehlen; for it would mean there was a link to one Sam Devereaux, who was way out of his league.

'Oh, I'm sure not. I don't think General Hawkins ever heard of what's-his-name. I know *I* haven't.' The chicken-shit was melting under Sam's shirt, all over his fevered back.

Koenig rose slowly from the milking stool, a second flatus loudly proclaiming his ascent. He spoke with quiet, intense hostility.

'The general has my reluctant respect. He has sent me a babbling idiot. Give me the papers, fool.'

'The papers —' Sam reached into his jacket pocket for another Xerox copy of the Shepherd Company's limited partnership agreement.

The German fingered the papers silently, squeezing each one as he flipped it. His audible reactions were blunt: a combination of farts and grunts.

'This is outrageous! A great injustice! Political enemies everywhere! All wishing only to destroy me!' Beads of saliva formed at the corners of Koenig's mouth.

'I agree wholeheartedly,' said Devereaux, eagerly nodding his head. 'I'd throw it away if I were you.'

'You would like that? All of you. You are all out to get me! My great contributions that kept peace in the world, enemies in constant touch, that opened hot lines and red lines and blue lines between the great powers – these are forgotten. Now you whisper behind my back. You tell lies about non-existent bank accounts, even my humble places of residence. You never concede that I earned every *Deutschmark* I possess! When I retired, none of you could tolerate it; you did not have me to kick around any longer! And now this! The injustice!'

'Oh, I understand.'

'You understand nothing! Give me something to write with, you idiot.'

He farted and signed.

CHAPTER FOURTEEN

The bells of the Angelus pealed in solemn, vibrant splendour. They echoed throughout St Peter's Square, floated above Bernini's marble guardians, and were heard in quiet celebration beyond the dome, deep in the Vatican gardens. Seated on a bench of white stone, looking up at the orange rays of the descending sun, was a corpulent man with a face best described as having weathered seven decades good-naturedly, if not always peacefully. The face was full; but the peasant quality of the bone structure under the folds of flesh would tend to deny that the face was pampered. The man's eyes were wide and large and brown and soft; they held nearly equal parts of strength, perception, resignation, and amusement.

He was dressed in the splendid white robes of his office. The highest office of the Holy Apostolic Catholic Church, the descendant of Peter himself, the Bishop of Rome, the spiritual commander of 400 million souls throughout the earth.

Pope Francesco I, the Vicar of Christ.

Born Giovanni Bombalini in a small village north of Padua in the first years of the century. It was a birth that was recorded sketchily, at best, for the Bombalinis were not affluent. Giovanni was delivered by a midwife who, as often as not, forgot to report the fruits of her labours (and her patient's labours) to the village clerk, secure in the knowledge that the church would do *something*; christenings made money. Actually Giovanni Bombalini's emergence into this world might never have been legally recorded at all except that his father had a wager with his cousin Frescobaldi, three villages to the north, that his second child would be a male. Bombalini Senior wanted to take no chances that his cousin Frescobaldi would renege on the bet, so he went to the village hall himself to report the birth of a male child.

As it happened, part of the wager was that Frescobaldi's wife - who was expecting in the same month - would *not* give birth to a boy. But of course she did, and the bet was cancelled. This child, Guido Frescobaldi, was born - according to the sketchy records - two days after *his* cousin, Giovanni.

Early in his life Giovanni showed signs of being different from the other children of the village. To begin with he did not care to learn his catechism by verbal repetition; he wanted to *read* it, *then* memorize it. This upset the village priest for it smacked of precociousness and somehow was an affront to authority, but the child would not be denied.

The ways of Giovanni Bombalini were indeed extraordinary. Although he never shirked his labours in the fields, he was rarely too tired to stay up half the night reading whatever he could get his hands on. When he was twelve he discovered the *biblioteca* in Padua, which was hardly the library in Milan, nor Venice, nor certainly Rome, but it was said by those who knew Giovanni that he read every book in Padua, then Milan, then Venice. By which time his priest recommended him to the holy fathers in Rome.

The church was Giovanni's answer to a prayer. And as long as he prayed a great deal - which was easier, though no less time-consuming than labouring in the fields - he was allowed to read more than he ever thought would be allowed him.

By the age of twenty-two, Giovanni Bombalini was an ordained priest. Some said the best-read priest in Rome, an *erudito fantastico*. But Giovanni did not possess the properly stern visage of a proper Vatican *erudito*; nor did he assume the proper attitudes of certainty with regard to everyday truths. He was forever finding exceptions and flexibilities in liturgical history, pointing out (some said mischievously) that the writings of the church found their strength in honest contradictions.

At twenty-six Giovanni Bombalini was a sharp pain in the large Vatican ass. Aggravated further by his matured appearance, which was the antithesis of the gaunt, academic image so desired by Rome's *eruditi*. He was, if anything, the caricature of a field peasant from the northern districts. Short of stature, stocky, and wide of girth, he looked like a farmhand more at home in the goat stables than in the marble halls of the various Vatican *collegia*. No amount of theological erudition, or good nature, or, indeed, deep belief in his church could counteract the combined aggravation of his mind and appearance. So posts were found for him in such unlikely locations as the Gold Coast, Sierra Leone, Malta, and, through an error, Monte Carlo. An exhausted Vatican dispatcher misread the name Montes Claros and inserted Monte Carlo – no doubt because he had never *heard* of Brazil's Montes Claros – and the fortunes of Giovanni Bombalini turned.

For into the cauldron of high stakes and high emotions wandered the simple looking priest with the bemused eyes, gentle humour, and a head packed with more knowledge than any twelve international financiers put together. He'd had little to do in the Gold Coast, Sierra Leone, and Malta, so he had occupied his time, when not praying or teaching the natives, by subscribing to scores of reading services and adding to his already extraordinary memory bank.

It is common knowledge that people who live with constant motion, and high risk, and a great deal of alcohol, occasionally need spiritual consolation. So Father Bombalini began to comfort a few stray lambs. And to the amazement of these first few strays, they found not so much a simple priest who outlined penance, but a most amusing fellow who could discourse at length on almost any subject: economic conditions of world markets, historical precedents for anticipated geopolitical events, and, particularly, food. (Here he favoured the more basic sauces, eschewing the artifices of the often inappropriate *haute cuisine*.)

Before too many months had passed, Father Bombalini was a regular guest at many of the larger hotel suites and great houses of the Côte d'Azur. This rather odd-looking, rotund prelate was a marvellous raconteur, and it always made everyone feel better to have him around before going out to covet - successfully - his neighbour's wife.

And a number of excessively large contributions to the church were made in Father Giovanni's name. With increasing frequency.

Rome could no longer overlook Bombalini. The exchequers of the Vatican treasury said so.

The war found Monsignor Bombalini in various Allied capitals and occasionally attached to various Allied armies. This was brought about for two reasons. The first was his adamant deposition to his superiors that he could not remain neutral in light of the known Hitlerian objectives. He catalogued his thesis with sixteen pages of historical, theological, and liturgical precedents; none but the Jesuits could understand it, and they were on his side. So Rome shut its eyes and hoped for the best. The second reason for his wartime travels was that the international rich of Monte Carlo in the thirties were now colonels and generals and diplomats and ambassadorial liaisons. They *all* wanted him. There were so many intra-Allied requests for his services that in Washington, J. Edgar Hoover marked Bombalini's file: *Highly Suspect. May be a fairy.*

The postwar years were a time of rapid acceleration up the Vatican ladder for Cardinal Bombalini. Much of his success was due to his close friendship with Angelo Roncalli, with whom he shared a number of unorthodox views, as well as a penchant for decent, but not necessarily exclusive, wine and a good game of cards after the evening prayers.

As he sat on the white stone bench in the Vatican gardens, Giovanni Bombalini - Pope Francesco - reflected that he missed Roncalli. They had accomplished much together; it had been good. And the similarities of their respective ascendencies to the chair of St Peter never ceased to amuse him. Roncalli, John, would have been amused, too; no doubt, was, of course.

They were both compromises offered by the stern,

orthodox constituencies of the Curia to quiet the fires of discontent within the global flock. Neither compromise expected to reign very long. But Roncalli had it easy; he had only theological arguments and undeveloped social reformers to contend with. He didn't have damn fool young priests who wanted to marry and have children and, when of other persuasions, run homosexual parishes! Not that any of these personally bothered Giovanni; there was absolutely *nothing* in theological law or dogma that actually prohibited marriage and offspring; and, as far as the other, if love of fellowman did not surmount biblical ambiguities, what had they learned? But, Mother of God, the fuss that was made!

There was so much to do – and the doctors had made it clear that his time was limited. It was the only thing they *were* clear about; they could isolate no specific illness, no particular malady. They just conferred and confirmed that his 'vital signs' were slowing down at an alarming rate. He had demanded openness from them; Mother of God, he had no fear of death! He welcomed the rest. He and Roncalli could plough the heavenly vineyards together and take up their baccarat again. At last count Roncalli owed him something over six hundred million lire.

He had told the doctors that they looked too long in their microscopes and too little at the obvious. The machine was wearing out; it was as simple as that. Whereupon they nodded pontifically and uttered sombrely: 'Three months, four at the most, Holy Father.'

Doctors. *Basta!* Veterinarians with *cugini* in the Curia! Their bills were outrageous! The goatherders of Padua knew more about medicine; they had to.

Francesco heard the footsteps behind him and turned. Walking up the garden path was a young papal aide whose name escaped him. The youthful priest carried a clipboard in his hand. There was a painted crucifix on the underside; it looked silly.

'Your Holiness asked that we resolve some minor matters before the vesper hour.'

'By all means, Father. What are they?'

The aide rattled off a series of inconsequential functions, ceremonial in nature, and Giovanni flattered the young prelate by requesting his opinion on most of them.

'Then there is a request from an American periodical, *Viva Gourmet*. I would not mention it to the Holy Father except that the inquiry was accompanied by a strong recommendation from the United States Armed Forces Information Service.'

'That is a most unusual combination, is it not, Father?'

'Yes, Your Holiness. Quite incomprehensible.'

'What was the request?'

'They had the effrontery to ask the Holy Father to submit to an interview with a lady journalist regarding the pontiff's favourite dishes.'

'Why is that an effrontery?'

The young prelate paused; he seemed momentarily perplexed. Then he continued with confidence. 'Because Cardinal Quartze said it was, Holy Father.'

'Did the learned cardinal give his reasons? Or, as usual, did he commune with God all by himself and simply deliver the divine edict?' Francesco tried not to overdo his perfectly natural reaction to Ignatio Quartze. The cardinal was a loathsome fellow in just about every department. He was an *erudito aristocratico* from a powerful Italian-Swiss family, who had the compassion of a disturbed cobra. Looked like one, too, thought Giovanni.

'He did, Holy Father,' replied the priest. And the instant he spoke, the aide was struck by a sudden embarrassment. 'He - he —'

'May I suggest, Father,' said the pontiff with graceful understanding, 'that our splendidly berobed cardinal offered the opinion that the pope's favourite dishes were less than impressive?'

'I - I —'

'I see he did. Well, Father, it is true that I subscribe to simpler cooking than does our cardinal with the unfortunate nasal drip, but it is not due to lack of knowledge. Merely lack of, perhaps, ostentation; not that our cardinal, who is afflicted with that unfortunate eye that strays to the right as he talks, is ostentatious. I don't believe it ever crossed his mind.'

'No, of course not, Holy Father.'

'But I think that during these days of high prices and widespread unemployment, it might be a fine idea for your pontiff to outline a number of inexpensive, though I assure you, quite excellent dishes. Who is the journalist? A lady, you say? Don't ever tell anyone I said it, Father, but they are not the best cooks.'

'No, surely not, Your Holiness. The nuns of Rome are strenuous —'

'Galvanizing, Father. Positively galvanizing! Who is the journalist from this gourmet periodical?'

'Her name is Lillian von Schnabe. She is American, from the state of California, married to an older man, a German immigrant who fled Hitler. As coincidence would have it, she is currently in Berlin.'

'I merely asked who she was, Father. Not her biography. How do you know all this?'

'It was in the recommendation from the United States Army Information Service. The military think highly of her, apparently.'

'More than apparently. So, her husband fled Hitler? One does not turn away from such compassionate women. Coupled with the state of food prices – a number of inexpensive papal dishes is called for. Set up an appointment, Father. You may tell our resplendent cardinal, who suffers from the unfortunate affliction of a high-decibelled wheeze, that we truly hope our decision is not an affront to him. *Viva Gourmet*. The Lord God has been good to me; it is a mark of recognition. I wonder why its correspondent is in Berlin? There's a monsignor in Bonn who makes an excellent *Sauerbraten*.'

'I swear, you've got feathers in your teeth!' said Lillian as Sam walked into the room.

'It's better than chickenshit.'

'What?'

'My business contact had a strange method of transportation.'

'What are you talking about?'

'I want to take a shower.'

'Not with *me*, honey!'

'I've never been so hungry in my life. They wouldn't even stop for a - what the hell is it? A strudel. Everything was *ein, zwei, drei*! *Mach schnell!* Christ, I'm starved! They really think they won the war!'

Lillian backed away from him. 'You are the filthiest, most foul-smelling man I've ever seen. I'm surprised they let you in the lobby.'

'I think we goose-stepped.' Sam noticed a large white business envelope on the bureau. 'What's that?'

'The front desk sent it up. They said it was urgent and they weren't sure you'd stop for messages.'

'I can only conclude your ex, the fruitcake, has been busy.' Devereaux picked up the envelope. Inside were airline tickets and a note. He didn't really have to read the note; the airline tickets said it all.

Algiers.

Then he read the note.

'*No!* Goddamn it, *no*! That's less than an hour from now!'

'What is?' asked Lillian. 'The plane?'

'What plane? How the hell do *you* know there's a plane?'

'Because MacKenzie called. From Washington. You can imagine his shock when I answered —'

'Spare me your inventive details!' roared Devereaux as he raced to the telephone. 'I've got several things to say to that devious son of a bitch! Even convicts get a day off! At least time for a meal and a shower!'

'You can't reach him now,' said Lillian quickly. 'That was one of the reasons he called. He'll be out for the rest of the day.'

Sam turned menacingly. Then he stopped. This girl could probably cut him in two. 'And I suppose he offered a suggestion as to why I should be on that plane. Once he got over the shock of hearing your lovely voice, of course.'

Lillian looked puzzled. It crossed Devereaux's mind that the puzzlement was not entirely genuine. 'Mac mentioned something about a German named Koenig. How anxious this Koenig was for you to leave Berlin – one way or the other.'

'The less controversial method being Air France to Paris and from Paris to Algiers?'

'Yes, he did say that. Although not in those exact words. He's terribly fond of you, Sam. He speaks of you as a son. The son he never had.'

'If there's a Jacob, I'm Esau. Otherwise, I'm fucked as Absalom.'

'Vulgarity isn't called for —'

'It's the only thing that *is* called for! What the hell is in Algiers?'

'A sheik named Azaz-Varak,' answered Lillian Hawkins von Schnabe.

Hawkins left the Watergate in a hurry. He had no desire to talk to Sam; he had absolute faith in Lillian, in all the girls, actually. They were doing their jobs splendidly! Besides, he was to meet with an Israeli major who, with any luck, could put the final pieces of the puzzle together for him. The puzzle being Sheik Azaz-Varak. By the time Devereaux reached Algiers a telephone call would have to be made. The Hawk could not make it without that final item which would ensure the last of the Shepherd Company's capitalization.

That Azaz-Varak was a thief on a global scale was nothing new. During the Second World War he sold oil at outrageous prices to the Allies and the Axis simultaneously, favouring only those who paid instantly in cash. This did not make him enemies, however; instead, his policies engendered respect, from Detroit to Essen.

But the war was ancient history. That war. It was Azaz-Varak's behaviour in a far more recent conflagration that interested Hawkins: the Mideast crisis.

Azaz-Varak was nowhere to be found.

While oaths were hurled across the lands of the Middle

East, and the world watched armies clash against armies, and crisis-laden conferences took place, and outrageous profits were made, the greediest sheik of them all claimed to have a case of shingles and went to the Virgin Islands.

Goddamn! It didn't make sense! So MacKenzie went back into Azaz-Varak's raw files and studied them with the eye of a professional. He began to find the pattern in the years between 1946 and 1948. Sheik Azaz-Varak had apparently spent a considerable amount of time in Tel Aviv!

According to the reports, his first few trips were made quite openly. It was supposed that Azaz-Varak sought Israeli women for his harem. Thereafter, however, Azaz-Varak continued to fly into Tel Aviv, but not openly, landing at night in outlying airfields that could accommodate his most modern and expensive private planes.

More women? Hawkins had researched exhaustively and was unable to unearth the name of a single Israeli female who ever went back to the sheikdom of Azaz-Kuwait.

Then, what had Azaz-Varak been doing in the state of Israel? And why had he travelled there so frequently?

MacKenzie's breakthrough came, strangely enough, from information supplied by naval intelligence on the island of St Thomas, where Azaz-Varak had fled during the Mideast war. There, he tried to buy up more property than anyone wished to sell. Rebuffed, he became furious.

The islanders had enough trouble. They did not need Arabs with harems and slaves. Jesus! *Slaves!* The very idea sent the bureau of tourism into apoplexy; visions of all that kitchen help in revolt were positively nauseating. Azaz-Varak was systematically prevented from buying two buckets of sand. When it was suspected he was trying to negotiate through second and third parties, covenants were included that would have made Palm Beach green with envy and the ACLU purple with rage. Simply put: no fucking Arabs could own, lease, sublease, visit, or trespass.

So in his frustration, the acquisitive sheik angrily, and hastily, brought in an American holding company called the Buffalo Corporation and tried to negotiate through it. There *were* laws and St Thomas was a United States possession. And it did not take much research on Hawkins's part to uncover the fact that the Buffalo Corporation – address: Albany Street, Buffalo, New York; telephone: unlisted – was a subsidiary of an unknown company called Pan-Friendship, main office: Beirut; telephone: also unlisted.

Subsequent overseas calls to several Israeli clearing-houses made stunningly clear what Azaz-Varak had been doing during all those visits to the Jewish homeland. He owned half the real estate in Tel Aviv, much of it in the poorer sections of town. The sheik was a Tel Aviv slumlord.

The Buffalo Corporation collected rents from all over the city. *And* if the Israeli major – who was in ordnance and supply – confirmed a report the Hawk had received from some old Cambodian buddies in the CIA, the Buffalo Corporation was also in another business. One that held most unfortunate implications for the owner of said Buffalo Corporation, insofar as he was the very Arab who scared hell out of the realtors in St Thomas.

The report was simple; all MacKenzie needed was one military official to corroborate it. For the CIA boys learned that a major expeditor of petro-chemicals and fuel for the army of Israel during the Mideast war was a little-known American company called the Buffalo Corporation.

Sheik Azaz-Varak not only owned half the real estate in Tel-Aviv, but at the height of the conflict, he fed the Israeli war machine so the maniacs in Cairo wouldn't damage his investments.

It was the sort of information that simply demanded a long-distance call, thought MacKenzie Hawkins. To the sheikdom of Azaz-Kuwait.

Devereaux appreciated the sympathy from the Air France stewardess, but he would have appreciated food more. There were no supplies in the galley of the 727, a condition that would be corrected in Paris. Apparently – and there was no way to be sure he understood correctly – the Boche catering trucks that serviced Air France had been tied up in a Russian induced traffic jam on the autobahn, and what had been left in the galley had been stolen by the Czechoslovakian ground crew in Prague. And besides, the food was better in Paris.

So Sam smoked cigarettes, caught himself chewing bits of tobacco, and tried to concentrate on the doings of MacKenzie Hawkins. His seatmate was some kind of Eastern religious, perhaps a Sikh, with brown skin tinged with grey, a very small black beard, a purple turban, and darting eyes that were as close as a human's could be to those of a rat. It made thinking about MacKenzie easier; there would be little conversation on the trip to Paris.

Hawkins had raised his third ten million. And now there was an Arabian sheik who was the fourth and final mark. Whatever it was that MacKenzie had culled from the raw files had the effect of thermonuclear blackmail. Christ! *Forty million!*

What was he going to *do* with it? What kind of 'equipment and support personnel' (whatever the hell *they* were) could possibly cost so much?

Granted one did not kidnap a pope with a dollar and a quarter in his pocket, but was it necessary to cover the Italian national debt to do it?

One thing was certain. The Hawk's plan for the kidnapping included the exchange of extraordinary sums of money. And whoever accepted such sums were *ipso facto* accessories to the most outrageous abduction in history! It was another avenue he, Sam, could explore. And a pretty good one at that. If he could obtain the names of even a few of Mac's suppliers, he could scare them right out of the picture. Certainly the Hawk was not going to say to someone: *Yes, I'll buy that railroad train because I'm going to kidnap this pope fellow and it'll be a big help.* No, that was hardly the way of an experienced general officer who had drugged half the pouch couriers in Southeast Asia. But if he, Sam, reached that same someone and said: *You know that train you're selling to that bearded idiot? It's going to be used to kidnap the pope. Have a good night's sleep* well, that was something else again. The train would not be sold. And if he could prevent a train from being sold, perhaps he could prevent other supplies from reaching the Hawk. MacKenzie was army; lines of supply were paramount to any operation. Without them whole strategies were altered, even abandoned. It was military holy writ.

Yes, reflected Devereaux, gazing out into the German twilight from the foodless Air France plane, it was a very decent avenue to explore. Coupled with his first consideration – finding out how the Hawk intended to pull off the kidnapping, and the second consideration – finding out what specific blackmailing material MacKenzie held over his investors, the suppliers were a third, powerful ingredient. In preventive medicine.

Sam closed his eyes, conjuring up visions of long ago. He was in the basement of his home in Quincy, Massachusetts. On the huge table in the centre of his room was his set of Lionel trains, going around and around, weaving in and out of the miniature shrubbery and over the tiny bridges and through the toy tunnels. But there was something strange about the sight. Except for the engine and the caboose, all the other vehicles were marked identically: 'Refrigerator Car. Food.'

At Orly Airport, the passengers to Algiers were told to remain on the plane. For Devereaux nothing mattered once he saw the white truck pull up alongside the aircraft and men in white coats transferring immaculate steel containers into the galley. He even smiled at Rat Eyes beside him, noticing as he did so that his seatmate's purple turban had slipped somewhat over his brown forehead. Sam might have said something – he'd learned long ago that even strangers appreciated it when you told them their zippers were open – but since several other turbaned acquaintances who'd boarded at Orly had come up to pay their respects and had said nothing, Devereaux felt it wasn't his place. Besides most of the other purple turbans seemed a touch lopsided. Perhaps it was a custom indigenous to the particular religious sect.

Regardless, all Sam could think about were the immaculate steel trays, now securely in the Air France galley broilers, sending out deliriously inviting wafts of *escalope de veau, tournedos, sauce Béarnaise*, and, if he was not mistaken, steak *au poivre*. God was in his heaven and on Air France as well. Good Lord! Devereaux vaguely calculated the hours since he'd eaten: It was nearing thirty-six.

Unintelligible words droned over the cabin loudspeakers; the 727 taxied out on to the field. Two minutes later they were airborne and the stewardesses went about the business of distributing the most meaningful literature Sam could think of: menus.

His order took up more time than anyone else in the cabin. This was partially due to the fact that he salivated and had to swallow as he spoke. There followed an agonizing hour. Normally it was not agonizing to Sam, for it was taken up with cocktails. But today he could not drink. His stomach was too empty.

At length, dinner approached. The stewardess went down the aisle spreading the miniature tablecloths, placing the napkin-enclosed silverware, and reconfirming the choice of dinner wines. Sam could not help himself; he kept craning his neck over the edge of the seat. The scents from the galley were driving him crazy. Every odour was a banquet to his nostrils; the juices ran down his throat at each recognizable smell.

And naturally it had to happen.

The weird looking Sikh beside him lunged from his seat and unravelled his purple turban. Out of the cloth fell a large, lethal revolver. It crashed to the deck of the aircraft; Rat Eyes lunged down, retrieved it, and screamed.

'Aiyee! Aiyee! Aiyee! Al Fatah! Al Fatah! Aiyee!'

It was the signal; a screeching symphony of 'Aiyees' and 'Fatahs' could be heard behind first class, throughout the tube of the long fuselage. From somewhere in his trousers, Rat Eyes pulled out an extremely long, murderous looking scimitar.

Sam stared numbly. In complete defeat.

So the man wasn't a Sikh. He was an Arab. A goddamn fucking Palestinian Arab.

What else?

The stewardess now faced the murderous blade; the barrel of the huge pistol was jammed between her breasts. She did her best, but the terror could not be concealed.

'On the wires! On the wires to your captain!' screeched the Palestinian. 'This aircraft will proceed to Algeria. This is the wishes of Al Fatah! To Algiers! Only Algiers! Or you will all die. *Die! Die!*'

'*Mais, oui, monsieur,*' screamed the stewardess. 'The aircraft *is* proceeding to Algiers! *That* is our destination, monsieur!'

The Arab was crestfallen. His wild, piercing eyes became temporary pools of dull mud, the frustration conveyed by the tiny dots of questioning chaos in the centre of the mud.

Then the eyes sprang back once more to the vivid, cruel, violent exuberance.

He slashed the air with the huge scimitar and waved the pistol maniacally.

His demonic, defiant screams were worthy of shattering the high-altitude glass, but fortunately did not.

'*Aiyee! Aiyee! Arafat!* Hear the word of *Arafat*! Jewish dogs and Christian pigs! There will be no food or water until we *land*! *That is the word of Arafat!*'

Deep within the recesses of Sam's subconscious a small voice whispered: *You're fucked, babe.*

CHAPTER FIFTEEN

The stage manager winced; two violins and three horns went sour during the crescendo of 'Musetta's Waltz'. The act's finale was ruined. Again.

He made a note for the conductor who he could see was smiling blissfully, unaware of the grating dissonance. It was understandable: the man's hearing wasn't so good anymore.

As the stage manager looked out, he saw that the spotlight operator had dozed off again; or had gone to the toilet. The shaft of light was angled down, immobile, into the pit – on a confused flautist – instead of on Mimi.

He made a note.

On the stage itself was another problem. Two problems. The swinging gates into the café had been hung upside down, the pointed tops inverted so that they vee'd up from the floor, providing the audience a clear view behind the scenery where numerous bare feet were being rubbed and not a few extras scratched themselves in boredom. The second problem was the step unit on stage left; it had become unhinged so that Rodolfo's leg plummeted down into the open space causing his tights to rip up to his crotch.

The stage manager sighed and made two more notes.

Puccini's *La Bohème* was being given its usual performance by the company. *Mannaggia!*

As he finished putting three exclamation points after his twenty-sixth note of the evening, the assistant box-office manager approached his lectern and handed him a message.

It was for Guido Frescobaldi, and because any distraction was preferable to watching the remainder of the act, the stage manager unfolded the paper and read it.

Instantly, involuntarily, he caught his breath. Old

Frescobaldi would have a fit - if it was possible for Guido to *have* a fit. There was a newspaper reporter in the audience who wanted to meet with Frescobaldi after the performance.

The stage manager shook his head sadly, recalling vividly Guido's tears and protestations when the last (and only) newspaper reporter interviewed him. There were two reporters actually: a man from Rome and a silent Chinese colleague. Both Communists.

It was not the interview that had upset Frescobaldi, it was the article that came out of it.

Impoverished Opera Artist Struggles for People's Culture as Cousin, the Pope, Lives in Indolent Luxury off the Honest Sweat of Oppressed Workers!

That had been for openers. The front page headlined the story in the Communist newspaper, *Il Popolo*. The article had gone on to say that diligent investigative reporting on the part of *Il Popolo*'s journalists - ever alert to the inequities of capitalism's unholy alliance with savage organized religion - had uncovered the crass injustice done to this look-alike relative of the world's most powerful and despotic religious leader. How one Guido Frescobaldi sacrificed for his art while his cousin, Pope Francesco, stole everyone blind. How Guido contributed his great talent for the good of the masses, never seeking material rewards, satisfied only that his contributions uplifted the spirit of the people. So different from his cousin, the pontiff, who contributed nothing but new methods to extract money from the frightened poor. Guido Frescobaldi was the earthly saint; his cousin the subterranean villain, no doubt with orgies in the catacombs, surrounded by treasures.

The stage manager did not know a great deal about Guido's cousin, or what he did in the catacombs, but he did know Frescobaldi. And *Il Popolo*'s reporter had etched a portrait that was somewhat at variance to the Guido they all knew. But it was *this* Guido the world outside of Milan read about. *Il Popolo* stated in an editorial that the shocking story was to be reprinted in all the Socialist countries, including China.

Oh, how Frescobaldi had screamed! His roars had been the protestations of a thoroughly embarrassed man. The stage manager hoped that he could catch Guido during the act change and give him the message, but it was not always easy to find Guido during an act change. And it was useless to put the note in the dressing room for he would never see it.

For the role of Alcindoro was Guido Frescobaldi's moment in the operatic sun. It was his single triumph in a lifetime devoted to his beloved *musica*. It was proof that tenacity really did overshadow talent.

Guido was usually so moved by the events on stage — as well as his own performance — that he waddled in a trance behind the scenery until the confusion of an act change was over, his eyes invariably moist, his head held high in the knowledge that he had given his all for the audience of La Scala Minuscola, the fifth-string company of the world-renowned opera house. It was both a training ground and a musical cemetery, allowing the inexperienced to flutter their vocal wings and the over-the-hill to stay occupied until the Great Conductor summoned them to that glorious festival in the sky.

The stage manager reread the note to Guido. In the audience that night was a lady journalist named Signora Greenberg who wished to chat with Frescobaldi. He had been recommended to her by no less a distinguished source than the United States Army *Informazione Servizio*. And the stage manager knew why this Signora Greenberg included the recommendation in her note. Ever since the Communists wrote that terrible article, Guido refused to talk to anyone from the newspapers. He had even grown a huge walrus moustache and beard to lessen the likeness between himself and the pontiff.

The Communists were stupid. *Il Popolo*, through habit, was always picking a fight with the Vatican, but they soon learned what everyone else knew: Pope Francesco was not a man to vilify. He was simply too nice a fellow.

Guido Frescobaldi was a nice fellow, too, thought the stage manager. Many a late night they had divided bottles of wine together; a middle-aged signaller of cues and the elder character actor who had given his life for music.

What a drama was in the *real* story of Frescobaldi! It was worthy of Puccini, himself!

To begin with, he lived only for his beloved opera; all else was inconsequential, necessary solely to keep body and musical soul together. He had been married years ago. And six years later his wife had left him, taking their six children with her back to her native village near Padua and the security of her father's not immodest farm. Though Frescobaldi's circumstances, which by tradition meant the circumstances of his family, had not been destitute. And if his own income was currently less than adequate for *him*, it was by choice, not necessity. The Frescobaldis were actually quite well off; their cousins, the Bombalinis, had been sufficiently wealthy to allow their third son, Giovanni, to enter the church, and God knew that took a little money.

But Guido turned his back on all things clerical, mercantile, and agricultural. He wanted only his music, his opera. He badgered his father and mother to send him to the academy in Rome, where it was soon discovered that Guido's passion far outdistanced his talents.

Frescobaldi had the Latin fire and the soul, perhaps, but he also possessed a rotten musical ear. And Papa Frescobaldi was getting nervous; so many Guido associated with were *non stabili* - they wore funny clothes.

So at the age of twenty-two, Papa told Guido to come home to the village north of Padua. He had been studying in Rome for eight years; no noticeable progress had been made. No jobs - at least in music - had been offered, no musical future seemed to hold promise.

Guido did not care, however. It was the total immersion in things musical that counted. Papa could not understand. But Papa would no longer pay, so Guido came home.

The elder Frescobaldi told his son to marry his nice village cousin, Rosa Bombalini, who was having a little trouble finding a husband, and Papa woud give Guido a *fonografo* for a wedding present. Then he could listen to all the music he wished. Also, if he did not marry Cousin Rosa, Papa would break his ass.

So for six years, while his cousin and brother-in-law, Father Giovanni Bombalini, studied in the Vatican and was sent to strange places, Guido Frescobaldi endured a forced marriage to the three hundred-pound bundle of self-indulgent hysteria named Rosa.

On the morning of his seventh anniversary, he gave up. He awoke screaming; he smashed windows, broke furniture, threw pots of linguini against the walls, and told Rosa that she and her six children were the most repulsive human beings he had ever met.

Basta!

Enough was enough!

Rosa gathered the children together and fled to the village farm; and Guido walked downtown to his father's pasta shop, picked up a bowl of tomato sauce, heaved it in Papa's face and left Padua forever. For Milan.

If the world would not let him be a great operatic tenor, he at least would be near great singers, great music.

He would clean toilets, sweep stages, sew costumes, carry spears. Anything.

He would make his life at La Scala!

And so it had been for over forty years with Frescobaldi. He had risen slowly but happily from toilets to brooms, from stitching to spears. Finally he was awarded those first few words on stage - *Not so much to sing, Guido! More like talk, you see?* - and the sheer openness of his emotion made him an instant favourite of less discriminating operagoers. Of La Scala Minuscula. Where the ticket scale was lower.

In his way Frescobaldi became a beloved fixture as well as a devoted participant. He was always available to help in rehearsals, to cue, to stand in, to recite, and his knowledge was formidable.

Only once in all the years did Guido cause any trouble for anyone, and it wasn't really his fault. That, of course, was the *Popolo* attempt to embarrass his cousin, the pope. Luckily, the Communist writer had not discovered Frescobaldi's early marriage to the pontiff's sister. It would have been difficult for him, however, because Rosa Bombalini had died of overeating three decades earlier.

Hurriedly, the stage manager made his way to Frescobaldi's dressing room. He was too late. The lady speaking to Guido surely was the Signora Greenberg. She was very American and, indeed, very well endowed. Her Italian was a little strange, however. Her words were drawn out like yawns, but the lady did not appear sleepy.

'You see, Signor Frescobaldi, the purpose will be to counteract those nasty things the Communists wrote.'

'Oh, yes, *please*!' cried Guido imploringly. 'They were infamous! There is no finer man in the world than my dear cousin, *Il Papa*. I weep for the embarrassment I caused!'

'I'm sure he doesn't feel that way. He speaks so well of you.'

'Yes – yes, he would,' replied Frescobaldi, the moisture clouding his blinking eyes. 'As children we would play in the fields together, when our families visited. Giovanni – excuse me, Pope Francesco – was the best of all the brothers and cousins. He was a good *man* even as a *boy*. Does that make sense? And brains!'

'He'll be happy to see you again,' said the Signora. 'We haven't scheduled the exact time yet, but he hopes you'll meet with him for the photographs.'

Guido Frescobaldi could not help himself. Although he lost not a dram of dignity, he wept – quietly, without a sound or a gesture. 'He is such a kind man. Did you know that when that terrible magazine came out he sent me a note, in his own hand. He wrote to me: "Guido, my cousin and dear friend: Why have you hidden yourself all these years? When you come to Rome, please call on me. We will play some bocce. I put a course in the garden. Always, my blessing, *Giovanni*."' Frescobaldi dabbed his eyes with the edge of the makeup towel. 'Not a hint of anger or even displeasure. But of course I would never disturb so great a personage. Who am I?'

'He knew it wasn't your fault. You understand that your cousin would rather not have it known that we're planning this anti-Communist story. With politics the way they are —'

'Not a *word!*' interrupted Guido. 'I say *nothing*. I wait only to hear from you and I shall come to Rome. If need be – and I am scheduled to perform – I shall allow my understudy to take my place. The audiences may throw vegetables, but for Francesco, *anything!*'

'He'll be touched.'

'Did you know,' said Frescobaldi, leaning forward in the chair, lowering his voice, 'that under this moustache of mine, the face is very like my exalted cousin's?'

'You mean you *really look alike?*'

'It was ever so since we were children.'

'It never would have crossed my mind. But now that you mention it, I do see a resemblance.'

The stage manager closed the door silently. It had been partially open; they had not seen him and there was no point in interrupting. Guido might be embarrassed; the dressing room was small. So Frescobaldi was going to see his cousin, the pope. *Buonissimo!* Perhaps he might beseech the pontiff to allocate some funds to La Scala Minuscola. They could use the money.

The singing was really terrible.

'Aiyee! Al Fatah! Arafat!'

The screaming Palestinian revolutionaries dashed through the exit doors and down the steps to the concrete of Dar el Beida airport. They hugged and kissed each other and slashed at the night air with their blades. One unfortunate had his finger sliced off in the rejoicing, but it did not cause much concern. Under the leadership of Rat Eyes the group made a dash for the fence that surrounded the field.

No one tried to stop them. Indeed, the searchlights were swung in their direction to help them see their way over the fence. The authorities understood that it was desirable for the idiots to leave the field this way. If they walked into the terminal and out through the doors, a large degree of face would be lost. Besides, the quicker they left the better. They were doing nothing for the tourist trade.

The instant the final Palestinian raced out of the aircraft, Sam had lurched into the Air France galley. To no avail. In the midst of crisis, Air France had kept its head, and its financial acumen. The gleaming metal trays were in place for the next contingent of passengers.

'I paid for some goddamned food!' yelled Sam.

'I'm sorry,' said the stewardess, smiling blankly. 'Regulations prohibit the serving of food after landing.'

'For God's sake, we were hijacked!'

'Your ticket reads Algiers. We are in Algiers. On the ground. After landing. There can be no food.'

'That's inhuman!'

'That is Air France, monsieur.'

Devereaux staggered through the Algerian customs. He held four American five-dollar bills in his hand, separated as though they were playing cards. Each of the four Algerian inspectors down the line took one, smiled, and passed him on to the next man. No luggage was opened; Sam grabbed his suitcase off the conveyor and looked frantically for the airport restaurant.

It was closed. For a religious holiday.

The taxi ride from the airport to the Aletti Hotel on Rue de l'Enur El Khettabi did nothing to calm his nerves or soothe his agonizingly empty stomach. The vehicle was ancient, the driver more so, and the road down into the city steep and filled with winding curves and hairpin turns.

'We're terribly sorry, Monsieur Devereaux,' said the dark-skinned desk clerk in overly precise English. 'All of Algiers is in a state of fasting until the sun rises in the morning. It is the will of Mohammed.'

Sam leaned over the marble counter and lowered his voice to a whisper. 'Look, I respect everyone's right to worship in his own way, but I haven't eaten and I've got a little money —'

'Monsieur!' The clerk's eyes widened in Algerian shock as he interrupted and drew himself up to his full height of roughly five feet. 'The will of Mohammed! The way of Allah!'

'Good Lord! I don't believe my *eyes!*' The shout came from across the Aletti lobby. The light was dim, the ceiling high. The figure was obscured in shadows. The only thing Sam knew was that the voice was deep and feminine. And deeply feminine. Perhaps he had heard it before, he could not be sure. How could he be sure of anything – at that moment – in such an unlikely spot as an Algerian hotel lobby during an Algerian religious holiday – in the last stages of starvation. All was beyond sureness.

And then the figure walked through the hazy pools of light, led by two enormous breasts that cleaved the air in majestic splendour.

Full and Round. Naturally; why did he even bother to act surprised? Ten million – thirty million, forty million dollars no longer shocked him. Why should the sight of Mrs MacKenzie Hawkins, number two?

She pressed the cool, wet towel on his forehead; he lay back on the bed. Six hours ago she had taken off his shoes and socks and shirt and told him to lie back and stop shaking. In truth, she'd *ordered* him to stop shaking. And while he was at it, to stop babbling incoherently about crazy things like Nazis and chicken droppings and wild-eyed Arabs who wanted to blow up airplanes because they flew where they were supposed to fly. Such talk!

But that had been six hours ago. And during the interim she had taken his mind off food, and MacKenzie Hawkins, and some sheik named Azaz-Varak,and – oh my God! – the *kidnapping of the pope*!

She had reduced the dimensions of the whole insanity to the simpler proportions of a terrifying nightmare.

Her name was Madge; he had remembered that. And she had sat next to him on the bean bag in Regina Greenberg's living room; and she had reached over to touch him every time she emphasized a point. He remembered that distinctly because each time she had leaned toward him, Full and Round seemed to burst out of her peasant blouse, as they seemed now about to burst out of the silk shirt she wore.

'Just a bit longer.' she said in her deep, somewhat breathless voice. 'The desk clerk promised you'd be the first tray out of the kitchen. Now just relax.'

'Tell me again.'

'About the food?'

'No. About how come you're here in Algiers. It'll take my mind off the food.'

'Then you'll just start babbling again. You simply won't believe me.'

'Maybe I missed something –'

'You're teasing me,' said Madge, leaning over dangerously, adjusting the towel. 'All right. Short and to the point. My late husband was the leading West Coast importer of African art. His gallery was the largest in California. When he died he had over $100,000 tied up in seventeenth-century Musso-Grossai statuary. What the hell am I going to do with five hundred statues of naked pigmies? I mean *really*! You'd do just what I'm doing. Try to stop the shipment and get your money back! Algiers is the clearing house for Musso-Grossai – Now, damn it! There you *go* again!'

Devereaux could not help himself. Tears of laughter rolled down his cheeks. 'I'm sorry. It's just that it's so much more *inventive* than a sudden London vacation from a philandering husband. Or a gourmet school in Berlin. My God, it's beautiful! Five hundred naked pigmies! Did you think it up, or did Mac?'

'You're too suspicious.' Madge smiled gently, knowingly, and lifted the towel from his forehead. 'That's no way to live. Here, I'll soak this with some cool water. Breakfast should be here in fifteen or twenty minutes.' She rose from the bed and looked over at the window in silent thought. The orange rays of the new day were streaming through the window. 'The sun's up.'

Devereaux watched her; the dawn's light washed over her striking features, heightening the sheen of her auburn hair and adding a soft, deep glow to her face. It was not a young face but it had something better than youth. An openness that accepted the years and could laugh gracefully at them.

There was a directness that touched Sam.

'You're a terrific looking person,' he said.

'So are you.' She replied quietly. 'You've got what an old friend of mine used to call a face you'd like to know. Your eyes level. My friend used to say "watch the eyes, especially in a crowd; see if they listen". Actually, Mac said it. A long time ago. I suppose that sounds silly, eyes listening.'

'It doesn't sound silly at all. Eyes do listen. I had a friend who used to go to Washington cocktail parties, and he'd repeat the word "hamburger" over and over again - just "hamburger", nothing else. He swore that ninety per cent of the time the people around him would say things like, "Very interesting. I'll check the statistics on that"; or "Have you mentioned it to the undersecretary?" He always knew who'd say those things because their eyes were moving so fast; you see, he wasn't very important.'

Madge laughed softly; their eyes locked and she smiled. 'He sounds very important to me.'

'You're a *nice* person, too.'

'Yes, I try to be.' She looked over at the window again. 'MacKenzie also said that too many people run from their perfectly natural inclination to be concerned human beings. As if concern was a sign of weakness. He said: "Goddamn, Midgey, *I'm* concerned and no son of a bitch better call *me* weak!" And no one ever did.'

'I suppose being concerned is another way of being nice,' added Devereaux, mulling over the latest homily.

'There's no better way,' said Madge, carrying the towel into the bathroom. 'I'll be out in a minute.'

She closed the door. Sam repeated the words to himself: *Too many people run from their perfectly natural inclination to be concerned human beings.* MacKenzie was a man of more complications than Devereaux cared to think about. At least, until breakfast arrived.

The bathroom door opened. Madge stood in the door frame and smiled deliberately, a sense of marvellous fun in her eyes, very much aware of the picture she presented. She no longer wore her skirt. Instead her breasts were now lovingly encased in an ivory-coloured brassiere made of webbed lace. Below, her short slip accentuated the curve of her hips and bore witness to the soft white flesh that touched – and wanted to be touched – between her upper thighs.

She walked around to the side of the bed and took his immobile hand. She sat down gracefully and leaned over, her incredible spheres touching him, sending electricity through him causing him to suddenly inhale very short breaths. She kissed him on the lips. She pulled back and undid his belt and with the swift, graceful movements of a dancer, pulled down his trousers.

'Why Major, you have been thinking nice thoughts –'

And the Algerian terrorist telephone rang.

The galaxy went out of whack again. Sanity vanished in a sudden rush of hysteria. Sweet reason and laced brassieres and soft flesh were no more. Instead, screams in Arabic, commands that threatened unbelievable violence should they be disobeyed.

'If you'll stop yelling about pigs and dogs and vultures for a second, maybe I can figure out what you're trying to say,' said Sam, holding the phone away from his ear. 'All *I* said was that I couldn't come down right now.'

'I am the emissary from Sheik *A*zaz-*Var*ak!'

'What the hell is that?'

'Dog!'

'It's a dog? You mean a puppy dog?'

'Silence! Azaz-Varak is the god of all khans! The possessor of the desert winds, the eyes of the falcon, the courage of all the lions of Judea, the prince of thunder!'

'Then what does he need me for?' ventured Sam hesitantly, reluctantly recognizing the name of the Hawk's fourth mark. The final ten million. Jesus! He thought about it now with no more emphasis than ten boxes of Pop Tarts!

'Silence, dog! Or both your ears will be cut from your head and placed with hot irons up your unspeakable.'

'Now, goddamn it, that's not friendly! You talk nicer or I'm going to hang up; there's a lady here.'

'Please, Mr Deveroo,' said the Arabic voice, suddenly

quite gentle with a trace of a whine. 'In the name of Allah for the love of Allah, do not be difficult. It will be *my* ears in unspeakable places if you are difficult. We must leave for Tizi Ouzou immediately.'

'Tizi - who?'

'Ouzou, Mr Deveroo.'

'Ouzou? Did you say Ouzoo?'

Suddenly, without any warning whatsoever, the most unexpected thing Sam could imagine happened. Madge grabbed the telephone from him.

'Give me that!' she ordered. 'I know Tizi Ouzou; my husband and I stayed there once. It's a dreadful place! - Listen here, whoever you are, you'd better have a damn good reason to ask my friend to go to Tizi Ouzou. It's the godforsaken end of nowhere! Without a decent hotel *or* restaurant, to say nothing about toilet facilities!'

The girl held the phone to her ear, nodding briefly every three or four seconds. The whine on the line became very audible.

'Really, Madge, I can handle —'

'Be quiet. This son of a bitch isn't even Algerian. ... Yes. Yes. ... All right. Then we'll *both* be down! ... Take it or leave it, you desert gnat, that's the only way it's going to be. ... They're *your ears*, sweetie. ... And one other thing. The minute we get there, I want a huge meal waiting for my friend here, do you understand? ... And no biscuits of camel dung, either! All right. Five minutes.'

She hung up and smiled at Devereaux, who was mostly naked and completely pale.

'That was very generous of you, but it's not necessary —'

'Don't be silly. You don't know these people; I do. You have to be firm, they're quite harmless, despite those goddamned knives. Besides, do you think I'd let you out of my sight for a minute? After I've seen what nice thoughts you've been thinking? And in your condition.' She leaned over and kissed him again. 'It's really very touching.'

Devereaux realized that in his weakened condition he

might be subject to hallucinations; but he was not prepared for the two robed Arabs that met them in the Aletti lobby.

Peter Lorre and Boris Karloff. Quite a bit younger than the more recent photographs Sam remembered, but otherwise unmistakable.

The next twenty minutes were a blur. Yet he *had* to be able to think clearly. Azaz-Varak (*who*ever and *where*ver he was) signified the last of the investors. He had to begin putting together the pieces of his counterstrategy.

Peter Lorre sat in the front seat next to Boris, who drove. The car sped through the streets and careened dangerously around the corners of early morning Algiers. They were halfway up a winding, steep hill when Devereaux realized they were heading for Dar el Beida airport.

'We going on a plane?' asked Sam apprehensively.

Madge answered beside him. 'Oh, sure, sweetie. Tizi Ouzou's like two hundred miles east. You wouldn't want to drive. Remember, I've *been* there.'

Devereaux looked at her. He wondered, and whispered. 'I remember. What I can't understand is why you're here. Do you know what you're involved with? Do you know what you're *doing*?'

'I'm trying to be helpful.'

'So was Rose Mary Woods.'

The interior of the helicopter was only slightly smaller than the main level of Pennsylvania Station. Pillows were everywhere and beside each seat was an elaborate water pipe attached to the wall with a kind of Bunsen burner underneath it. An open galley was at the rear.

And after three minutes in the air, Sam was given the first sustenance he could recall. A small cup of acrid, black liquid that vaguely smelled of coffee, but more of bitter liquorice mixed with stale sardines.

He drank it in one swallow, grimaced, and looked at the tiny person wrapped in sheets who had poured it for him. The tiny person manipulated several wheels around the water pipe in the wall and held a match to the burner beneath. A long rubber tube with a mouthpiece was reeled from somewhere and held out for Sam.

He took it and wondered. It probably would not do him any good, but on the other hand it was something to put in his mouth, and nothing of that nature at this point could be any worse than the numbed agony he was experiencing. He inserted the mouthpiece between his teeth and drew on it.

It wasn't smoke exactly; it was more a vapour. Sweet and pungent at the same time. Really very pleasant. Actually quite delightful. Rather diverting in its way.

He drew more heavily; and then more rapidly; he looked across at Madge, sitting opposite him in a bank of pillows. 'Would you mind, my dear?' he heard himself saying calmly. 'Please remove all your clothes.'

'I'd go easy on that,' replied the girl in her most provocative, breathless whisper.

Was she whispering? Her voice seemed to arrive at his ears on different levels of sound.

'Your blouse first, if you please.' Again he was not quite positive he had said what he heard himself saying. 'Then perhaps if you would remove your skirt while performing a small, undulating dance. That would be very accommodating.'

'Put that damn thing down.'

'It's up?' He could actually smell her perfume. And the pains were gone from his stomach. Instead he could feel a surging force of great strength pulsating throughout his body. He was capable of giant deeds; he was - what was it? - the possessor of the desert winds. A prince of thunder, a hurler of lightning. With the courage of all the lions of Judea.

'That's not a Lucky Strike you're pulling on. It's pure hashish.'

'Who ...?' The information reached that small section of his brain that was functioning. *What the hell was he doing?* He spat out the mouthpiece and tried to stabilize the aircraft; it had to be the helicopter because *something* was suddenly going around and around. The lion of Judea was shrinking; a mangy pussycat was taking its place.

And then he heard the whining words of Peter Lorre, who had walked back from the pilot's area. 'We are on a heading south-south-east of Tizi Ouzou.'

'How come?' Madge was upset and did not bother to conceal it. 'You said Tizi, not someplace else. I've got friends on Rue Joucif, you fly! My late husband did a lot of favours for the Algerian government!'

'A thousand nights of blissful pardons, lady of Deveroo, but my government is Azaz-Kuwait. My sheik is the sheik of all sheiks, the god of all khans, the eyes of the falcon, the courage —'

'*When you're calling mee, calling meee, calling meeee!*' Sam suddenly found himself bursting forth in song; at least, it sounded like him. It *was* a song.

'Shut up, Major!' shouted Madge.

'*Alone - alonnnnne on this night that was meant for —*'

'Will you be quiet!' yelled the girl.

'It seemed appropriate,' mumbled Sam.

'Where are we going?' asked Madge of the whining Arab, who was looking at Devereaux as though the American should be watched closely.

'Seventy miles south-east of Tizi Ouzou is a stretch of desert that is traversed only by Bedouin tribes. It is very remote and lends itself to confidential rendezvous. An eagle's tent has been spread for the sheik of all sheiks, the god of all khans. Azaz-Varak, the magnificent, is flying in from his holiest of kingdoms to meet with the unspeakable dog named Deveroo.'

When I'm calling yoooo - Deverooo - only yooooo —'

'*Will you shut up!*'

CHAPTER SIXTEEN

There were maps everywhere, covering the Watergate bed, spilling over the coffee table, scattered about the floor, propped up against the bureau mirror, and draped over the hotel sofa. There were gasoline road maps, railroad maps, elevation charts, geological and vegetation carto-analyses; even aerial photographs from sequential altitudes of 500, 1,500, 5,000, and finally 20,000 feet.

These plus 363 ground-level photographs of every inch of the terrain under study.

Nothing could be left to chance.

Five minutes ago he had made his final decision. The real estate broker from the highly confidential, international firm of Les Châteaux Suisses des Grands Siècles would be arriving imminently. Naturally, secretly; the first law of Les Châteaux Suisses was absolute secrecy.

Mac had selected a remote château in the canton of Valais, south of Zermatt, in the countryside near Champoluc. The surrounding lands - two hundred acres - were in the cartographical shadow of the Matterhorn and were virtually inaccessible.

What was uppermost in his mind were two factors. The first was terrain. It would have to come as close as possible to duplicating Ground Zero, as Hawkins had decided to name it. Every turn and curve and rise of the road; each slope and hill that might play a part in the approach to or the escape from Ground Zero would have to be simulated as precisely as possible. Manoeuvres were useless if the training grounds did not reflect the combat zone.

The second factor was the inaccessibility. His base of operations, as Mac had come to think of the leased property, had to be completely concealed from the outlying country roads as well as from the air. The area had to be one where huge pieces of equipment could be hidden in seconds; where a complement of at least a dozen men could live and train for a minimum of eight weeks.

The château in question possessed these specifics. And it was not that far from Zürich. The Shepherd Company's capital would be transferred to Zürich. Devereaux would have to see to this centralization of finances. As well as the vetting of the château's lease.

There was a discreet knock at the hotel door. MacKenzie stepped carefully over the maps and photographs on the floor and went to it. He stood close to the panel and spoke.

'Monsieur D'Artagnan?' Les Châteaux Suisses used pseudonyms all the time.

'*Oui, mon général*,' was the quiet reply from the corridor.

Hawkins opened the door and a middle-aged, nondescript, portly man entered. Even his slightly waxed moustache was nondescript, thought MacKenzie. He'd be a tough fellow to spot in a crowd; there was absolutely nothing outstanding about him.

'I see you have pursued the information we sent you,' said Monsieur D'Artagnan in an accent formed west of Alsace-Lorraine. He was obviously a man who wasted no time on the amenities, and the Hawk was grateful for that.

'Yes, I have. I've made my decision.'

'Which property?'

'Château Machenfeld.'

'Ahh, *Le Machenfeld! Magnifique extraordinaire!* What history has been played on its rolling fields; what battles won and lost in front of its towering parapets of granite! And the indoor plumbing has been kept most functioningly modern. An exquisite choice. I congratulate you. You and your coterie of religious brothers will be very happy.' D'Artagnan removed the fattest envelope Hawkins had ever seen from his inner jacket pocket. The highly secretive firm did not carry briefcases, Mac remembered; so much confidential information crammed into one repository was too dangerous. The brokers carried only those papers of immediate concern.

'Are those the leasing arrangements?'

'*Oui, mon général*. All completed and ready for your chosen and agreed-upon mark. And the six months' deposit, of course.'

'Well, before we get to that, let me go over the conditions --'

'There are *new* ones, monsieur?'

'No. I just want to make sure you understand the old ones.'

'But, my *général*, everything *was* understood,' said D'Artagnan, smiling. 'You dictated the specifications; I transcribed them myself, as is our policy, and you approved the transcript. Here. See for yourself.' He handed Hawkins the papers. 'I think you know we would never alter our clients' demands. We have only to fill in the specific château and cross-check to make sure the demands are not in conflict with the owner's conditions of lease. I have done so with all potential locations; there are no conflicts.'

MacKenzie took the papers and picked his way between the maps and photographs to the sofa. With one hand he removed two huge elevation charts and sat down.

'I want to be positive that what I'm reading is what I heard.'

'Ask any questions you wish. As is the policy of Les Châteaux Suisses des Grands Siècles, each broker is completely familiar with all conditions. And when our business is concluded, the papers are microfilmed and placed in the company vaults in Geneva. We suggest you make similar arrangements with your copies. Untraceable.'

Hawkins read aloud. 'Whereas the party of the first part, hereafter known as the lessee, takes possession *in-nomen-incognitum*. . . .' Mac's eyes skimmed downward. 'In the absence of ... *communicatum-directorum* between the party of ... and the party of.... Goddamn! You boys got your training in clandestine operations.'

D'Artagnan smiled; the waxed moustache stretched a little. 'Ask your questions, monsieur.'

And so it began.

Les Châteaux Suisses des Grands Siècles was nothing if not thorough and specific - in the language of a lease that would never from that moment on see the light of day.

To begin with all identities were held sacrosanct, never to be divulged to any individual, organization, court, or government. No law, national or international, superseded the agreement; *it* was the only law. Payments were made to the firm either in cash or treasurer's cheques; in the case of the Shepherd Company, from a Cayman Island depository.

Whenever explanations of 'source' were desirable, they would be expedited where necessary and in the interests of controlling outside curiosity. In the case of the Shepherd Company, the sole explanation of 'source' was a loose federation of international philanthropists interested in the study and promulgation of an historic religiosity.

All supplies, equipment, transportation, and services would be expedited in complete confidentiality by Les Châteaux Suisses des Grands Siècles and consigned to branch offices in Zermatt, Interlaken, Chamonix, or Grenoble. Any and all deliveries of consequence to Le Château Machenfeld would be made between the hours of midnight and 4 a.m. Drivers, technicians, and labourers, where possible, would be from the ranks of the Shepherd Company's brotherhood, who would be sent down from Le Machenfeld to the branch offices. In the absence thereof, only employees of Les Châteaux Suisses who had no less than ten years' acceptable service with the firm would be assigned the deliveries.

All payments were to be made in advance, based on book

retail value, with a surcharge of 40 per cent for the confidential services of Les Châteaux Suisses.

'That's a lot of per cent,' said MacKenzie.

'It's a very wide boulevard,' replied D'Artagnan. 'We don't avail ourselves to those who drive in narrow streets. We think our consultation fee is ample proof of this.'

It was, thought the Hawk. The 'consultation fee' - applied against whatever lease was arrived at, *if* a lease *was* signed - was $500,000.

'You do mighty fine work, Mr D'Artagnan,' said Hawkins, taking up a fountain pen.

'You're in good hands. In a few days you will, as it were, vanish from the earth.'

'Don't worry. Everybody I know - that's *everybody* - will be extremely grateful never to hear from me again. Seems I generate complications.' The Hawk laughed quietly to himself. He signed his name: *George Washington Rappaport*.

D'Artagnan left with MacKenzie's treasurer's cheque drawn on the Cayman Island's Admiralty Bank. The amount was for $1,495,000.

The Hawk picked up a handful of photographs and walked back to the hotel sofa. As he sat down, however, he knew he could not dwell on the majesty of Machenfeld. There were other immediate considerations. Machenfeld would be worthless without the personnel to train within its borders. But former Lieutenant General MacKenzie Hawkins, twice winner of the Congressional Medal of Honour, knew where he was going and how to get there. Ground Zero was several months away. But the journey had begun.

He wondered how Sam and Midgey were doing. Goddamn, that boy was getting around!

The helicopter descended, dropping straight down and causing torrential clouds of sand to blast up in increasingly furious layers from the desert floor. So thick was the enveloping storm that the only way Sam knew they had landed was the jarring thud of the undercarriage as it met and was swallowed by the dunes.

They had been in the air somewhat longer than had been anticipated. There had been a minor navigational problem: The pilot was lost. It had to be the pilot since it was unthinkable to admit the possibility that the eagle's tent of Azaz-Varak was in the wrong place. But at last, they saw the complex of canvas below.

The sand settled and Peter Lorre opened the hatch. The desert sun was blinding. Sam held Madge's arm as they stepped out of the aircraft; if the sun was blinding, the sand was boiling. 'Where the hell are we?'

'Aiyee!' 'Aiyee!' 'Aiyee!' 'Aiyee!'

The screams were everywhere, and from everywhere there was rushing movement. Turbaned Arabs, their sheets flying in the wind like a hundred white sails, raced out of the various tents towards them. Peter Lorre and Boris Karloff flanked Sam, gripping his arms as if displaying an animal carcass. Madge stood in front, somewhat protectively, thought Devereaux uncomfortably, as though she were about to give instructions to a slaughterhouse butcher. The racing battalion of sheets and turbans formed two single lines that created a corridor leading slightly uphill in the sand to the largest of the tents, about fifty yards away.

Peter Lorre's nasal shriek filled the air. '*Aiyee!* The eye of the falcon! The hurler of lightning! The god of all khans and the sheik of all sheiks!' He turned to Sam and screamed even louder. '*Kneel! Unworthy white hyena!*'

'*What?*' Devereaux wasn't arguing; he just thought the sand would melt his trousers.

'It is better to kneel,' said the deep-throated Boris Karloff, 'than to find yourself standing on stumps.'

The sand was, indeed, uncomfortable. And Sam, in an instant of real human concern, wondered what Madge was going to do; she wore a very short skirt above her desert boots. He squinted and looked at her.

He need not have indulged in human concern, he thought. Madge was not kneeling at all. Instead she had moved slightly to the side and was standing erect. She was spectacular.

'Bitch,' he whispered.

'Keep your head,' she answered quietly. 'That's meant figuratively – I think.'

'*Aiyee!* Behold the prince of thunder and lightning!' shrieked Peter Lorre.

There was movement at the tent at the end of the corridor of abus and turbans. Two minions swept back the front flap and prostrated themselves on the ground, their faces in the sand. From the shadowed recesses emerged a man who was a major disappointment, a walking anticlimax, to the dramatic preparations for his entrance.

The prince of thunder and lightning was a spindly little Arab; peering out from the shrouds was about the ugliest face Devereaux had ever seen. Below the outsized, narrow, hooked nose, Azaz-Varak's lips were curled – actually *curled* – so that his thin black moustache seemed fused to his nostrils. The pallor of his skin (what could be seen) was a sickly beige, which served to emphasize the dark, deep circles under his heavy-lidded eyes.

Azaz-Varak approached, lips pressing, nostrils sniffing, head bobbing. He looked only at Madge. When he spoke there was a certain authority in his whine.

'The wives of the lion's lair, the royal harem – none understand the awesome responsibilities that befall my generous person. Would you like a camel, lady?'

Madge shook her head with a certain authority of her own. Azaz-Varak continued to stare.

'Two camels? The aeroplane?'

'I'm in mourning,' said Madge respectfully but firmly. 'My wealthy sheik passed away just after the last crescent moon. You know the rules.'

The heavy-lidded eyes of Azaz-Varak were filled with disappointment; his curled-up lips smacked twice as he replied. 'Ahh, it is the awesome burdens of our faith. You have two crescents of the calendar to survive. May your sheik rest with Allah. Perhaps you will visit my palaces when your time has passed.'

'We'll see. Right now, my escort is hungry. Allah wants him to protect me; he can't do that if he faints.'

Azaz-Varak looked at Sam as though studying the pre-slaughtered carcass. 'He has two functions, then. One worthy, one despicable. Come, dog. To the eagle's tent.'

'That's where the food is, isn't it?' Devereaux smiled his best, most ingratiating smile as he scrambled to his feet.

'You will partake of my table when our business is concluded. Pray to Allah that it is finished before the northern snows come to the desert. Did you bring the unmentionable agreement?'

Devereaux nodded. 'Did you bring any hot corned beef?'

'*Silence!*' shrieked Peter Lorre.

'Lady,' said Azaz-Varak, addressing Madge, 'my servants will see to your every wish. My palaces are lovely; you would like them.'

'It's tempting. We'll see where I am in a month or so.' She winked at Azaz-Varak. His lips went through a series of wet pressings before he snapped his fingers and proceeded towards the eagle's tent.

The minutes stretched into quarter hours, those to the inevitable hour, and then two more of them. Devereaux honestly believed he had reached the end. A promising legal career was being snuffed out, starved out, in the middle of some godforsaken stretch of desert, seventy miles south of a ridiculously named place called Tizi Ouzou in North Africa.

What made the ending so ludicrous was the sight of Azaz-Varak poring over each sentence of the Shepherd Company's limited partnership papers, with eight to ten screeching Arabs looking over his shoulder, arguing vehemently among themselves. Every page was treated as though it were the only page; every convoluted and unnecessary – legalism torn apart for a meaning that was not there. Sam saw clearly the terrible irony: the esoteric, legalistic nonsense that was the essence of every lawyer's livelihood was keeping him from his own survival.

An insane thought went through his pained brain: if all legal documents were written to be understood between meals all meals postponed until said understanding was clear the state of justice would be on a much higher plane. And most lawyers of his acquaintance out of work.

Every now and then one of Azaz-Varak's ministers would carry over a page and point to a particular paragraph, asking him in excellent English what it meant. Invariably Devereaux would explain that it was a standard clause – which invariably it was – and not important.

If it was not important, why was the language so confusing? Only significant items were in confusing words; otherwise there was no need for the confusion.

And, too, good things were stated clearly; unworthy things were often obscured. Did standard mean unworthy?

And so it went. Until at one point Sam screamed.

Nothing else; he simply screamed.

Azaz-Varak and his gaggle of ministers looked over at him. They nodded as if to say, 'Your point is well taken.' And then went back to screaming at each other.

At the instant the darkness started to cloud his vision, his last look at living things, thought Sam, he heard the words, whined by the sheik of sheiks.

'The northern snows have reached the desert, unspeakable one. These foul papers are like camels' prints in storms of sand: They are without meaning. Not any meaning that would bring the wrath of Allah, or certain international authorities. My generous, all-knowing person has signed them. Not that I subscribe to the despicable suggestion made to my ear, but only to help unite the world in love, you hated dog.'

Azaz-Varak rose from the mountain of pillows beneath

him. He was escorted to a screened-off section of the enormous tent by several hunched-over ministers and disappeared beyond the silks.

Peter Lorre came up to Sam, the limited partnership agreement in his hands. He gave it to Devereaux and whispered, 'Put this in your pocket. It is better that the eye of the falcon not fall on it again.'

'Is falcon edible?'

Perplexed, the tiny Arab looked at Sam. 'Your eyeballs are swimming in their sockets, Abdul Deveroo. Have the faith of the Koran, first paragraph, book four.'

'What the hell is that?' Sam could hardly speak.

'"The feasts were brought among the unbelieving infidels and no longer were they unbelieving."'

'Does that mean we eat?'

'It does. The god of all khans has ordered his favourite: boiled testicle of camel braised with the stomach of desert rat.'

'*Aiyeeeeee!*' Devereaux blanched and leaped up from the floor of the eagle's tent. The spring had been sprung; there was nothing left but self-annihilation. The end was at hand; the forces of destruction called for his finish in an explosion of violence.

So be it. He would meet it swiftly. Surely. Without thought, only blinding fury. He ran around the pillows and over the rugs and out on to the sand. It was sundown; his end would come with the orange sun descending over the desert horizon.

Boiled testicles! Stomach of rat!

'Madge! *Madge!*'

If he could only reach her! She could bring back news of his demise to his mother and Aaron Pinkus. Let them know he died bravely.

'*Madge!* Where are you?!'

When the words came he felt stirrings of bewilderment that were contradictory to the last thoughts of those who were about to perish.

'Hi, sweetie! Come on over. Look what I've got *here*. It's a *gas!*'

Sam turned, his ankles deep in sand, his caked lips trembling. Fifty yards away a group of Arabs were gathered around the front of the helicopter, all peering into the pilot's cabin.

In a trance of confusion, Devereaux staggered towards the bewildering sight. The Arabs squealed and grumbled but let him through. He gripped the ledge of the window and peered inside. It was easy; the aircraft had sunk into the dune upon landing.

It was not his eyes, however, that were assaulted. It was his ears.

There was a continuous, deafening crackle of static from the helicopter's panel that filled the small enclosure like jack hammers in a wind tunnel. Madge was in the co-pilot's seat, her blouse neckline lowered another several buttons.

Then he heard the words riding through the static and Sam froze, his hunger and exhaustion replaced momentarily by a kind of hypnotic terror.

'Midgey! Midgey, girl! You still there?'

'Yes, Mac, still here. It's just Sam. He's finished with what's-his-name.'

'*Goddamn!* How is he?'

'Hungry. He's a very hungry boy,' said Madge, expertly manipulating switches and dials on the radio panel.

'There'll be plenty of time for rations later. An army travels on its stomach, but first it's got to evacuate the fire zone! Before it gets its ass shot off! Does he have the papers?'

'They're sticking out of his pocket —'

'He's a fine young attorney, that boy! He'll go far! Now, get out of there, Midgey. Get him to Dar el Beida and on that plane for Zermatt. Confirm, and over and out!'

'Roger confirm, Mac. Out.' Midge whipped through several dozen switches as though she were a computer programmer. She turned her face to Devereaux and beamed.

'You're going to have a nice rest, Sam. Mac says you really deserve a vacation.'

'Who? Where ...?'

'Zermatt, sweetie. It's in Switzerland.'

PART THREE

The smooth-running corporation is largely dependent on its executive personnel, whose backgrounds and allegiances are compatible with the overall objectives of the structure and whose identities can be submerged to the corporate image.

Shepherd's Laws of Economics:
Book CXIV, Chapter 92

CHAPTER SEVENTEEN

Cardinal Ignatio Quartze, his thin, aristocratic features bespeaking generations of *noblesse oblige*, stormed across the rugs of his Vatican office to the large balconied window overlooking St Peter's Square. He spoke in fury, his lips compressed in anger, his nasal voice searing like the screech of a bullet.

'The Bombalini peasant goes too far! I tell you he is a disgrace to the college which – God help us all – elevated him!'

The cardinal's audience was a plump, boyish-looking priest who sat, as languorously as his habit allowed, in a purple velvet chair in the centre of the room. His pink cheeks and pursed, thick lips bespoke, perhaps, a less aristocratic background than his superior but no less a love of luxury. His speech was more a purr than a voice.

'He was and remains only a compromise, Cardinal. You were assured his health would not permit an extended reign.'

'Every *day* is an extension beyond endurance!'

'He has certain ... humilities that serve us. He has quieted much hostile press. The people look upon him warmly; our worldwide contributions are nearly as high as they were with Roncalli.'

'Please! Not that name! What good is a treasury that expands and contracts like a thousand concertinas because the Holy See subsidizes everything he can put his fat peasant hands on! And we don't need a friendly press. Division is far better to solidify our own! Nobody understands.'

'Oh, but I do, Cardinal. I really do ...'

'Did you see him today?' continued Quartze as if the priest had not spoken. 'He openly humiliated me! In audience! He questioned my African allocations.'

'A patently obvious ploy to appease that terrible black man. He's forever complaining.'

'And afterwards he tells jokes *jokes*, mind you to the Vatican guard! And waddles into the museum crowds and eats an ice *eats* an *ice*, mind you offered by some Sicilian brood mare! Next he'll drop lire in the men's room and all the toilet seats will be stolen! Such indignities! What he does to the bones of St Peter! They will turn to dust!'

'It cannot be very long, my dear Cardinal.'

'Long enough! He'll deplete the treasury and fill the Curia with wild-eyed radicals!'

'You are the next pontiff. The negative reactions of the broad middle hierarchy support you. They are silent, but resentments run deep.'

The cardinal paused; his mouth curved slightly downward as he stared out into the square, his jaw jutted forward below the dark hollows of his deep-set eyes. 'I do believe we have the delegates. Ronaldo, get me the plans for my villa at San Vincente. It calms my nerves to study them.'

'Of course,' said the priest, rising from the purple chair. 'You must remain calm. And when summer comes you will be rid of the Bombalini peasant. He will stay at Castel Gandolfo for at least six weeks.'

'The *plans*, Ronaldo! I'm very upset. Yet in the midst of chaos, I remain the most controlled man in the Vatican . The plans, you transvestite!' screamed the cardinal.

The moment the papal aide with the ever present clipboard left the room, Pope Francesco I got out of the elevated, high-backed, white velvet chair (a repository that would have frightened Saint Sebastian) and sat next to the lady from *Viva Gourmet* on the couch. He was struck immediately by the beauty of her voice; it was warm and lilting. Very lovely. It befitted such a healthy looking woman.

The aide had suggested that the interview be limited to twenty minutes; the pontiff had suggested that it should end when concluded. The lady journalist had reddened slightly with embarrassment, so Giovanni put her at ease by switching to English and asking her if she thought there was a market for clipboards with crucifixes painted on the underside. She had laughed while the aide, who did not understand English, stood by the door, his clipboard clutched to his breast like a plastic stigmata.

The aide would have to be replaced, thought the pope. He was another young prelate seduced by the pretensions of Ignatio Quartze. The cardinal was too obvious; he was moving his charges into the papal apartments before the papal funeral was arranged. But Francesco had made up his mind: the Church was not going to be left in the pontifical hands of Ignatio Quartze. To begin with, they held the chalice at Mass as though wringing the neck of a chicken.

The interview with *Viva Gourmet*'s Lillian von Schnabe was productive and pleasant. Giovanni expounded on two of his favourite subjects: that good, substantial meals could be created from inexpensive stock and flavoured with simple, spiced sauces; and that in these difficult days of high prices it was a mark of distinction – to say nothing of Christian brotherhood – to share one's table with one's neighbour.

Mrs von Schnabe saw immediately what he was trying to communicate. 'Is this a form of "the loaves and the fishes", Your Holiness?'

'Let us say He was not preaching to the wealthier sections of Nazareth. A number of His miracles were based in sound psychological principles, my dear. I open my basket of fruit, you open your basket of pasta; we have fruit *and* pasta. The simple addition alone gives variety. Variety we rightly equate with more rather than less.'

'And the diet's improved,' agreed Lillian, nodding.

'*Perfetto*. You see? Two *principii*: reduce the cost and share the supply.'

'That sounds almost socialistic, though, doesn't it?'

'When stomachs are empty and prices are high, labels are foolish. In the *Borsa Valori* – the stock exchange, you call it they are not prone to open baskets; they sell them. It is fitting that they do so, considering the nature of their labours. But I do not address such people. They eat at the Grand Hotel, on each other's expense accounts. I believe that, too, is a derivative of the "loaves and fishes" principle.'

They discussed numerous recipes based on the village dishes from the pope's past. Giovanni could see that the nice lady with the lovely voice was impressed. He had done his nutritional homework; carbohydrates, proteins, starch, calories, iron, and all kinds of vitamins were to be found in his recipes.

Lillian filled half a notebook, writing as rapidly as the pope spoke, stopping him occasionally to clarify a word or phrase. After nearly an hour had passed, she paused and asked a question Giovanni did not understand.

'What about your own *personal* requirements, Your Holiness? Are there any restrictions or specific necessities called for in the meals brought to you?'

'*Che cosa?* What do you mean?'

'We are what we eat, you know.'

'I sincerely hope not. I am in my seventh decade, my dear. An excess of onion or olive or pimento. ... But such information is not needed for your article. People my age quite naturally gravitate to and regulate their personal needs in this area.'

Lillian put her pencil down. 'I didn't mean to pry, but you're so fascinating a man – and I *am* considered one of the best nutritional experts in America. I suppose I just wanted to approve of the way your kitchen treats you.'

Ahh, thought Giovanni Bombalini, *how many years it has been since a lovely person of the opposite gender has been concerned about him! He could not remember, it was so long ago! Pinched-faced nuns and officious nurses, yes. But so attractive a lady, with such a lovely voice. ...*

'Well, my dear, these outrageous doctors *do* insist on certain foods. ...'

Lillian picked up her pencil.

And they talked for another fifteen minutes.

At the end of which time there was a knock on the door of the papal apartment. Francesco rose from the couch and returned to the elevated, high-backed, white velvet chair that belonged in one of those Cinecittà biblical spectaculars.

An agitated Cardinal Ignatio Quartze stood in the doorway, a handkerchief dabbing his aquiline nose, noises emerging from his throat. 'I am sorry to interrupt, Holy Father,' he said in both Italian and high dudgeon, giving the word 'holy' a rather profane but eminently courteous connotation, 'but I've just been informed that Your Holiness has seen fit to disagree with my instructions regarding the convocation of the Bankers for Christ.'

'"Disagree" is too strong a term. I merely suggested that the convocation committee reconsider. To occupy the Sistine Chapel for two days at the height of the spring tourist season seems unwarranted.'

'If you will forgive my contrary observation, the Sistine is the most favoured *and* frequented site we possess. All convocations of merit convene there.'

'Thus denying thousands every year of its beauty. I'm not sure there's merit in that.'

'We are *not* an amusement park, Pope Francesco.' Strange noises continued to come from the area of the cardinal's throat; he blew his nose with aristocratic vigour.

'I sometimes wonder,' replied Giovanni. 'We sell such a diversity of baubles everywhere. Did you know there's a stand featuring rhinestone rosary beads?'

'*Please*, Your Holiness. The Bankers for Christ. They *expect* the Sistine. We are finalizing extremely important matters.'

'Yes, my dear Cardinal, I received the memorandum. "Accruals for Jesus" is somewhat laboured, I think, but I suppose there are certain tax advantages.' Giovanni's attention was suddenly drawn to Lillian. She had closed her notebook politely but firmly; she was anxious to leave. *Ahh*, it had been such a pleasant interlude! And Quartze was not going to spoil it; he could wait. He addressed the attractive lady with the lovely voice. In English, of course; a language only barely understood by Quartze. 'How rude we are. Do forgive us. The agitated cardinal with the propellers in his nasal passages has once again found my judgements lacking.'

'Then I would have to say *his* judgement left much to be desired,' said Lillian, rising from the couch and placing her notebook in her purse. She looked into Giovanni's eyes and spoke softly with feeling. 'I suppose this isn't a proper thing to say but since I'm not Catholic, I'll say it anyway. You're one of the most attractive men I've ever met. I hope you're not offended.'

Giovanni Bombalini, Pope Francesco, Vicar of Christ felt the stirrings of memories of fifty years ago. And they were good. In a profoundly sacred sense – for which he was grateful. 'And you, my dear, possess an honesty – however erroneous your present opinion – that walks in the warm light of God.'

'If I do, it's because I was taught by someone quite like you, I think. Although a few would recognize the similarity.'

'I am flattered. This – someone, give him the blessings of a farmhand-priest.'

Lillian smiled. She started for the door, where Quartze's handkerchief fluttered a tattoo in front of his agitated face and the sounds of mucus still could be heard beyond his aquiline nose and very thin lips. The prelate sidestepped to let her pass, doing his best to ignore her. So Lillian paused briefly, forcing him to look at her. When he did so, she winked.

As she closed the door the words from Pope Francesco were clear and firm. For in his anger, the pontiff raised his voice, in English.

'Talk to me not of the Sistine, Ignatio! Instead, discuss these plans I requested for your waterfront home at San Vincente! What are "security arrangements"? They include a *steam bath*?'

Hawkins had reserved both seats in the first-class section of the Lufthansa 747. Since he needed elbow room, there was no point in inconveniencing a fellow passenger. This way, he was able to place the folders beside him for quick referrals.

He had specifically chosen the night flight to Zürich. The travellers, by and large, would be diplomats, bankers, or corporate executives used to transatlantic flights; they would use the night for sleep, not socializing. He would have a minimum of interruptions.

For selections would have to be made, offers of recruitment dispatched immediately from Zürich.

MacKenzie's briefcase contained assorted personnel profiles from which he would choose his troops. They were the last of the files he had Xeroxed at the G-2 archives. Those fortunate enough to be chosen would be his brigade; his personal army that would be privileged to engage in the most unusual manoeuvre in modern military history.

And each soldier would return from the engagement one of the richest men in his part of the world.

For, where possible, they would be from separate parts of the world. For the inviolate condition of recruitment was that none would ever acknowledge the existence of the others once the engagement was completed. It would be better if they came from different places.

The dossiers in the Hawk's briefcase were those of the most accomplished double and triple agents in the US Army data banks. And there was a common denominator running through each file: All were in forced retirement.

The state of double and triple agenting was at a low ebb. The experts described in the dossiers had not had really gainful employment for some time, and for such men inactivity was anathema. It meant not only a loss of prestige within the community of international criminals, but also a reduced scale of living.

The prospects of $500,000 per man would not be lightly dismissed. And each potential recruit was worth it. Each was the best at his speciality.

It was all a question of logistics. Think - then *out*-think. Every function handled by an expert, every move timed to the split second.

And that required a commander who demanded flawless precision from his troops. Who trained them to perform at peak efficiency levels. Who did not stint when it came to equipment and simulation; who would duplicate as far as technically possible the *exact conditions* projected for the assault. In essence, a general officer of the first rank. Himself. *Goddamn!*

Once the brigade was selected and assembled, Mac would outline the basic strategy. Then he would allow his officers to offer suggestions and refinements. A good commander always listened to his subordinate officers but, of course, reserved final judgement for himself.

The weeks of training would show where the strengths and weaknesses lay; the objective was merely to eliminate all weakness.

The fewer troops the better, but not so few as to impair the efficiency of the mission. Which was why there was only one payment for each soldier: $500,000. There would be no rewards if they were caught. At least, not the kind they were after. There *would* be certain family allotments in the case of capture. It was the sort of thing all armies had learned to take for granted. Men performed better under combat conditions if their minds were free of concern about their families. It was a good thing, too. It was another proof of separation between the species.

The Shepherd Company would bank funds for dependants in advance of Ground Zero; to be deducted, of course, from all final payments upon the successful completion of the operation.

Goddamn! He was not only pro, he was a very thorough pro at that! If those idiots in the Pentagon had turned over the whole US Army to him, they would not be having all that trouble with volunteer enlistments. The Pentagon pricky-shits did not really understand 'the book'. If a soldier took the book for what it was and didn't try to bend it politically, or find ambiguities to hide behind - well, it was a goddamned good book. Flawed but workable.

He had no time to think about pricky-shits. He had about

refined his brigade. The required areas of expertise were seven: camouflage, demolition, sedative medicines, native orientation, aircraft technology, escape cartography, and electronics.

Seven experts. He had narrowed the dossiers down to twelve. Before he reached Zürich he knew he would have the seven. It was just a question of reading and rereading. He would send out his offers from Zürich, not from the Château Machenfeld; nothing could be traced to Machenfeld.

He even had to be careful in Zürich. Not with regard to traces, however; he could handle that problem. But he had to make damn sure he didn't run into Sam Devereaux. Sam was due within hours of his own arrival; he wasn't ready for Sam's kind of panic. He could handle *that* problem better within the confines of Machenfeld.

But then, thought the Hawk, he didn't really have anything to worry about. Devereaux was the girls' problem and they had – each and every one – carried out their assignments with real know-how.

Goddamn! They were splendid! A man had to count himself fortunate, indeed, to have such a quartet of fine women behind him. 'Behind every great man. . . .' they said. Behind *him* there wasn't *one* fine lass, there were *four*.

And a grander, more upstanding group of girls there never were! Sam was a lucky fellow and he didn't know it. Hawkins made a mental note to tell him when he saw Sam at Machenfeld.

Tomorrow, if the schedule held.

Devereaux walked down the station platform looking for the correctly numbered railway car. The task was made difficult because he could not stop belching. He had eaten his way from Tizi-whatever-the-hell-it-was, through Algiers, past Rome, into Zürich. Madge had seen him off at Dar el Beida airport admitting no more than their good-byes than she had saying hello in the Aletti Hotel room.

But Sam had made up his mind not to speculate any further about the girls. Whatever propelled them to do what they did for the Hawk could be left to Krafft-Ebing; he had other things to concentrate on.

The capitalization of forty million dollars was committed. Hawkins now had his marbles (no, he did not have his marbles, but that was another question), and he would start playing the game. The Hawk would begin his final arrangements, make his purchases, recruit his – what was it? – 'support personnel'.

Jesus! Support personnel!

So he could kidnap the pope!

Oh, my God! The whole world was an enormous fruitcake!

There was only one thing to bear in mind, one objective to keep in focus: How to stop MacKenzie Hawkins.

Two objectives: Stay out of jail himself. And out of the homicidal clutches of the Mafia, the Peerage, the Nazis, and particularly those Arabs who wanted to stuff his unmentionables into unspeakables.

He found his compartment, the sort made famous by Rex Harrison and Margaret Lockwood. Shadows and black velvet collars and the incessant *therumping* of the metal wheels against the metal tracks below signifying the ineviatable approach of terror. And large windows on the sliding doors, with curtains suddenly drawn back revealing the faces of evil.

Night Train, Orient Express – with slow dissolves to hands inching into folds of dark overcoats, ever so slowly withdrawing the black steel of murderous pistols. The train started.

'Well, ah declare! Ah said to myself, Ah simply *don't beleeeeve it*! It's the *mayjor*! Right here in *l'il ole Zürich*!'

There was no reason to be the least astonished. After all, *Titanics* was on schedule.

Regina Sommerville Hawkins Clark Madison Greenberg stood in the corridor outside the railroad compartment and spoke through the wood-framed window. She slid the door open and filled the small enclosure with remembrances of magnolia blossoms. Sam sat down calmly by the window, amazed at his own casualness. 'Your timing's nothing short of brilliant. The train rolls and so do you. If I tried to get off at Lucerne I have an idea you'd start screaming "rape"!

'Why, what a peculiar thing to say. I hope you haven't forgotten the Beverly Hills Hotel; I never will.'

'My memories have no beginnings, no middles, no ends. The world fornicates in a thousand broken mirrors; we abuse ourselves in the reflections of Sodom and Gomorrah. . . .

'Now, tell me why you just *happen* to be in Zürich. At the Hauptbahnhof, on this particular train, in this particular car.'

'Oh, that's easy. Manny's shooting a picture in Geneva. For UA. I think it's so porn they had to make it outside the States.'

'That's Geneva; this is Zürich. You can do better than that. Let's have it for Hawkins's Harem. A little imagination, please.'

'Honestly! Now you're downright offensive!' Regina swept her vicuña back and placed her hands defiantly on her hips. Two cannons had Devereaux in their sights. 'I don't think you've got a damn thing to complain about. We root ourselves up out of *very* comfortable circumstances, traipse *all* over the world, subject ourselves to every kind of inconvenience - *rush, rush, rush* - check on everything - look after you, body *and* soul - make sure no one hurts you - see to your every comfort —. Oh, Lawdy, what more could we do?! And for what? Abuse! Just plain, big ole abuse!'

Regina dropped her defiant pose and began to cry. She opened her purse, withdrew a Kleenex, and sat down opposite Sam, dabbing her eyes.

A lost, hurt little girl.

'Hey, come on. That's not fair.'

As are most men, Sam was helpless before a tearful woman.

Regina sobbed; her chest throbbed. Devereaux got out of his seat and knelt in front of her. 'It's okay. It's all right. Don't cry, please.'

Between subsiding gasps, the girl looked at him gratefully. 'Then you don't hate me? Say you don't hate me.'

'How could I hate you? You're lovely – and sweet – and for Christ's sake, please stop crying.'

She put her face next to his and her lips against his ear. 'I'm sorry. It's just that I'm exhausted. The pressure's been simply God-awful. I've stayed by the telephone night and day, always worryin' – and, of course, wonderin'. I really missed you.'

Ginny's coat was like a warm, comforting blanket between them. The huge, soft lapels came close to enveloping Devereaux's arms. She took both his hands and guided them between the folds of thick fabric and placed them on the softer, warmer, more comforting swells of loveliness that were beneath the silk of her blouse.

'That's better. Stop crying now.' It was all he could think to say, so he said it softly.

She whispered into his ear, causing all kinds of things to happen to his metabolism. 'Do you remember those marvellous old English movies that took place on trains like this?'

'Sure. Rex Harrison saving Margaret Lockwood from the evil Conrad Veidt —'

'I think you can slide the door closed and lock it. And there are curtains. ...'

Devereaux rose from the floor. He locked the door, closed the curtains, then turned back to Regina. She had removed her vicuña coat and spread it invitingly over the soft seat of the railroad compartment.

Beneath them the *therumping* sounds of the metal against metal signified the inexorable journey, the beat somehow sensual. Outside, the lovely countryside of Switzerland whipped by, bathed in a Swiss twilight.

'How much time do we have before we reach Zermatt?' he asked.

'Enough,' she replied, smiling. She began unbuttoning her silk blouse. 'And we'll know. It's the last stop.'

CHAPTER EIGHTEEN

Hawkins registered at Zürich's Hotel D'Accord with a counterfeit passport. He'd purchased it in Washington from a CIA agent who realized the courts would not let him write a book when he retired; the man also offered a selection of wigs and hidden cameras but MacKenzie demurred. On settling into the room, his first act was to go right down to the lobby again and negotiate with the head switch-board operator: cash for cooperation. Since the cash was one hundred dollars, it was agreed that all his calls and cablegrams would be routed through her board.

He returned to the room and spread the seven dossiers (his final selections) over the coffee table. He was immensely pleased. These men were the most devious, experienced *provocateurs* in their fields. It was now merely a question of enlisting them. And MacKenzie knew he was an exceptionally qualified recruiter.

Four he knew he could reach by phone. Three by cable. Admittedly, the telephone contacts would be difficult, for in no case would one call find the expert in. But he would reach them by using various codes from the past. One call would be made to a Basque fishing village on the Bay of Biscay; another to a similar coastal town in Crete. A third would be placed to Stockholm, to the sister of the espionage expert who was currently living as a minister of the Scandinavian Baptist Church. The fourth call would be to Marseilles where the man sought was employed as a tugboat pilot.

And the geographical diversity! In addition to those he could reach by telephone (Biscay, Crete, Stockholm and Marseilles), there were the cablegrams: to Athens, Rome, and Beirut. What a spread! It was an intelligence director's dream!

MacKenzie took off his jacket, threw it on the bed, and withdrew a fresh cigar from his shirt pocket. He chewed the end to its proper consistency and lighted up. It was just nine-fifteen; the afternoon train to Zermatt was at four-fifteen.

Seven hours. Now that was a good omen if ever one existed! Seven hours and seven subordinate officers to recruit.

He carried the three dossiers to the desk and arranged the files in front of the telephone. The cablegrams would be sent first.

At precisely twenty-two minutes to four the Hawk replaced the telephone and made a red check mark on the dossier titled *Marseilles*. It was the last of the phone contacts; he needed only two replies – to the cables to Athens and Beirut. Rome had responded two hours ago. Rome had been out of work longer than the others.

The calls had gone smoothly. In each case the initial conversations with the middlemen – and women – had been reserved, polite, general, almost abstract. And with each MacKenzie employed just the right words, quietly, confidentially. Each expert he had wanted to reach called him back.

There had been no hitches with anyone. His proposals were couched in the same universally understood language; the term *yellow mountain* the springboard. It was the highest score an agent could make for himself. The *yellow mountain* figure was a 'five hundred key' with advance funds banked against contingencies. The *security controls* included 'inaccessible clearing-houses' that maintained no connections with international regulatory agencies. The *time factor* was between six and eight weeks, depending on the 'technological refinements called for in the sophisticated engineering process'. And finally, as leader, his own background encompassed wholesale service to entire governments in most of Southeast Asia, proof of which could be confirmed by several accounts in Geneva.

He had done his research well. To a man, they all needed

to mine the *yellow mountain*.

Hawkins got up from the desk and stretched. It had been a long day and it wasn't over yet. In twenty minutes he would have to leave for the railroad station. Between now and then he would speak with the switchboard operator and give her instructions for those callers who might try to reach him. The instructions would be simple: he had reserved the room for a week; he would return to Zürich in three days. The callers could contact him there, or leave numbers where they could be reached. MacKenzie did not want to return to Zürich, but Athens and Beirut were exceptional recruits.

The telephone rang. It was Athens.

Six minutes later Athens was in.

One more to go.

The Hawk moved his untouched luggage to the door and repacked his briefcase, leaving Beirut's dossier in a separate, easily accessible spot. He looked at his watch: three minutes to four. There was no point in procrastinating any longer. He had to leave for the station. Returning to the desk he dialled the switchboard operator and told her he wanted to leave a few simple instructions —

The operator interrupted politely.

'Yes, of course, mein Herr. But may I take them later? I was about to ring your room. An overseas call has just come in for you. From Beirut.'

Goddamn!

Sam opened his eyes. The sun was streaming through the huge French doors: the breeze billowed the drapes of blue silk. He looked around the room. The ceiling was at least twelve feet high, the fluted columns in the corners and the intricately carved mouldings of dark wood everywhere bespoke the word 'château.' It all came into focus. He was in a place called Chateau Machenfeld, somewhere south of Zermatt. Outside the thick, sculptured door of his room was a wide hallway with Persian prayer rugs scattered over a glistening dark floor, and muted candelabra on the walls. The hallway led to an enormous winding staircase and a proliferation of crystal chandeliers above a great hall the size of a respectable ballroom. There, among priceless antiques and Renaisssance portraits, was the entrance - gigantic double doors of oak opening on a set of marble steps that led to a circular drive large enough to handle a funeral for the chairman of General Motors.

What had Hawkins *done*? How did he do it? My God, why? What was he going to use such a place for?

Devereaux looked at the sleeping Regina, her dark brown hair lying in waves over the pillow, her California-tanned face half buried under the eiderdown quilt. If she had any answers, she wouldn't tell him. Of all the girls, Ginny was the most outrageously manipulative; she had orchestrated him down to the moment of sleep. Partially, granted only partially, because he was fascinated by her. There was a will of steel beneath the soft magnolia exterior; she was a natural leader who, as all natural leaders, took delight in her leadership. She used her gifts, mental and physical, with imagination and boldness, and a considerable dash of humour. She could be the strong and moral proselytizer one moment, and the lost little girl in the middle of burning Atlanta the next. She was the laughing, provocative siren in the plantation moonlight, and with the flick of a switch, a conspiratorial, whispering Mata Hari giving orders to a suspicious looking chauffeur in the shadows of the Zermatt railroad station.

'*Mack Feldmann's ass is in the bitter seltzer!*'

To the best of Sam's recollection those had been the words Ginny had whispered to the strange man in the black beret, with the gold front tooth, whose catlike eyes riveted themselves to the front of her blouse.

'*Mack's in felt!*' had been the whispered reply. '*His sight's in an auto bomb's flower pot!*'

With that less-than-articulate rejoinder, Ginny had nodded, grabbed Devereaux's arm, and propelled him into the Zermatt street.

'Carry your suitcase in your left hand and whistle something. He'll turn into an alley and we'll wait at the corner for him to bring out the car.'

'Why all the nonsense? The left hand. The whistling —'

'Others are checking. To make sure we're not being followed.'

The *Orient Express* syndrome was being somewhat overdone, Sam had thought at the time, but nonetheless he'd switched the suitcase to his left hand and started whistling.

'Not *that*, you ninny!'

'What's the matter? It's some kind of hymn —'

'Over here it's called "Deutschland Über Alles"!'

He'd switched to 'Rock of Ages' as another man, this one in a real Conrad Veidt overcoat complete with velvet lapels, came up to Regina and spoke softly.

'*Your warts are in the wagon.*'

'*Mack Feldmann's ass surely has sweet shekels,*' she had answered quietly, rapidly. And within seconds a long black automobile raced out of the dark alley and they had climbed in.

That was how the tortuous, two-hour drive had begun. Miles of winding, uphill roads cut out of the Swiss mountains and forests, intermittently illuminated by the eerie wash of moonlight. Until they reached some kind of massive gate that wasn't a gate; it was an honest-to-god *portcullis*. In front of a *moat*.

A real moat! With heavy planks and the sounds of water below. Then another winding, uphill road that ended in the enormous circular drive in front of the largest country house Sam had seen since he toured Fontainebleau with the Quincy Boy Scouts. And even Fontainebleau didn't have parapets. This place did, certainly high and definitely stone, with the sort of cutout patterns one associated with *Ivanhoe*.

Quite a place, Château Machenfeld. And he had only seen it at night. He wasn't sure he wanted to see it in daylight. There was something frightening about the mere thought of such a massive edifice when related to one MacKenzie Hawkins.

But where did the château fit in? What was it for? If it was going to be the son of a bitch's command post, why didn't he just rent Fenway Park and be done with it? It had to take an army of minions to keep the place running; minions talked. Ask anyone at Nuremberg or in Sirica's courtroom.

But Regina wouldn't talk. (Of course, she wasn't a minion; in no way did the word fit.) Yet he had tried. All the way down from Zürich – well, perhaps not every moment – and half the night in Machenfeld – perhaps less than half – he had done his best to get her to tell him what she knew.

They had sparred verbally, each talking obliquely, neither coming to grips with any positive statements that could lead to any real conclusions. She admitted – she had no choice – that all the girls had agreed to turn up in the right places at the right times so that he, Sam, would have company and not be led into temptations that could be debilitating on such a long businees trip. And have someone trustworthy to take messages for him. And watch out for him. And where goddamned cotton-pickin' hell was the harm in *that*? Where was he going to find such a concerned group of ladies who had his best interests at heart? And kept him on schedule?

Did she know what the *business trip* was about?

Lawdy, no! She never asked. None of the girls asked.

Why not?

Landsakes, honey! The Hawk had told them not to.

Couldn't any of them draw ... certain inferences? I mean, my God, his itinerary wasn't exactly that of a New England shoe salesman.

Honeychile! When they were married to the Hawk – individually, of course – he was always involved with top-secret army things they all knew they shouldn't ask questions about.

He wasn't *in* the army now!

Well-live-and-die-in-Dixie! That's the *army's* fault!

And so it went.

And then he began to understand. Regina was no patsy. None of the girls was. *Fall guy* was not in their collective vocabulary. If Ginny, or Lillian, or Madge, or Anne knew anything concrete they weren't about to say so. If they perceived a lack of complete integrity, each put on blinkers, and her own particular activity remained unrelated to any larger action. None certainly would discuss anything with *him*.

There was another problem in the midst of the Hawk's insanity: Sam genuinely liked the girls. Whatever the whack-a-doo furies were that drove them to do MacKenzie's bidding, each was her person, each an individual, each – God help him – had an honesty he found refreshing. So, if he did spell out what he knew, the instant he did so they were accessories. To a *conspiracy*. It didn't take a lawyer to know that. What was he thinking about; he *was* a lawyer.

As of this ... point in time ... each girl was clean. Maybe not like a hound's tooth; maybe not even like a wino's bridgework, but legally it could be argued that each had operated in a vacuum. There was no conspiracy under the circumstances.

Thank you, Mr Defence Attorney. The bench suggests that you reclaim your tuition from law school.

Sam got out of the ridiculously oversized, canopied bed as quietly as possible. He saw his shorts halfway across the room towards the French doors, which was where he was heading, anyway, and briefly wondered why they were so far from the bed. Then he remembered, and he smiled.

But this was morning, a new day, and things were going to be different. Ginny had given him one specific to hang on to: Hawkins would arrive by late afternoon or early evening. He would use the time until then to learn whatever he could about Château Machenfeld. Or more precisely, what the Hawk was planning for Château Machenfeld as it related to one Pope Francesco, Vicar of Christ.

It was time for him to mount his own counterstrategy. Hawkins was good, no question about it. But he, Sam Devereaux from the Eastern Establishment's Quincy-Boston axis, wasn't so bad, either. Confidence! Mac had it; so did he.

As he put on his shorts, the obvious first move in his counterstrategy came into focus. It wasn't just obvious, it was blatant; bells rang! Such an extraordinary place (mansion, estate, compound, small country) as Machenfeld would demand an unending series of supplies to keep it functioning. And suppliers were like minions, they could see, and hear, and bear witness. The Hawk's proclivity for massiveness could be the most vulnerable aspect of his plans. Sam had considered disrupting Mac's supply lines as *one* of his options, from a military point of view, but he had no idea how positively logical it was. It might be all he needed.

He'd circulate rumours as massively dangerous, as gigantically outrageous, as the sight of Machenfeld itself. He'd start with the servants, then the suppliers, then everyone else who came near the château, until a state of isolation was brought about and he could come to grips with a deserted Hawkins, and - *what the hell was that noise?*

He walked rapidly to the French doors and through them to the small balcony beyond. It overlooked the rear of Château Machenfeld. He assumed it was the rear; there was no circular drive below. Instead, there were gardens in spring bloom, with gravelled paths and latticed arbours and scores of small fishponds carved out of rock. Beyond the gardens were green fields that merged into greener, darker forests, and in the distance were the majestic Alps.

The noise continued, spoiling the view. He could not, at first, determine where it came from, and so he squinted in the sunlight. And instantly wished to hell he hadn't. Because he could now see what was making the noise.

One, two, three ... five, six ... eight, nine! Nine assorted - *insanely* assorted - vehicles were slowly going down a dirt road that bordered the fields, progressing south towards the surrounding forests.

There were two long black limousines, a huge earth-moving bulldozer, an outsized tractor with pronged forks in front, and five - goddamn it, yes, five motorcycles!

It didn't take a lot of imagination to get the picture. The Hawk was about to enter manoeuvres! He had bought himself his own personal *papal motorcade*! Plus equipment that could shove the ground around into any design he liked: The route of said papal motorcade!

But he hadn't even arrived at Machenfeld! How the hell was he able to – and what the hell was *that*?

In his anger and confusion, Devereaux gripped the balcony, shaking his head in frustrated bewilderment. His eyes were arrested by an extraordinary sight fifty yards away.

Within a kind of patio, outside a pair of open doors that looked like the entrance to some sort of enormous kitchen, stood a large man wearing a chef's hat, who was in the process of checking off items from a thick sheaf of papers in his hand. In front of the man was a mountain of crates and cartons and boxes that must have reached the height of fifteen feet!

Lines of supply, *shit*!

There wasn't anything left in Europe for Hawkins to buy. There was enough food down there to eliminate half the famine on the Ganges! The son of a bitch had requisitioned enough rations for an army, goddamn it, an army setting out on a two-year bivouac!

Limousines, motorcycles, bulldozers, tractors, food for the entire Lost Battalion! Sam's counterstrategy move number one was shot to hell by a parade of nine idiotically assorted vehicles and some gasping eccentric in a chef's hat.

The only state of isolation in the foreseeable future was from any and all lines of supply. They were totally unnecessary.

That left the minions. The dozen or so servants that had to be around to keep Machenfeld afloat. Kitchens, gardens, fields (that probably meant barns, maybe livestock), and at least thirty to forty rooms with cleaning and waxing and polishing and dusting. Christ! There *had* to be a staff of twenty!

He'd begin right away. Perhaps with the drivers of the nine vehicles; convince them to get the damn things off the château's grounds before it was too late. Then he'd rapidly go from one group of servants to another. Let them know in ominous terms, which meant legal terms, that if they knew what was good for them they'd get the hell out of

Machenfeld before all the agents of Interpol descended.

All the food in Switzerland wouldn't do the Hawk any good if there was no one on the premises. To *run* the premises. And a few well-chosen words to those manning the vehicles, words like 'international violations', 'personal accountability', and 'life imprisonment', would surely cause that stream of motorcycles and limousines and trucks to barrel-ass back over the moat into safer territory.

Sam was so preoccupied with his new strategy that he wasn't really aware that his undershorts kept sagging, causing him to hold them up with a free hand. He was forced to be aware of it now because as he gripped the railing his shorts had plummeted down to his ankles. Swiftly, he retrieved his modesty, noting with a degree of self-satisfaction that the games with Ginny Greenberg must have been pretty damned exciting indeed. But it was no time for pleasant reminiscence; there was work to do. His watch read nearly eleven; he hadn't realized he'd slept so long - the games were not only exciting, but exhausting. He had barely five or six hours to get everybody out. Such a large staff of servants probably had lots of personal belongings. That would mean transportation, perhaps more complicated than he had considered. But one thing had to be clear: when the minions left the grounds of Machenfeld, they were *not to return*. For *any* reason. Anything less would weaken his basic premise: Machenfeld was a threat to everyone who remained, therefore no one was to do so.

Evacuation!

The château was to be deserted!

Then what the hell was MacKenzie going to do?

Stew in his cigar juice, *that's* what he was going to do!

It was merely a question of logistics and execution.

Goddamn! Logistics and execution! He was beginning to *think* like the Hawk! And have the confidence of the Hawk! Be bold! Be outrageous! Take fate by the balls and. . . .

Shit! Before anything could happen, he had to get dressed. He raced through the French doors into the room. Ginny stirred and moaned a little and then buried her head farther into the eiderdown quilt. He stepped out of the torn underwear, and crossed quietly to his suitcase which was on an overstuffed armchair against the velour-covered wall.

It was empty.

There wasn't a goddamned thing in his suitcase.

He looked around for the closet.

Closets. There were four.

Empty. Except for Ginny's dresses.

Shit!

He ran as quietly as possible to the sculptured door and opened it.

Sitting across the wide hallway was the black beret with the gold front tooth and catlike eyes which were now focused on Sam's lower extremities. In the confusion that, perhaps, was understandable. The sneer was not.

'Where are my clothes?' whispered Devereaux, partially closing the door, leaning against it.

'In the *launtree*, mein Herr,' replied the black beret in an accent formed in some Swiss canton run by Hermann Göring.

'Everything?'

'Courtesy of Château Machenfeld. All was dirty.'

'That's ridiculous!' Sam tried to keep his voice low. He did not want to wake Ginny. 'Nobody asked me —'

'You were asleep, mein Herr,' interrupted the black beret, grinning suggestively, his gold tooth gleaming. 'You were very tired.'

'Well, now I'm very angry! I want my clothes back. Right away!'

'I cannot do that.'

'Why not?'

'It is the *launtree's* day off.'

'What? Then why did you take them?'

'I told you, mein Herr. They were dirty.'

Sam stared at the catlike eyes across the hallway. They had narrowed ominously; and the gold tooth was no longer seen because the grin had disappeared, replaced by an adamant mouth. Sam closed the door. He had to think. Quickly. As Mac would say, he had to weigh his options. And he had to get out.

He did not consider himself a brawler, yet he was not a physical coward. He was a pretty big fellow, and regardless of what Lillian said in Berlin, he was in fair shape. Still, all things considered it was a good guess that the black-bereted maniac across the hall could beat the shit out of him. Even naked, he could not leave by the stairs.

Option One considered and rejected.

That left the windows, more specifically the small balcony beyond the French doors. He grabbed his shorts off the floor, put them on, held them up, and walked silently outside. The room was three storeys off the ground, but directly below was another balcony. With sheets, or drapes, tied together he could make it with reasonable safety.

Option Two was feasible.

He went back inside and studied the drapes. As his mother in Quincy would say, they were spring drapes. Silk, billowy, not strong. Option Two was fading. Then he looked at the bed sheets, ignoring the inviting sight of Regina who was now more outside the eiderdown quilt than under. If the sheets were combined *with* the drapes, this would probably hold him. Option Two was re-emerging.

Battle dress.

That was a problem. There was nothing *but* dresses.

So, assuming Option Two succeeded and he reached the ground, he had Options Three and Four to consider. And as he considered them there was a sinking feeling in his stomach. He could race around Machenfeld in underwear that kept falling down to his ankles or he could put on one of Ginny's Balenciaga prints and hope the zipper held.

A man running around spreading alarms in dishevelled underwear, *or* a Paris original, was not likely to be taken too seriously. There might even be Options Five and Six to contend with: be locked up, or raped.

Shit!

He had to keep his head; he had to get hold of himself and think things out. Slowly. He could not allow a minor item like clothing to stand in the way of evacuation. What would the Hawk do?What was that goddamned term he used so frequently?

Support personnel! That was it!

Sam raced back out on the balcony. The man in the chef's hat was still checking off items on his list. It'd probably take him a week.

'*Psssst! Psssst!*' Devereaux leaned over the railing, remembering at the last instant not to let go of the underwear. 'Hey, *you*!' he whispered loudly.

The man looked up, startled at first, then smiled broadly. '*Ahh! Bonjour, monsieur! Ça va?*' he shouted.

Sam held his finger to his lips. 'Shhh!' He gestured for the chef to come closer.

He did so, carrying his papers, making a last notation as he walked. '*Oui, monsieur?*'

'I'm being held prisoner!' whispered Devereaux with solemn urgency and much authority. 'They've taken my clothes. I need *clothes*. And when I get down I want you to get everyone who works here into the kitchen. I've got some very important things to say. I'm a lawyer. *Avocat*.'

The man in the chef's hat cocked his head. '*Je ne comprends pas, monsieur. Désirez-vous le petit déjeuner?*'

'Who? – No. I want clothes. *See?* All I've got is this, *these*.' Sam stretched his torn undershorts so they could be seen between the rails; then he pointed to his legs. 'I need pants, *trousers*! Right away. *Please!*'

The expression on the man's face changed from bewilderment to suspicion. Perhaps even distaste mingled with hostility. '*Vos sous-vêtements sont très jolis*,' he said, shaking his head, turning back towards the patio and the crates of food.

'Wait! Wait a minute!'

'The chef is French, mein Herr, but not *that* French.' The

voice came from below, from the balcony directly underneath. The speaker was an immense, bald man with shoulders nearly as wide as the depth of the railing. 'He thinks you are making a most peculiar offer. I can assure you he's not interested.'

'Who the hell are *you*?'

'My name is unimportant. I leave the château when the new master of Machenfeld arrives. Until then his every instruction is my command. His instructions do not include your clothing.'

Devereaux had an overpowering urge to let his shorts fall and copy Hawkins's action on the roof of the diplomatic mission in Peking, but he controlled himself. The man on the balcony below was huge. And obviously couldn't take a joke. So instead he leaned over and whispered the words conspiratorially.

'Heil Hitler, you fucker!'

The man's arm shot forward; his heel clicked like the bolt of a rifle. '*Jawohl! Sieg heil!*'

'Oh, shit!' Sam turned and walked back into the room. In exasperation, he kicked off his shorts. Then he absently studied them as they lay on the floor. Perhaps it was the angle of the fabric, he was not sure. But suddenly they looked strange.

He bent down and picked them up.

Christ! What games?

The elastic waist had been cut deliberately in three places! The incisions were *incisions*, not tears. There were no loose threads or stretched cloth. Someone had taken a sharp instrument and sliced the goddamn things! On purpose. Immobilizing him by the simplest method possible!

'Lawdy! What's all that shoutin' about?' Regina Greenberg yawned and stretched, modestly pulling the eiderdown quilt over her enormous breasts.

'You bitch,' said Devereaux in quiet anger. 'You devious bitch!'

'What's the matter, honeychile?'

'Don't "honeychile" me, you Southern retardant! I can't get *out* of here!'

Ginny blinked and yawned again. She spoke with calm authority. 'You know, Mac once said something that's been a comfort to me all through the years. He said, when the mortars are falling all around you and things look terrible – and, believe me, there were times when the world looked pretty terrible to me – he said, think of the good things you've done, the accomplishments, the contributions. Don't ponder your mistakes or your sorrows; that only puts you in a depressed state of mind. And a depressed state of mind is not equipped to take advantage of that one moment that could arise and save your ass. It's all a question of mental attitudes.'

'What the hell has that bullshit got to do with the fact that I don't have any clothes?'

'Not an awful lot, I guess. It's just that you sounded so depressed. That's no way to face the Hawk.'

Devereaux started to answer blindly, angrily. Then he stopped, looked at the sincerity in Ginny's eyes and began again. 'Wait a minute. "Face the Hawk." You mean you want me to fight him? *Stop* him?'

'That's your decision, Sam. I only want what's best for everyone.'

'Will you help me?'

Ginny was pensive for a moment, then replied firmly. 'No, I won't do that. Not in the way you're thinking. I owe MacKenzie too much.'

'Lady!' burst out Devereaux. 'Do you have *any idea* what that lunatic is up to?'

Mrs Hawkins number one looked at him with an expression of suddenly imposed innocence. 'A lieutenant doesn't question a general officer, Major. He can't be expected to understand the intricacies of command —'

'Then what the hell are we talking about?'

'You're a smart fellow. The Hawk wouldn't have promoted you if you weren't. I just want him to have the finest advice he can get. So he can do whatever it is he wants to do the best way possible.' Ginny rolled over under the eiderdown quilt. 'I'm really very sleepy.'

And Devereaux saw them on the bedside table next to her head.

A pair of scissors.

CHAPTER NINETEEN

'Sorry about the clothes,' said the Hawk in the huge drawing room. Sam glared and retied the curtain sash he used as a belt around the eiderdown quilt. 'You'd think the laundry would have more than one key, wouldn't you? These big fancy places don't trust anyone; shows the kind of house guests they must be used to, I suppose.'

'Oh, shut up,' mumbled Devereaux, who found it necessary to double-loop the sash because the silk kept slipping. 'The laundress *will* be here in the morning, I presume.'

'I'm sure of it. She's one of the few who go home at night. To the village. That'll change, of course; there'll be a lot of changes.'

'Just tell me there'll be *one* change and I'll go back and have dinner with Azaz-Varak.'

'Come on now, Sam, you've got a one-track mind. Let's get on to other things. You sure you don't want a shirt and a pair of trousers? Just take me a minute to go upstairs. ...' Hawkins made a gesture past a dozen or so overstuffed, antimacassared armchairs towards the great hall.

'No! I don't want anything from you! – I take that back. I *do* want something. I want you to call off this crazy business and let me go home!'

MacKenzie bit off the chewed end of his cigar, spitting it between the feet of a suit of armour. 'You *will* go home, I promise you that. The minute you centralize the company finances and make a few deposits that can be tapped under certain conditions, I'll drive you to the airport myself. That's the word of a general officer.'

'It's the reasoning of a brain soaked in linseed oil! Do you have any idea what you're asking me to do? That's not chopped liver you're talking about, it's *forty million dollars.* I'm marked for life! They'll have a record sheet on me in every Interpol headquarters and police station in the civilized world! You don't put your name on forty million dollars' worth of bank transfers and expect to go back to a normal law practice. Word gets out.'

'That's not so, and you know it. All that Swiss banking stuff is confidential.'

Devereaux looked around to make sure no one else was within hearing. 'Even if it's supposed to be, it's not *going* to be once a ... certain attempt is made to snatch a ... certain person in Rome! And that's *all* it will be! An attempt! You'll have your ass in a net, and every contact you've made since China will be put under a microscope and my name will surface and so will forty fucking million dollars in Zürich and that's the *ballgame*!'

'Now, goddamn, boy, we've been over that! Your job's finished now. Or will be soon's you take care of the money. You don't have to be involved anymore. And you're *clean*, son. You're a hundred per cent Clorox!'

'I'm not.' Devereaux choked as he whispered and clutched the eiderdown quilt. 'I just *told* you: The minute *you're* nailed, *I'm* nailed!'

'For what? Say you happened to be right – which I don't for a second consider remotely possible – what can they nail you for? Banking funds for an old soldier who told you he was raising money to support an organization dedicated to spreading religious brotherhood? Let me ask you a question, Mr Attorney. Could you, under oath, testify to any wrongdoing?'

'You're *insane*!' broke in Sam, stumbling slightly as he stepped forward. 'You *told* me! You're going to kidnap —' Devereaux stopped and made charade-like gestures that included hauling a body over his shoulder and the sign of the cross.

'Well, *hell*, boy, there are *oaths* and there are *oaths*! Be reasonable. Anyway, that's hearsay. Not admissible.'

Sam closed his eyes; he began to understand what martyrdom was all about. He continued, his whisper strained but controlled. 'I walked out of those archives with that fucking briefcase chained to my wrist!'

'Outside of that,' mumbled MacKenzie. 'Anyhow, that's army stuff; neither of us has much use for the army. Anything else?'

Devereaux thought. 'Circumstantially, it's the mother-loving end. There hasn't been a single aboveboard transaction.'

'That's objective,' said Hawkins, shaking his head, confirming his own judgement. 'There's been no violence; no one's lied. No theft, no collusion. Everything voluntary. And if the particular methods *seem* unusual, that's the prerogative of every individual investor, as long as he doesn't infringe on the rights of others.' Mac paused and held Sam's eyes. 'There's something else, too. You said yourself that a lawyer's first responsibility was to his client, not abstract moral dilemmas.'

'I said that?'

'You surely did.'

'That's not bad —'

'It's goddamned eloquent, that's what it is. You've got a silver tongue in your head, young man.'

Sam stared back at the Hawk, trying to see beneath his guile. But it wasn't guile; he meant what he said. And since personal sincerity was the momentary leveller, Devereaux decided to be personally sincere.

'Listen to me,' he said quietly. 'Say you go through with this – this insanity, because that's what it is, you know. Say you really do it. You actually kidnap the pope and get away with it. Even for a few days. Do you know what might happen? What you could trigger?'

'Surely do. Four hundred million green samolians from four hundred million howling mackerel snappers. No offence intended, just a harmless phrase.'

'*No*, you gung-ho son of a bitch! There'd be international *revulsion*! And *recrimination*. And then mainly *accusations*!

Governments would point their fingers at other governments! Presidents and chairmen and prime ministers would use blue lines and red lines and then very *hot* lines. And before you know it, some asshole recites a code from a tiny black box in a briefcase because he didn't like what some other asshole said. Jesus, Mac! You could start World War Three!'

'*Goddamn!* Is that what you've been thinking about?'

'It's what I've tried *not* to think about.'

Hawkins threw his cigar into the cavern that was the Machenfeld fireplace and stood arms akimbo, a flame dying in his eyes. 'Sam, boy, you couldn't be farther from the truth. You know, son, war isn't what it used to be. Hasn't any spirit to it anymore. Bugles and drums, and men caring for men, and hating an enemy because he can hurt the things you love. That's all gone now. Now it's buttons and shifty-eyed policitians who blink a lot and wave their hands without meaning very much. I hate war. I never thought I'd hear myself say it, but I'm saying it and learning it now. I'd never allow a war.'

Devereaux bored into the Hawk's eyes; he would not let MacKenzie look away. 'Why should I believe that? Everything you've done reeks of con. Immense con. Why should a war stop you?'

'Because, young man,' replied Hawkins quietly, returning Sam's stare in full measure, 'I just told you the truth.'

'All right. Suppose you provoke one without meaning to?'

'*Goddamn!* Now you're pushing me too far!' MacKenzie strode from the fireplace to a second suit of armour to the right of the mantel. The face piece was open so he slammed it shut. 'I put in damned near forty years and got fucked by the plastic men! *Your* words, boy! Now, I don't feel sorry for myself because I knew what I was doing, and was accountable for my actions! But, goddamn, don't ask me to feel sorry for *them* or be accountable for their *stupidity*!'

So much for personal sincerity, thought Devereaux. Like Options One, Two, Three, and Four in the morning, it was shot to hell. This time in a burst of self-righteousness. There was nothing for it but to find another way. One would present itself, Sam was convinced of that. The Hawk had a way to go before the pontiff of the Catholic Church blessed the edelweiss at Machenfeld. Something would turn up; and Option Seven – Options Five and Six happily avoided – was coming into focus. For the moment he had to calm MacKenzie down and under no circumstances lose his confidence. And then Mac did have a point. A legal point.

He, Sam, was clean. Legally clean. In every other way the mud was an inch thick, but in evidentiary considerations, he was not a good case for any prosecutor.

'Okay, Mac, I'm not going to fight you. You were screwed and I did say it, and I believe you. You hate war. Maybe that's good enough. I don't know anymore. Personally, I just want to go back home to Quincy, and if I read about you in the papers, I'll remember the words of a scarred but honest warrior spoken in this room.'

'A tongue of silver, boy! I admire that.'

'As long as it's not a head of lead, I'll accept that. Do you have the papers for the Zürich bank?'

'Don't you want to hear the amount I've ... accrued for your participation? How do you like that "accrued"? I'm a corporate president, you know; we don't fuck around with second-rate vocabularies.'

'I'm impressed. What's the entry figure?'

'The what?'

'The accrual; that's the noun root of the verb "to accrue".'

'Smartass shavetail. What do you say to a half a million dollars?'

Sam could not say anything. He was numb. He saw his hand move in astonishment, and he watched it with a certain fascination, not sure if the appendage belonged to him. It must have; when he thought about jiggling the fingers, they jiggled.

A half a million dollars.

What was there to think about? It was as insane as everything else. Including the fact that he was not indictable.

It was Monopoly time. Let's buy *Boardwalk* and *Park Place*.

Stop. Go To Jail.

Why worry?

It didn't do any good anyway.

'That's reasonable - severance pay,' Sam said.

'That's all you've got to *say*? With what I banked for you in New York, you can hire that Jewish fella and he'll be happy to take the job.' MacKenzie was the injured party. He obviously expected Devereaux to practise a little bit of his well-advertised overreaction.

'Let's say I'll erupt with enthusiasm when I'm looking at those figures - in a bank book - in Boston - with my mother sitting across the room complaining about the new management at the Copley Plaza. Okay?'

'Do you know something?' said Hawkins, his eyes squinting. 'You're kind of weird.'

'*I'm* kind of. ...' Devereaux did not finish the sentence. There was no point.

There was the abrupt, episodic clicking of high heels. Regina Greenberg walked through the cathedral arch into the drawing room. She was dressed in a beige pants suit, the rather severe jacket buttoned over Titanics. She looked, well, rather efficient, thought Sam. She smiled briefly and addressed Hawkins.

'I've met with the staff. Five will stay. Three couldn't; they'd have to live in the village and I explained that wasn't acceptable.'

'I hope they weren't hurt.'

Ginny laughed confidently. 'Hardly. I spoke to each individually, and gave all three two months' wages.'

'The rest understand the conditions?' MacKenzie reached into his pocket for a fresh cigar.

'And their bonuses,' said Ginny. 'Minimum three months. All with families to explain that they've been hired for resident staff work in France for the duration. No questions are to be asked.'

'No different from overseas duty,' commented the Hawk,

nodding his head. 'And the money's a hell of a lot better than combat pay – without a weapon in sight.'

'The logistics are in your favour, too,' continued Ginny. 'Only two of the five are married. Not too happily, I gather. They won't miss, or be missed.'

'We'll have to get women, though,' countered MacKenzie, 'for R and R. I'll scout the grounds later; spec out tent arrangements – far enough away from the manouevres, of course. And the counsellor here is going into Zürich to take care of several financial items for me. What do you think, Sam? How long do you figure it will be before you're finished?'

Devereaux had to force himself to consider the Hawk's question. He was stunned by the obvious control MacKenzie wielded over Ginny. According to the data banks, she had divorced MacKenzie over twenty years ago; yet here she was deferring to him like a schoolgirl with a crush on her teacher.

'What did you say?' Sam knew the question but wanted a few seconds to evaluate.

'How long will Zürich take?'

'A day. Maybe a day and a half, with no hitches. A lot will depend on the account clearances. I think the transfers are coded through Geneva, but I may be wrong about that.'

'Can "hitches" be eliminated with a little honey in the pot?'

'Probably. Relinquishing-of-interest could apply. The time period's minor but the sums aren't. The depositories would pick up several thousand – on paper. That might act as a general incentive.'

'Goddamn, son, you hear yourself? You hear how *good* you are?'

'Elementary bookkeeping. A trial lawyer figures litigation with banks is prime meat. They've got more ways to lie to themselves – and everybody else – than anyone since tribes started to barter. A decent attorney simply picks the lie he knows will suit him best.'

'You hear that, Ginny? Isn't that boy something?!'

'You're mighty impressive, Sam; I've got to admit it. And, Mac, since the m*ay*jor here's got everything under control, maybe I could go up to Zürich with him and kind of keep him company.'

'Why, that's a splendid idea! Don't know why I didn't think of it.'

'I can't imagine how it escaped you,' said Devereaux quietly. 'You're all heart.'

From all points of the compass the Hawk's subordinate officers arrived. They were met at the Zermatt railroad station by the bereted, gold-toothed, cat-eyed chauffeur whose name was Rudolph. And Rudolph had a hectic two days.

Crete showed up first, without incident. That is, he managed to cross international boundaries under the scrutiny of very professional authorities without incident (but with a forged passport) and got as far as the Zermatt station, where his troubles erupted. For Rudolph refused to acknowledge Crete to be Crete in spite of the proper identity markings on his clothing, and consequently would not let him into his Italian taxi.

Because, for reasons that escaped Hawkins, none of the G-2 data bank entries on Crete had established the fact that he was Black. Yet there it was. Crete was a brilliant aeronautical engineer, a Soviet sympathizer as long as the Ruskies paid him, a defected espionage agent complete with a doctor's degree and very black skin. Rudolph was totally bewildered, so MacKenzie had to use some very harsh language over the telephone with Rudolph, and finally the bereted maniac let the *Schwarzer* in the back seat of his car.

Marseilles and Stockholm were next. They flew in together out of Paris because they met each other on the previous night at Les Calavados on the Boulevard Georges Cinque and renewed an old acquaintanceship that went back to the days when both were making money from the Allies and the Axis. They were delighted to discover that they were both on a trip to the same yellow mountain in Zermatt. Rudolph had no trouble with Stockholm and Marseilles because they spotted him before he spotted them and they criticized him for his stupidity at being obvious.

Beirut did not take the train from Zürich; he hired an ambulance, instead. He had his reasons; they went back to several contraband run-ins with the Zürich police. So he flew in to Geneva, drove a rented car in the name of a socially elite transvestite, dropped it in Lausanne, contacted l'Hôpital des Deux Enfants in Montreux and leased the ambulance, ordering it to transport him as a coronary wishing to spend his last days in Zermatt. He timed everything to the Zürich train however and all would have gone smoothly except for Rudolph. Unfortunately, Rudolph had a flat tyre on the back roads of Machenfeld, and in his subsequent haste to reach the Bahnhof on time he had a minor collision in the railroad station's parking lot. With the ambulance.

Therefore it was difficult for Rudolph to identify the highly agitated coronary patient, who climbed out of the rear door yelling about imbeciles, with the figure whose markings identified him as Beirut.

But Rudolph was beginning to shrug more and more. The master of Machenfeld, he was beginning to suspect, was not all there in the head. And neither were the people he was sent up to Zermatt to meet.

And the lovely lady of his late-night dreams, the beautifully breasted Fräulein, had left the château for several days. Things were not the same.

Rome and Rudolph got along splendidly. Rome lost his luggage on the train. The combined chaos of finding his three suitcases and his contact from the château proved a strain nearly too much for Rome. Rudolph sympathized and allowed him to sit in the front seat on the trip to the château.

Biscay was extremely secretive. Once he displayed the coded identification (a pair of white gloves with black roses stitched on the back) Biscay excused himself to go to the men's room and disappeared through a window. After an hour, Rudolph's impatience turned to curiosity and the curiosity, in turn, became panic when he discovered the men's room empty. He tried to remain inconspicuous as he looked in nooks and crannies and luggage bins. Biscay followed him discreetly. And it was only after Rudolph called Machenfeld in panic that Biscay, listening from an adjacent booth, decided that his contact was authentic.

Biscay sat in the back seat, and Rudolph did not say a single word all the way to Machenfeld.

The last to arrive was Athens. If Biscay was suspicious, Athens was paranoid. To begin with, he pulled the emergency cord on the train, stopping it in the freight yards just outside the station. Conductors and engineers ran through the cars looking for the emergency, while Athens jumped off and raced over the tracks to the platform, where he concealed himself behind a concrete pillar. It was not difficult for Athens to spot Rudolph.

The train finally proceeded into the station. Rudolph examined all the disembarking passengers; Athens could see his anxiety. When there was no one left on the platform but railroad personnel, Athens approached Rudolph from the rear and tapped him on the shoulder. As he did so, he displayed his identification (a red kerchief) and gestured for Rudolph to follow him.

At which point, Athens raced back to the end of the platform, jumped down on to the tracks and started running towards the freight yard. He soon outdistanced Rudolph and started a series of *I-See-You's* between the immobile cars.

Five minutes later a distraught Rudolph was being comforted by the energetic Athens as they walked out of the freight yards towards the taxi.

And as MacKenzie Hawkins watched the car approach from the ramparts of Machenfeld, he congratulated himself once more on his professionalism. Seventy-two hours had passed since he had begun making his coded contacts from the D'Accord; and in that seventy-two hours every one of his subordinate officers was physically on the premises.

Goddamn!

Based on the accepted principle that larceny goes a long way in the banking business, Sam's trip to Zürich - more specifically his trip to the Staats Bank to centralize the Shepherd Company's capital – was so successful so rapidly that he would be able to catch the early afternoon train back to Zermatt. And since Regina Greenberg was out shopping, he left a message for her at the Hotel D'Accord: *Have gone bowling. Will be home late.*

He wanted those hours on the train by himself; to think, to refine. For Option Seven was becoming more sharply defined as the hours passed. Due mainly to the papers he carried out of the bank given him by a perspiring trust officer who was considerably richer than he was before he'd met Sam.

Among the fourteen documents, four pertained to the account transfers from Geneva, the Cayman Islands, Berlin, and Algiers – minus accrued interest, of course; one listed the total assets of the Shepherd Company, with its bond of confidentiality, its codes of release and the account number; one was in the name of the family Devereaux (Sam did not explain it and the banker had asked no questions, treating the item as though it did not exist); and eight separate documents defined eight separate trusts.

One of these accounts was larger than the others and within it were four individual sets of figures ... obviously meant for four individuals. It did not take much reflection on Devereaux's part to identify them: Mrs Hawkinses one, two, three, and four.

That left seven trusts, each with an identical maximum figure.

Seven.

The Hawk's *support personnel.*

MacKenzie had recruited seven men to kidnap the pope. (Sam couldn't imagine that any were women; the Hawk's four ex-wives were capable of *anything* calling for feminine skills.) These seven were his – what was it? – subordinate officers. MacKenzie had allowed that his subordinate officers would be arriving at Machenfeld shortly.

'What do you mean "subordinate officers"?' Devereaux had asked.

'The troops, son, the troops!' The Hawk had replied, the flame reignited in his eyes.

'What do you mean "shortly"?'

'We're on blue alert, boy. That means all posts are manned, contact expected from here on in.'

'Like in a few days?'

'Maybe sooner, depending on enemy counterpersonnel blockades. Our troops will have to cross hostile territory on their way to base camp.'

'What the fuck are you talking about?'

'Nothing you have to be concerned with. Just bring back that money stuff from Zürich. Before I give my first briefing on the mission, I want my subordinate officers to see for themselves just how thoroughly command centre has taken care of their interests. It'll give 'em a real sense of purpose, of comradeship; it emanates from the top, you know. It always has.'

That was the other reason why Option Seven was coming into focus. *Bring back that money stuff ... before I give my first briefing ... command centre has taken care of their interests.*

The Hawk's troops had been recruited without knowing precisely what the war was all about. Militarily speaking there was nothing unusual in that, but considering the enormity of the projected enemy's resources – namely, the whole world – a few well-chosen words like, '*Do you realize what this maniac intends to do? Kidnap the pope!*' and '*You're dealing with a certified mental case!*' and '*You're commander is a fruitcake!*' and '*This lunatic shot the jade balls off a Chinese monument.*' – things like that could very well make the support personnel look to other fields of endeavour.

It was a question of timing. And psychology. If Sam read him correctly, Hawkins was going to hit his subordinate officers with a double-barrelled salvo: a highly technical, strategically 'feasible' description of the abduction, *and* bona fide documents from the Staats Bank du Zürich that guaranteed each man a fortune, *regardless of outcome*! It would be a tough act to cripple, but that's what Option Seven was all about.

Sam would reach the subordinate officers *first*. He would shoot off canons of doubt regarding the Hawk's fundamental sanity. There was nothing more frightening to criminal underlings than the possibility that their employers were unbalanced. Lack of balance meant lack of judgement, no matter how well disguised. And lack of judgement could spell ten-to-twenty-to-life; in this case, probably a long rope and a blindfold.

Even the criminal element in Europe had to have heard of the paranoid general who was thrown out of China. It wasn't that long ago. And when he had finished this part of his oral summation, Sam would place his high card on the table.

High? There were none higher. It was irresistible.

For on the train to Zermatt he would go through the documents from the Staats Bank du Zürich, specifically the trust accounts, and write out all the numbers and the sequential codes of release, and put them on seven pieces of paper.

He would give each man a card with the information written on it. Each could leave Château Machenfeld without so much as sitting through a meal, head for Zürich - *and claim his money*.

Each subordinate officer would make a fortune! For doing absolutely nothing. Irresistible!

Giovanni Bombalini, the Vicar of Christ, walked out into his beloved garden to be alone. He did not wish to see anyone, or talk with anyone. He was angry with the world, *his* world, and when one was angry it was always best to meditate.

He sighed. If he was to be truthful with himself, he had to admit he was angry with God. It was so senseless! He raised his eyes to the afternoon sky and a single word emerged plaintively from his lips.

'Why?'

He lowered his head and continued down the path. The

sprays of lilies were in spring bloom, greeting life.

As he was about to leave it.

The doctors had just delivered their collective report. His vital signs were diminishing with increased acceleration. He had no more than six or seven weeks.

Death itself was easy. Good heavens, it was a relief! *Life* was the struggle. But struggle or no, he had not consolidated the necessary forces to carry on his and Roncalli's work. He needed more time; he needed the authority of the office to bring divergent factions closer together. Why could not God understand that?

Eh, my beloved Lord? Why? Just a little more time? I promise not to lose my temper. Nor will I insult the nasal-toned – pardon, most Holy Father – the cardinal or his band of antediluvian thieves. Six months would do nicely. Then I shall rest in the arms of Christ with grateful devotion. Five months, perhaps? Much could be accomplished in five months ....

Giovanni tried with all his heart to perceive a heavenly response. If there was one, it was too weak to get through his vital signs.

Perhaps, dear Father, if you would speak to the Holy Virgin? She might find more eloquent words to convey my supplication. It is said that women are more persuasive in these matters....

Still nothing. Just a minor pain in his knees which meant the weight was hard on his old bones and he should sit for a while. What was it that lovely *giornalista* had said? There were certain exercises —

Basta! All he needed was to collapse doing push-pulls. Ignatio Quartze would roll his body under the bed and they would not find him for a week. In the meantime, Quartze would pack the Curia.

The pontiff reached his favourite white bench and lowered himself on the cool stone. A breeze came from the garden walls, fluttering the leaves of the tree above him. Was it a sign? It *was* refreshing. Then the breeze stopped; the still air returned and the fluttering of leaves was replaced by footsteps clattering over the path.

It was the new papal aide. A young Black priest from the diocese of New York City, a brilliant student who had done much good work in the Harlem districts. Francesco had sought out just such a deserving young prelate – over considerable opposition. It was a small part of a large design.

'Your Holiness?'

'Yes, my son. You look agitated. What's the matter?'

'I think I did something quite wrong. I was bewildered and you weren't in your rooms and there didn't seem to be anything else to do. I'm very sorry.'

'Well, now, we don't know the extent of this calamity until you describe it. You didn't, by any chance, find Cardinal Quartze in my closet and call the guards?'

The Black priest smiled. Ignatio had made clear his disapproval of the aide's appointment. Francesco took every opportunity to lessen the insult.

'No, Your Holiness. I heard your private telephone ringing. The one in the drawer of your bedside table; it just kept ringing.'

'It would, my son,' interrupted the pontiff. 'It is not connected to the Vatican switchboard. A minor indulgence. So you answered it. Who was calling? Only a few old friends and an associate or two of long standing have the number. There is no great harm in what you did. Who was it?'

'A monsignor in Washington, Holy Father. He was very upset —'

'Ahh, Monsignor Patrick Dennis O'Gilligan! Yes, he calls frequently. We play chess together long distance.'

'He was very excited – and he thought I was *you.* He didn't give me a chance to speak. He rattled on so fast I couldn't stop him.'

'Yes, that sounds like Paddy; he's had his problems. The Berrigans again? Those two keep busy —'

'No, Holy Father. Much worse. The *President* called him. Something about the confidence of the confessional, and whether it was *admissible*. He wants to *convert*, Holy Father!'

'Che cosa? Madre di Dio!'

'It gets worse, Your Holiness. Sixteen White House aides want to find Jesus right away. Under certain conditions of Vatican privilege and something called Christian immunity.'

Giovanni sighed. There was *so much* to do.

Four months, oh Lord?

CHAPTER TWENTY

The unfamiliar faces had one thing in common, thought Sam. Very muscular bodies. As though each enjoyed the outdoors, kept in trim by moving rocks under the eyes of the penitentiary guards. And speaking of eyes, that was another thing in common. All their eyes seemed a little sleepy at first, the lids half closed. But it was only appearance. On closer examination the eyes could be seen spinning in their sockets like pinballs caught between magnets; very little went unobserved.

There was a tall, blond man who looked like he jumped out of a television commercial for Scandinavian cigars; a Black who nodded silently a great deal and spoke an English refined in university lecture rooms; another dark-skinned fellow with distinctly sharp, northern features whose accent was like all those people in formal clothes at the Savoy; two Frenchmen who had something to do with boats; a long-haired man in very tight trousers who strutted when he walked like a tango dancer, aware of his ass – unmistakably Italian; and finally, a rather wild-eyed Greek who wore a red kerchief and kept telling jokes no one quite understood.

There was a soft-spoken politeness among them that was positively unctuous, complemented by manners that seemed born of breeding and wealth, were it not for the shifty eyes. They certainly were very much at home in the huge drawing room of Château Machenfeld, where the Hawk had everyone gather before the late dinner.

Gathered, but in the interests of international security, not introduced. No names were used.

Sam had returned to the château at seven. It would have been an hour earlier but he had to walk the last three miles because no taxi out of Zermatt was allowed to travel beyond certain zones and Rudolph was nowhere to be found. When Sam called information for Machenfeld's telephone number, he discovered there was no such place.

It all might have taken the heart out of him, but Option Seven kept him going. He knew when a case was won.

MacKenzie had greeted him with mixed feelings. The Hawk was pleased that he had brought back the financial papers so promptly, but felt that his treatment of Regina was most ungentlemanly. She was a fine girl, and now Sam could not properly say good-bye to her.

Why not?

Because her luggage had been sent to the airport. Ginny was on her way back to California, with a stop in Rome to look at the museums.

So much for Ginny, thought Devereaux. He was a little sad, but there was Option Seven to think about. And he began to think the timing was perfect.

MacKenzie told him that there would be no business discussed the first evening. Just social chitchat and strolls through the gardens and cocktails and dinner and brandy. Why? Because the troops would like a chance, he believed, to size each other up, check their rooms for bugs, oil their weapons, and generally assure themselves that Machenfeld was no Interpol trap. Sam could expect to hear noises during the night; most of the men would carry out their own surveillance, and that was good because they would undoubtedly run into one another and realize further that everything was on the up-and-up.

In the morning, when all were refreshed, the Hawk would hold his first briefing. Before he did that, however, he would certainly take the time to say good-bye to Sam. He was going to miss his young friend, no question about it. But the word of a general officer was his bond; it was the glue that held his battalions together.

Devereaux's work was finished. Rudolph would drive him into Zermatt, where he'd take the morning train to Zürich and the late-afternoon flight to New York.

There was one thing Sam should be aware of, however, just in case he became nervous or was afflicted with hypertension. For the next month or so, several associates of the Shepherd Company's first investor, Mr Dellacroce, would stay in close touch with him. Their names were Fingers and Meat, Hawkins believed; it was just a temporary arrangement, no offence intended.

Yes. Sam understood. There was no point in MacKenzie being redundant.

Devereaux had terminated the conversation, saying he would shave and shower the sweat of three mountain miles off him, and return for cocktails.

In his room, Sam found the scissors Ginny had used on his underwear and cut out seven strips of paper five inches long, one inch wide. He wrote out the identical message on each.

Vitally important you meet with me in my room – third floor, rear of house, last door in the north hallway on the right. 2.00 a.m. sharp. Your life depends on it. I am a friend. Remember two o'clock this morning!

He folded the strips of paper neatly so they fitted into the palm of his hand and put them in his jacket pocket. He then removed the seven index cards from his briefcase, the ones with the account numbers and sequential codes-of-release written on them and put them in his trousers pocket. They were his high cards. Irresistible!

He returned to the drawing room downstairs and put to use all the social graces a fine Boston upbringing provided. He shook hands with the men.

And passed each his message.

By one thirty in the morning he was ready. The Italian came first, his hands encased in sheer, skintight black gloves, his feet laced in balletlike slippers with ridged rubber soles. And then, one by one, the rest showed up in apparel not much different. There was a proliferation of gloves, and soft shoes or sneakers, and black sweaters, and narrow trousers with thick belts holding thicker knives, and small holsters with single straps across small pistols, and in several cases coils of wire.

Altogether a very professional group of psychopaths, thought Sam, as he told them with quiet, not completely heartfelt authority to relax and get comfortable, and smoke if they wished.

Since they all *were* relaxed, and most smoking already, he wasn't sure it was a good opening. But the best summations were those that built from quiet even awkward beginnings.

So he began. Softly, at first. Starting with man as a tribal being, looking to the heavens for meaning beyond his daily battle for survival, finding solace in that which he could not really comprehend, because there was comfort in primitive faith. There was structure, an organization to natural phenomena, and that meant there had to be a force, a mind, a profound all-knowing intelligence that conceived the whole. Yet could never be truly understood.

There was beauty in that lack of understanding, for men strove beyond themselves for the all-seeing, all-knowing force that created the earth, created *them*, knew *them* – loved *them*.

Without this search, man was an animal. With it he reached out, and compassion became a part of him.

Sam explained that symbols and titles were not important in themselves, for correlations could be drawn between all religions. The essence was the differentiation between good and evil. But symbols and titles held mystical meaning, and profound comfort, for millions everywhere. Faith. The poor and the oppressed prayed to them, held them in reverence and hope. And for millions these symbols were the warm light in their unceasing winters of darkness.

Devereaux paused. It was the moment for a crescendo.

'Gentlemen, facing you is a crime of such monstrous proportions, a crime of such profound evil – a crime which *cannot possibly succeed* and can only lead each of you to your death, or to a life endured, not lived, in a brutal prison cell. For within the walls of this château is a man who would rob you of your most priceless possessions! Your *freedom*! Your *very lives*! For he conceives the *impossible*. In his unbalanced – woefully unbalanced – mind he is convinced he can overcome the swift and terrible reaction, the vengeance, of the entire world! He expects to lead you into the gaping jaws of oblivion. He intends to kidnap the pontiff of the Catholic Church! He is, in a word, *insane*!'

Sam stopped. He bored his eyes into the face of each man. Cigarettes were suspended in midair, mouths were open in disbelief, eyelids were stretched stares conveying a paralysis born of shock.

He had them! The jury was in the palm of his hand! The phrases had come out like thunder!

It was time for his high cards. Those irresistible figures and sequential code words that would make each man in the room rich. Very, very rich. For doing nothing but avoiding the risk of oblivion.

'Gentlemen, I realize the state of shock you're in and it pains me to see it. It pains me to have caused it. As that great Roman, Marcus Aurelius, observed: We must all do what we have to do, at the moment fate demands that we do it. But as the Indian prophet, Baga Nishyad, also observed: Buckets filled with tears can be spread over grain and the rice will grow like jewels. I do not have jewels, gentlemen, but I do have riches for each of you. Deserved rewards. Sums of money that will lessen your pain, and send you back to the lands of your choice, to live in freedom, freedom from fear, from oblivion. And from want. Here. I pass among you these small index cards. Each is a passport to your personal nirvanas. Let me explain.'

And Sam did.

And the seven subordinate officers studied the cards, glancing at one another as they did so.

'Do you speak French?' asked one of the Frenchmen.

Devereaux laughed – a touch too gaily he felt. 'Not really.'

'Thank you,' said the Frenchman, turning to the others. '*Vous parlez tous français?*'

To a man they nodded affirmatively.

So they all began speaking French.

Quietly. Rapidly. Until seven heads nodded once again affirmatively. Sam was touched; he knew they were trying to find a way to thank him.

Which was why he was bewildered when two of the men suddenly approached and grabbed him, spun him around, and began wrapping his wrists in wire.

'What the hell are you doing?' he yelled. 'What are you doing to my hands? And what the hell is that?'

He gestured his head at the red kerchief the Greek had whipped from his neck and was now twirling.

'And what the hell are they?!'

He referred to a number of metallic cracks that sounded strangely like weapons being inspected.

'We have that compassion you spoke of, monsieur,' said the Frenchman. 'We offer the choice of a blindfold before we execute him.'

'*What!?*'

'Be brave, signore,' said the Italian. 'We all know this business. We accept the odds or we do not play.'

'Ya,' added the Viking. 'It is a game. Some vin. Some lose. You lost.'

'*Whaaat?!*'

'Take him down to the patio,' said the second Frenchman. 'We'll tell the staff it's target practice.'

'*Mac! Maac! Maaac!*' He was led down the hallway. Several pairs of hands clapped themselves over his mouth; he bit them. '*For Christ's sake! Hawkins! Where the fuck are you?!*'

Again the hands clamped over his face. The cordon marched with precision down the hallway towards the magnificent winding staircase. Devereaux again forced his mouth open and bit furiously at the flesh around his teeth; hands and arms whipped back momentarily. It was enough for Sam to kick out behind him and for an instant free himself.

He raced and plunged bodily down the curving steps, tumbling over and over as he fell.

'Hawkins! You son of a bitch, get out here! These maniacs want to shoot me!'

He bounced over the treads, careened against the wall, and plummeted shoulders over backside down into the last straightaway. His shouts were progressively blurred, but the overall meaning was unmistakable.

'Blindfolds – ouch! Pistols! Goddamn – you – oh – ohh –. Hawkins! Uhu! Jesus – my head!'

He reached the bottom of the staircase, a dishevelled heap. The Hawk strode through the cathedral arch from the drawing room, a cigar clenched between his teeth, several folded maps in his hand. He looked at Sam on the floor and then up at the band of subordinate officers.

'*Goddamn*, boy! This changes *everything*!'

Once again his clothes were taken. Only now there weren't even any dresses in the closet. His meals were brought up by Rudolph.

The Hawk explained that it had taken a command counterdecision to save his life; and the troops did not like it one bit.

'For a fact, I nearly had a mutiny on my hands before the brigade set its colours,' Hawkins had told him the next morning.

'Set its what? Never mind, don't tell me.'

'I mean it, son. I had to take stern measures and let them know right off that in matters of extreme prejudice, no authority – regardless of consensus – exceeded that of a field general. It was touch and go for a while, but I've handled the roughest in my day. Those pups, good as they are, weren't any match. It's in the eyes, boy. Always the eyes.'

'I don't understand,' Devereaux had moaned sincerely. 'I spelled everything out beautifully. I unravelled the whole ball of wax. The background, the motive. Jesus! Even the money! I had them!'

'You had nothing,' the Hawk replied concisely. 'You made two big mistakes. To begin with, you assumed that such a group of men, such a fine contingent of officers, would accept money surreptitiously, without earning it —'

'Get off it!' Devereaux had roared his interruption. 'You can't sell the honour-among-thieves bullshit because I won't buy it!'

'I think you're misjudging, boy, but if that's the way you see it, there's your second mistake to consider.'

'What mistake?'

'One of the oldest traps in Interpol is to set up a hot bank account and send someone after it. I'm surprised you didn't know that. You set up seven all at once.'

Sam had retreated under the eiderdown quilt and pulled it over his head. Unfortunately, he could not block out MacKenzie's words.

'You know, Sam, life is a series of compartments, some related to each other, most separate. But every once in a while these parallel compartments, as I call them, have to acknowledge one another's existence. Now, you saved my life in Peking. You brought to bear your skills and your experience and kept me from that oblivion I hear you talked about. And last night, here in Switzerland, I saved *your* life. Using what skills and experience *I* have. We're even. Our compartments in this area aren't parallel anymore. So don't fuck up, son. I can't be responsible. And that's the word of a general officer.'

By the end of two weeks, Sam was sure he'd lose what was left of his sanity. The mere thought of clothes drove him mad. Throughout his life clothes were an accepted part of living – sometimes pleasant, even ego-fulfilling – but they had not been a subject he ever dwelled on for any length of time.

That's a nice jacket; the price is okay. Get it. Shirts? His mother said he should get shirts. What's wrong with Filene's? So I'm a lawyer. Okay, J. Press. Shirts and grey flannels. Socks? His bureau drawer somehow always had socks in it. And shorts and handkerchiefs. A suit was a pretty big occasion, the few times in his adult life when he went out and bought one. Still, he'd never been tempted to have one tailor-made. And in the goddamned army, his civilian jackets and trousers were on hand only because they meant a change from the goddamned uniform. No. Clothes had never been a major factor in his life.

They were now.

But necessity - part of which was not losing one's sanity - was the mother of invention. And truer words were never said. So Sam began to invent, and the thesis of his invention was that he was undergoing a sincere change of position.

It had to be gradual, based on available alternatives. Since he was so completely, intrinsically, *legally* enmeshed in the Shepherd Company's operations and since all avenues of separation had been blocked, what was the point of fighting any longer? Life *was* compartmentalized; and he was locked into a big vault named MacKenzie Hawkins - which also held some forty million dollars, which was a lot of chopped liver.

Maybe, just maybe, his negative approach was self-defeating, all things considered. Perhaps, just perhaps, he should be putting his energies into productive channels; find areas where he could contribute. After all, there was one indelible bottom line. If the Shepherd Company got blown up, a hell of a lot of shrapnel would find its way into the hide of the second and only other corporate officer of record.

These were the conjectures he began to put into words - haltingly, without much conviction at first - during MacKenzie's daily visits at the start of the third week. But he realized that simply saying them was not very persuasive. The Hawk had to see his mind working, observe the transformation.

By Wednesday he had built up to the following:

'Mac, have you considered the legal aspects after - you know, after --'

'Ground Zero's good enough. What legal aspects? Seems to me you've obliged nicely in that department.'

'I'm not so sure. I've been involved in a fair amount of plea bargaining. From Boston to Peking.'

'What are you talking about?'

'Nothing. I was just - oh, nothing.'

By Thursday, this: 'There could be consequences after ... this Ground Zero ... that you haven't thought out. A cancer could be growing on the presidency of the Shepherd Company that ultimately may cripple the office.'

'Spell it out, boy.'

'Well. ... No, never mind. It's conjecture. What was all that noise this afternoon? It sounded very exciting.'

The Hawk squint-eyed him before being pulled into the question. 'Goddamn, it was exciting,' he answered after several seconds. 'Nothing like the evolvement of precision in manoeuvres! It fires up a man's heart! What the hell were you talking about? This cancer stuff.'

'Oh forget it. The old legal brain was just wandering. Are the manoeuvres really all that ... top drawer?'

'Yeah ...' Hawkins rolled the cigar from one side of his mouth to the other. 'They're all right, I guess.'

On Friday: 'How was the practice today? Sounded great.'

'Practice? Goddamn, it's not practice, it's manoeuvres!'

'Sorry. How were they?'

'A little sloppy; we've got some minor difficulties.'

'Sorry, again. But I've confidence in you. You'll straighten things out.'

'Yeah ...' The Hawk paced at the foot of the bed, his cigar a mashed pulp. 'I may have to pick up a few diversion troops. Two or three, that's all. I wasn't concentrating. And, goddamn, Sam, I would have been on-the-barrel-sight except for the trouble you've caused!'

'I told you. I really regret all that. *I* wasn't concentrating —'

MacKenzie stopped and blurted out the words. 'Do you mean that?'

'Yes,' replied Devereaux slowly, with conviction. 'The first thing a lawyer learns is to deal with facts, hard evidence. All of it, not just the bits and pieces. I isolated. I'm truly sorry.'

'I won't pretend to understand that bullshit, but if you feel the way I think you're saying, what the hell were you talking about yesterday? And, damn it, the day before. Those "consequences" after Ground Zero.'

Bingo! as they said in Boston, thought Devereaux to himself. But he showed no emotion; he was the calm, probing attorney with his client's best interests at heart. 'All right. I'll spell it out. I know those trust accounts, Mac. Excluding the one major trust, which I gather is yours, your seven men can draw (or have their consigners draw) up to three hundred thousand on the basis of the first code releases. The second code releases are on a printout sheet in one of the other documents. The printout requires your countersignature and I assume you'll send it to Zürich just before you leave for Ground Zero. Am I right so far?'

'I really skull-sessioned that trust business. What's wrong?'

'Nothing. Yet. With the second release each man has a total of five hundred thousand, correct? That's his fee, right? A half a million for Ground Zero. Everybody the same.'

'Not bad for six weeks' work.'

'There are other things to consider. Plea bargaining on a large scale can include more than immunity. And not just through writing a book, although I understand a lot of cash is funnelled through publishers these days.'

'What are you talking about?' The Hawk squashed his cigar out on the bedpost.

'What's to prevent any or all of your subordinate officers from going straight to the authorities - through intermediaries, of course - and making separate deals? After the fact. They have your money; they avoid prosecution because they cooperate. Remember, we're talking about one of the biggest scores in history. They could make a few thousand on top of what they've got.'

MacKenzie's squinting eyes suddenly widened in relief. And self-satisfaction. There was definitely a sense of triumph in his grin. 'Is that what you've troubled yourself over, boy?'

'Don't make light of it —'

'Hell, no, I won't. And I didn't. None of my men would do anything like that. Because they're going to want to disappear like jackrabbits running from a brush fire. They won't surface anywhere for fear of colliding with *each other*.'

'Now *I* don't understand,' said Sam dejectedly.

The Hawk sat on the bed. 'I've covered all that, son. Sort of in the same way I lashed you to the loaded howitzer. You gave me the idea. I intend to say good-bye to each officer separately. And with each I'm going to hand him an open-faced bearer bond worth an additional half million. And tell him *he's* the *only* one getting it. Because like a good general officer I've kept my combat logs, and in rereading them I realized the mission could not have been successful without *his* particular strategic contributions. They're hung. Both ways. A man won't inform on a crime that couldn't have been committed without *his expertise* - especially when it's worth an additional half million - and he sure as shit doesn't want his fellow conspirators to know he got preferential treatment to the tune of half a million.'

'My God!' Sam could not stop the admiration from creeping into his voice.

'Clausewitz makes it clear that you don't engage the Berber in the same way you do battle with the king's dragoons. It's a question of applicable tactics.'

Devereaux, once again, was struck by the Hawk's sheer boldness. He spoke softly, barely above a whisper, 'You're talking about - Jesus! - three and a half million dollars!'

'That's correct; you add real quick. And a million apiece for the girls, that's four more million. Plus the original compensation for the officers, another three and a half. And for your information, though I should probably reconsider, I've got another bearer bond for you. That's a million on your paysheet.'

'*What?*'

'I kind of suspected you never understood the forty-mill capitalization. I didn't just come up with a figure, you know. That sum was arrived at after very careful deliberation. I got a booklet from the Securities and Exchange Commission which told what to look for in sound corporate financing. You see, before the company even *markets* its services, we have a preoperation salary outlay of close to fifteen million;

then there was the capitalization expenses, including travel and front money and finder's fees – I kinda screwed you on that, son, but I knew you had good things coming – and the corporate real estate and the equipment indigenous to the marketing sources ....'

Involuntarily, Sam's ears distorted the sound waves. Isolated phrases such as 'aircraft purchases estimated at five million', and 'shortwave communication relays coming in at a million-two', and 'refurbishing, and supplies', and 'additional company offices' – all these came through with sufficient clarity to make Sam wonder where he was. Stark naked under an eiderdown quilt somewhere in Switzerland, or fully clothed in a boardroom somewhere in the Chrysler Building. Unfortunately for the state of his stomach, everything came together with the Hawk's brief summation.

'This SEC booklet was very specific about liquid assets available for reserve capital. It recommended a point spread of twenty to thirty per cent. Then I checked out the custom-of-the-trade practices with limited partnership agreements and found that the overcalls were generally ten to fifteen per cent, which struck me as inadequate. So I skulled a bit and decided on twenty-five per cent. And that's what we've got. The budget projections prior to marketing come to just about thirty million. Taking that as the base figure, you add ten for contingency. That makes forty million and that's what I raised. Damned sound economics, I'd say.'

Devereaux was temporarily speechless. His mind was racing but no words came. MacKenzie the military fruitcake was suddenly Hawkins the conglomerate financier. And that was more frightening than anything he had previously considered. Military principles (or lack thereof) when combined with industrial principles (of which there was a lack thereof) did a military-industrial complex make. The Hawk was a walking military-industrial complex!

If there was strident urgency in Sam's stopping MacKenzie before, it was tripled now.

'You're invincible,' said Sam finally. 'I rescind all my previous reservations. Let me join you, really join you. Let me earn my silly million.'

CHAPTER TWENTY-ONE

Each officer had been assigned a colour, in French. Not only was French spoken by everyone, but the sounds of the colour words were more distinctive in French than in any other language.

The American Negro from Crete was *Noir*, of course. The Viking from Stockholm, *Gris*; the Frenchman from Biscay was *Bleu*; while his countryman from Marseilles was *Vert*; the dark-skinned non-Black from Beirut was *Brun*; Rome was *Orange*; and finally, Athens was *Rouge*, in honour of his ever present kerchief. To instil a sense of discipline and identity among the men, the Hawk further insisted that the word 'Captain' precede each colour.

This aspect of authority and identity was desirable because MacKenzie's second command by necessity stripped his men of their specific individualities. For Ground Zero's assault was to be made in stocking masks. Head and face hair were to be at a minimum; skins powdered or bleached to medium Caucasian hues, and all ambulation which, no doubt, had been studiously disguised, drastically changed.

The men accepted the order without question. Razors and scissors and bleaching agents went to work; none had any desire to stand out any more distinctly from his fellow officers than basic nature dictated. There was security in anonymity, and they knew it.

The manoeuvres progressed into the fourth week. The forest road bordering the Machenfeld field had been shaped to conform as accurately as possible to the site of Ground Zero; boulders had been moved, trees uprooted, whole areas of bush transplanted. A second location had been selected and cosmeticized: a winding, narrow, back road that descended a relatively steep hill in the woods.

In redesigning both these sites the men worked from enlarged photographs – 123 photographs, to be exact – sent by an agreeable tourist in Rome by the name of Lillian von Schnabe. However, Mrs von Schnabe did not take credit for her films. As a matter of fact, the rolls were sent undeveloped by two relays of couriers unknown to each other and delivered to a bewildered Rudolph in Zermatt. In several cases of tampons. Rudolph put the strange cargo in the trunk of his Italian taxi, underneath the tools. A man had his dignity to consider.

On the third day of the fourth week the Hawk scheduled the first complete run-through of the assault. By necessity it was a start-stop hold-to-position exercise as the men switched around, assuming the pivotal roles of the adversary. Motorcycles raced, limousines sped, figures in stocking masks leaped from their stations to perform the tasks assigned. Using a stopwatch, MacKenzie clocked each phase of the manoeuvre; he had developed eight basic phases for the entirety, from incursion to escape. And goddamn, his officers were progressing beautifully! They knew that the overall success of Ground Zero depended on the complete success of each individual assignment within each specific phase. The concept of failure was not attractive.

Which was why the captains objected unanimously to the Hawk's prime tactical innovation: total absence of hand weapons. A well-placed knife or a rapidly exercised garrotte had served them all in past skirmishes, more often than not being the difference between survival and capture. But MacKenzie was adamant: It would be both guarantee and proof that no harm would come to the pope until the ransom was paid. Therefore, all pistols, knives, coils, foot studs, knee cleats, finger points – even pig-iron knuckles – were eliminated. Forbidden, too, were any forms of hand-to-hand above the level of basic jukato.

Eventually, they accepted the limitations. 'In Sweden there is a saying,' intoned Captain Gris in his Nordic lilt. 'One Volvo in the garage is worth a lifetime of passes on the

Scandinavian railroad. I shall accommodate the commander.'

'Oui,' agreed Captain Bleu, the Frenchman from Biscay. 'For the recompense involved, I shall sing them to sleep with Gascogne lullabies, if it is required.'

But lullabies were not required. Instead, sleep was to be induced by half-inch hypodermic needles dispensing solutions of sodium pentothal. Each officer would be outfitted with a thin bandolier across his chest, which carried tiny hypodermic needles in small rubber receptacles - where once had been bullets. They were easy to extract swiftly. If administered properly, within a three-inch diameter on the lower right area of the neck, the anaesthetic would take effect in seconds. The problem was merely to immobilize the victims for those brief moments until the drug caused collapse. It was not a difficult problem and since there'd be considerable noise from the vehicles, even a partial scream or two might go unnoticed.

So the officers, heeding the words of wisdom from Gris and Bleu, re-evaluated their objections to the Hawk's order. In a way it was a challenge; and none were interested in lifetime passes on the Scandinavian railroad. Not when he could own a fleet of Volvos.

Each captain's expertise was called on. Captain Gris and Bleu were masters of camouflage and escape cartography. Captain Rouge was an expert in demolition; he had personally blown up six piers in the Corinth strait when it was rumoured the American fleet was sailing in. Sedative medicines were a speciality of the Englishman, Captain Brun, who had darkened his skin for a life in Beirut; most narcotics held interest for him. Aircraft technology and electronics were covered brilliantly. The first, of course, was the bailiwick of Captain Noir, whose exploits in Houston - and Moscow - were legend. The second was the province of Captain Vert, who found it necessary in Marseilles to devise an extraordinary variety of radio communications. It was such a busy port; and Interpol was always underfoot.

Lastly, native orientation was left to Captain Orange, who

knew Rome like the back of his constantly gesturing hand. He would write out full descriptions of eight innocuous-looking sets of clothing that blended into the current dress, and further, he would provide a minimum of four separate methods of transportation, using public conveyances where feasible, to the site of Ground Zero. For during the final days of the fourth week, each captain was to travel to Rome and personally survey the assault area.

The airfield at Zaragolo would be no problem; they agreed to that. And neither would the helicopter at Ground Zero. It could be flown in the night before the assault. Gris and Bleu assured them the camouflage would be undetectable.

Goddamn, thought MacKenzie as he snapped the stopwatch at the end of the manoeuvre's Phase Eight. Twenty-one minutes! In another day or so it would get to the optimum eighteen. He felt a surge of pride in his once bemedalled chest. His machine was emerging as one of the finest ministrike forces in the military books.

Even the three privates (the diversionary-troops) were splendid. They had but two functions: scream and lie still. But as was proper for the lowest enlisted ranks, they knew nothing. They had been recruited by Captain Brun from the poppy fields high in the Turkish hills, to which they would return the instant Ground Zero was terminated. They'd been hired to perform at a fixed price, did not care to know anything and, naturally, were housed by themselves in enlisted quarters and did not eat at the officers' mess.

They were called simply: Privates One, Two, and Three.

The run-through completed, the officers gathered around the Hawk beside the huge blackboard he'd set up on an A-frame in the field. Sweat was pouring through their stocking masks. Those in priestly habits took them off carefully, studying them for repairs that might be needed; and the inevitable cigarettes and matches came out of pockets. No lighters; fingerprints could be lifted from lighters.

The three privates, naturally, went off by themselves. In sight but not within hearing. Enlisted personnel were not privy to tactical analyses; it was not proper.

The analyses began. Although immensely pleased Hawkins did not dwell on the positive; he told them their mistakes, marking up the blackboard with his criticisms with such sharp authority that the officers cowered like rebuked children.

'Precision, gentlemen! Precision is everything! You must never allow your concentration to lapse, even for a second! Captain Noir, you're cutting your time too close between Phase One and your station in Phase Six. Captain Gris, you had trouble with your cassock over the uniform. Practise it, man! Captains Rouge and Brun, your execution of Phase Five was just plain sloppy! Take out that radio equipment! Go over your moves! Captain Orange! Yours was the most serious lapse of all!'

'*Che cosa?* I make *no* mistakes!'

'Phase Seven, Captain! Without the proper execution of Phase Seven, the whole mission goes up in mortar smoke! That's the *exchange*, soldier! You're the one who speaks Italian best. I put this Frescobaldi in the pope's car and take the pope. Where the hell were *you*?'

'In position, *Generale*!'

'You were on the wrong side of the road! And Captain Bleu, for an expert at camouflage, you stuck out like a plucked duck in your Phase Four station! *Cover*, man! Use the foliage for cover!

'Now, as to this latrine rumour that some of you are unhappy over Phase Eight, the escape routes to Zaragolo; that a few of you figure we should have two copters at Ground Zero. Well, let me tell you, there's no contingency for radar, gentlemen. One small bird with Italian air force markings, flying low, can get through. Two choppers would be picked up on a scanner. I don't think any of you cotton to having your asses a thousand feet in the air, surrounded by the whole guinea air force. No offence, Captain Orange.'

The captains looked at each other. They'd obviously discussed Phase Eight among themselves, and since the small helicopter at target centre was lifting out only the

Hawk, the pope, and the two pilots, they had grumbled. But the commander painted a convincing picture. The escape routes on the ground had been exhaustively analysed by Gris and Bleu, who were not only the best in the business, but who would be using them as well. It was conceivable that the ground was safer.

'We withdraw our objections,' said Captain Vert.

'Good,' said MacKenzie. 'Now let's concentrate on —'

It was as far as he got. For in the distance, across the south field, running through the grass was the figure of Sam Devereaux in sweat pants, shouting at the top of his lungs.

'One, two, three, four! What do we like to *jog* for? *Good* health, *good* health! Five, six, seven, eight! Get the weight! Out of the freight! Four, three, *two*, *one*! Jogging is a lot of fun!'

'*Mon Dieu!*' cried Captain Bleu. 'The soft-headed one never stops! He has carried on so for five days now!'

'Before we rise in the morning!' added Gris. 'During rest periods, whenever there is a peaceful moment he is below the window, shouting.'

The other captains joined in a chorus of agreement. They had accepted the general's decision not to shoot the idiot, even grudgingly allowed that there was no harm in letting the fool out of the room to exercise – as long as two guards from the Machenfeld staff were assigned to him. The jackass wasn't going anywhere; not in sweat pants, with no top, over a high barbed-wire fence that led only to impenetrable Swiss mountain forests. But they had drawn the line regarding the clown's participation in Ground Zero.

So here he was, trying to impress them with his training. A pathetically poor athlete who cannot make the team, but will not stop trying.

'All right. All right,' said the Hawk, suppressing a laugh. 'I'll talk to him again, make him quiet down. He's just doing it for your benefit, you know. He really wants to join the big fellas.'

He was driving them all crazy, and he knew it. Of course

there were times when he thought he might collapse from exhaustion, but the knowledge that his grotesqueries were having their desired effect kept him going. Everyone avoided him, some actually ran at the sight of him. His insane behaviour had become an irritating, aggravating joke. Already three dogs which had appeared out of nowhere to guard him were taken from the corridor outside his room to the staff quarters below because of their incessant barking. And he made it a point to run by the staff area repeatedly. The hounds, themselves weary of being screamed at for their perfectly natural reaction, now merely raised their heads and stared with hatred at him from behind the gates as he passed by.

As did the staff – and MacKenzie's officers. Sam was a loud nuisance, a joke that had worn thin. What was happening, of course, was that he was being taken for granted. And in a few days he would take advantage of that scorn.

Although he was not allowed to eat with Mac and his band of psychopaths, the Hawk was considerate enough to continue visiting him every day in the late afternoon when Sam was brought back to his room and the sweat pants removed. Devereaux understood. Hawkins needed a sounding board for his enthusiasms. And, bragging, he dropped the information that he and his men would be away for a day or two to execute a surveillance check of Ground Zero. They would then return for any last-minute alterations of strategy.

But Sam shouldn't be concerned. He would not be lonely at Machenfeld. What with the guards, and the dogs, and the staff.

Sam smiled. For when the Hawk and his freaks left the château, it was his own personal Ground Zero. He had begun to prime his guards, the wild-eyed Rudolph and some obvious killer with no name. He had convinced Rudolph and No Name on several occasions to sit in the middle of a field as he ran around it. It was not difficult; they were grateful to be stationary. They simply sat in the grass with two ominous looking pistols trained on him as he jogged and intermittently stopped to perform callisthenics. On each occasion he had gradually widened the distance between him and his guards so that this afternoon he was nearly 250 yards away from them.

The army had taught him *something* about small weapons; he knew that there was no handgun that was any damned good beyond thirty yards. Not in terms of accuracy; scatter shot was something else, but he had to take *some* chances. Stopping the Hawk was the kind of objective that in war made heroes of unheroic soldiers. What had MacKenzie said? 'It's commitment. Nothing takes its place. All the ammo in the world can't be a substitute....'

Sam was committed. The prospects of World War III loomed larger every day.

His plan was simple, and relatively safe. He had been tempted to give it an option number, but his options had not been noticeably successful so he decided against it. He would jog here in the south field, as he was doing now, where the bordering forest was thickest and the grass higher than in the other pastures. He would widen the distance between himself and the guards as he had done this afternoon and institute intermittent callisthenics. Among them pushups. Which naturally brought him close to the ground, below the level of the grass.

At the proper moment, he would crawl away as fast as he could towards the forest, then race to the fence. However, when he reached the fence, he would *not* climb it. Instead, he would remove the sweat pants - properly torn - and throw them over. And then, if all went as it should, if Rudolph and No Name were racing in several directions at once, he would scream as though severely hurt and get the hell out of the area. Into the thickest woods.

Rudolph and No Name would naturally run to the spot at the fence, see the sweat pants on the other side, and undoubtedly take the appropriate actions: One would go over the fence, while the other raced back to the château for the dogs.

At which point Sam would wait until he heard the

barking. Then he would return to Machenfeld, go in through the door, steal clothes and a weapon. From that point to an automobile in the circular drive, and a pistol to threaten the gatekeeper, had to be clear sailing.

It had to be!

What could go wrong?

The Hawk wasn't the only one capable of strategies. He'd learn not to mess with a Boston lawyer who worked for Aaron Pinkus!

The shouts interrupted his thoughts. He was within sight of the manoeuvre area; he could see the strange looking road signs and the vehicles. Rudolph and No Name were yelling at him to come back. Naturally, he would oblige; he was not permitted to observe manoeuvres.

'*Sorry fellas!*' he yelled breathlessly as he reversed direction, his legs pounding the soft earth. 'Let's head down to the gate and back and call it a day!'

Rudolph and No Name grimaced and got up from the grass. Rudolph gave him a finger; No Name a thumb to the teeth.

Sam made it a point every afternoon to end his jogging with a run down to the main gate. It was a good idea to study the premises as thoroughly as possible in anticipation of his escape. It was conceivable that he might have to operate the mechanism himself, depending upon the state of panic at the moment. If it was maximum (as MacKenzie would say) the gate might even be left open.

He contemplated this possibility as his feet clattered over the boards of the moat, when suddenly his musings were replaced by a feeling of discomfort. For down at the gate a long, black limousine was being admitted with much bowing and obsequious grinning on the part of the gatekeeper. And when he heard the words shouted from the driver's seat as the automobile was expertly whipped out of the gate towards him, he froze and instantly considered drowning himself in the Machenfeld moat.

'I don't belive it!' yelled Lillian Hawkins von Schnabe at the wheel. 'Sam Devereaux in *sweat pants*! God almighty, you took my advice. You're toning up that wreck of a vessel you live in!'

And if he considered drowning himself at Lillian's words, the next voice he heard drove him to the railing.

'You surely look better than you did in London!' shouted Anne from Santa Monica, Mrs Hawkins number four – Sloping yet Argumentative. 'Your little trip must have done you a world of good!'

CHAPTER TWENTY-TWO

Devereaux's escape plan did not become unglued as had Options One to Four. Neither was it bypassed as Options Five and Six had been. Nor had it exploded in a torrent of abuse as was the fate of Option Seven. It was, however, postponed.

He suddenly had two additional guards to contend with, one of whom was as much a shock to the Hawk as both were to Sam. MacKenzie admitted it. Casually, without letting it upset his schedule; merely using the reality to bolster his overall strength – turning a liability into an asset.

'Annie's got a problem, counsellor,' the Hawk said back in Devereaux's room. 'I think you might give it some legal thought. Do something about it when this is over.'

'All problems pale into insignificance —'

'Not hers. You see, Annie's family – the whole goddamn family – spent more time *in* prison than *out* of it. Mother, father, brothers – she was the only girl – they had record sheets that took up most of the precinct files in Detroit.'

'I never came across any of that. It's not in the data banks.' Devereaux was momentarily sidetracked from his own concerns. MacKenzie wasn't trying to con him, now. There was no fire in the eyes, only sadness. Truth. But there *hadn't* been any mention of a criminal record in Anne's dossier. If he remembered correctly, she'd been listed as the only daughter of two obscure Michigan school teachers who wrote poetry in medieval French. Parents deceased.

'Course not,' said the Hawk. 'I changed all that for the

army. And everybody else, mainly her. It was a big hangup for the girl; it was holding her back.' MacKenzie lowered his voice, as if the words were painful, but nevertheless a reality that could not be brushed aside. 'Annie was a hooker. She fell into poor ways – very artificial ways for her – when she was growing up. She worked the streets. She didn't know any better then. She had no home life, most of the time no home. When she wasn't hooking she'd spend her time in libraries, looking at all the pretty magazines, imagining what it would be like to live decent. She was constantly trying to improve herself, you know. She never stops reading, even now, always after bettering herself. Because underneath there's a very fine person. There always was.'

Sam's memory went back to the Savoy. Anne in bed with a huge, glossy paperback of *The Wives of Henry VIII* on her lap. Then later, the words spoken with such conviction in the foyer doorway as she was about to get dressed. Words that meant a great deal to her. Devereaux looked up at the Hawk and repeated them quietly. '"Don't change the outside too much or you'll mess up the inside." She said you told her that.'

MacKenzie seemed embarrassed. It was obvious he had not forgotten. 'She had problems. Like I just said, underneath there was a very fine person she didn't recognize. Hell, *I* did. Anybody would.'

'What's her legal problem?' Sam asked.

'This goddamned gigolo-waiter husband of hers. She's stuck with that fucker for six years; helped him go from a hot-pants beach boy to owning a couple of restaurants. She *built* those restaurants. She's damned proud of them! And she likes the life. Overlooking the water, all those boats, nice people. She lives decent now, and *she did it*.'

'So?'

'He wants her out. He's got himself another woman and he doesn't want any lip from Annie. A quiet divorce and just get the hell out.'

'She doesn't want the divorce?'

'That's immaterial. She doesn't want to lose the

restaurants! It's principle, Sam. They represent everything she's worked for.'

'He can't simply take them. There's the property settlement to consider, and California laws are rough as hell.'

'So's he. He went back to Detroit and dug up her police record.'

Sam paused. 'That's a legal problem,' he said.

'You'll work on it?'

'There's not much I can do here. It's a confrontation problem, big attack variety. Fire for fire, dig up counter-accusations.' Devereaux snapped both his fingers – the legal *Wunderkind* making a brilliant decision. 'Tell you what. Let me out of here and I'll fly straight to California! I'll hire out one of the best LA private detectives – like on television – and really go after this prick!'

'Good thinking, boy,' replied the Hawk, clucking his tongue in respect. 'I like that aggressive tone; you bear it in mind for later. Say, in a month or two.'

'Why not *now*? I could —'

'I'm afraid you can't. That's out of the question. You're here for the duration. Talk with Annie, though. Learn what you can. Maybe Lillian can help; she's a resourceful filly.'

With these words MacKenzie dispensed with his liability and gained an asset: Sam now had two additional people to keep an eye on him. He might outwit Rudolph and No Name; the girls were something else again.

Within hours after their arrival, however, it was apparent to Sam that Lillian would have very little time to pay attention to him. In her usual forthright manner she plunged into furious activity, commandeering two of the Machenfeld staff to help her. The work began first thing in the morning when the brigade went out for manoeuvres.

Upstairs. In the top floor rooms and on the ramparts of the château.

There was the banging of hammers and the whirring of

saws and the cracking of plaster. Furniture was carried up and down the long winding staircase; those pieces too large or too awkward were raised and lowered by pulleys and ropes over the outside walls. Scores of potted plants and bushes and small trees were placed around the battlements – seen from the ground by Sam for he was not permitted above the third floor. Paints and brushes and panels of wood were transported daily by Lillian and her two helpers and when Sam could no longer politely ignore her labours, he asked her what she was doing.

'A little arranging, that's all,' she replied.

Finally, crates of crushed stone and washed gravel were hoisted up the wall, accompanied by several concrete benches and (if Sam was not mistaken, and being from Boston he was not) a marble *prayer stall.*

It was suddenly very clear to Devereaux exactly what Lillian was doing. She was turning the top floor and the ramparts of Château Machenfeld into a full-fledged papal residence! Complete with apartments and gardens and prayer stalls!

Oh, my God! A papal residence!

Anne, on the other hand, spent most of her time with Sam. Since MacKenzie had deemed it improper for the girls to eat at the officers' mess – it was diversionary for women to break bread with a strike force prior to combat – Anne and Lillian were assigned their meals in Devereaux's room, Sam under the eiderdown quilt, of course. But Lillian was rarely there; she spent most of her time upstairs – arranging.

So Sam and Anne were thrown together. On a surprisingly platonic basis. True, he had made no pass, but she made no offer either. It was as though both understood the insanity whirling around them, neither wanting the other to be involved, each, in a very real sense, protecting the other. And the more they talked together, the more Sam began to understand what MacKenzie meant about Anne. She was the most genuine, guileless person he had ever met in his life. All the girls were devoid of artifice, but there was something different about Annie. Whereas the others had reached certain plateaux, conscious of their worth, Anne was not satisfied. There was about her a delightfully irreverent sense of purpose that proclaimed for all the world to hear that she *could* expand, *could* experience – but *good heavens*! one did not have to be *gloomy* about it.

Devereaux recognized his imminent danger; he could get really sidetracked. He began to think that he had been looking for this girl for about fifteen years.

And he *couldn't* think about that. Another plan had come into focus. One he knew would work.

The very day Hawkins and his brigade of banana captains took off for Ground Zero!

The last sweet and sour strains of the orchestra filled the theatre. Guido Frescobaldi took his curtain calls, wiping a tear from his eyes. He had to shed his art and think of things plenipotentiary now. He had to hurry to his dressing room and lock up his makeup box.

The call had come! He was going to Rome! He was going to be embraced by his beloved cousin, the most beloved of all popes, Giovanni Bombalini, Francesco, Vicar of Christ! Ohh! Such blessings had come to him! To be reunited after all these years!

But he could say nothing. Absolutely *nothing*. That was part of the arrangements. It was the way Bombalini – *Madre di Cristo* – Pope Francesco wished it, and one did not question the ways of so munificent a pontiff. But Guido did wonder just a little bit. Why did Giovanni insist that he tell the management that small lie that he was going to visit family in Padua, not Rome? Even his friend, the stage manager, had winked when he told him.

'Perhaps you might ask your *family* to pray to Saint Peter for a little sacred lire, Guido. The box office has not been good this season.'

What did the stage manager know? And when did he know it?

It was not like the Giovanni of old to be secretive. And yet who was he, Frescobaldi, to doubt the wisdom of his beloved cousin, the pope.

Guido reached his small dressing room and began to take off his costume. As he did so his eyes fell on his Sunday church suit, pressed and hanging neatly in the centre of the wall. He was going to wear it on the train to Rome. And he suddenly felt ungrateful and ashamed of himself.

Giovanni was being so *good* to him. How could he even *think* a compromising thought?

The lady journalist who was bringing them together had asked for all his measurements. Every last one. When he asked why, she told him. And he had wept.

Giovanni was buying him a new suit.

The Hawk and his subordinate officers returned from Rome. The final check of Ground Zero had gone off without a hitch; no alterations were required.

Further, all intelligence data had been gathered and processed. Using basic surveillance techniques employed in hostile territories, Hawkins had donned an enemy uniform (in this case a black suit and a clerical collar) and obtained a Vatican pass, and identification that certified him to be a Jesuit doing an efficiency study for the treasury. He had free access to all calendars and personnel schedules. From apartments to barracks.

They all confirmed the Hawk's projections.

The pope would leave for Castel Gandolfo on the same day he had chosen for the past two years. He was an organized man; time was to be allocated properly with regard to needs and functions. Castel Gandolfo expected him, and he would be there.

The pope would use the same modest motorcade he had employed previously. He was not a wasteful or pretentious man. One motorcycle point with two front and rear flanks. Basic. The limousines were restricted to two: his own, in which his most personal aides accompanied him; and a second, for secretaries and lesser prelates, who carried his current working papers.

The route of the motorcade was the scenic road he had spoken of with feeling whenever he mentioned Gandolfo: the beautiful Via Appia Antica, with its rolling hills and remnants of ancient Rome along the way.

Via Appia Antica. Ground Zero.

The two Lear jets had been delivered to Zaragolo. It was an airfield for the rich. The small Fiat sedan, which was the diversion equipment for the Turk privates, had been purchased by Captain Noir, in the name of the Ethiopian embassy. It was parked in an all-night garage next to a police station, where the crime rate was at a minimum.

Guido Frescobaldi was on his way to Rome. Regina would handle him. She'd put him up at a *pensione* she rented called The Doge, on the Via Due Macelli, right near the Spanish Steps, and take good care of the old man until the morning of the assault. And first thing that morning she'd load him up with a thiopental solution that would keep him on a harmless high for damn near twelve hours.

The Hawk planned to pick Guido up in the Fiat on his way to Ground Zero. Of course, Regina would have him properly dressed by then, with a very large overcoat that covered his fancy clothes. Skirts, really.

There was only one last item to take care of. The two limousines used in manoeuvres had to be driven to a place called Valtournanche, several miles northwest of the Alpine town of Champoluc. To a little-used private airfield frequented by the jetsetters heading for their ski chalets. The limousines were a natural. They were registered to nonexistent Greeks, and the Swiss *never* bothered Greeks who could afford such automobiles.

Lillian could take care of the transfer. Oversee it, actually. She could use the two men who had helped her shape up the pope's BOQ. Once the cars were in position they could vanish along with Lillian. Mac, of course, would give them bonuses.

He'd get rid of Rudolph, too, and that psycho, what's-his-name, the minute they were back from Ground Zero and the pope was safely - secretly - in his quarters. The chef had to stay; what the hell, even if he did find out who he was cooking for, he was a French Huguenot wanted by the police in sixteen countries.

That left Anne. And Sam, of course.

He could handle Sam. Sam was so lashed to that loaded howitzer he was part of the casing. But he couldn't figure out Annie. What was the girl up to? Why wouldn't she leave? Why had she used his own oath against him?

'You gave your solemn word that if ever any of us came to you in need, you'd never abandon us. You'd never allow an injustice to be done if you could prevent it. I'm here. I'm in need, and an injustice has been done. I've nowhere else to go. Please let me stay.'

Well, of course, he had to. After all, it was the word of a general officer.

But *why*? Could it be Sam?

Goddamn!

So he would die in Gandolfo. It could be worse, thought Giovanni Bombalini, gazing out the windows of his study. A half century ago all he had to look forward to was a gravesite in the Gold Coast, preceded by a long, drawn-out Last Rites ceremony delivered half in Latin, half in Kwa with swarms of flies circling his head. Gandolfo certainly held advantages over that exit.

He would be able to work better, too, at Gandolfo; use the weeks left to straighten out his own affairs, which were minimum, and do his best to set a course for the immediate future of the Church. He would bring with him several hundred analyses of the most powerful dioceses throughout the world and issue scores of promotions; balancing, but balancing in favour of younger, more vigorous perspectives.

Which often had nothing to do with youth.

He had to keep reminding himself that the intractable old guard was not to be scorned, and should not be. The old war-horses had gone through ecclesiastical battles unknown to the vast majority of those who screamed for reform and change. It was not easy to alter the philosophies of a lifetime. But the *fine* old war-horses knew when to step aside and graze in the pastures, ready with an affectionate eye to offer advice when asked, compassion regardless. The others – the Ignatio Quartzes of the world – needed a push.

Pope Francesco decided that among his last acts would be a little pushing. It would take the form of a Last Rites Dissertation to be read to the Curia after his death, and then made public. It was a bit presumptuous, he supposed, but if God did not want him to complete it, He could always summon him at His will.

He had begun the dissertation, dictating to the young Black priest. And he had sent a papal memorandum to every office in the Vatican appointing his young aide as executor of his personal effects in the event he was called to the arms of Christ.

Giovanni was told that Ignatio Quartze threw up for nearly an hour after receiving the papal instruction. It must have wreaked havoc with the cardinal's nasal passages.

'Your Holiness?' The young Black aide came through the door of the bedroom carrying a suitcase. 'I can't find the miniature chessboard. It's not in the drawer with the telephone.'

Giovanni thought for a moment, then coughed an embarrassed laugh. 'I'm afraid it's in the bathroom, Father. Since Monsignor O'Gilligan solved his conversion problems by explaining penance, he's been an absolute terror in his moves. Concentration was required.'

'Yes, sir.' The young priest smiled as he put down the suitcase. 'I'll put it in the vestment trunk.'

'Are we about packed? I say "we", but you've done the work.'

'Almost, Holy Father. The pills and the tonics will stay in my briefcase.'

'A little fine brandy could do just as well.'

'I have that, too, Your Holiness.'

'You are truly a man of God, my son.'

CHAPTER TWENTY-THREE

RIGIRATI! COSTRUZIONE!

The large metal sign was secured to the centre of the wooden barrier, that stretched across the width of the back country road.

It looked very official, right down to the last tiny red reflector, and the imposing insignia of Rome's municipal government. It also officially closed off a section of the Via Appia Antica to all approaching vehicles, offering instead a detour cut out of the forest down the Appian hill. And since this particular stretch of the Appian road was the narrowest on the entire route, there was no feasible alternative to the detour if the vehicles in question were larger than the smallest Fiat. Not even the size of the Fiat sedan which the Hawk had driven out of the garage next to the police station and which now lay overturned at the bottom of the hill.

Any larger automobile would not have room to turn around. To reverse direction a driver would have to steer his car backward for the better part of a mile, over countless potholes and around numerous blind curves. Of course the same driver might opt for negotiating the wide expanses of fields that regularly interrupted the Appian forests, but they were filled with rocks and mounds and intermittent stone walls, some built in ancient times. The fields were not only treacherous, but it was against the law to drive on them.

These thoughts went through Captain Noir's head, his black face powdered under the stocking mask, as he lay motionless in the bushes off the side of the road beyond the barrier. He had heard the sounds of the motorcycles in the distance.

All was ready.

Ground Zero had arrived.

The location was perfect. Only trees and fields and hills; the general had planned well. The abduction could probably be carried out on this isolated stretch of road without the detour but in some ways the detour was the most important aspect of Ground Zero. The vehicles *could* turn around by inches – but they wouldn't. They would use the detour.

Still, in case they didn't, Captain Noir held in his hand a piercing, high-frequency whistle. Its use meant that Plan Able, Phase One, Positions One to Three were aborted, instantly implementing Plan Baker, Phase Double Zero, Positions One Hundred and One to One Hundred and Ten: abduction farther up Appia.

Down the road beyond the barrier, the blue helmet with the white cross enamelled on the steel stood out like an enormous jewel in the Italian sunlight. It was on the head of the motorcycle patrolman in front of the papal column; the Vatican point, as the general termed him. The uniformed officer was travelling at medium speed; any faster on the old road would be uncomfortable for those in the limousines.

The patrolman spotted the barrier with the large official sign and drove up to it. Captain Noir held his breath. The officer jumped off his motorcycle, kicked out the stand, and walked up to the obstruction. He raised his eyebrows in bewilderment, looked beyond the barricade for signs of construction and grumbled unintelligibly.

He turned and held up his hands. The lead automobile had reached a point approximately a hundred feet from the barrier.

The patrolman returned to his idling bike, mounted, swung the bars, drove swiftly to the lead limousine, and spoke excitedly to those inside.

The rear door opened; a priest in a black cassock got out. He and the patrolman walked back towards the barrier, their attention on the sloping road down the Appian hill.

There was rapid, indistinguishable chatter between them; and then a series of gestures that conveyed only indecision. The priest turned, picked up the cloth of his cassock, and trotted back past the lead car to the papal limousine.

Captain Noir could not see too well, but the slight Appian breeze carried the sounds of more excited chatter. Noir swallowed and gripped the high-frequency whistle in his hand.

Then to his great relief he heard laughter. And the priest returned to the lead car, nodded his head, gesturing to the left at the patrolman, and climbed back into the limousine.

An adventurous decision had just been made; the general knew his enemy.

The motorcade turned left down the hill, led by the patrolman. All the vehicles entered cautiously, at very slow speeds, and when the two rear motorcycles reached the first curve on the slope, Noir got out of the grass and raced to the barrier, pulling it across the opening of the detour. He ripped off the top sign revealing the second:

DINAMITE! FERMA! PERICOLO!

He had done it! By God, he'd done it! He had escaped from Machenfeld and was on his way to Rome, and if everything held firm, no one would know he was gone until morning! Then it would be too late! The Hawk would be on his way to Ground Zero!

There was no way they could know he was gone. Unless they broke down the door to his room, which was highly unlikely under the circumstances. Anne wasn't talking to him; she'd stamped off to her room in the south wing. He had provoked an argument that could be heard on the peaks of the Matterhorn, eliciting language from her she must have learned from her felonious family.

Rudolph and No Name wanted absolutely nothing to do with him. Especially proximity. After the battle with Anne he had proceeded to complain to his guards of sudden, agonizing pains in his groin. He had doubled up and screamed.

'Oh, Jesus! It's Kuwaiti encephalitis! *I saw it in the Algerian desert five weeks ago! Oh, my God! I caught it! The testicles swell like basketballs, but heavier! I've got to have a doctor! Get me a doctor!'*

'No doctor. No outside communications until the master of Machenfeld returns.' Rudolph was stern.

'Then you better watch it!' Sam continued. 'It's highly contagious!'

Whereupon he had fainted, clutching himself through the sweat pants. Panicked, No Name and Rudolph moved back swiftly against the wall in the drawing room. Revived but in agony, Sam crawled out of the room and up the staircase. To meet his Maker in peace, and with enormous testicles.

Rudolph and No Name stayed well behind until Sam reached his room and closed the door. When he opened the door for one last time – he saw that his guards were far down the hallway with double handkerchiefs tied around their faces, aerosol cans of disinfectant billowing clouds of spray around them.

The coast was clear! For a beautiful, foolproof exit from Machenfeld.

Lillian and two of the staff were driving the limousines to an airfield somewhere south. He'd overheard the Hawk explaining the route to Mrs Hawkins number three; the trip was four hours long and it was vital that she position the vehicles on a road by the west highway of the airfield.

An airfield!

That meant aeroplanes! And aeroplanes flew to Rome!

And even if they didn't – or wouldn't – there were telephones! And radios!

His new plan had jelled instantly. He would be inside the trunk of the second limousine, the one being driven by a member of the château staff. It had been a simple matter to jam the lock of the vehicle's trunk while he had been saying goodbye to Lillian, helping her with the suitcases.

As soon as his guards disappeared in the cloud of disinfectant, Sam tied three blankets together, scaled down to the ground from the balcony, raced to the limousine in the drive, and crawled into the trunk.

Once inside, he wrapped the blankets around his upper body, grateful he still had his sweat pants, and waited. He was counting on nature to provide him with a shortcut to his objective and he was not disappointed.

The limousines sped through the gate and the trip had begun. After three and a half hours of bouncing, plunging, climbing, and racing through the Swiss mountains, Sam heard the rapid blasts of the limousine's horn. Within seconds there'd been a corresponding reply in the distance, from the lead automobile, and the car slowed down and stopped. The driver got out quickly. Devereaux could hear the footsteps outside the trunk. And then he'd heard the unmistakable muted splashing.

He opened the trunk, climbed silently out, and hit the urinating Swiss with a jack handle.

Before a half minute had passed, Devereaux had removed the man's trousers, jacket, shirt, and shoes. Pulling on the trousers and the jacket – enough to obscure him in the night darkness – he had raced around to the door and leaped into the driver's seat, tapping the horn twice as a signal to resume the trip.

Lillian honked back, and started off immediately.

The airfield at Valtournanche (that's what the sign had said) did present a minor problem, but it was more than compensated for by the extraordinary sum of money Sam found in the jacket he had taken from the Swiss. Five thousand dollars, American! The Hawk must have given the staff member a bonus!

It automatically gave birth to another, incredible plan! A magnificent finale!

He could stop the Hawk without the police! Without the authorities! Stop him cold, dismantle Ground Zero and disperse the brigade all at the same time! With no firing squads or hangmen or life imprisonment in the offing! It was perfect. Beyond error.

There was a curve in the road on the west border of the airfield. Sam slowed his limousine, and the instant Lillian's vehicle rounded the turn, he stopped the car, turned off the ignition, grabbed the shirt and the shoes, jumped out, and raced into the woods.

He waited in the darkness for the inevitable. Lillian's automobile could be heard in reverse gear. She and her escort got out and ran back to the abandoned second car.

'Isn't that the limit!' Lillian was angry. 'The ungrateful worm chickened at the last moment! And after Mac gave him all that money. Well, it doesn't surprise me. His neck muscles had no tone; it's always a sign of weakness. Come on! Get in! We're almost there.'

An hour later Devereaux, dressed in a leather jacket and baggy trousers oddly too large for his frame, was counting out $2,500 to a stunned pilot in a Valtournanche hangar, the fee for a rushed, unscheduled flight to Rome. Sam had chosen a man quite a bit smaller than himself, with no apparent muscle tone whatsoever. Pilots who took this kind of employment were not generally considered to be of the highest moral character. He didn't care to be rolled and dropped off into an Alpine mountain pass.

But he had made it! They were airborne! They'd reach Rome well before dawn. And then he, Sam Devereaux, the finest young attorney in Boston, would deliver the best summation of his career.

*

Captains Gris and Bleu, dressed in tight-fitting police uniforms, stood erect and motionless behind the trunks of two Appian maples on opposite sides of the winding road – motionless except for their right hands, which they flexed at their sides, thumbs caressing the short hollow needles that protruded from the inverted rings.

As the commander had predicted, the two motorcycles at either side of the papal limousine had dropped back and now rode parallel in front of the bikes flanking the rear. And again, as the commander had projected, the noise was deafening.

One by one the vehicles passed. As the final two patrolmen came between the two maple trees, Gris and Bleu leaped out, hammerlocked both men with their left arms, and each plunged a small needle into his man's neck.

Within seconds the patrolmen were limp.

Gris and Bleu lowered the motorcycles between their legs and dragged each body off into the underbrush. Together they entered the woods and raced diagonally downhill through the tangled foliage to position themselves for their next assignment. Secreted in these positions were the cassocks they would slip over their uniforms.

Captains Orange and Vert lay on their stomachs across from one another hidden by the tall weeds. Their posts were at the start of the second curve on the descending side road. Through the dense reeds they saw – and smiled as they did so – that the two final motorcycles failed to appear. Their other team of patrolmen struggled to keep their bikes upright, riding behind the second limousine.

Captain Orange crossed himself as the pontiff's vehicle passed.

Captain Vert spat. It was long past time for the Church to install a *French* pope; the Italians were pigs about that.

The papal car turned into the final downhill curve. Orange and Vert sprang up and out and executed the practised manoeuvres with lightning-swift dispatch against the motorcycle escorts.

The patrolmen collapsed; the papal limousine was entering the turn at the base of the Appian hill. There were only seconds remaining before the detonations of Phase Four, the smoke bombs from the overturned Fiat. Orange and Vert ran to their next assignment – the most prestigious of all: Phase Seven. Phases Five and Six, the destruction of the communications equipment and the sedation of the papal entourage, would be occurring any second.

Phase Seven was the zenith of Ground Zero: the exchange of the popes. Guido Frescobaldi for Giovanni Bombalini.

The explosions from the Fiat were positively frightening; the screams of the hysterical Turks terrifying. The Hawk grinned in appreciation. *Goddamn!* What a beautiful sight! All that smoke and noise and – well, the screams were overdone.

The motorcade stopped in shock, agitated voices swelling. One motorcycle and two limousines in an isolated back country road bordered by a steep hill on the south side and a tall, thick forest on the north.

Optimum, observed the Hawk, holding a weaving Guido Frescobaldi in the bushes.

Captain Noir reached his post and signalled Captains Rouge and Brun; they were strung out at ten-yard intervals, prepared for the moment to implement Phase Five: the destruction of all communications equipment.

It came.

The single Vatican policeman jumped off his motorcycle and ran towards the smoking Fiat with the trapped, screaming passengers. Every door of both limousines was swung open. The drivers and the priests screamed and waved their hands and shouted orders at everyone and no one, then ran towards the overturned car.

Now!

Dressed as priests, Noir, Rouge, and Brun dashed from their hidden recesses. Brun and Rouge plunged into the front seat of the first limousine, ripping out every wire in sight. Noir raced to the second automobile, the papal car, and dived through the open door towards the equipment.

Suddenly a hand lashed out over the seat, followed by an arm extending from a white cassock. But the hand and the arm were not white. They were *black*!

And the grip that held Noir's neck – accompanied by the swift, hard rabbit punches that hammered his head – was a street tactic Noir knew well. It was indigenous to a plot of turf called Harlem!

Noir wrenched his aching, pounding head and was suddenly, astoundingly, face to face with a brother!

A *brother* in the honkey white robes of the Church!

It went against Noir's grain to coldcock a brother, but there was nothing for it. The Catholic kid was good, but he hadn't taken advanced training above 138th Street and Amsterdam. Noir twisted his thumb and forefinger into the sensitive flesh; the Black priest screamed and released Noir's head as Noir yanked him halfway over the seat. He sighed as he chopped the Catholic kid at the base of the skull. He immediately went about his business, ripping wires and smashing dials. The fat old honkey in white robes – the *man*, himself, figured Noir – leaned forward and pulled the kid into the back seat, cradling the kid's head as if the kid was really hurt.

'He'll be okay, pops. I don't know how you boys do it. I *swear* I don't! The Baptists got his turf tide up in ribbons. They've got *rhythm*! Course, you've got the cops....'

Son of a bitch! What the hell else could go wrong? What other delays were concealed in the blinding sunlight of Rome's Leonardo da Vinci Airport? It was a nightmare being played out in the bright morning without benefit of sleep!

The goddamned, dwarf son of a bitch of a pilot from Valtournanche insisted that his aircraft be cleared by the narcotic inspectors! Nobody gave a damn if a plane flew in six vaults of stolen gold, or undeclared diamonds, or eyes-only defence plans for all of NATO, as long as there wasn't a joint on board! No amount of protesting on Sam's part made any difference whatsoever – Well, yes it did. It caused him to be stripped and searched.

'Per favore, signore. Where is your underwear? Where did you leave it? – Search the plane again!'

'That's crazy!' screamed Devereaux. 'How could a pair of shorts —'

'Che cosa?' inquired the capitano suspiciously.

'Shorts!' Sam outlined a pair of briefs. 'Where could I hide ...'

'Ah haaa,' interrupted the capitano. 'The mountain Swiss wear long underwear. With pockets. And flaps. And many buttons. Buttons are hollow.'

'I'm not Swiss! I'm American!'

The capitano's eyebrows shot up as he lowered his voice. 'Ah haaa — Mafia, signore?'

And so it went until Sam had dispensed ten one-hundred-dollar American bills, which happened to coincide with the end of the capitano's shift, whereupon Sam was released.

'Where can I get a taxi?'

'Have your money exchanged first, signore. No taxi has change for American one-hundred-dollar bills.'

'I don't have any hundreds left. Only five hundreds.'

'Then they will call the police. For certainly such money cannot possibly be authentic. You will need lire.'

Oh, my God, the police! thought Sam. The police and hysterical taxi drivers were the last thing he wanted. They definitely were not part of his grand finale to thwart the Hawk.

And so he spent the better part of an hour in the exchange line only to be told by the lady with a moustache that bills of such denominations had to be examined by specto-graphs.

'Thank you, signore,' said the face of fur finally. 'We have processed these under four different machines. They are very nice. Here is your lire. Do you have an empty suit-case?'

It was 9.45. Still time! A taxi into Rome took about an hour when one considered the traffic, and then perhaps a half hour to get to the southern outskirts where he could pick up the Via Appia.

The ride down the Appia couldn't be more than twenty minutes or so. He would recognize the signs he had seen during manoeuvres, he was sure of that. He'd reach Ground Zero with at least a half hour to spare!

He'd stop the Hawk, prevent World War III, eliminate the spectre of life imprisonment, and go home to Boston with a real Swiss bank account!

Goddamn! If he had two cigars, he'd smoke them both at the same time!

He ran across the terminal to the door under the signs that read Taxi in three languages. He raced breathlessly on to the concrete.

Up and down the whole area were hundreds of immobile dollies filled with luggage. Groups of men were gathered in the street, close to riot.

Sam approached a tourist. 'What's going on?'

'Goldanged guinea bastards called a cab strike!' Sam backed away. He had several hundred thousand lire stuffed in his pockets like football pads. There had to be somebody in one of the parking lots with an automobile.

He found him. At twenty minutes past eleven. And offered money. The faster he drove the more thousands of lire he would get. The man agreed.

11.32! He would make it!

He had to!

It was the summation of his life!

Why was he kidding himself? It was his life.

Gris and Bleu pulled at the clerical ropes around their cassocks. They were on their knees, concealed by the dense underbrush and cascading branches at the base of the hill by the edge of the old road. Both were prepared to spring through the foliage to execute Phase Six, the immobilization of the motorcade. The overturned Fiat was directly in front of them, the smoke billowing everywhere, the five papal aides, the two chauffeurs and the remaining patrolman all making genuine attempts to reach the screaming Turks.

The numbers presented no problem. Once Gris and Bleu joined the smoke-engulfed mêlée, they would work swiftly, their church habits adding to the confusion. It would be a simple matter to incapacitate one adversary, then another. Rouge would join them on the west flank, intercepting anyone who might discover the conspiracy prematurely, and make a dash for the limousines.

Now!

Gris and Bleu lunged out of the brush into the confusion of smoke, screams, and flailing arms, their wide cassocks billowing, rings at the ready.

One by one the members of the papal entourage collapsed to the ground, beatific smiles on their peaceful faces.

'Tie them! Give me some cord!' yelled Gris to the Turks as the three 'victims' crawled out of the windows and from under the car.

'Not tight, you maniacs!' added Bleu harshly. 'Remember what the commander said!'

'*Mon Dieu!*' roared Bleu suddenly, grabbing Gris's shoulder, pointing to the ground beyond the rising smoke. '*Qu'est-ce que c'est que ça?*'

In the middle of the road, halfway to the limousines, lay Rouge flat on his back, one arm raised, the wrist bent, as though frozen in mid-pirouette. The stocking mask could not disguise the expression of Olympian repose underneath. In the confusion, he had tripped over his cassock, plunging his needle into his stomach.

'Quick!' yelled Gris. 'The antidote! The general thinks of everything!'

'He has to,' said Bleu.

'*Now!*' ordered the Hawk, holding Guido Frescobaldi, who had suddenly raised his voice in song.

Across the dirt road, Mac could see Orange crossing himself as he leaped out of the bushes towards the papal limousine. It was wasted motion, he thought; the pope was not going to attempt any escape. He had helped his aide down on the seat and was getting out of the car, his face wrathful.

The Hawk took Frescobaldi by the hand, and led him towards the limousine.

'I bid you good day, sir,' said the Hawk to the pope. It was a proper military salutation for a surrender.

'*Animale!*' roared the pontiff in a roll of thunder that reverberated throughout the Appian forests and hills. '*Uccisore! Assassino!*'

'What's that?'

'*Basta*!' The thunder cracked again. And the lightning was in Francesco's eyes; the eyes of a giant in the body of a mortal. 'Take my life! You kill my beloved children! The children of God! You slay the *innocenti*! Send me to Jesus! Kill me, too! And may God have mercy on your soul!'

'Oh, for Chri— for heaven's sake, shut up! Nobody's going to kill anybody.'

'I see what I see! The children of God are slain!'

'That's plain horseshit! Nobody's hurt, and nobody's going to get hurt.'

'They are all *morto*,' said Francesco, with less conviction, his eyes darting everywhere in bewilderment.

'No more than you are. We wouldn't be tying them up if they were, would we? Orange! Over here!'

'Sì, Generale.' Orange came around the hood of the limousine, crossing himself repeatedly.

'Get that coloured boy out of the car. Must be a house guest of the pope here.'

'That man is a *priest*. My personal aide!'

'You don't say? Must be a fine lad with the choirs. Easy, Orange,' said MacKenzie as the Italian pulled the unconscious Black prelate from the automobile. 'Put him in the brush and loosen that big robe. It's too damn hot for ponchos.'

'You mean,' asked Giovanni incredulously, 'they're all alive?'

'Certainly, they're alive,' replied MacKenzie, signalling Vert to prepare Frescobaldi for the exchange; the pope's double sat serene.

'I don't believe you! You've murdered them!' roared the pope suddenly.

'Will you keep quiet!' The Hawk did not ask a question. 'Listen to me. I don't know how you handle your command, but I assume you can tell if a soldier's alive or not.'

'Che cosa? ...'

'Captain Gris!' yelled MacKenzie to the masked Scandinavian tying up a priest by the hubcaps of the first limousine. 'Lift that man up and bring him here, please.'

Gris complied. MacKenzie took the pontiff's right hand.

'Here! Put your fingers on the side of the throat next to the collar bone. Now, see? Do you get pulse?'

The pope's eyes narrowed, his concentration on the touch. 'The heart —. Yes. You speak the truth. The others? They are the same? The hearts beat?'

'I gave you my word,' said the Hawk sternly. 'I must reprimand you, sir. Opposing commands do not lie when capture is secure. We're not animals, sir. But we haven't much time.' The Hawk gestured for Vert to bring over the narcotized Frescobaldi. 'I'm afraid we'll have to change some of your clothes. I'll have to —'

MacKenzie stopped. Pope Francesco was staring at Frescobaldi. It was the first moment he had taken cognizance of the singer who was clean shaven and now, without his moustache, looked more like Giovanni Bombalini than did Bombalini himself.

'Guido! It is Guido Frescobaldi!' The pontiff's voice could have been heard in the Bay of Naples, so loud was his roar. 'Guido, my own flesh! My blood! It is Guido! *Madre di Dio!* You are a part of this – this heresy?!'

Signor Guido Frescobaldi smiled.

'Che gelida ... manina ... a rigido esanine ... ah, la-la ... la-laaa. ...'

'It's him, all right, but he's been a little out of things since this morning. And will be for a while longer. Come on, now. We've got to get some of that hardware off you and on him. Captain Orange? Captain Vert? Give Mr Francesco a hand.'

'There!' The Hawk spoke in the tones of a victorious general officer. He held the grinning Guido Frescobaldi by the shoulders, admiring the final result. 'He looks real fine, doesn't he?'

Francesco, transfixed, could not help himself. '*Jesus et Spiritus Sanctus.* The ugly Frescobaldi is myself. It is a miracle of God.'

'Two like-spits in the gunnery pool, Mr Pope!'

The pontiff was barely audible. 'You put ... Frescobaldi ... in the *chair* of *St Peter*?'

'For about two hours with luck – by my calculations.'

'But *why*?'

'Nothing personal. I understand you're a very nice fellow.'

'But why? In the name of God, *why*? That is no answer.'

'Didn't expect it to be,' replied the Hawk. 'I just don't want you screaming your head off. You've got a mighty loud voice.'

'Then I shall be – screaming my head out – if you do not tell me ... *Aiyeeeee!* ...'

'All right! All *right*! We're kidnapping you. Holding you

for ransom. You'll be fine; no harm will come to you and that's the word of a general officer.'

The conference was interrupted by Captains Gris and Bleu, who raced up and snapped to attention.

'The area is secured, General,' barked Gris.

'All sedations are completed,' added Bleu. 'We are prepared to move.'

'Good! Let's move then. *Troops!* Evacuate the area! Prepare to execute escape procedures! By your numbers! *Move*!'

As if on cue, the sounds of the revving helicopter could be heard from the camouflaged area fifty yards away from the centre of Ground Zero.

And then there was another sound. From the road at the top of the Appian hill: A car screeching to a halt.

'*Stop!*' came a plaintive wail from the woods. 'For Christ's sake, *stop*!'

'*What?*'

'*Mon Dieu!*'

'*Che cosa?!*'

'*I say!*'

'*Tokig!*'

'*Bakasi!*'

'*Shit!*'

Sam stumbled down the old dirt road on the hill. He came racing around the last curve and fell to one knee.

Giovanni Bombalini watched in astonishment; automatically he gave the kneeling figure his rather confused benediction, '*Deus et filius —*'

'Will you shut up!' MacKenzie glared at Francesco. '*Goddamn*, Sam! What the hell are you doing here? You're supposed to be sick as a *dog* —'

'*Listen* to me, everybody!' broke in Sam. 'Everyone gather around!' He struggled to his feet; the captains stood where they were, their faces betraying a certain insensitivity. 'Escape! Run for your lives! Leave this man alone! It's a trap! Machenfeld has fallen! It happened last night! Hundreds of Interpol police are swarming. ...' Sam's jaw was suddenly a gaping orifice as he stared at the Hawk. '*What did you say?*'

'You're a real pistol, son. I respect your moxie, like I said before. But I can't say you have much respect for my know-how.' MacKenzie snapped one of the straps that crisscrossed his chest over his field jacket. It was attached to a large leather case that was lashed over his hip. 'No assault operation ever stays out of contact with its command centre. Not since 1971, anyway. Hell, I used to patch relays from Ly Sol in Cambodia right straight down to the Mekong units.'

'*What?*'

'Tri-arced, high-frequency radio contact, boy. Set a schedule and receive-send simultaneously. You're *dated*, Sam! As of an hour ago the only thing swarming around Machenfeld were butterflies. I don't know how you did it, but you're mighty lucky you got here alone.... Come to think of it, you'd be a damned fool to get here any other way. – All right, men! Resume Phase Eight! – Come on, Sam. You're going for a ride. And I tell you this now, boy. Any more trouble and I'm going to open a door at two thousand feet and you can fly by yourself!'

'Mac, you can't! Think of World War *Three*!'

'Think of a nice free-fall – without a parachute – straight into a plate of spaghetti!'

And then there was another sound. A frightening one. From the top of the hill. From the road again.

The captains and the Turks froze.

The Hawk whipped his head around – and up – towards the Via Appia.

The pontiff said one word.

'*Carabinieri.*'

The whining, jarring, two-note scream of the Italian state police sirens could be heard in the distance. Drawing nearer.

'*Goddamn! How?!* What the hell *happened*? Sam, you *didn't*!'

'My God, *no*! I didn't! I *wouldn't*!'

'I think there is a – miscalculation, signore,' said Pope Francesco softly.

'*What?* What mother – what miscalculation?'

'The motorcade was to stop at the small village – well, not so *much* a village – of Tuscabondo. It is a mile or so past the *deviazione*, your detour.'

'Jesus!'

'He can be merciful, Signor Generale.'

'Those bastards will be swarming the hills, the fields. Goddamn!'

'And the air, Generale,' said Captain Orange excitedly, breaking out in a sweat under his mask. 'The *carabinieri* have fleets of *elicotteri*. They are the *pazzi* of the sky!'

'Jesus H. Christ!'

'*Figlio di Santa Maria – Figlio di Dio* – He is the way, *Generale*.'

'I told you to shut up. *Men!* Check your maps! Quickly! Gris and Bleu, evaluate escape routes E-Eight and E-Twelve. Our previous routes were faster but more exposed. Deliver your decision in one minute! Orange and Vert. Give me Frescobaldi! Join the others! Sam, you stay here!'

The screams of the sirens were nearer, almost at the intercept point of the Appia. Frescobaldi, weaving in MacKenzie's grip, sang louder.

'Signore.' Giovanni Bombalini took a step towards MacKenzie. 'You speak the word of a general. You have great sincerity when you say it.'

'What? Yes, of course. You're not much different, I suspect. Command's a big responsibility.'

'Indeed it is. And truth is responsibility's right arm.' The pope looked once more at the unconscious figures of his motorcade, each body comfortably stretched out, none harmed. 'And compassion, naturally.'

The Hawk was barely listening. He was holding Frescobaldi, keeping an alert eye on a stunned Sam Devereaux, and watching Captains Gris and Bleu make their final evaluations over the maps. 'What are you talking about?'

'You say you have no wish to inflict harm on my person.'

'Of course not. Wouldn't get much ransom for a corpse. Well, maybe with *your* people —'

'And Frescobaldi is as strong as an ox,' said the pope, as much to himself as to MacKenzie, while studying the half-conscious Guido. 'He always was. Signor Generale, if I said I would go with you without interference, perhaps even in the spirit of cooperation, would you grant me a small request? As one commander to another?'

The Hawk squinted at the pontiff.

'What is it?'

'A brief note, only several words - in English - to be left with my aide. I would want you to read it, of course.'

MacKenzie took out a combat pad from his field jacket, ripped off a page, unclipped the waterproof pencil and handed both to Francesco. 'You've got fifteen seconds.'

The pope put the paper against the limousine and wrote swiftly. He gave the page back to the Hawk.

> *I am safe. With God's blessing I shall reach you as the chess-playing O'Gilligan reaches me.*
>
> *Honkey.*

'If it's a code, it's pretty piss-poor. Go ahead, put it in the coloured fella's pocket. I like that part that says you're safe.'

Giovanni ran to the figure of his papal aide, stuffed the note under his cassock and returned to the Hawk. 'Now, Signor Generale, you waste time.'

'What?'

'Put Frescobaldi in the limousine! Hurry! Inside is a briefcase. With my pills. Get it, please.'

'*What?*'

'You would last five minutes in the Curia! Where is the *elicottero*?'

'The copter?'

'Yes.'

'Over there. In a clearing.'

Captains Gris and Bleu had completed their swift conference. Gris called out. 'We have briefed the men, General. We go! We meet at Zaragolo!'

'Zaragolo!' said the pontiff. 'The airport at Monti Prenestini?'

'Yes,' answered the Hawk, staring with sudden concentration on Pope Francesco. 'What about it?'

'Tell them to stay north of Rocca Priora! There are battalions of police in Rocca Priora.'

'That's east of Frascati —'

'Yes!'

'You heard him, Captains! Outflank Rocca Priora! *Now, scramble!'* roared the Hawk.

'No!' screamed Sam, backing away on the road, looking up at the hill. 'Everybody's crazy! You're out of your minds! I'm going to stop you. All of you!'

'Young man!' Giovanni stood erect and addressed Sam pontifically. 'Will you please be quiet and do as the general says?!'

Noir emerged from the clearing. 'The bird's ready, General! We've got a clean lift-off area.'

'We've also got an extra passenger. Get the counsellor, Captain. You might show him a needle, if you can manage it.'

'With real pleasure,' said Noir.

'One dosage, Captain!'

'Shit!'

And so Giovanni Bombalini, the Holy Father of the Catholic Church, and MacKenzie Hawkins, two-time winner of the Congressional Medal of Honour, put Guido Frescobaldi into the papal limousine and ran like hell through the Appian forest to the helicopter.

It was difficult for Francesco. The pontiff swore mildly at Sebastian, the patron saint of athletes, and finally in desperation pulled up the skirts of his habit, displaying rather thick peasant legs, and damn near beat MacKenzie to the aircraft.

The Lear jet soared above Zaragolo's cloud cover, Captain Noir at the controls, Captain Rouge in the co-pilot's seat. The Hawk and the pope sat in the forward section, across from one another, each by a window.

Bewildered, MacKenzie glanced over at Francesco. He knew from long years of experience that when command was stymied, the best thing to do was to do nothing, unless the combat at hand required immediate counter-strike.

Such was not the case now. The problem was that Francesco did not behave like any enemy the Hawk had ever fought.

Goddamn!

There he sat, his heavy robes unbuttoned down to his undershirt, his shoes off, and his hands folded casually across his wide girth, looking out of the Lear's window like some kind of happy delicatessen proprietor on his first aeroplane ride. It was amazing. And confusing.

Goddamn!

Why?

MacKenzie realized that there was no point in wearing his stocking mask any longer. The others had to, for their own protection, but for him it made no difference.

He removed it with a grateful sigh. Francesco looked over at him, not unpleasantly. The pope nodded his head, as if to say, Nice to meet you face to face.

Goddamn!

MacKenzie reached into his pocket for a cigar. He lifted one out, bit off the end, and pulled out a book of matches.

'*Per favore*?' Francesco was leaning towards him.

'What?'

'A cigar, Signor Generale. For me. Do you mind?'

'Oh, no, not at all. Here you are.' Hawkins extracted a second cigar from the pack and handed it to the pontiff. And then, as an afterthought, reached into his other pocket for the clipper.

But it was too late.

Francesco had bitten off the end, spat it out – somehow

without offence - taken the matches from Mac's hand, and struck one.

Pope Francesco, the Vicar of Christ, lighted up. And as the circles of aromatic smoke rose above his head, the pontiff sat back in the seat, crossed his legs under his habit, and enjoyed the scenery below.

'*Grazie*,' Francesco said.

'*Prego*', replied MacKenzie.

PART FOUR

The ultimate success of any corporation is dependent upon its major product or service. It is imperative that the projected consumer be convinced through aggressive public relations techniques that the product, or service, is essential – to his very existence, if possible.

Shepherd's Laws of Economics:
Book CCCXXI, Chapter 173

CHAPTER TWENTY-FOUR

Sam sat in the cushioned, wrought iron chair at the northwest corner of the Machenfeld gardens. Anne had picked the spot after careful deliberation; it was the area of the gardens that provided the best view of the Matterhorn whose peak could be seen in the distance.

It had been three weeks now since the awful thing:

Ground Zero.

The captains and the Turks had departed – for unknown parts of the world, never to be heard from again. The staff had been reduced to one cook, who helped Anne and Sam with the housecleaning and the gardens. MacKenzie was not very good at either chore, but he did take turns driving into the village for the newspapers. Too, he checked daily with the high-priced doctor he had flown in from New York, just in case. The doctor, a specialist in internal medicine, had no idea why he was being paid such extraordinary sums of money to do absolutely nothing but live lavishly in a lakeside residence, and so in the spirit of the AMA he accepted the unreported cash and did not complain.

Francesco (Sam could not bring himself to say pope) had settled comfortably into the sealed-off top-floor apartments and could be seen daily walking on the ramparts through his rooftop gardens.

MacKenzie had really done it! He had won the biggest military objective of his career.

And he was currently, through a convoluted series of extraordinarily complex, untraceable conduits, making his ransom demands of the Vatican. Ultrahigh-frequency radio codes arcing from the Alps to Beirut to Algiers; relayed by desert and ocean towers from Marseilles, to Paris, to Milan, and so on to Rome.

According to the schedules he had imposed, the Vatican reply was to be radioed out of Rome and relayed from Beirut by 5 p.m.

MacKenzie had left Machenfeld to drive to the isolated transmission centre - a lone cabin high in the upper Alps, in which was installed the finest, most sophisticated radio equipment obtainable. It had been delivered to Machenfeld by Les Châteaux Suisses but put into operation by the Hawk himself. No one but MacKenzie knew the location of the mountain retreat.

Oh, my God! Five o'clock this afternoon! Sam forced his thoughts away from the awful thing.

There was movement up at the château. Anne had walked out the terrace door carrying the usual large, glossy picture book under her arm and a silver tray with glasses on it in her hands. She started across the lawn to the gardens. Her walk was firm, feminine; a graceful, natural dancer oblivious to the subtle rhythms inherent in her grace. Her light brown hair fell casually, framing the clear pink skin of her lovely face. Her wide, bright blue eyes reflected whatever light they faced.

He had learned something from all the girls, thought Devereaux. Something different and individually their own - gifts to him. And if a normal life was ever to return, he would be grateful for their gifts.

But perhaps he had learned the most important thing from Anne: Try for improvement - but don't deny what's past.

There was laughter on the lawn. Anne was looking up at the ramparts where Francesco, dressed in a colourful ski sweater, was leaning over the parapet.

It had become their private game, Anne's and Francesco's. Whenever the Hawk was out of sight they held conversations. And Sam was sure - because Anne would not deny it - that she had made numerous trips up to his private apartments bringing him glasses of chianti, which was specifically forbidden from his diet. Anne and Francsco had become good friends.

Several minutes later that judgement was confirmed. Anne placed the silver tray with the drinks on the table next to Sam. Her eyes were smiling.

'Did you know, Sam, that Jesus was a very practical, down-to-earth person. When he washed Mary Magdalene's feet, he was letting everybody know she was a human being. Maybe a very fine one, in spite of what she used to do. And that people shouldn't throw rocks at her because maybe their feet weren't so clean, either.'

MacKenzie climbed the final precipice by means of an Alpine hook. The last two hundred yards of the spiralling summit road were too deep with mountain snow for the motorcycle, so it was faster to make the final ascent directly. It was eleven minutes to five, Zürich time.

The signals would commence in eleven minutes. From Beirut. They would be repeated after an interval of five minutes, to double-check for decoding errors. At the end of the second series he would confirm reception by transmitting the air-clearance code to the relay in Beirut: four dashes, repeated twice.

Once inside, the Hawk started the generators and watched with satisfaction as the myriad wheels spun with a smooth whirring sound within the casing, and the dials began registering *output*.

When the two green lights went on, signifying maximum performance, he plugged in the single electric heater, feeling the warmth of the glowing coils. He reached over to the powerful shortwave equipment, flipped on the receiving switches and turned the amplifier spools to high volume. Three minutes to go.

He walked to the wall. Slowly he began to turn a handle, hearing the gears mesh. Outside, beyond the iron grillework of the tiny window, he could see a webbed disc swing out and up on its track.

He returned to the radio receiving panel and revolved the parallel megacycle and tetracycle dials with delicate precision. The voices of a dozen languages emerged from the amplifiers. When the needles were in the exact parallel cycle points there was a silence. One minute to go.

MacKenzie took out a cigar from his pocket and lighted up. He inhaled with real contentment and blew out the smoke in ring after ring.

Suddenly the signals were there. Four short, high-pitched dashes; repeated once. The channel was cleared.

He picked up a pencil, his hand poised above a page of notepaper, prepared to write out the code as it was beamed from Beirut.

The message terminated, the Hawk had five minutes to decode. To convert the signals into numbers, then transfer the numbers into letters and the letters into words.

When he had finished, he stared in disbelief at the Vatican reply.

It was impossible!

Obviously, he had made several errors in receiving the Beirut transmission.

The signals began again.

The Hawk started writing on a fresh page of notepaper.

Carefully.

Precisely.

The transmission ended as it began: four dashes, repeated once.

MacKenzie put the decoding schedule in front of him. He believed he had memorized it thoroughly, but this was no time to make a mistake. He cross-checked every dot, every dash.

Every word.

There were no errors.

The unbelievable had happened.

Relative to the insane request regarding the contribution of four hundred million American dollars, by assessing worldwide dioceses on the basis of one dollar per communicant, the treasury of the Holy See is in no position to consider such a request. Or any request at all for this particular charity. The Holy Father is in excellent health and sends his blessings in the name of the Father, the Son, and the Holy Spirit.

Ignatio Quartze,
Cardinal Omnipitum,
Keeper of the Vatican Treasury

The Shepherd Company suspended operations.

MacKenzie Hawkins walked the grounds of Château Machenfeld, smoking his cigars, staring blankly at the infinite beauty of the Alps.

Sam made an accounting of the corporation's monetary assets, exclusive of the properties and equipment. Of the original capitalization of $40,000,000, there remained $12,810,431.02.

Plus a contingency expense fund of $150,000, which had not been touched.

Not bad at all. Especially since the investors, to a panicked vulture, refused reimbursement. They wanted nothing whatsoever to do with the Shepherd Company or any of its management personnel. None would even bother to file for tax losses as long as Shepherd's corporate executives promised - on the Bible, *Burke's Peerage*, *Mein Kampf*, and the Koran - never to get in touch with him again.

And Francesco, now sporting a Tyrolean hat along with his favourite ski sweater, was allowed out of the top-floor apartments. For the sake of everybody's sanity, it was agreed to refer to him as Zio Francesco, somebody's uncle.

Since he showed no inclination to go anywhere or do anything other than enjoy the company, Zio Francesco roamed freely. There was someone always nearby, but not to prevent escape; for assistance. He was, after all, in his seventies.

The cook was especially taken with him, for he spent long periods in the kitchen, helping with the sauces, and every once in a while asking permission to fix a particular dish.

He made one request of the Hawk. The Hawk refused it.

No! Absolutely no! Zio could not telephone his apartment in the Vatican! It made no difference whatsoever that his telephone was private or unlisted *or* concealed in the drawer of his bedside table! Telephone calls could be traced.

Not if they were radioed, insisted Francesco. The Hawk had impressed them all, frequently, by telling them about his complicated methods of communicating with Rome. Of course, a simple telephone call would not have to be nearly so complex. One little relay, perhaps.

No! All that spaghetti had gone to Zio's head. His brain was soft.

The Hawk's was softer, perhaps, suggested Francesco. What progress was the general making? Were not matters at a stalemate? Had not Cardinal Quartze outflanked him?

How could a telephone call change that?

How could it make things any worse? persisted Francesco. The Hawk could be at the radio, his hand on a switch, prepared to break the connection should Zio say anything improper. Was it not more advantageous to the general for at least two people to know he was alive? That the deception was *truly* a deception? There certainly was nothing to lose, for the Hawk had already lost. And possibly there was something to gain. Perhaps four hundred million American dollars.

Besides, Guido needed help. This was no criticism of his cousin, who was not only strong as a bull but a most gentle and thoughtful person. But he was new at the job and would certainly listen to his cousin Giovanni Bombalini. Helped, of course, by Giovanni's personal aide, the young American priest from Harlem.

The situation might *not* be remedied overnight – for there were matters of health and logistics to be considered. But when all was said and done, what alternative did the Hawk *have*?

He obviously had none. And so MacKenzie came down from the Alpine cabin one afternoon carrying three canvas-wrapped cartons of radio equipment and proceeded to install the instruments in a Machenfeld bedroom.

When all was completed, the Hawk issued an irrevocable command. Only he and Zio Francesco were allowed inside during radio transmissions.

That was fine with Anne and Sam. They had no desire to be there. The cook thought everybody was crazy and went back to the kitchen.

And at least twice a week from then on – very late at night – the huge disc antenna was wheeled out and raised above the battlements. Neither Sam nor Anne knew what was being said or whether anything was being accomplished, but often when they sat in the gardens to talk and look at the glorious Swiss moon, they heard great peals of laughter from the upstairs room. The Hawk and the pope were like small boys thoroughly enjoying a new game.

A secret game, played in their personal clubhouse.

Sam sat in the garden absently looking at his copy of *The Times*. Life at Château Machenfeld had become routinized. For instance, every morning one of them would drive into the village to pick up the newspapers. Coffee in the gardens with the newspapers was a wonderful way to start the day. The world was such an unholy mess; life was so peaceful at Machenfeld.

The Hawk, having discovered the existence of riding trails on the property, purchased several fine horses and rode frequently, sometimes for hours at a time. He'd found something he'd been looking for, thought Sam.

Francesco discovered oil painting. He would trek over the fields in his Tyrolean hat with Anne or the cook, set up his easel and paints, and render for posterity his impressions of the Alpine splendours. That is, when he wasn't in the kitchen, or teaching Anne to play chess, or debating – always pleasantly – with Sam over points of law.

There was one thing about Francesco that nobody talked about, but all knew had something to do with his attitude. Francesco had not been a well man when he was taken out of the Appian hills. Not well at all. It was the reason Mac had insisted on the availability of the New York specialist.

But as the weeks went by, Francesco seemed to improve in the Alpine air.

Would it have been the same, otherwise?

No one, of course, would speculate, but Francesco had said something at dinner one evening that registered on them all.

'Those doctors. I shall outlive every one of them! They would have had me buried a month ago.'

The Hawk responded with a coughing fit.

And Sam? What of him?

Whatever it was, he knew that it included Anne.

He looked at her now in the late morning sun, sitting in the chair reading the newspaper, the ever present book on the table beside her. *A Pictorial History of Switzerland* was the title today.

She was so lovely, so gloriously – herself. She'd help him become a better lawyer, by making the law seem not so important.

Now he began to think of other things.

Like reading quietly. Understanding. Evaluating.

Like – Judge Devereaux.

Oh, Boston was going to like Anne! His mother would like her, too. And Aaron Pinkus. Aaron would approve wholeheartedly.

If Judge Devereaux ever got back to Boston.

He'd think about that – tomorrow.

'Sam?' said Anne, looking over at him.

'What?'

'Did you read this article in the *Tribune*?'

'What article? I haven't seen the *Tribune*.'

'Here.' She pointed but did not give him the paper. She was engrossed. 'It's about the Catholic Church. All kinds of things. The pope has called a Fifth Ecumenical Council. And there's an announcement that a hundred and sixty-three opera companies are being subsidized, to elevate the spirit of creativity. And a famous cardinal – my God, Sam – it's that Ignatio Quartze! The one Mac yells about.'

'What about him?'

'It seems he's retiring to some villa called San Vincente. Something to do with papal disputes over Vatican allocations. Isn't that strange?'

Devereaux was silent for several moments before he replied. 'I think our friends have been very busy up on the ramparts.'

In the distance were the sounds of galloping hooves. Seconds later MacKenzie Hawkins emerged on the dirt road from beyond the trees and the fields where only weeks ago manoeuvres were held. He reined in his horse and trotted up to the northwest corner of the gardens.

'Goddamn! Isn't it a glorious day? You can see the peak of the Matterhorn!'

There was the music of a triangle coming from the other direction. MacKenzie waved; Devereaux and Anne turned and saw Francesco on the terrace outside the kitchen door, the triangle and the silver bar in his hands. He was dressed in a large apron, the Tyrolean hat firmly on his head.

Zio Francesco called out.

'Lunch, everybody! The *speciale di giorno* is *fantastico*!'

'I'm hungry as a horse!' roared back the Hawk as he patted his mount. 'What've you got, Zio?'

Francesco raised his voice to the Alpine hills. And there was music in his words.

'My dear friends. It's *Linguini Bombalini*!'

EPILOGUE

MacKenzie Hawkins, pleasantly surfeited with Zio's linguini and the splendid *chianti classico* Francesco had his cousin, Frescabaldi, ship to the railroad station in Zermatt, the Hawk wandered across the Alpine pasture to the edge of the field, its glorious view of the majestic mountains as always moving him. It was another ritual that had become part of his day. A few minutes alone, really alone, without even his horse beneath him, or the sound of human voices, only the rustle of the tall grass caressed by the gentle Alpine breezes. He needed these moments, for a man had to face both his accomplishments and his failures by himself, accepting the results without regret as long as he knew he had done his best with what was in him.

Regarding Zio, he had both lost and he had won. He had hardly reached the four hundred million dollars he envisioned, but what was left of the forty million capitalization wasn't exactly C-rations. Yet he had won something else, something far more important, a restored, healthy, *vital* Pope Francesco the First, the Pontiff who wanted more than anything else to finish the job started by John the Twenty-Third. To blow the cobwebs out of the Catacombs and bring his church into the twenty-first century. Zio would have to go back, they both had agreed to that without telling the others – sometime soon, somehow. They could work it out. Somehow.

Well, that was just goddamned *fine* for Uncle Zio, but what about *him*, what about the Hawk? What the hell was *he* supposed to do? Sit on his ass in Edelweiss and let the world pass as he *vegetated*?

'Find another cause, Mac, perhaps a somewhat more earthly one,' had suggested Francesco. 'The world abounds with them, and you have extraordinary talents my son – '

'Cut the "my son" crap, Zio.'

'Sorry, it goes with the office. If I had so many "sons", I'd make an extraordinary mockery of celibacy – which I intend to bring up one day. It's really so unnatural, so foolish, and nothing explicit in the Scriptures.'

'Maybe I should just keep you here before they hang you in St Peter's Square.'

'No, no, I must go back . . . But what about you, my friend. What *will* you do?'

The Hawk had not replied, for he had no answer then. He thought about it now, gazing at the breath-taking skyline of the snow-capped Alps, when suddenly, an eagle swooped down from some unseen high altitude perch in search of ground-bound prey that would sustain it.

An *eagle*. A lone eagle, soaring in splendour and splendid freedom, the master of the air and the earth, its wingspread incredible and mesmerizing. The magnificent bird circled in the winds, descending lower and lower, then abruptly dove with marvellous speed into a field below . . . Something *happened*! The eagle's massive wings were flapping furiously – it was caught, something had snared it, binding it to the ground! Then, in agonizing moments, the bird broke free, its movements frantic until it found the unencumbered air and soared aloft.

MacKenzie stared across at the would-be killing field, wondering what had caused the near tragic occurrence. The answer came in seconds: two men were racing out of a nearby cluster of brush, obviously annoyed that their decoyed trap malfunctioned. They picked up the lethal animal-covered instrument, one throwing it into the grass in disgust.

The incident brought back memories to the Hawk, images from long ago when he was a young officer posted to a Ranger training base somewhere in the hills of Nebraska or

Iowa, or was it Kansas? – no it was Nebraska. The eagle itself was not the sole prodder of these memories, but the great bird was a large part of it because of what it somehow historically stood for in pictures and symbols, even in name. Full headdresses crowning the heads of once powerful chiefs, the single, double and triple feathers earned by deeds of bravery by the young tribal males.

The American Indian.

There had been an Indian reservation perhaps twenty miles from the secret training base, certainly no secret to the Indians who pathetically came to beg whatever they could from the strapping, well-fed troops. So pathetic were these pilgrimages, that many of the young Rangers, the Hawk among them, trekked over to the reservation to get a clearer understanding. It was a *disgrace*! These original inhabitants, the *owners* of the land, lived in abject poverty, scandalously shafted by the white invader! Naturally the Rangers stole the Quartermaster bare and until the soldiers left for scaling cliffs on D-Day, the Indians lived better than any of them could remember.

The *American Indian* – screwed by the same kind of pricky shits who threw General MacKenzie Hawkins out of the army! That noble savage would be his *cause*! It might take months, even years, but *goddamn*, it was a quest worth serving.

The Hawk turned and raced back across the field, the tall grass whipped by his gathering speed. He saw Francesco by the vegetable garden, watering his precious herbs. 'Zio, *Zio*, I've *got* it!'

'What have you got, my son – forgive me, I mean Mac?'

'I'm going to free our American Indians, I mean *really* set them *free*!'

'They are in *chains*?' asked the bewildered Francesco, his watering-can drenching his Lederhose.

'Worse, they're in economic bondage, shafted by the white pricky shits!'

'Sometimes you can be obtuse, MacKenzie – '

'Don't you *see*, Zio? It's my grail, my quest, my *cause*! Hell, it might take me a long time, maybe even a few years, but the right *shaftees* are there, I know it, I *feel* it!'

'May this humble country priest bless in advance those you would free from this bondage? . . . In the name of the Father, the Son, and the Holy Ghost, pray to your Maker, my children. The Hawk is on your horizon.'

ROBERT LUDLUM

THE OSTERMAN WEEKEND

Encore

PART ONE
Sunday Afternoon

1

Saddle Valley, New Jersey, is a Village.

At least real estate developers, hearing alarm signals from a decaying upper middle-class Manhattan, found a Village when they invaded its wooden acres in the late 1930s.

The white, shield-shaped sign on Valley Road reads

SADDLE VALLEY
VILLAGE INCORPORATED 1862
Welcome

The 'Welcome' is in smaller lettering than any of the words preceding it, for Saddle Valley does not really welcome outsiders, those Sunday afternoon drivers who like to watch the Villagers at play. Two Saddle Valley police cars patrol the roads on Sunday afternoon.

It might also be noted that the sign on Valley Road does not read

SADDLE VALLEY, NEW JERSEY

or even

SADDLE VALLEY, N.J.

merely

SADDLE VALLEY

The Village does not acknowledge a higher authority; it is its own master. Isolated, secure, inviolate.

On a recent July Sunday afternoon, one of the two Saddle Valley patrol cars seemed to be extraordinarily thorough. The white car with blue lines roamed the roads just a bit faster than usual. It went from one end of the Village to the other – cruising into the residential areas – in front of, behind and to the sides of the spacious, tastefully landscaped one-acre lots.

This particular patrol car on this particular Sunday afternoon was noticed by several residents of Saddle Valley.

It was meant to be.

It was part of the plan.

John Tanner, in old tennis shorts and yesterday's shirt, sneakers and no socks, was clearing out his two-car garage with half an ear cocked to the sounds coming from his pool. His twelve-year-old son, Raymond, had friends over, and periodically Tanner walked far enough out on the driveway so he could see past the backyard patio to the pool and make sure the children were all right. Actually, he only walked out when the level of shouting was reduced to conversation – or periods of silence.

Tanner's wife, Alice, with irritating regularity, came into the garage through the laundry-room entrance to tell her husband what to throw out next. John hated getting rid of things, and the resulting accumulation of junk exasperated her. This time she motioned toward a broken lawn spreader which had lain for weeks at the back of the garage.

John noticed her gesture. 'I could mount it on a piece of wrought iron and sell it to the Museum of Modern Art,' he said. 'Remnants of past inequities. Pre-gardener period.'

Alice Tanner laughed. Her husband noted once again, as he had for so many years, that it was a nice laugh.

'I'll haul it to the curb. They pick up Mondays.' Alice reached for the relic.

'That's okay. I'll do it.'

'No, you won't. You'll change your mind halfway down.'

Her husband lifted the spreader over a Briggs and Stratton rotary lawn mower while Alice sidled past the small Triumph she proudly referred to as her 'status symbol'. As she started pushing the spreader down the driveway, the right wheel fell off. Both of them laughed.

'That'd clinch the deal with the museum. It's irresistible.'

Alice looked up and stopped laughing. Forty yards away, in front of their house on Orchard Drive, the white patrol car was slowly cruising.

'The gestapo's screening the peasants this afternoon,' she said.

'What?' Tanner picked up the wheel and threw it into the well of the spreader.

'Saddle Valley's finest is on the job. That's the second or third time they've gone down Orchard.'

Tanner glanced at the passing patrol car. The driver, Officer Jenkins, returned his stare. There was no wave, no gesture of greeting. No acknowledgement. Yet they were acquaintances, if not friends.

'Maybe the dog barked too much last night.'

'The baby-sitter didn't say anything.'

'A dollar fifty an hour is hush money.'

'You'd better get this down, darling.' Alice's thoughts turned from the police car. 'Without a wheel it becomes father's job. I'll check the kids.'

Tanner, pulling the spreader behind him, went down the driveway to the curb, his eyes drawn to a bright light about sixty yards away. Orchard Drive, going west, bore to the left around a cluster of trees. Several hundred feet beyond the midpoint of the bend were Tanner's nearest neighbors, the Scanlans.

The light was the reflection of sun off the patrol car. It was parked by the side of the road.

The two policemen were turned around in their seats, staring out the rear window, staring, he was sure, at *him*. For a second or two, he remained motionless. Then he started to walk toward the car. The two officers turned, started the engine and sped off.

Tanner looked after it, puzzled, then walked slowly back toward his house.

The Saddle Valley police car raced out toward Peachtree Lane; there it slowed and resumed cruising speed.

Richard Tremayne sat in his air-conditioned living room watching the Mets blow a six-run lead. The curtains of the large bay windows were open.

Suddenly Tremayne rose from his chair and went to the window. The patrol car was there again. Only now it was hardly moving.

'Hey, Ginny!' he called to his wife. 'Come here a minute.'

Virginia Tremayne walked gracefully down the three steps into the living room. 'What is it? Now you didn't call me to tell me your Mets or Jets hit something?'

'When John and Alice were over last night . . . were he and I . . . all right? I mean, we weren't too loud or anything, were we?'

'You were both plastered. But pleasant. Why?'

'I know we were drunk. It was a lousy week. But we didn't do anything outlandish?'

'Of course not. Attorneys and newsmen are models of decorum. Why do you ask?'

'Goddamn police car's gone by the house for the fifth time.'

'Oh.' Virginia felt a knot in the pit of her stomach. 'Are you sure?'

'You can't miss *that* car in the sunlight.'

'No, I guess you can't . . . You said it was a rotten week. Would that awful man be trying to . . .'

'Oh, Jesus, no! I told you to forget that. He's a loudmouth. He took the case too personally.' Tremayne continued looking out the window. The police car was leaving.

'He did threaten you, though. You said he did. He said he had connections . . .'

Tremayne turned slowly and faced his wife. 'We all have connections, don't we? Some as far away as Switzerland?'

'Dick, please. That's absurd.'

'Of course it is. Car's gone now . . . probably nothing. They're due for another raise in October. Probably checking out houses to buy. The bastards! They make more than I did five years out of law school.'

'I think you're a little edgy with a bad head. That's what I think.'

'I think you're probably right.'

Virginia watched her husband. He kept staring out the window. 'The maid wants Wednesday off. We'll eat out, all right?'

'Sure.' He did not turn round.

His wife started up into the hall. She looked back at her husband; he was now looking at her. Beads of perspiration had formed on his forehead. And the room was cool.

The Saddle Valley patrol car headed east toward Route Five, the main link with Manhattan twenty-six miles away. It stopped on a road overlooking Exit 10A. The patrolman to the right of the driver took a pair of binoculars from the glove compartment and began scanning the cars coming off the exit ramp. The binoculars had Zeiss-Ikon lenses.

After several minutes he tapped the sleeve of the driver, Jenkins, who looked over through the open window. He motioned the other man to give him the binoculars, and put them to his eyes, tracking the automobile specified by his fellow officer. He spoke one word: 'Confirmed.'

Jenkins started the car and headed south. He picked up the radio-phone. 'Two car calling in. Heading south on Register Road. Tailing green Ford sedan. New York plates. Filled with niggers or PR's.'

The crackling reply came over the speaker. 'Read you, two car. Chase 'em the hell out.'

'Will do. No sweat. Out.'

The patrol car then turned left and sped down the long incline into Route Five. Once on the highway, Jenkins pressed the accelerator to the floor and the car plunged forward on the smooth surface. In sixty seconds the speedometer read ninety-two.

Four minutes later the patrol car slowed down rounding a long curve. A few hundred yards beyond the curve stood two aluminum-framed telephone booths, glass and metal reflecting the harsh glare of the July sun.

The police car came to a stop and Jenkins' companion climbed out.

'Got a dime?'

'Oh, Christ, McDermott!' Jenkins laughed. 'Fifteen years in the field and you don't carry the change to make contact.'

'Don't be a smartass. I've got nickels, but one of them's an Indian head.'

'Here.' Jenkins took a coin from his pocket and handed it to McDermott. 'An ABM could be stuck and you wouldn't use a Roosevelt dime to alert operations.'

'Don't know that I would.' McDermott walked to the phone booth, pushed in the squeaky, shiny door, and dialed '0'. The booth was stifling, the still air so close that he kept the door open with his foot.

'I'll head down to the U-turn,' yelled Jenkins from the car window. 'Pick you up on the other side.'

'Okay . . . Operator. A collect call to New Hampshire. Area Code three-one-two. Six-five-four-oh-one. The name is Mr Leather.'

There was no mistaking the words. McDermott had placed a call to the state of New Hampshire and the telephone operator put it through. However, what the operator could not know was that this particular number did not cause a telephone to ring in the state of New Hampshire. For somewhere, in some underground complex housing thousands upon thousands of trunk lines, a tiny relay was activated and a small magnetized bar fell across a quarter-inch space and made another connection. This connection caused – not a bell – but a low humming sound to emanate from a telephone two hundred and sixty-three miles *south* of Saddle Valley, New Jersey.

The telephone was in a second-floor office in a red brick building fifty yards inside a twelve-foot-high electrified fence. The building was one of perhaps ten, all connected with one another to form a single complex. Outside the fence the woods were thick with summer foliage. The location was McLean, Virginia. The complex was the Central Intelligence Agency. Isolated, secure, inviolate.

The man sitting behind the desk in the second-floor office crushed out his cigarette in relief. He'd been waiting anxiously for the call. He noted with satisfaction that the small wheels of the recording device automatically started revolving. He picked up the telephone.

'Andrews speaking. Yes, operator, I accept the charges.'

'Leather reporting,' came the words rerouted from the state of New Hampshire.

'You're cleared. Tape going, Leather.'

'Confirming the presence of all suspects. The Cardones just arrived from Kennedy Airport.'

'We knew he landed . . .'

'Then why the hell did we have to race down here?'

'That's a rotten highway, Route Five. He could have an accident.'

'On Sunday afternoon?'

'Or any other time. You want the statistics on accidents for that route?'

'Go back to your Goddamn computers . . .'

Andrews shrugged. Men in the field were always irritated over one thing or another. 'As I read you, all three suspects are present. Correct?'

'Correct. Tanners, Tremaynes and the Cardones. All accounted for. All waiting. The first two are primed. We'll get to Cardone in a few minutes.'

'Anything else?'

'Not for now.'

'How's the wife?'

'Jenkins is lucky. He's a bachelor. Lillian keeps looking at those houses and wants one.'

'Not on our salary, McDermott.'

'That's what I tell her. She wants me to defect.'

For the briefest of seconds Andrews reacted painfully to McDermott's joke. 'The pay's worse, I'm told.'

'Couldn't be . . . There's Jenkins. Be in touch.'

Joseph Cardone drove his Cadillac into the circular drive and parked in front of the stone steps leading to the huge oak door. He turned off the engine and stretched, bending his elbows beneath the roof. He sighed and woke his boys of six and seven. A third child, a girl of ten, was reading a comic book.

Sitting beside Cardone was his wife, Betty. She looked out the window at the house. 'It's good to get away, but it's better to get home.'

Cardone laughed and put his large hand on his wife's shoulder. 'You must mean that.'

'I do.'

'You must. You say it every time we come home. The exact words.'

'It's a nice home.'

Cardone opened the door. 'Hey, Princess . . . get your brothers out and help your mother with the smaller bags.' Cardone reached in and withdrew the keys from the ignition. He started toward the trunk. 'Where's Louise?'

'She probably won't be here till Tuesday. We're

three days early, remember? I gave her off till then.'

Cardone winced. The thought of his wife's cooking was not pleasant. 'We eat out.'

'We'll have to today. It takes too long to defrost things.' Betty Cardone walked up the stone steps, taking the front-door key out of her purse.

Joe dismissed his wife's remark. He liked food and he did not like his wife's preparation of it. Rich debutantes from Chestnut Hill couldn't begin to cook like good South Side Italian mamas from Philadelphia.

One hour later he had the central air-conditioning going full blast throughout the large house, and the stuffy air, unchanged for nearly two weeks, was becoming bearable again. He was aware of such things. He'd been an exceptionally successful athlete – his route to success, both social and financial. He stepped out on the front porch and looked at the lawn with the huge willow tree centered in the grass within the circular drive. The gardeners had kept it all up nicely. They should. Their prices were ridiculous. Not that price ever concerned him any more.

Suddenly there it was again. The patrol car. This was the third time he'd seen it since leaving the highway.

'Hey, you! Hold it!'

The two officers in the car looked briefly at one another, about to race away. But Cardone had run to the curb.

'Hey!'

The patrol car stopped.

'Yes, Mr Cardone?'

'What's with the police routine? Any trouble around here?'

'No, Mr Cardone. It's vacation time. We're just checking against our schedules when residents return. You were due this afternoon, so we just wanted to make sure it was you. Take your house off the check list.'

Joe watched the policeman carefully. He knew the officer was lying, and the policeman knew he knew.

'You earn your money.'

'Do our best, Mr Cardone.'

'I'll bet you do.'

'Good day, sir.' The patrol car sped off.

Joe looked after it. He hadn't intended to go to the office until mid-week, but that had to be changed now. He'd go into New York in the morning.

On Sunday afternoons, between the hours of five and six, Tanner closeted himself in his study, a walnut-paneled room with three television sets, and watched three different interview shows simultaneously.

Alice knew her husband had to watch. As Director of News for Standard Mutual, it was part of his job to be aware of the competition. But Alice thought there was something sinister about a man sitting alone in a half-lit room watching three television sets at the same time, and she constantly chided him for it.

Today, Tanner reminded his wife that he'd

have to miss next Sunday – Bernie and Leila would be there, and nothing ever disturbed an Osterman weekend. So he sat in the darkened room, knowing all too well what he was going to see.

Every Director of News for every network had his favorite program, the one to which he gave extra attention. For Tanner it was the Woodward show. A half hour on Sunday afternoon during which the best news analyst in the business interviewed a single subject, usually a controversial figure currently in the headlines.

Today Charles Woodward was interviewing a substitute, Undersecretary Ralph Ashton from the State Department. The Secretary himself was suddenly unavailable, so Ashton had been recruited.

It was a gargantuan mistake by the Department. Ashton was a witless, prosaic former businessman whose main asset was his ability to raise money. That he was even considered to represent the Administration was a major error on someone's part. Unless there were other motives.

Woodward would crucify him.

As Tanner listened to Ashton's evasive, hollow replies, he realized that a great many people in Washington were soon going to be telephoning each other. Woodward's polite inflections couldn't hide his growing antagonism toward the Undersecretary. The reportorial instinct was being frustrated; soon Woodward's tones would turn to ice and Ashton would be slaughtered. Politely, to be sure, but slaughtered nevertheless.

It was the sort of thing Tanner felt embarrassed watching.

He turned up the volume of the second set. In ponderous, nasal tones a moderator was describing the backgrounds and positions of the panel of experts who were about to question the UN delegate from Ghana. The black diplomat looked for all the world as if he were being driven to the guillotine in front of a collection of male Madame Defarges. Very white, well-paid Madame Defarges.

No competition there.

The third network was better, but not good enough. No competition there either.

Tanner decided he had had enough. He was too far ahead to worry, and he'd see Woodward's tape in the morning. It was only five-twenty, and the sun was still on the pool. He heard his daughter's shouts as she returned from the country club, and the reluctant departure of Raymond's friends from the backyard. His family was together. The three of them were probably sitting outside waiting till he finished watching and started the fire for the steaks.

He'd surprise them.

He turned off the sets, put the pad and pencil on his desk. It was time for a drink.

Tanner opened the door of his study and walked into the living room. Through the rear windows, he saw Alice and the children playing follow-the-leader off the pool diving board. They were laughing, at peace.

Alice deserved it. Christ! She deserved it!

He watched his wife. She jumped – toes pointed – into the water, bobbing up quickly to make sure that eight-year-old Janet would be all right when she followed her.

Remarkable! After all the years he was more in love with his wife than ever.

He remembered the patrol car, then dismissed the thought. The policemen were simply finding a secluded spot in which to rest, or listen to the ball game undisturbed. He'd heard that policemen did that sort of thing in New York. Then why not in Saddle Valley? Saddle Valley was a lot safer than New York.

Saddle Valley was probably the safest place in the world. At least it seemed that way to John Tanner on this particular Sunday afternoon.

Richard Tremayne turned off his one television set within ten seconds after John Tanner had shut off his three. The Mets had won it after all.

His headache had left him and with it his irritability. Ginny had been right, he thought. He was simply edgy. No reason to take it out on the family. His stomach felt stronger now. A little food would fix him up again. Maybe he'd call Johnny and Ali and take Ginny over for a swim in the Tanners' pool.

Ginny kept asking why they didn't have one of their own. Heaven knew they had an income several times that of the Tanners. Everybody could see that. But Tremayne knew why.

A pool would be that one symbol too much. Too much at age forty-four. It was enough that they had moved into Saddle Valley when he was only thirty-eight. A seventy-four-thousand-dollar house at thirty-eight years of age. With a fifty-thousand-dollar down payment. A pool could wait until his forty-fifth birthday. It would make sense then.

Of course what people – clients – didn't think about was that he had graduated from Yale Law in the top five percent of his class, had clerked for Learned Hand, had spent three years at the bottom of his present firm's ladder before any real money came his way. When it came, however, it came rapidly.

Tremayne walked out to the patio. Ginny and their thirteen-year-old daughter Peg were cutting roses near a white arbor. His entire backyard, nearly half an acre, was cultivated and manicured. There were flowers everywhere. The garden was Ginny's pastime, hobby, avocation – next to sex, her passion. Nothing really replaced sex, thought her husband with an unconscious chuckle.

'Here! Let me give you a hand,' shouted Tremayne as he walked toward his wife and daughter.

'You're feeling better,' said Virginia, smiling.

'Look at these, daddy! Aren't they beautiful?' His daughter held up a bunch of red and yellow roses.

'They're lovely, sweetheart.'

'Dick, did I tell you? Bernie and Leila are flying east next week. They'll be here Friday.'

'Johnny told me . . . An Osterman weekend. I'll have to get in shape.'

'I thought you were practicing last night.'

Tremayne laughed. He never apologized for getting drunk, it happened too seldom, and he was never really difficult. Besides, last night he had deserved it. It *had* been a rotten week.

The three of them walked back to the patio. Virginia slipped her hand under her husband's arm. Peggy, growing so tall, her father thought, smiled brightly. The patio phone rang.

'I'll get it!' Peg dashed ahead.

'Why not?' shouted her father in mock exasperation. 'It's never for us!'

'We've simply got to get her her own telephone.' Virginia Tremayne pinched her husband's arm playfully.

'You're both driving me on welfare.'

'It's for you, mother. It's Mrs Cardone.' Peggy suddenly covered the receiver with her hand. '*Please* don't talk too long, mother. Carol Brown said she'd call me when she got home. You know, I told you. The Choate boy.'

Virginia Tremayne smiled knowingly, exchanging a conspiratorial look with her daughter. 'Carol won't elope without telling you, darling. She may need more than her week's allowance.'

'Oh, mother!'

Richard watched them with amusement. It was comfortable and comforting at the same time. His wife was doing a good job with their child. No one could argue with that. He knew there were those who criticized Ginny, said she dressed a little . . . flamboyantly. He'd heard that word and knew it meant something else. But the kids. The kids all flocked around Ginny. That was important these days. Perhaps his wife knew something most other women didn't know.

Things . . . 'things' were working out, thought Tremayne. Even the ultimate security, if Bernie Osterman was to be believed.

It was a good life.

He'd get on the phone with Joe if Ginny and Betty ever finished with their conversation. Then he'd call John and Ali. After Johnny's television shows were over. Perhaps the six of them could go over to the Club for the Sunday buffet.

Suddenly the memory of the patrol car flashed across his mind. He dismissed it. He had been nervous, edgy, hung over. Let's face it, he thought. It *was* Sunday afternoon and the town council *had* insisted that the police thoroughly check out the residential areas on Sunday afternoons.

Funny, he mused. He didn't think the Cardones were due back so early. Joe must have been called by his office to get in on Monday. The market was crazy these days. Especially commodities, Joe's speciality.

Betty nodded yes to Joe's question from the telephone. It solved the dinner problem. The buffet wasn't bad, even if the Club had never learned the secret of a good antipasto. Joe kept telling the manager that you had to use Genoa salami, not Hebrew National, but the chef had a deal with a Jewish supplier, so what could a mere member do? Even Joe, probably the richest of them all. On the other hand he was Italian – not

Catholic, but nevertheless Italian – and it had only been a decade since the Saddle Valley Country Club first let Italians join. One of these days they'd let Jews in – that'd be the time for some kind of celebration.

It was this silent intolerance – never spelled out – that caused the Cardones, the Tanners and the Tremaynes to make it a special point to have Bernie and Leila Osterman very much in evidence at the Club whenever they came east. One thing could be said for the six of them. They weren't bigots.

It was strange, thought Cardone as he hung up the phone and started toward the small gym on the side of his house, strange that the Tanners had brought them all together. It had been John and Ali Tanner who had known the Ostermans in Los Angeles when Tanner was just starting out. Now Joe wondered whether John and Ali really understood the bond between Bernie Osterman and him and Dick Tremayne. It was a bond one didn't discuss with outsiders.

Eventually it would spell out the kind of independence every man sought, every worried citizen might pray for; there were dangers, risks, but it was right for him and Betty. Right for the Tremaynes and the Ostermans. They had discussed it among themselves, analyzed it, thought it through carefully, and collectively reached the decision.

It might have been right for the Tanners. But Joe, Dick and Bernie agreed that the first signal had to come from John himself. That was paramount. Enough hints had been dropped and Tanner had not responded.

Joe closed the heavy, matted door of his personal gymnasium, turned on the steam dials and stripped. He put on a pair of sweatpants and took his sweatshirt off the stainless-steel rack. He smiled as he noticed the embroidered initials on the flannel. Only a girl from Chestnut Hill would have a monogram sewn on a sweatshirt.

J. A. C.

Joseph Ambruzzio Cardone.

Giuseppe Ambruzzio Cardione. Second of eight children from the union of Angela and Umberto Cardione, once of Sicily and later South Philadelphia. Eventually, citizens. American flags alongside countless, cosmeticized pictures of the Virgin Mary holding a cherubic Christ-child with blue eyes and red lips.

Giuseppe Ambruzzio Cardione grew into a large, immensely strong young man who was just about the best athlete South Philadelphia High had ever seen. He was president of his senior class and twice elected to the All-City Student Council.

Of the many college scholarships offered he chose the most prestigious, Princeton, also the nearest to Philadelphia. As a Princeton halfback he accomplished the seemingly impossible for his alma mater. He was chosen All-American, the first Princeton football player in years to be so honored.

Several grateful alumni brought him to Wall Street. He'd shortened his name to Cardone, the last vowel pronounced very slightly. It had a kind of majesty, he thought. Like Cardozo. But no one was fooled; soon he didn't care. The market was expanding, exploding to the point where *everyone* was buying securities. At first he was merely a good customers' man. An Italian boy who had made good, a fellow who could talk to the emerging new-rich with money to spend; talk in ways the new-rich, still nervous about investments, could understand.

And it had to happen.

The Italians are sensitive people. They're more comfortable doing business with their own kind. A number of the construction boys – the Costellanos, the Latronas, the Battellas – who had made fortunes in industrial developments, gravitated to Cardone. Two syllables only. 'Joey Cardone,' they called him. And Joey found them tax shelters, Joey found them capital gains, Joey found them security.

The money poured in. The gross of the brokerage house nearly doubled, thanks to Joey's friends. Worthington and Bennett, members, NY Stock Exchange, became Worthington, Bennett and Cardone. From that point it was a short leap to Bennett-Cardone, Ltd.

Cardone was grateful to his *compares*. But the reason for his gratitude was also the reason why he shuddered just a bit when a patrol car appeared too frequently around his house. For a few of his *compares*, perhaps more than a few, were on the fringes – perhaps more than the fringes – of the underworld.

He finished with the weights and climbed on his rowing machine. The perspiration was pouring out and he felt better now. The menace of the patrol car began to diminish. After all, ninety-nine percent of the Saddle Valley families returned from vacations on Sunday. Who ever heard of people coming back from a vacation on a Wednesday? Even if the day were listed as such at the police station, a conscientious desk sergeant might well consider it an error and change it to Sunday. No one returned on Wednesday. Wednesday was a business day.

And who would ever take seriously the idea that Joseph Cardone had anything to do with the Cosa Nostra? He was the living proof of the work ethic. The American Success Story. A Princeton All-American.

Joe removed his sweatshirt and walked into the steam room, now dense with vapor. He sat on the bench and breathed deeply. The steam was purifying. After nearly two weeks of French-Canadian cooking, his body needed purifying.

He laughed aloud in his steam room. It was good to be home, his wife was right about that. And Tremayne told him the Ostermans would be flying in Friday morning. It'd be good to see Bernie and Leila again. It had been nearly four months. But they'd kept in touch.

Two hundred and fifty miles south of Saddle Valley, New Jersey, is that section of the nation's capital known as Georgetown. In Georgetown the pace of life changes every day at 5:30 P.M. Before, the pace is gradual, aristocratic, even delicate. After, there is a quickening – not sudden, but with a growing momentum. The residents, for the most part men and women of power and wealth and commitment to both, are dedicated to the propagation of their influence.

After five-thirty, the games begin.

After five-thirty in Georgetown, it is time for stratagems.

Who is where? . . . Why are they there?

Except on Sunday afternoon, when the power-brokers survey their creations of the previous week, and take the time to restore their strength for the next six days of strategy.

Let there be light and there *was* light. Let there be rest and there *is* rest.

Except, again, not for all.

For instance, not for Alexander Danforth, aide to the President of the United States. An aide without portfolio and without specified activities.

Danforth was the liaison between the all-securities communications room in the underground levels of the White House and the Central Intelligence Agency in McLean, Virginia. He was the compleat power-broker because he was never in evidence, yet his decisions were among the most important in Washington. Regardless of administrations, his quiet voice was heeded by all. It had been for years.

On this particular Sunday afternoon, Danforth sat with the Central Intelligence Agency's Deputy Administrator, George Grover, beneath the bougainvillea tree on Danforth's small backyard patio, watching television. The two men had reached the same conclusion John Tanner had reached two hundred and fifty miles north: Charles Woodward was going to make news tomorrow morning.

'State's going to use up a month's supply of toilet tissue,' Danforth said.

'They should. Whoever let Ashton go on? He's not only stupid, he *looks* stupid. Stupid and slippery. John Tanner's responsible for this program, isn't he?'

'He is.'

'Smart son of a bitch. It'd be nice to be certain he's on our side,' Grover said.

'Fassett's assured us.' The two men exchanged looks. 'Well, you've seen the file. Don't you agree?'

'Yes. Yes, I do. Fassett's right.'

'He generally is.'

There were two telephones on the ceramic table in front of Danforth. One was black with an outdoor plug-in jack on the ground. The other was red and a red cable extended from inside the house. The red phone hummed – it did not ring. Danforth picked it up.

'Yes . . . Yes, Andrews. Good . . . Fine. Ring Fassett on Redder and tell him to come over. Has Los Angeles confirmed the Ostermans? No change? . . . Excellent. We're on schedule.'

Bernard Osterman, CCNY, Class of '46, pulled the page out of his typewriter and glanced at it. Adding it to the bottom of a thin sheaf of papers, he stood up. He walked around his kidney-shaped pool and handed the manuscript to his wife, Leila, who sat naked in her lounge chair.

Osterman was naked too.

'You know, an undressed woman's not particularly attractive in sunlight.'

'You think you're a portrait in beige? . . . Give.' She took the pages and reached for her large, tinted glasses. 'Is this the finish?'

Bernie nodded. 'When are the kids getting home?'

'They'll call from the beach before they start back. I told Marie to make sure they phone. I wouldn't want Merwyn to find out about naked girls in sunlight at his age. There's enough aversion to that in this town.'

'You've got a point. Read.' Bernie dove into the pool. He swam back and forth rapidly for three minutes . . . until he was out of breath. He was a good swimmer. In the Army they made him a swimming instructor at Fort Dix. 'Speed-Jew' they had called him at the Army pool. But never to his face. He was a thin man, but tough. If CCNY had had a football team instead of a joke, he would have been its captain. An end. Joe Cardone told Bernie he could have used him at Princeton.

Bernie had laughed when Joe told him that. In spite of the surface democratization of the Army experience – and it was surface – it had never occurred to Bernard Osterman, of the Tremont Avenue Ostermans, Bronx, New York, to vault time-honored barriers and enter the Ivy League. He might have been able to, he was bright and there was the GI Bill, but it simply never entered his thinking.

It wouldn't have been comfortable then – in 1946. It would be now; things had changed.

Osterman climbed up the ladder. It was good that he and Leila were going to the east coast, back to Saddle Valley for a few days. It was somehow akin to taking a brief, concentrated course in pleasant living whenever they returned. Everyone always said the east was hectic, pressurized – far more so than Los Angeles; but that wasn't so. It only seemed that way because the area of action was more confined.

Los Angeles, *his* Los Angeles, which meant Burbank, Hollywood, Beverly Hills, was where the real insanity was practiced. Men and women racing crazily up and down the aisles of a palm-lined drug store. Everything on sale, everything labeled, everyone competing in their psychedelic shirts and orange slacks.

There were times when Bernie just wanted to see someone dressed in a Brooks Brothers suit and a button-down broadcloth. It didn't really mean anything, not actually; he didn't give much of a damn what costumes the tribes of Los Angeles wore. Perhaps it was just the continual, overbearing assault on the eyes.

Or perhaps he was entering one of his downswings again. He was wearying of it all.

Which was unfair. The palm-lined drug store had treated him very well.

'How is it?' he asked his wife.

'Pretty good. You may even have a problem.'

'What?' Bernie grabbed a towel from a stack on the table. 'What problem?'

'You could be stripping too many layers away. Too much pain, maybe.' Leila flipped over a page as her husband smiled. 'Be quiet a minute and let me finish. Perhaps you'll snap out of it.'

Bernie Osterman sat down in a webbed chair and let the warm California sun wash over his body. There was still a smile on his lips; he knew what his wife meant and it was comforting to him. The years of formula writing hadn't destroyed his ability to strip away the layers – when he wanted to.

And there were times when there was nothing more important to him than to want to. To prove to himself that he could still do it. The way he used to back in the days when they lived in New York.

They were good days. Provocative, exciting, filled with commitment and purpose. Only there was never anything else really – just commitment, just purpose. A few flattering reviews written by other intense young writers. He'd been called *penetrating* then; *perceptive, incisive.* Once, even, *extraordinary.*

It hadn't been enough. And so he and Leila came to the palm-lined drug store and willingly, happily trained their talents for the exploding world of the television residual.

Someday, though. Someday, thought Bernard Osterman, it would happen again. The luxury of sitting down with all the time in the world to really do it. Make a big mistake if he had to. It was important to be able to think like that.

'Bernie?'

'Yes?'

Leila draped a towel over her front and pushed the latch on the lounge chair so the back raised itself. 'It's beautiful, sweetie. I mean really very beautiful, and I think you know it's not going to work.'

'It does work!'

'They won't sit still for it.'

'Fuck 'em!'

'We're being paid thirty thousand for a one-hour drama, Bernie. Not a two-hour exorcism ending in a funeral home.'

'It's not an exorcism. It happens to be a sad story based on very real conditions, and the conditions don't change. You want to drive down to the barrio and take a look?'

'They won't buy it. They'll want rewrites.'

'I won't make them!'

'And they'll hold the balance. There's fifteen thousand coming to us.'

'Son of a bitch!'

'You know I'm right.'

'Talk! All Goddamned talk! This season we'll have *meaning*! *Controversy*! . . . Talk!'

'They look at the figures. A rave in *The Times* doesn't sell deodorant in Kansas.'

'Fuck 'em.'

'Relax. Take another swim. It's a big pool.' Leila Osterman looked at her husband. He knew what that look meant and couldn't help smiling. A little sadly.

'OK, fix it then.'

Leila reached for the pencil and yellow pad on the table next to her chair. Bernie stood up and approached the edge of the pool.

'You think Tanner might want to join us? You think maybe I can approach him?'

His wife put down her pencil and looked up at her husband.

'I don't know. Johnny's different from us . . .'

'Different from Joe and Betty? Dick and Ginny? I don't see he's so different.'

'I wouldn't jump at him. He's still a newshawk. Vulture they used to call him, remember? The vulture of San Diego. He's got a spine. I wouldn't want to bend it. It might snap back.'

'He thinks like we do. He thinks like Joe and Dick. Like us.'

'I repeat. Don't jump. Call it the well-advertised woman's intuition, but don't jump . . . We could get hurt.'

Osterman dove into the pool and swam thirty-six feet under water to the far end. Leila was only half right, he thought. Tanner was an uncompromising newsman but he was also a sensible and sensitive human being. Tanner wasn't a fool, he saw what was happening – everywhere. It was inevitable.

It all came down to individual survival.

It reduced itself to being able to do what one wanted to do. To write an 'exorcism' if he was capable of it. Without worrying about deodorants in the state of Kansas.

Bernie surfaced and held on to the side of the pool, breathing deeply. He pushed himself off and slowly breast-stroked back toward his wife.

'Did I box you into a corner?'

'You never could.' Leila spoke while writing on the yellow pad. 'There was a time in my life when I thought thirty thousand dollars was all the money in the world. Brooklyn's house of Weintraub was not Chase Manhattan's biggest client.' She tore off a page and secured it under a Pepsi-Cola bottle.

'I never had that problem,' said Bernie, treading water. 'The Ostermans are really a silent branch of the Rothschilds.'

'I know. Your racing colors are puce and pumpkin orange.'

'Hey!' Bernie suddenly grasped the ledge and looked excitedly at his wife. 'Did I tell you? The trainer called this morning from Palm Springs. That two-year-old we bought did three furlongs in forty-one seconds!'

Leila Osterman dropped the pad on her lap and laughed. 'You know, we're really too much! And you want to play Dostoyevski!'

'I see what you mean . . . Well, someday.'

'Sure. In the meantime keep an eye on Kansas and the other on those cockamamie horses of yours.'

Osterman chuckled and plunged toward the opposite side of the pool. He thought once more about the Tanners. John and Ali Tanner. He'd cleared their names with Switzerland. Zurich was enthusiastic.

Bernard Osterman had made up his mind. Somehow he'd convince his wife.

He was going to talk seriously to John Tanner next weekend.

Danforth walked through the narrow front hallway of his Georgetown house and opened the door. Laurence Fassett, of the Central Intelligence Agency, smiled and extended his hand.

'Good afternoon, Mr Danforth. Andrews called me from McLean. We've only met once before – I'm sure you don't remember. It's an honor, sir.'

Danforth looked at this extraordinary man and returned the smile. The CIA dossier said Fassett was forty-seven, but to Danforth he seemed much younger. The broad shoulders, the muscular neck, the unwrinkled face beneath the short-cropped blond hair: this all reminded Danforth of his own approaching seventieth birthday.

'Of course I remember. Come in, please.'

As Fassett stepped into the hallway, his gaze fell on several Degas watercolors on the wall. He took a step closer. 'These are beautiful.'

'Yes, they are. Are you an expert, Mr Fassett?'

'Oh, no. Just an enthusiastic amateur . . . My wife was an artist. We used to spend a lot of time in the Louvre.'

Danforth knew he shouldn't dwell on Fassett's wife. She had been German – with ties in East Berlin. She had been killed in East Berlin.

'Yes, yes, of course. Come this way, please.

Grover's out back. We were watching the Woodward program on the patio.'

The two' men walked out onto the flagstone and brick backyard. George Grover rose from his chair.

'Hello, Larry. Things are beginning to move.'

'Looks that way. It can't be too quick for me.'

'Nor for any of us, I shouldn't think,' said Danforth. 'Drink?'

'No, thank you, sir. If you don't mind, I'd rather make this as quick as possible.'

The three men sat down around the ceramic table. 'Then let's pick up from where we are right now,' Danforth said. 'What is the immediate plan?'

Fassett looked bewildered. 'I thought it had all been cleared through you.'

'Oh, I've read the reports. I just want the information first-hand from the man in charge.'

'All right, sir. Phase one is complete. The Tanners, the Tremaynes and the Cardones are all in Saddle Valley. No immediate vacations planned, they'll be there throughout the coming week. This information is confirmed from all our sources. There are thirteen agents in the town and the three families will be under constant surveillance . . . Intercepts have been placed on all telephones. Untraceable.

'Los Angeles has established the Ostermans' flight on Friday to be Number 509, arriving Kennedy at 4:50 Eastern Daylight Time. Their usual procedure is to take a taxi directly out to the suburbs. The cab will be followed, of course . . .'

'If, by then, they're adhering to normal patterns,' interrupted Grover.

'If they're not, they won't be on that plane . . . Tomorrow we bring Tanner down to Washington.'

'He has no inkling at the moment, does he?' asked Danforth.

'None at all – other than the patrol car, which we'll use if he balks tomorrow morning.'

'How do you think he'll take it?' Grover leaned forward on his seat.

'I think it'll blow his mind.'

'He may refuse to cooperate,' Danforth said.

'That's not likely. If I do my job, he won't have a choice.'

Danforth looked at the intense, muscular man who spoke so confidently. 'You're anxious that we succeed, aren't you? You're very committed.'

'I have reason to be.' Fassett returned the old man's stare. When he continued it was in a matter-of-fact tone. 'They killed my wife. They ran her down on the Kurfürstendamm at two o'clock in the morning – while I was being "detained". She was trying to find me. Did you know that?'

'I've read the file. You have my deepest sympathy . . .'

'I don't want your sympathy. Those orders came from Moscow. I want them. I want Omega.'

PART TWO

Monday
Tuesday
Wednesday
Thursday

2

Monday – 10:15 A.M.

Tanner left the elevator and walked down the thickly carpeted corridor toward his office. He'd spent twenty-five minutes in the screening room watching the Woodward tape. It confirmed what the newspapers had reported: Charles Woodward had exposed Undersecretary Ashton as a political hack.

There had to be a lot of embarrassed men in Washington, he thought.

'Quite a show, wasn't it?' his secretary said.

'Out-of-sight, as my son would put it. I don't think we can expect many dinner invitations to the White House. Any calls?'

'From all over town. Mainly congratulations; I left the names on your desk.'

'That's comforting. I may need them. Anything else?'

'Yes, sir. The FCC called twice. A man called Fassett.'

'Who?'

'Mr Laurence Fassett.'

'We've always dealt with Cranston down there.'

'That's what I thought, but he said it was urgent.'

'Maybe the State Department's trying to get us arrested before sundown.'

'I doubt it. They'd at least wait a day or two; it'd look less political.'

'You'd better get him back. To the FCC everything's urgent.' Tanner crossed into his office, sat down at his desk, and read through the messages. He smiled; even his competition had been impressed.

The telephone intercom buzzed. 'Mr Fassett's on one, sir.'

'Thanks.' Tanner pushed the appropriate button. 'Mr Fassett? Sorry I was out of the office when you called.'

'It's my place to apologize,' said the polite voice at the other end of the line. 'It's just that I have a difficult schedule today, and you're a priority.'

'What's the problem?'

'Routine but urgent is the best way I can describe it. The papers you filed with us in May for Standard's news division were incomplete.'

'What?' John remembered something FCC's Cranston had said to him a few weeks ago. He also recalled that Cranston had said it was unimportant. 'What's missing?'

'Two signatures of yours for one thing. On pages seventeen and eighteen. And the breakdown of projected public service features for the six-month period commencing in January.'

John Tanner did remember now. It had been Cranston's fault. Pages seventeen and eighteen had been missing from the folder sent from Washington for Tanner's signature – a point which the network's legal department had made to Tanner's office – and the service feature blanks were to be left open for another month, pending network decisions. Cranston, again, had agreed.

'If you'll check, you'll find your Mr Cranston omitted the pages you refer to and the specific service features were postponed. He agreed to that.'

There was a momentary pause from Washington. When Fassett spoke his voice held a touch less politeness than it had previously.

'In all deference to Cranston, he had no authority to make such a decision. Surely you have the information now.' It was a statement.

'Yes, as a matter of fact, we do. I'll send it out Special Delivery.'

'I'm afraid that's not good enough. We'll have to ask you to get down here this afternoon.'

'Now, wait a minute. That's kind of short notice, isn't it?'

'I don't make the rules. I just carry them out. As of two months ago Standard Mutual Network is operating in violation of the FCC code. We can't allow ourselves to be put in that position. Regardless of who's responsible, that is a fact. You're in violation. Let's get it cleared up today.'

'All right. But I warn you, if this action is in any way a harassment emanating from the State Department, I'll bring down the network attorneys and label it for what it is.'

'I not only don't like your insinuation, but I don't know what you're talking about.'

'I think you do. The Woodward Show yesterday afternoon.'

Fassett laughed. 'Oh, I heard about that. The *Post* did quite a story on it . . . And I think you can put your mind at ease. I tried to reach you twice last Friday.'

'You did?'

'Yes.'

'Wait a minute.' Tanner pushed the *hold* button and then the *local*. 'Norma? Did this Fassett try to get me Friday?'

There was a short silence while Tanner's secretary checked Friday's call sheet. 'Could be. There were two calls from Washington, an Operator thirty-six in DC for you to reach if you returned by four. You were in the studio till five-thirty.'

'Didn't you ask who was calling?'

'Of course I did. The only answer I got was that it could wait until Monday.'

'Thanks.' Tanner got back on the line with Fassett. 'Did you leave an operator's number?'

'Operator three-six, Washington. Till 4:00 P.M.'

'You didn't give your name or identify the agency . . .'

'It was Friday. I wanted to get out early. Would you have felt better if I'd left an urgent call you couldn't return?'

'Okay, okay. And this can't wait for the mails?'

'I'm sorry, Mr Tanner. I mean I'm really *very* sorry, but I have my instructions. Standard Mutual's not a small local station. The filing should have been completed weeks ago . . . Also,' here Fassett laughed again, 'the way you keep stepping on exposed toes, I wouldn't want to be you if some wheels in the State Department found out your whole damn news department was in violation . . . And that's no threat. It couldn't be. We're both at fault.'

John Tanner smiled at the telephone. Fassett was right. The filing *was* overdue. And there was no sense risking bureaucratic reprisals. He sighed. 'I'll catch the one o'clock shuttle and be at the FCC by three or a little after. Where's your office?'

'I'll be with Cranston. We'll have the papers, and don't forget the schedules. They're only projections, we won't hold you to them.'

'Right. See you then.' Tanner pushed another button and dialed his home number.

'Hi, darling.'

'I've got to hop down to Washington this afternoon.'

'Any problems?'

'No. "Routine but urgent" was the description. Some FCC business. I'll catch a shuttle back to Newark by seven. I just wanted you to know that I'd be late.'

'Okay, darling. Do you want me to pick you up?'

'No, I'll get a cab.'

'Sure?'

'Very. It'll make me feel good to think Standard's paying the twenty bucks.'

'You're worth it. By the way, I read the reviews

on the Woodward Show. You're a regular triumph.'

'That's what I wrote across my jacket. Tanner the Triumph.'

'I wish you would,' said Alice quietly.

Even in jest she could never let it go. They had no real money problems, but Alice Tanner forever thought her husband was underpaid. It was the only serious argument between them. He could never explain that to seek more from a corporation like Standard Mutual meant just that much more obligation to the faceless giant.

'See you tonight, Ali.'

'Bye. I love you.'

As if in silent deference to his wife's complaint, Tanner commandeered one of the news cars to take him to La-Guardia Airport in an hour. No one argued. Tanner was, indeed, a triumph this morning.

During the next forty-five minutes, Tanner tied together a number of administrative loose ends. The last order of business was a call to Standard Mutual's legal department.

'Mr Harrison, please . . . Hello, Andy? John Tanner. I'm in a hurry, Andy; I've got to catch a plane. I just want to find out something. Do we have anything pending with the FCC I don't know about? Any problems? I know about the public service features but Cranston said we could hold on those . . . Sure, I'll wait.' Tanner fingered the telephone cord, his thoughts still on Fassett. 'Yes, Andy, I'm here . . . Pages seventeen and eighteen. The signatures . . . I see. Okay. Thanks. No, no problems here. Thanks again.'

Tanner replaced the phone and got out of his chair slowly. Harrison had added fuel to his vague suspicions. It all seemed just a bit too contrived. The FCC filing had been complete except for the final two pages on the fourth and fifth copies of the document. They were merely duplicates, important to no one, easily Xeroxed. Yet those pages had been missing from the file. Harrison had just commented:

'I remember, John. I sent you a memo about it. It looked to me as though they had been deliberately left out. Can't imagine why . . .'

Neither could Tanner.

3

Monday – 3:25 P.M.

To Tanner's amazement, the FCC sent a limousine to meet his plane.

Cranston's offices were on the sixth floor of the FCC Building; at one time or another every major network news director had been summoned there. Cranston was a career man – respected by the networks as well as the changing administrations – and because of this Tanner found himself resenting the unknown Laurence Fassett, who could say with indignation, '. . . Cranston had no authority to make such a decision.'

He'd never heard of Laurence Fassett.

Tanner pushed open the door to Cranston's waiting room. It was empty. The secretary's desk was bare – no pads, no pencils, no papers of any kind. What light there was came from Cranston's office door. It was open and he could hear the quiet whirr of an air conditioner. The window shades in the office were down, probably to keep out the summer sunlight. And then, against the office wall, he saw the shadow of a figure walking toward the door.

'Good afternoon,' said the man as he came into view. He was shorter than Tanner by several inches, probably five ten or eleven, but very broad in the shoulders. His blond hair was cut short, his eyes set far apart beneath bushy light-brown eyebrows. He was, perhaps, Tanner's age, but without question a more physical man. Even his stance had a potential spring to it, thought Tanner.

'Mr Fassett?'

'That's right. Won't you come in?' Fassett, instead of retreating into Cranston's office, crossed in front of Tanner to the door and locked it. 'We'd rather not have any interruptions.'

'Why not?' asked Tanner, startled.

Laurence Fassett looked about the room. 'Yes. Yes. I see what you mean. Good point. Come in, please.' Fassett walked in front of Tanner into Cranston's office. The shades of the two windows overlooking the street were pulled all the way down; Cranston's desk was as bare as his secretary's, except for two ashtrays and one other item. In the center of the cleared surface was a small Wollensak tape recorder with two cords – one in front of Cranston's chair, the other by the chair in front of Cranston's desk.

'Is that a tape recorder?' asked the news director, following Fassett into the office.

'Yes, it is. Won't you sit down, please?'

John Tanner remained standing. When he spoke it was with quiet anger. 'No, I will *not* sit down. I don't like any of this. Your methods are very unclear, or maybe *too* clear. If you intend putting anything I say down on tape, you know perfectly well I won't allow it without the presence of a network attorney.'

Fassett stood behind Cranston's desk. 'This is not FCC business. When I explain, you'll understand my . . . methods.'

'You'd better explain quickly, because I'm about to leave. I was called by the FCC to deliver the public service hours projected by Standard Mutual – which I have in my briefcase – and to sign two copies of our filing which *your* office omitted sending. You made it clear that you would be with Cranston when I arrived. Instead, I find an office which obviously is not in use . . . I'd say you'd better have a good explanation or you'll be hearing from our attorneys within an hour. And if this is any kind of reprisal against Standard Mutual's news division, I'll blast you from coast to coast.'

'I'm sorry . . . These things are never easy.'

'They shouldn't be!'

'Now hold it. Cranston's on vacation. We used his name because you've dealt with him before.'

'You're telling me you intentionally lied?'

'Yes. The key, Mr Tanner, is in the phrase you employed just now . . . "I was called by the FCC," I believe you said. May I present my credentials?' Laurence Fassett reached into his breast pocket and withdrew a small plastic case. He held it across the desk.

Tanner opened it.

The top card identified Laurence C. Fassett as an employee of the Central Intelligence Agency.

The other card was Fassett's priority permit to enter the McLean complex at any hour of day or night.

'What's this all about? Why am I here?' Tanner handed back Fassett's identification.

'That's the reason for the tape recorder. Let me show you. Before I explain our business I have to ask you a number of questions. There are two switches which can shut off the machine. One here by me, the other there by you. If at any time I ask you a question you do not care to answer, all you have to do is push the OFF switch and the machine stops. On the other hand – and, again, for your protection – if I feel you are including private information which is no concern of ours, *I* shall stop the machine.' Fassett started up the recorder with his switch and then reached across the desk for the cord in front of Tanner's chair and stopped it. 'See? Quite simple. I've been through hundreds of these interviews. You've got nothing to worry about.'

'This sounds like a pretrial examination without benefit of counsel or mandate of subpoena! What's the point? If you think you're going to intimidate me, you're crazy!'

'The *point* is one of completely positive identification . . . And you're absolutely right. If it was our intention to intimidate anyone, we picked about as vulnerable a subject as J. Edgar Hoover. And even *he* doesn't have control of a network news program.'

Tanner looked at the CIA man standing politely behind Cranston's desk. Fassett had a point. The CIA wouldn't allow itself to use so blatant a tactic on someone in his position.

'What do you mean, "completely positive identification"? You know who I am.'

'It should give you some idea of the magnitude of the information I'm empowered to deliver. Just extraordinary precaution in line with the importance of the data . . . Did you know that in the Second World War an actor – a corporal in the British army, to be exact – impersonated Field Marshal Montgomery at high-level conferences in Africa and even some of Montgomery's Sandhurst classmates didn't catch on?'

The news director picked up the cord and pushed the ON and OFF switches. The machine started and stopped. John Tanner's curiosity – mingled with fear – was growing. He sat down. 'Go ahead. Just remember, I'll shut off the tape and leave any time I want to.'

'I understand. That's your privilege – up to a point.'

'What do you mean by that? No qualifications, please.'

'Trust me. You'll understand.' Fassett's reassuring look served its purpose.

'Go ahead,' said Tanner. The CIA man picked up a manila folder and opened it. He then started the machine.

'Your full name is John Raymond Tanner?'

'Incorrect. My legal name is John Tanner. The Raymond was a baptismal name and is not registered on my birth certificate.'

Fassett smiled from across the desk. 'Very good.'

'Thank you.'

'You currently reside at 22 Orchard Drive, Saddle Valley, New Jersey?'

'I do.'

'You were born on May 21, 1924, in Springfield, Illinois, to Lucas and Margaret Tanner?'

'Yes.'

'Your family moved to San Mateo, California, when you were seven years old?'

'Yes.'

'For what purpose?'

'My father's firm transferred him to Northern California. He was a personnel executive for a department-store chain. The Bryant Stores.'

'Comfortable circumstances?'

'Reasonably so.'

'You were educated in the San Mateo public school system?'

'No. I went through the second year of San Mateo High and transferred to a private school for the final two years of secondary school. Winston Preparatory.'

'Upon graduation you enrolled at Stanford University?'

'Yes.'

'Were you a member of any fraternities or clubs?'

'Yes. Alpha Kappa fraternity. The Trylon News Society, several others I can't recall . . . Photography club, I think, but I didn't stay. I worked on the campus magazine, but quit.'

'Any reason?'

Tanner looked at the CIA man. 'Yes. I strenuously objected to the Nisei situation. The prison camps. The magazine supported them. My objection still stands.'

Fassett smiled again. 'Your education was interrupted?'

'Most educations were. I enlisted in the Army at the end of my sophomore year.'

'Where were you trained?'

'Fort Benning, Georgia. Infantry.'

'Third Army? Fourteenth Division?'

'Yes.'

'You saw service in the European theater of operations?'

'Yes.'

'Your highest rank was First Lieutenant?'

'Yes.'

'OCS training at Fort Benning?'

'No. I received a Field Commission in France.'

'I see you also received several decorations.'

'They were unit citations, battalion commendations. Not individual.'

'You were hospitalized for a period of three weeks in St Lô. Was this a result of wounds?'

Tanner looked momentarily embarrassed. 'You know perfectly well it wasn't. There's no Purple Heart on my Army record,' he said quietly.

'Would you explain?'

'I fell out of a jeep on the road to St Lô. Dislocated hip.'

Both men smiled.

'You were discharged in July of 1945 and returned to Stanford the following September?'

'I did . . . To anticipate you, Mr Fassett, I switched from an English major to the journalism school. I graduated in 1947 with a Bachelor of Arts degree.'

Laurence Fassett's eyes remained on the folder in front of him. 'You were married in your junior year to one Alice McCall?'

Tanner reached for his switch and shut off the machine. 'This may be where I walk out.'

'Relax, Mr Tanner. Just identification . . . We don't subscribe to the theory that the sins of the parents are visited upon their daughters. A simple yes or no will suffice.'

Tanner started the machine again. 'That is correct.'

At this point, Laurence Fassett picked the cord off the desk and pushed the OFF switch. Tanner watched the reels stop, and then looked at the CIA man.

'My next two questions concern the circumstances leading up to your marriage. I presume you do not care to answer them.'

'You presume correctly.'

'Believe me, they aren't important.'

'If you told me they were, I'd leave right now.' Ali had been through enough. Tanner would not allow his wife's personal tragedy to be brought up again, by anyone.

Fassett started the machine again. 'Two children were born to you and Alice Mc . . . Tanner. A boy, Raymond, now age thirteen, and a girl, Janet, now eight.'

'My son is twelve.'

'His birthday is day after tomorrow. To go back

a bit, your first employment after graduation was with *The Sacramento Daily News*.'

'Reporter. Rewrite man, office boy, movie critic and a space salesman when time permitted.'

'You stayed with the Sacramento paper for three and a half years and then obtained a position with *The Los Angeles Times*?'

'No. I was in Sacramento for . . . *two* and a half years – I had an interim job with the *San Francisco Chronicle* for about a year before I got the job at *The Times*.'

'On *The Los Angeles Times* you were quite successful as an investigative reporter . . .'

'I was fortunate. I assume you're referring to my work on the San Diego waterfront operations.'

'I am. You were nominated for a Pulitzer, I believe.'

'I didn't get it.'

'And then elevated to an editorial position with *The Times*?'

'An assistant editor. Nothing spectacular.'

'You remained with *The Times* for a period of five years . . .'

'Nearer six, I think.'

'Until January of 1958 when you joined Standard Mutual in Los Angeles?'

'Correct.'

'You remained on the Los Angeles staff until March of 1963 when you were transferred to New York City. Since that time you have received several promotions?'

'I came east as a network editor for the seven

o'clock news program. I expanded into documentaries and specials until I reached my present position.'

'Which is?'

'Director of News for Standard Mutual.'

Laurence Fassett closed the folder and shut off the tape recorder. He leaned back and smiled at John Tanner. 'That wasn't so painful, was it?'

'You mean that's it?'

'No, not . . . *it*, but the completion of the identity section. You passed. You gave me just enough slightly wrong answers to pass the test.'

'What?'

'These things,' Fassett slapped the folder, 'are designed by the Interrogations Division. Fellows with high foreheads bring in other fellows with beards and they put the stuff through computers. You couldn't possibly answer everything correctly. If you did it would mean you had studied too hard . . . For instance, you were with *The Sacramento Daily News* for three years almost to the day. Not two and a half or three and a half. Your family moved to San Mateo when you were eight years, two months, not seven years old.'

'I'll be Goddamned . . .'

'Frankly, even if you had answered everything correctly, we might have passed you. But it's nice to know you're normal. In your case, we had to have it all on tape . . . Now, I'm afraid, comes the tough part.'

'Tough compared to what?' asked the news editor.

'Just rough . . . I have to start the machine

now.' He did so and picked up a single sheet of paper. 'John Tanner, I must inform you that what I am about to discuss with you comes under the heading of classified information of the highest priority. In no way is this information a reflection on you or your family and to that I do so swear. The revealing of this information to anyone would be against the interests of the United States Government in the severest sense. So much so that those in the government service aware of this information can be prosecuted under the National Security Act, Title eighteen, Section seven-nine-three, should they violate the demands of secrecy . . . Is everything I've said so far completely clear?'

'It is . . . However, I am neither bound nor am I indictable.'

'I realize that. It is my intention to take you in three stages toward the essential, classified information. At the end of stages one and two you may ask to be excused from this interview and we can only rely on your intelligence and loyalty to your government to keep silent about what has been said. However, if you agree to the third stage, in which identities are revealed to you, you accept the same responsibility as those in government service and can be prosecuted under the National Security Act should you violate the aforementioned demands of secrecy. Is that clear, Mr Tanner?'

Tanner shifted in his seat before speaking. He looked at the revolving wheels of the tape recorder and then up at Fassett. 'It's clear, but

I'll be damned if I agree to it. You don't have any right calling me down here under false pretenses and then setting up conditions that make me indictable.'

'I didn't ask if you agreed. Only if you understood clearly what I said.'

'And if that's a threat, you can go to hell.'

'All I'm doing is spelling out conditions. Is that a threat? Is it any more than you do every day with contracts? You can walk out any time you like until you give me your consent to reveal names. Is that so illogical?'

Tanner reasoned that it wasn't, really. And his curiosity now had to be satisfied.

'You said earlier that whatever this thing is, it has nothing to do with my family? Nothing to do with my wife? . . . Or me?'

'I swore to it on this tape.' Fassett realized that Tanner had added the 'or me' as an afterthought. He was protecting his wife.

'Go ahead.'

Fassett rose from the chair and walked toward the window shades. 'By the way, you don't have to stay sitting down. They're high-impedance microphones. Miniaturized, of course.'

'I'll sit.'

'Suit yourself. A number of years ago we heard rumors of a Soviet NKVD operation which could have widespread damaging effects on the American economy should it ever amount to anything. We tried to trace it down, tried to learn something about it. We couldn't. It remained rumor. It was a better-kept secret than the Russian space program.

'Then in 1966 an East German intelligence officer defected. He gave us our first concrete knowledge of the operation. He informed us that East German Intelligence maintained contact with agents in the West – or a cell – known only as *Omega*. I'll give you the geographical code name in a minute . . . or maybe I won't. It's in step two. That's up to you. Omega would regularly forward sealed files to East German Intelligence. Two armed couriers would fly them to Moscow under the strictest secrecy.

'The function of Omega is as old as espionage itself, and extremely effective in these days of large corporations and huge conglomerates . . . Omega is a doomsday book.'

'A what?'

'Doomsday book. Lists containing hundreds, perhaps by now thousands, of individuals marked for the plague. In this case not bubonic, but blackmail. The men and women on these lists are people in decision-making positions in scores of giant companies in key fields. Many have enormous economic power. Purchasing as well as refusal-to-purchase power. Forty or fifty, acting in concert, could create economic chaos.'

'I don't understand. Why would they? Why should they?'

'I told you. Blackmail. Each of these people is vulnerable, exploitable for any of a thousand reasons. Sex, extracurricular or deviate; legal misrepresentation; business malpractice; price-fixing;

stock manipulation; tax evasion. The book touches a great many people. Men and women whose reputations, businesses, professions, even their families could be destroyed. Unless they comply.'

'It's also a pretty low view of the business world, and I'm not at all sure it's an accurate one. Not to the extent you describe it. Not to the point of economic chaos.'

'Oh? The Crawford Foundation made an in-depth study of industry leadership in the United States from 1925 to 1945. The results are still classified a quarter of a century later. The study determined that during this period thirty-two percent of the corporate financial power in this country was obtained by questionable, if not illegal, means. *Thirty-two percent!*'

'I don't believe that. If it's true it should be made public.'

'Impossible. There'd be legal massacre. Courts and money are not an immaculate combination . . . Today it's the conglomerates. Pick up the newspaper any day. Turn to the financial pages and read about the manipulators. Look at the charges and countercharges. It's a mother lode for Omega. A directory of candidates. None of those boys lives in a deep freeze. Not one of them. An unsecured loan is granted, a stock margin is expanded – temporarily – girls are provided to a good customer. Omega digs just a little with the right people and a lot of slime gets in the bucket. It's not very hard to do. You just have to be accurate. Enough so to frighten.'

Tanner looked away from the blond man who spoke with such precision. With such relaxed confidence. 'I don't like to think you're right.'

Suddenly, Fassett crossed back to the table and turned off the tape recorder. The wheels stopped. 'Why not? It's not just the information uncovered – that could be relatively harmless – but the way it's applied. Take *you*, for instance. Suppose, just suppose, a story based on occurrences around twenty some-odd years ago outside Los Angeles were printed in the Saddle Valley paper. Your children are in school there, your wife happy in the community . . . How long do you think you'd stay there?'

Tanner lurched out of his chair and faced the shorter man across the desk. His rage was such that his hands trembled. He spoke with deep feeling, barely audible.

'That's filthy!'

'That's Omega, Mr Tanner. Relax, I was only making a point.' Fassett turned the recorder back on and continued as Tanner returned warily to his chair. 'Omega exists. Which brings me to the last part of . . . stage one.'

'What's that?'

Laurence Fassett sat down behind the desk. He crushed out his cigarette, while Tanner reached into his pocket and withdrew a pack. 'We know now that there's a time table for Omega. A date for the chaos to begin . . . I'm not telling you anything you don't know when I admit that my agency is often involved in exchange of personnel with the Soviets.'

'Nothing I don't know.'

'One of ours for two or three of theirs is the normal ratio . . .'

'I know that, too.'

'Twelve months ago on the border of Albania such an exchange took place. Forty-five days of haggling. I was there, which is why I'm here now. During the exchange our team was approached by several members of the Soviet Foreign Service. The best way I can describe them to you is to call them moderates. The same as our moderates.'

'I understand what our moderates oppose. What do the Soviet moderates oppose?'

'Same thing. Instead of a Pentagon – and an elusive military-industrial complex – it's the hard-liners in the Presidium. The militarists.'

'I see.'

'We were informed that the Soviet militarists have issued a target date for the final phase of Operation Omega. On that date the plan will be implemented. Untold hundreds of powerful executives in the American business community will be reached and threatened with personal destruction if they do not follow the orders given them. A major financial crisis could be the result. An economic disaster is not impossible . . . It's the truth.

'That is the end of stage one.'

Tanner got out of his chair, drawing on his cigarette. He paced up and down in front of the desk. 'And with that information I have the option to get out of here?'

'You do.'

'You're too much. Honest to Christ, you're too much! . . . The tape's running. Go on.'

'Very well. Stage two. We knew that Omega was made up of the very same type of individual it will attack. It had to be, otherwise the contacts could never have been made, the vulnerabilities never established. In essence, we basically knew what to look for. Men who could infiltrate large companies, men who worked either in or for them, who could associate with their subjects . . . As I mentioned previously, Omega is a code name for a cell or a group of agents. There is also a geographical code name; a clearing house for the forwarding of information. Having passed through this source, the authenticity is presumably established because of its operational secrecy. The geographical code name for Omega is difficult to give an accurate translation of, but the nearest is "Chasm of . . . Leather" or "Goat Skin".'

'"Chasm of Leather"?' Tanner put out his cigarette.

'Yes. Remember we learned this over three years ago. After eighteen months of concentrated research we pinpointed the "Chasm of Leather" as one of eleven locations throughout the country . . .'

'One of them being Saddle Valley, New Jersey?'

'Let's not get ahead of ourselves.'

'Am I right?'

'We placed agents within these communities,' continued the CIA man, disregarding Tanner's question. 'We ran checks on thousands of citizens

– a very expensive exercise – and the more we researched, the more evidence we turned up that the Village of Saddle Valley was the "Chasm of Leather". It was a thorough job. Watermarks on stationery, analysis of dust particles the East German officer brought out in the sealed folders he gave us when he defected, a thousand different items checked and rechecked . . . But mainly, the information about certain residents unearthed in the research.'

'I think you'd better get to the point.'

'That will be *your* decision. I've just about concluded stage two.' Tanner remained silent, so Fassett continued. 'You are in a position to give us incalculable assistance. In one of the most sensitive operations in current US–Soviet relations, you can do what no one else can do. It might even appeal to you, for as you must have gathered from what I've said, the moderates on both sides are at this moment working together.'

'Please clarify that.'

'Only fanatics subscribe to this type of insurgency. It's far too dangerous for both countries. There's a power struggle in the Soviet Presidium. The moderates must prevail for all our sakes. One way to accomplish this is to expose even part of Omega and kill the target date.'

'How can I do anything?'

'You know Omega, Mr Tanner. You know Omega very well.'

Tanner caught his breath. For a moment he believed his heart had stopped. He felt the blood rush to his head. He felt, for an instant, somewhat sick.

'I find that an *incredible* statement.'

'I would, too, if I were you. Nevertheless, it's true.'

'And I gather this is the end of stage two? . . . You bastard. You son of a bitch!' Tanner spoke hardly above a whisper.

'Call me anything you like. Hit me if you want to. I won't hit back . . . I told you, I've been through this before.'

Tanner got out of the chair and pressed his fingers against his forehead. He turned away from Fassett, then whipped around. 'Suppose you're wrong?' he whispered. 'Suppose you Goddamn idiots have made another *mistake*!'

'We haven't . . . We don't claim to have flushed Omega out completely. However, we *have* narrowed it down. You're in a unique position.'

Tanner walked to the window and started to pull up the shade.

'Don't *touch* that! Hold it *down*!' Fassett leaped from his chair and grabbed Tanner's wrist with one hand and the string of the shade with his other. Tanner looked into the agent's eyes.

'And if I walk out of here now, I live with what you've told me? Never knowing who's in my house, who I'm talking to in the street? Living with the knowledge that you think someone might fire a rifle into this room if I lift up the shade?'

'Don't over-dramatize. These are merely precautions.'

Tanner walked back to his side of the desk but

did not sit down. 'Goddamn you,' he said softly. 'You know I can't leave . . .'

'Do you accept the conditions?'

'I do.'

'I must ask you to sign this affidavit.' He took out a page from the manila folder and placed it in front of Tanner. It was a concise statement on the nature and penalties of the National Security Act. It referred to Omega in unspecific terms – Exhibit A, defined as the tape recording. Tanner scribbled his name and remained standing, staring at Fassett.

'I shall now ask you the following questions.' Fassett picked up the folder and flipped to the back pages. 'Are you familiar with the individuals I now specify? Richard Tremayne and his wife, Virginia . . . Please reply.'

Astounded, Tanner spoke softly. 'I am.'

'Joseph Cardone, born Giuseppe Ambruzzio Cardione, and his wife, Elizabeth?'

'I am.'

'Bernard Osterman and his wife, Leila?'

'Yes.'

'Louder, please, Mr Tanner.'

'I said, yes.'

'I now inform you that one, two, or all three of the couples specified are essential to the Omega operation.'

'You're out of your mind! You're insane!'

'We're not . . . I spoke of our exchange on the Albanian border. It was made known to us then that Omega, Chasm of Leather, operated out of a Manhattan suburb – and that confirmed our analysis. That Omega was comprised of couples – men and women fanatically devoted to the militaristic policies of the Soviet expansionists. These couples were well paid for their services. The couples specified – the Tremaynes, the Cardones, and the Ostermans – currently possess coded bank accounts in Zurich, Switzerland, with amounts far exceeding any incomes ever reported.'

'You can't mean what you're saying!'

'Even allowing for coincidence, and we have thoroughly researched each party involved, it is our opinion that you are being used as a very successful cover for Omega. You're a newsman above reproach.

'We don't claim that all three couples are involved. It's conceivable that one or possibly two of the couples are being used as decoys, as you are. But it's doubtful. The evidence – the Swiss accounts, the professions, the unusual circumstances of your association – point to a cell.'

'Then how did you disqualify me?' asked Tanner numbly.

'Your life from the day you were born has been microscopically inspected by professionals. If we're wrong about you, we have no business doing what we're doing.'

Tanner, exhausted, sat down with difficulty in the chair. 'What do you want me to do?'

'If our information is correct, the Ostermans are flying east on Friday and will stay with you and your family over the weekend. Is that right?'

'It *was.*'

'Don't change it. Don't alter the situation.'

'That's impossible now . . .'

'It's the only way you can help us. *All* of us.'

'Why?'

'We believe we can trap Omega during this coming weekend. *If* we have your cooperation. Without it, we can't.'

'How?'

'There are four days remaining before the Ostermans arrive. During this period our subjects – the Ostermans, the Tremaynes, and the Cardones – will be harassed. Each couple will receive untraceable telephone calls, cablegrams routed through Zurich, chance meetings with strangers in restaurants, in cocktail lounges, on the street. The point of all this is to deliver a common message. That John Tanner is *not* what he appears to be. You are something else. Perhaps a double agent, or a Politbureau informer, or even a bona fide member of my own organization. The information they receive will be confusing, designed to throw them off balance.'

'And make my family a set of targets. I won't permit it! They'd kill us!'

'That's the one thing they won't do.'

'Why not? If anything you say is true – and I'm by no means convinced that it is. I *know* these people. I can't believe it!'

'In that event, there's no risk at all.'

'Why not?'

'If they – any one or all couples – are not involved with Omega, they'll do the normal thing. They'll report the incidents to the police or the

FBI. We'll take over then. If one or two couples make such reports and the other or others do not, we'll know who Omega is.'

'And . . . supposing you *are* right. What then? What are your built-in guarantees?'

'Several factors. All fool-proof. I told you the "information" about you will be false. Whoever Omega is will use his resources and check out what he learns with the Kremlin itself. Our confederates there are prepared. They will intercept. The information Omega gets back from Moscow will be the truth. The truth until this afternoon, that is. You are simply John Tanner, news director, and no part of any conspiracy. What will be added is the trap. Moscow will inform whoever runs a check on you to be suspicious of the *other* couples. *They* may be defectors. We divide. We bring about a confrontation and walk in.'

'That's awfully glib. It sounds too easy.'

'If any attempt was made on your life or the lives of your family, the entire Omega operation would be in jeopardy. They're not willing to take that risk. They've worked too hard. I told you, they're fanatics. The target date for Omega is less than one month away.'

'That's not good enough.'

'There's something else. A minimum of two armed agents will be assigned to each member of your family. Twenty-four-hour surveillance. They'll never be more than fifty yards away. At any time.'

'Now I know you're insane. You don't know

Saddle Valley. Strangers lurking around are spotted quickly and chased out! We'd be sitting ducks.'

Fassett smiled. 'At this moment we have thirteen men in Saddle Valley. Thirteen. They're daily residents of your community.'

'Sweet Jesus!' Tanner spoke softly. 'Nineteen-eighty-four is creeping up on us, isn't it?'

'The times we live in often call for it.'

'I don't have a choice, do I? I don't have a choice at all.' He pointed to the tape recorder and the affidavit lying beside it. 'I'm hung now, aren't I?'

'I think you're over-dramatizing again.'

'No, I'm not. I'm not dramatizing anything . . . I have to do exactly what you want me to do, don't I? I *have* to go through with it . . . The only alternative I have is to disappear . . . and be hunted. Hunted by you and – if you're right – by this Omega.'

Fassett returned Tanner's look without a trace of deceit. Tanner had spoken the truth and both men knew it.

'It's only six days. Six days out of a lifetime.'

4

Monday – 8:05 P.M.

The flight from Dulles Airport to Newark seemed unreal. He wasn't tired. He was terrified. His mind kept darting from one image to another, each visual picture pushing the previous one out into the distance. There were the sharp staring eyes of Laurence Fassett above the tape recorder's turning reels. The drone of Fassett's voice asking those interminable questions; then the voice growing louder and louder.

'Omega!'

And the faces of Bernie and Leila Osterman, Dick and Ginny Tremayne, Joe and Betty Cardone.

None of it made sense! He'd get to Newark and suddenly the nightmare would be over and he'd remember giving Laurence Fassett the public service features and signing the absent pages of the FCC filing.

Only he knew he wouldn't.

The hour's ride from Newark to Saddle Valley was made in silence, the taxi driver taking his cue from his fare in the back seat who kept lighting cigarettes and who hadn't answered him when he'd asked how the flight had been.

SADDLE VALLEY
VILLAGE INCORPORATED 1862
Welcome

Tanner stared at the sign as it caught the cab's headlights. As it receded he could only think of the words 'Chasm of Leather'.

Unreal.

Ten minutes later the taxi pulled up to his house. He got out and absently handed the driver the fare agreed upon.

'Thanks, Mr Tanner,' said the driver, leaning over the seat to take the money through the window.

'What? What did you say?' demanded John Tanner.

'I said "Thanks, Mr Tanner".'

Tanner leaned down and gripped the door handle, pulling the door open with all his strength.

'How did you know my name? You tell me how you knew my *name*!'

The taxi driver could see beads of perspiration rolling down his passenger's face, the crazy look in the man's eyes. A weirdo, thought the driver. He carefully moved his left hand toward the floor beneath his feet. He always kept a thin lead pipe there.

'Look, Mac,' he said, his fingers around the pipe. 'You don't want nobody to use your name, take the sign off your lawn.'

Tanner stepped back and looked over his shoulder. On the lawn was the wrought-iron lantern, a weatherproof hurricane lamp hanging from a crossbar by a chain. Above the lamp, reflected in the light, were the words:

THE TANNERS
22 ORCHARD DRIVE

He'd looked at that lamp and those words a thousand times. *The Tanners. 22 Orchard Drive.* At that moment they, too, seemed unreal. As if he had never seen them before.

'I'm sorry, fella. I'm a little on edge. I don't like flying.' He closed the door as the driver began rolling up the window. The driver spoke curtly.

'Take the train then, Mister. Or walk, for Christ's sake!'

The taxi roared off, and Tanner turned and looked at his house. The door opened. The dog bounded out to meet him. His wife stood in the hall light, and he could see her smile.

5

Tuesday – 3:30 A.M. *California Time*

The white French telephone, with its muted Hollywood bell, had rung at least five times. Leila thought sleepily that it was foolish to have it on Bernie's side of the bed. It never woke him, only her.

She nudged her husband's ribs with her elbow. 'Darling . . . Bernie. Bernie! It's the phone.'

'What?' Osterman opened his eyes, confused. 'The phone? Oh, the Goddamn phone. Who can hear it?'

He reached over in the darkness and found the thin cradle with his fingers.

'Yes? . . . Yes, this is Bernard Osterman . . . Long distance?' He covered the phone with his hand and pushed himself up against the headboard. He turned toward his wife. 'What time is it?'

Leila snapped on her bedside lamp and looked at the table clock. 'Three-thirty. My God!'

'Probably some bastard on that Hawaiian series. It's not even midnight there yet.' Bernie was listening at the phone. 'Yes, operator, I'm waiting . . . It's very long distance, honey. If it *is* Hawaii, they can put that producer on the typewriter; we've had it. We never should have touched it . . . Yes, operator? Please hurry, will you?'

'You said you wanted to see those islands without a uniform on, remember?'

'I apologize . . . Yes, operator, this *is* Bernard Osterman, damn it! Yes? Yes? Thank you, operator . . . Hello? I can hardly hear you. Hello? . . . Yes, that's better. Who's this? . . . What? What did you say? . . . Who *is* this? What's your name? I don't understand you. Yes, I *heard* you, but I don't understand . . . Hello? . . . Hello! Wait a minute! I said *wait* a minute!' Osterman shot up and flung his legs over the side of the bed. The blankets came after him and fell on the floor at his feet. He began punching the center bar on the white French telephone. 'Operator! Operator! The Goddamn line's dead!'

'Who was it? Why are you shouting? What did they say?'

'He . . . the son of a bitch grunted like a bull. He said, he said we were to watch out for the . . . *Tan One*. That's what he said. He made sure I heard the words. *The Tan One*. What the hell is that?'

'The *what*?'

'The Tan One! That's all he kept repeating!'

'It doesn't make sense . . . Was it Hawaii? Did the operator say where the call came from?'

Osterman stared at his wife in the dim light of the bedroom. 'Yes. I heard that clearly. It was overseas . . . It was Lisbon. Lisbon, Portugal.'

'We don't know anyone in Portugal!'

'Lisbon, Lisbon, Lisbon . . .' Osterman kept

repeating the name quietly to himself. 'Lisbon. Neutral. Lisbon was neutral.'

'What do you mean?'

'*Tan One* . . .'

'Tan . . . tan. Tanner. Could it be John Tanner? John Tanner!'

'Neutral!'

'It's John Tanner,' said Leila quietly.

'Johnny? . . . What did he mean, "Watch out"?' Why should we watch out? Why place a call at three-thirty in the morning?'

Leila sat up and reached for a cigarette. 'Johnny's got enemies. The San Diego waterfront still hurts because of him.'

'San Diego, sure! But Lisbon?'

'*Daily Variety* said last week that we're going to New York,' continued Leila, inhaling smoke deeply. 'That we'd probably stay with our ex-neighbors, the Tanners.'

'So?'

'Perhaps we're too well advertised.' She looked at her husband.

'Maybe I'll call Johnny.' Osterman reached for the phone.

Leila grabbed his wrist. 'Are you out of your *mind*?'

Osterman lay back down.

Joe opened his eyes and glanced at his watch: six-twenty-two. Time to get up, have a short workout in his gym and perhaps walk over to the Club for an hour's practice on the golf range.

He was an early riser, Betty the opposite.

She would sleep till noon whenever she had the chance. They had two double beds, one for each of them, because Joe knew the debilitating effects of two separate body temperatures under the same set of covers. The benefits of a person's sleep were diminished by nearly fifty percent when he shared a bed all night with somebody else. And since the purpose of the marriage bed was exclusively sexual, there was no point in losing the benefits of sleep.

A pair of double beds was just fine.

He finished ten minutes on the exercycle and five with seven-and-a-half-pound handbells. He looked through the thick glass window of the steam bath and saw that the room was ready.

A panel light above the gym's wall clock flashed on. It was the front doorbell. Joe had the device installed in case he was home alone and working out.

The clock read six-fifty-one, much too early for anyone in Saddle Valley to be ringing front doorbells. He put the small weights on the floor and walked to his house intercom.

'Yes? Who is it?'

'Telegram, Mr Cardione.'

'Who?'

'Cardione, it says.'

'The name is Cardone.'

'Isn't this Eleven Apple Place?'

'I'll be right there.'

He flicked off the intercom and grabbed a towel from the rack, draping it around him as he walked rapidly out of the gym. He didn't like what he had just heard. He reached the front door and opened it. A small man in uniform stood there chewing gum.

'Why didn't you telephone? It's pretty early, isn't it?'

'Instructions were to deliver. I had to drive out here, Mr Cardione. Almost fifteen miles. We keep twenty-four-hour service.'

Cardone signed for the envelope. 'Why fifteen miles? Western Union's got a branch in Ridge Park.'

'Not Western Union, Mister. This is a cablegram . . . from Europe.'

Cardone grabbed the envelope out of the uniformed man's hand. 'Wait a minute.' He didn't want to appear excited, so he walked normally into the living room where he remembered seeing Betty's purse on the piano. He took out two one-dollar bills and returned to the door. 'Here you are. Sorry about the trip.' He closed the door and ripped open the cablegram.

L'UOMO BRUNO PALIDO NON E AMICO DEL ITALIANO. GUARDA BENE VICINI DI QUESTA MANIERA. PROTECIATE PER LA FINA DELLA SETTIMANA.

DA VINCI

Cardone walked into the kitchen, found a pencil on the telephone shelf and sat down at the table. He wrote out the translation on the back of a magazine.

The light-brown man is no friend of the Italian. Be cautious of such neighbors. Protect yourself against the end of the week. Da Vinci.

What did it mean? What 'light-brown . . . neighbors'? There were no blacks in Saddle Valley. The message didn't make sense.

Suddenly Joe Cardone froze. The light-brown neighbor could only mean John Tanner. The end of the week – Friday – the Ostermans were arriving. Someone in Europe was telling him to protect himself against John Tanner and the upcoming Osterman weekend.

He snatched up the cablegram and looked at the dateline.

Zurich.

Oh, Jesus Christ! Zurich!

Someone in Zurich – someone who called himself Da Vinci, someone who knew his real name, who knew John Tanner, who knew about the Ostermans – was warning him!

Joe Cardone stared out the window at his backyard lawn. Da Vinci, Da Vinci!

Leonardo.

Artist, soldier, architect of war – all things to all men.

Mafia! Oh, Christ! Which of them?

The Costellanos? The Battellas? The Latronas, maybe.

Which of them had turned on him? And *why*? He was their *friend*!

His hands shook as he spread the cablegram on the kitchen table. He read it once more. Each sentence conjured up progressively more dangerous meanings.

Tanner!

John Tanner had found out something! But *what*?

And why did the message come from Zurich?

What would any of them have to do with Zurich?

Or the Ostermans?

What had Tanner discovered? What was he going to do? . . . One of the Battella men called Tanner something once; what was it?

'*Volturno!*'

Vulture.

'. . . no friend of the Italian . . . Be cautious . . . Protect yourself . . .'

How? From *what*? Tanner wouldn't confide in him. Why should he?

He, Joe Cardone, wasn't syndicate; he wasn't *famiglia*. What could *he* know?

But 'Da Vinci's' message had come from Switzerland.

And that left one remaining possibility, a frightening one. The Cosa Nostra had learned about Zurich! They'd use it against him unless he was able to control the 'light-brown man', the Italian's enemy. Unless he could stop whatever it was John Tanner was about to do, he'd be destroyed.

Zurich! The Ostermans!

He had done what he thought was right! What he had to do to *survive.* Osterman had pointed that out in a way that left no doubts. But it was in other hands now. Not his. He couldn't be touched any more.

Joe Cardone walked out of the kitchen and returned to his miniature gymnasium. Without putting on gloves he started pounding the bag. Faster and faster, harder and harder.

There was a screeching in his brain.

'Zurich! Zurich! Zurich!'

Virginia Tremayne heard her husband get out of bed at six-fifteen, and knew immediately that something was wrong. Her husband rarely stirred that early.

She waited several minutes. When he didn't return, she rose, put on her bathrobe, and went downstairs. He was in the living room standing by the bay window, smoking a cigarette and reading something on a piece of paper.

'What *are* you doing?'

'Look at this,' he answered quietly.

'At what?' She took the paper from his hand.

Take extreme caution with your editorial friend. His friendship does not extend beyond his zeal. He is not what he appears to be. We may have to report his visitors from California.

Blackstone

'What is this? When did you get it?'

'I heard noises outside the window about twenty minutes ago. Just enough to wake me up. Then there was the gunning of a car engine. It kept racing up and down . . . I thought you heard it, too. You pulled the covers up.'

'I think I did. I didn't pay any attention . . .'

'I came down and opened the door. This envelope was on the doormat.'

'What does it mean?'

'I'm not sure yet.'

'Who's Blackstone?'

'The commentaries. Basis of the legal system . . .' Richard Tremayne flung himself down in an armchair and brought his hand up to his forehead. With the other he rolled his cigarette delicately along the rim of an ashtray. 'Please . . . Let me think.'

Virginia Tremayne looked again at the paper with the cryptic message. '"Editorial friend." Does that mean? . . .'

'Tanner's onto something and whoever delivered this is in panic. Now they're trying to make me panic, too.'

'Why?'

'I don't know. Maybe they think I can help them. And if I don't, they're threatening me. All of us.'

'The Ostermans.'

'Exactly. They're threatening us with Zurich.'

'Oh, my God! They know! Someone's found out!'

'It looks that way.'

'Do you think Bernie got frightened? Talked about it?'

Tremayne's eye twitched. 'He'd be insane if he did. He'd be crucified on both sides of the Atlantic . . . No, that's not it.'

'What is it, then?'

'Whoever wrote this is someone I've either worked with in the past or refused to handle. Maybe it's one of the current cases. Maybe one of the files on my desk right now. And Tanner got wind of it and is making noises. They expect me to stop him. If I don't, I'm finished. Before I can afford it . . . Before Zurich goes to work for us.'

'They couldn't *touch* you!' said Tremayne's wife with fierce, artificial defiance.

'Come on, darling. Let's not kid each *other*. In polite circles I'm a merger analyst. In the boardrooms I'm a corporate raider. To paraphrase Judge Hand, the merger market is currently insane with false purchase. False. That means fake. Buying with paper. Pieces of fiction.'

'Are you in trouble?'

'Not really – I could always say I was given wrong information. The courts like me.'

'They respect you! You've worked harder than any man I know. You're the best damned lawyer there is!'

'I'd like to think so.'

'You *are*!'

Richard Tremayne stood at the large bay window looking out at the lawn of his seventy-four-thousand-dollar ranch house. 'Isn't it funny. You're probably right. I'm one of the best there is in a system I despise . . . A system Tanner would rip apart piece by piece on one of his programs if he knew what really made it go. That's what the little message is all about.'

'I think you're wrong, I think it's someone you've beaten who wants to get even. Who's trying to frighten you.'

'Then he's succeeded. What this . . . Blackstone is telling me isn't anything I don't know. What I *am* and what I *do* makes me Tanner's natural enemy. At least, he'd think so . . . If only he knew the truth.'

He looked at her and forced a smile. 'They know the truth in Zurich.'

6

Tuesday – 9:30 A.M. *California Time*

Osterman wandered aimlessly around the studio lot, trying to get his mind off the pre-dawn phone call. He was obsessed by it.

Neither he nor Leila had slept again. They'd kept trying to narrow down the possibilities and when those were exhausted they explored the more important question of why.

Why had *he* been called? What was behind it? Was Tanner onto another one of his exposés?

If he was, it had nothing to do with him. Nothing to do with Bernie Osterman.

Tanner never talked in specifics about his work. Only in generalities. He had a low pressure point when it came to what he considered injustice, and since the two men often disagreed on what constituted fair game in the marketplace, they avoided specifics.

Bernie thought of Tanner as a crusader who had never traveled on foot. He'd never gone through the experience of watching a father come home and announce he had no job the next day. Or a mother staying up half the night sewing wonders into a worn-out garment for a child going to school in the morning. Tanner could afford his indignation, and he had done fine work. But there were some things he would never understand. It was why Bernie had never discussed Zurich with him.

'Hey, Bernie! Wait a minute!' Ed Pomfret, a middle-aged rotund, insecure producer, caught up with him on the sidewalk.

'Hello, Eddie. How's everything?'

'Great! I tried reaching you at your office. The girl said you were out.'

'Nothing to do.'

'I got the word, guess you did, too. It'll be good working with you.'

'Oh? . . . No, I didn't get the word. What are we working on?'

'What's this? Jokes?' Pomfret was slightly defensive. As if he was aware that Osterman thought he was a second-rater.

'No jokes. I'm wrapping up here this week. What are you talking about? Who gave you the word?'

'That new man from Continuity phoned me this morning. I'm handling half of the segments on *The Interceptor* series. He said you were doing four running shots. I like the idea.'

'What idea?'

'The story outline. Three men working on a big, quiet deal in Switzerland. Right away it grabbed me.'

Osterman stopped walking and looked down at Pomfret.

'Who put you up to this?'

'Put me up to what?'

'There's no four shots. No outlines. No deal. Now tell me what you're trying to say.'

'You've got to be joking. Would I kid powerhouses like you and Leila? I was tickled to death. Continuity told me to phone you, ask for the outlines!'

'Who called you?'

'What's his name . . . That new exec Continuity brought from New York.'

'Who?'

'He told me his name . . . Tanner. That's it. Tanner. Jim Tanner, John Tanner . . .'

'John Tanner doesn't work here! Now, who told you to tell me this?' He grabbed Pomfret's arm. 'Tell me, you son of a bitch!'

'Take your hands off me! You're crazy!'

Osterman recognized his mistake: Pomfret was no more than a messenger boy. He let go of the producer's arm. 'I'm sorry, Eddie. I apologize . . . I've got a lot on my mind. Forgive me, please. I'm a pig.'

'Sure, sure. You're uptight, that's all. You're very uptight, man.'

'You say this fellow – Tanner – called you this morning?'

'About two hours ago. To tell you the truth, I didn't know him.'

'Listen. This is some kind of a practical joke. You know what I mean? I'm not doing the series, believe me . . . Just forget it, okay?'

'A joke?'

'Take my word for it, okay? . . . Tell you what; they're talking to Leila and me about a project here. I'll insist on you as the money-man, how about it?'

'Hey, thanks!'

'Don't mention it. Just keep this little joke between the two of us, right?'

Osterman didn't bother to wait for Pomfret's grateful reply. He hurried away down the studio street, toward his car. He had to get home to Leila.

A huge man in a chauffeur's uniform was sitting in the front seat of his car! He got out as Bernie approached and held the back door open for him.

'Mr Osterman?'

'Who are you? What are you doing in . . .'

'I have a message for you.'

'But I don't want to hear it! I want to know why you're sitting in my car!'

'Be very careful of your friend, John Tanner. Be careful what you say to him.'

'What in God's name are you talking about?'

The chauffeur shrugged. 'I'm just delivering a message, Mr Osterman. And now would you like me to drive you home?'

'Of course not! I don't know you! I don't understand . . .'

The back door closed gently. 'As you wish, sir. I was simply trying to be friendly.' With a smart salute, he turned away.

Bernie stood alone, immobile, staring after him.

7

Tuesday – 10:00 A.M.

'Are any of the Mediterranean accounts in trouble?' Joe Cardone asked.

His partner, Sam Bennett, turned in his chair to make sure the office door was shut. 'Mediterranean' was their code word for those clients both partners knew were lucrative but dangerous investors. 'Not that I know of,' he said. 'Why? Did you hear something?'

'Nothing direct . . . Perhaps nothing at all.'

'That's why you came back early, though?'

'No, not really.' Cardone understood that even for Bennett not all explanations could be given. Sam was no part of Zurich. So Joe hesitated. 'Well, partly. I spent some time at the Montreal Exchange.'

'What did you hear?'

'That there's a new drive from the Attorney General's office; that the SEC is handing over everything they have. Every possible Mafia connection with a hundred thousand or more is being watched.'

'That's nothing new. Where've you been?'

'In Montreal. That's where I've been. I don't like it when I hear things like that eight hundred miles from the office. And I'm Goddamned reluctant to pick up a telephone and ask my partner if any of our clients are currently before a grand jury . . . I mean, telephone conversations aren't guaranteed to be private any more.'

'Good Lord!' Bennett laughed. 'Your imagination's working overtime, isn't it?'

'I hope so.'

'You know damned well I'd have gotten in touch with you if anything like that came up. Or even looked like it *might* come up. You didn't cut a vacation short on those grounds. What's the rest?'

Cardone avoided his partner's eyes as he sat down at his desk. 'Okay. I won't lie. Something else did bring me in . . . I don't think it has anything to do with us. With *you* or the company. If I find out otherwise, I'll come to you, all right?'

Bennett got out of the chair and accepted his partner's non-explanation. Over the years he'd learned not to question Joe too closely. For in spite of his partner's gregariousness, Cardone was a private man. He brought large amounts of capital into the firm and never asked for more than a proper business share. That was good enough for Bennett.

Sam walked to the door, laughing softly. 'When are you going to stop running from the phantom of South Philadelphia?'

Cardone returned his partner's smile. 'When it stops chasing me into the Bankers' Club with a hot lasagna.'

Bennett closed the door behind him, and Joe

returned to the ten-day accumulation of mail and messages. There was nothing. Nothing that could be related to a Mediterranean problem. Nothing that even hinted at a Mafia conflict. Yet something had happened during those ten days; something that concerned Tanner.

He picked up his telephone and pushed the button for his secretary. 'Is this everything? There weren't any other messages?'

'None you have to return. I told everyone you wouldn't be back until the end of the week. Some said they'd call then, the others will phone you Monday.'

'Keep it like that. Any calls, I'll be back Monday.'

He replaced the phone and unlocked the second drawer of his desk, in which he kept an index file of three-by-five cards. The Mediterranean clients.

He put the small metal box in front of him and started fingering through the cards. Perhaps a name would trigger a memory, a forgotten fact which might have relevance.

His private telephone rang. Only Betty called him on that line; no one else had the number. Joe loved his wife, but she had a positive genius for irritating him with trivial matters when he wished no interruptions.

'Yes, dear?'

Silence.

'What is it honey? I'm jammed up.'

Still his wife didn't answer.

Cardone was suddenly afraid. No one but Betty had that number!

'Betty? Answer me!'

The voice, when it came, was slow, deep and precise.

'John Tanner flew to Washington yesterday. Mr Da Vinci is very concerned. Perhaps your friends in California betrayed you. They've been in contact with Tanner.'

Joe Cardone heard the click of the disconnected telephone.

Jesus! Oh, Jesus! Oh, Christ! It was the Ostermans! They'd turned!

But *why*? It didn't make sense! What possible connection could there be between Zurich and anything *remotely* Mafia? They were light-years apart!

Or were they? Or was one using the other?

Cardone tried to steady himself but it was impossible. He found himself crushing the small metal box.

What could he do? Who could he talk to?

Tanner himself? Oh, God, of course not!

The Ostermans? Bernie Osterman? Christ, no! Not *now*.

Tremayne. Dick Tremayne.

8

Tuesday – 10:10 A.M.

Too shaken to sit in a commuter's seat on the Saddle Valley express, Tremayne decided to drive into New York.

As he sped east on Route Five toward the George Washington Bridge, he noticed a light blue Cadillac in his rear view mirror. When he pulled to the left, racing ahead of the other cars, the Cadillac did the same. When he returned to the right, squeezing into the slower flow, so did the Cadillac – always several automobiles behind him.

At the bridge he neared the tollbooth and saw that the Cadillac, in a faster adjacent lane, came parallel. He tried to see who the driver was.

It was a woman. She turned her face away; he could only see the back of her head. Yet she looked vaguely familiar.

The Cadillac sped off before he could reflect further. Traffic blocked any chance he had to follow. He was certain the Cadillac had followed him, but just as surely, the driver did not want to be recognized.

Why? Who was she?

Was this woman 'Blackstone'?

* * *

He found it impossible to accomplish anything in his office. He canceled the few appointments he had made, and, instead, reexamined the files of recent corporate mergers he had favorably gotten through the courts. One folder in particular interested him: *The Cameron Woolens*. Three factories in a small Massachusetts town owned for generations by the Cameron family. Raided from the inside by the oldest son. Blackmail had forced him to sell his share of the company to a New York clothing chain who claimed to want the Cameron label.

They got the label, and closed the factories; the town went bankrupt. Tremayne had represented the clothing chain in the Boston courts. The Cameron family had a daughter. An unmarried woman in her early thirties. Headstrong, angry.

The driver of the Cadillac was a woman. About the right age.

Yet to select one was to dismiss so many other possibilities. The merger builders knew whom to call when legal matters got sticky. Tremayne! He was the expert. A forty-four-year-old magician wielding the new legal machinery, sweeping aside old legal concepts in the exploding economy of the conglomerates.

Was it the Cameron daughter in the light blue Cadillac?

How could he know? There were so many. The Camerons. The Smythes of Atlanta. The Boyntons of Chicago. The Fergusons of Rochester. The corporate raiders preyed upon old families, the moneyed families. The old moneyed families pampered themselves, they were targets. Who among them might be Blackstone?

Tremayne got out of his chair and walked aimlessly around his office. He couldn't stand the confinement any longer; he had to go out.

He wondered what Tanner would say if he called him and suggested a casual lunch. How would Tanner react? Would he accept casually? Would he put him off? Would it be possible – if Tanner accepted – to learn anything related to Blackstone's warning?

Tremayne picked up the phone and dialed. His eyelid twitched, almost painfully.

Tanner was tied up in a meeting. Tremayne was relieved; it had been a foolish thing to do. He left no message and hurried out of his office.

On Fifth Avenue, a Checker cab pulled up directly in front of him, blocking his path at the corner crossing.

'Hey, mister!' The driver put his head out the window.

Tremayne wondered whom he was calling – so did several other pedestrians. They all looked at one another.

'You, mister! Your name Tremayne?'

'Me? Yes . . .'

'I got a message for you.'

'For me? How did you? . . .'

'I gotta hurry, the light's gonna change and I got twenty bucks for this. I'm to tell you to walk east on Fifty-fourth Street. Just keep walking and a Mr Blackstone will contact you.'

Tremayne put his hand on the driver's shoulder. '*Who* told you? Who gave you . . .'

'What do I know? Some wack sits in my cab since nine-thirty this morning with the meter on. He's got a pair of binoculars and smokes thin cigars.'

The 'Don't Walk' sign began to blink.

'What did he say! . . . Here!' Tremayne reached into his pocket and withdrew some bills. He gave the driver a ten. 'Here. Now, *tell* me, please!'

'Just what I said, mister. He got out a few seconds ago, gave me twenty bucks to tell you to walk east on Fifty-fourth. That's all.'

'That's *not* all!' Tremayne grabbed the driver's shirt.

'Thanks for the ten.' The driver pushed Tremayne's hand away, honked his horn to disperse the jaywalkers in front of him, and drove off.

Tremayne controlled his panic. He stepped back onto the curb and retreated under the awning of the storefront behind him, looking at the men walking north, trying to find a man with a pair of binoculars or a thin cigar.

Finding nobody, he began to edge his way from store entrance to store entrance, toward Fifty-fourth Street. He walked slowly, staring at the passersby. Several collided against him going in the same direction but walking much faster. Several others, heading south, noticed the strange behavior of the blond man in his expensively cut clothes, and smiled.

On the Fifty-fourth Street corner, Tremayne stopped. In spite of the slight breeze and his lightweight suit, he was perspiring. He knew he had to head east. There was no question about it.

One thing was clear. Blackstone was not the driver of the light blue Cadillac. Blackstone was a man with binoculars and thin cigars.

Then who was the woman? He'd seen her before. He knew it!

He started east on Fifty-fourth, walking on the right side; no one signaled him, no one even looked at him. Then across Park Avenue to the center island.

No one.

Lexington Avenue. Past the huge construction sites. No one.

Third Avenue. Second, First.

No one.

Tremayne entered the last block. A dead-end street terminating at the East River, flanked on both sides by the canopies of apartment house entrances. A few men with briefcases and women carrying department store boxes came and went from both buildings. At the end of the street was a light tan Mercedes-Benz sedan parked crossways, as if in the middle of a turn. And near it stood a man in an elegant white suit and Panama hat. He was quite a bit shorter than Tremayne. Even thirty yards away, Tremayne could see he was deeply tanned. He wore thick, wide sunglasses and was looking directly at Tremayne as Tremayne approached him.

'Mr . . . Blackstone?'

'Mr Tremayne. I'm sorry you had to walk such

a distance. We had to be sure, you see, that you were alone.'

'Why wouldn't I be?' Tremayne was trying to place the accent. It was cultivated, but not the sort associated with the northeastern states.

'A man who's in trouble often, mistakenly, looks for company.'

'What kind of trouble am I in?'

'You *did* get my note?'

'Of course. What did it mean?'

'Exactly what it said. Your friend Tanner is very dangerous to you. And to us. We simply want to emphasize the point as good businessmen should with one another.'

'What business interests are you concerned with, Mr Blackstone? I assume Blackstone isn't your name so I could hardly connect you with anything familiar.'

The man in the white suit and hat and dark glasses took several steps toward the Mercedes.

'We told you. His friends from California . . .'

'The Ostermans?'

'Yes.'

'My firm has had no dealings with the Ostermans. None whatever.'

'But you have, haven't you?' Blackstone walked in front of the hood and stood on the other side of the Mercedes.

'You can't be serious!'

'Believe me when I say that I am.' The man reached for the door handle, but he did not open the door. He was waiting.

'Just a minute! Who *are* you?'

'Blackstone will do.'

'No! . . . What you said! You couldn't . . .'

'But we do. That's the point. And since you now know that we do, it should offer some proof of our considerable influence.'

'What are you driving at?' Tremayne pressed his hands against the Mercedes' hood and leaned toward Blackstone.

'It's crossed our minds that you may have cooperated with your friend Tanner. That's really why we wanted to see you. It would be most inadvisable. We wouldn't hesitate to make public your contribution to the Osterman interests.'

'You're crazy! Why would I cooperate with Tanner? On what? I don't know what you're talking about.'

Blackstone removed his dark glasses. His eyes were blue and penetrating, and Tremayne could see freckles about his nose and cheekbones. 'If that's true then you have nothing to worry about.'

'Of course it's true! There's no earthly reason why I should work with Tanner on anything!'

'That's logical.' Blackstone opened the door of the Mercedes. 'Just keep it that way.'

'For God's sake, you can't just *leave*! I see Tanner every day. At the Club. On the train. What the hell am I supposed to think, what am I supposed to say?'

'You mean what are you supposed to look for? If I were you, I'd act as if nothing had happened. As if we'd never met . . . He may drop hints – if you're telling the truth – he may probe. Then you'll know.'

Tremayne stood up, fighting to remain calm. 'For all our sakes, I think you'd better tell me whom you represent. It would be best, it really would.'

'Oh, no, counselor.' A short laugh accompanied Blackstone's reply. 'You see, we've noticed that you've acquired a disturbing habit over the past several years. Nothing serious, not at this time, but to be considered.'

'What habit is that?'

'Periodically you drink too much.'

'That's ridiculous!'

'I said it wasn't serious. You do brilliant work. Nevertheless, at such times you haven't your normal control. No, it would be a mistake to burden you, especially in your current state of anxiety.'

'Don't go. Please! . . .'

'We'll be in touch. Perhaps you'll have learned something that will help us. At any rate, we always watch your . . . merger work with great interest.'

Tremayne flinched. 'What about the Ostermans? You've got to *tell* me.'

'If you've got a brain in your legal head, you won't say a thing to the Ostermans! Or hint at anything! If Osterman is cooperating with Tanner, you'll find out. If he's not, don't give him any ideas about *you*.' Blackstone climbed into the driver's seat of the Mercedes and started the motor. He said, just before he drove off, 'Keep your head, Mr Tremayne. We'll be in touch.'

Tremayne tried to marshal his thoughts; he

could feel his eyelid twitch. Thank Christ he hadn't reached Tanner! Not being prepared, he might have said something – something asinine, dangerous.

Had Osterman been such a gargantuan fool – or coward – to blurt out the truth about Zurich to John Tanner? Without consulting them?

If that were the case, Zurich would have to be alerted. Zurich would take care of Osterman. They'd crucify him!

He had to find Cardone. They had to decide what to do. He ran to a corner telephone.

Betty told him Joe had gone in to the office. Cardone's secretary told him Joe was still on vacation.

Joe was playing games. The twitch above Tremayne's left eye nearly blinded him.

9

Tuesday – 7:00 A.M.

Unable to sleep, Tanner walked into his study, his eyes drawn to the gray glass of the three television sets. There was something dead about them, empty. He lit a cigarette and sat down on the couch. He thought about Fassett's instructions: remain calm, oblivious, and say nothing to Ali. Fassett had repeated the last command several times.

The only real danger would come if Ali said the wrong thing to the wrong person. There *was* danger in that. Danger to Ali. But Tanner had never withheld anything from his wife. He wasn't sure he could do it. The fact that they were always open with each other was the strongest bond in their strong marriage. Even when they fought, there was never the weapon of unspoken accusations. Alice McCall had had enough of that as a child.

Omega, however, would change their lives, for the next six days, at any rate. He had to accept that because Fassett said it was best for Ali.

The sun was up now. The day was beginning and the Cardones, the Tremaynes and the Ostermans would soon be under fire. Tanner wondered what they'd do, how they'd react. He hoped that all three couples would contact the authorities and prove Fassett wrong. Sanity would return.

But it was possible that the madness had just begun. Whichever the case, he would stay home. If Fassett was right, he'd be there with Ali and the children. Fassett had no control over that decision.

He would let Ali think it was the flu. He'd be in touch with his office by phone, but he would stay with his family.

His telephone rang regularly; questions from the office. Ali and the children complained that the constant ringing of the telephone was enough to drive them crazy, so the three of them retreated to the pool. Except for a few clouds around noon, the day was hot – perfect for swimming. The white patrol car passed the house a number of times. On Sunday Tanner had been concerned over it. Now he was grateful. Fassett was keeping his word.

The telephone rang again. 'Yes, Charlie.' He didn't bother to say hello.

'Mr Tanner?'

'Oh, sorry. Yes, this is John Tanner.'

'Fassett calling . . .'

'Wait a minute!' Tanner looked out his study window to make sure Ali and the children were still at the pool. They were.

'What is it, Fassett? Have you people started?'

'Can you talk?'

'Yes . . . Have you found out anything? Has any of them called the police?'

'Negative. If that happens we'll contact you immediately. That's not why I'm calling you . . . You've done something extremely foolish. I can't emphasize how careless.'

'What are you talking about?'

'You didn't go in to your office this morning . . .'

'I certainly did *not*!'

'. . . But there must be no break from your normal routine. No altering of your usual schedule. That's terribly important. For your own protection, you *must* follow our instructions.'

'That's asking too much!'

'Listen to me. Your wife and children are at this moment in the swimming pool behind your house. Your son, Raymond, did not go to his tennis lesson . . .'

'I told him not to. I told him to do some work on the lawn.'

'Your wife had groceries delivered, which is not customary.'

'I explained that I might need her to take notes for me. She's done that before . . .'

'The main point is you're not doing what you usually do. It's vital that you keep to your day-to-day routine. I can't stress it enough. You cannot, you *must* not call attention to yourself.'

'I'm watching out for my family. I think that's understandable.'

'So are we. Far more effectively than you can. None of them have been out of our sight for a single minute. I'll amend that. Neither have you.

You walked out into your driveway twice: at nine-thirty-two and eleven-twenty. Your daughter had a friend over for lunch, one Joan Loomis, aged eight. We're extremely thorough and extremely careful.'

The news director reached for a cigarette and lit it with the desk lighter. 'Guess you are.'

'There's nothing for you to worry about. There's no danger to you or your family.'

'Probably not. I think you're all crazy. None of them have anything to do with this Omega.'

'That's possible. But if we're right, they won't take any action without checking further. They won't panic, too much is at stake. And when they do check further they'll immediately suspect each other. For heaven's sake, don't give them any reason not to. Go about your business as if nothing happened. It's vital. No one could harm your family. They couldn't get near enough.'

'All right. You're convincing. But I went out to the driveway three times this morning, not twice.'

'No, you didn't. The third time you remained in the garage doorway. You didn't physically walk out onto the driveway. And it wasn't morning, it was twelve-fourteen.' Fassett laughed. 'Feeling better now?'

'I'd be an awful liar if I didn't admit it.'

'You're not a liar. Not generally at any rate. Your file makes that very clear.' Fassett laughed again. Even Tanner smiled.

'You're really too much, you know that. I'll go into the office tomorrow.'

'When it's all over, you and your wife will have

to get together with me and mine for an evening. I think they'd like each other. Drinks will be on me. Dewars White Label with a tall soda for you and Scotch on the rocks with a pinch of water for your wife.'

'Good God! If you start describing our sex life . . .'

'Let me check the index . . .'

'Go to hell,' Tanner laughed, relieved. 'We'll take you up on that evening.'

'You should. We'd get along.'

'Name the date, we'll be there.'

'I'll make a point of it on Monday. Be in touch. You have the emergency number for after hours. Don't hesitate to call.'

'I won't. I'll be in the office tomorrow.'

'Fine. And do me a favor. Don't plan any more programs on us. My employers didn't like the last one.'

Tanner remembered. The program Fassett referred to had been a Woodward Show. The writers had come up with the phrase *Caught in the Act* for the letters CIA. It was a year ago, almost to the week. 'It wasn't bad.'

'It wasn't good. I saw that one. I wanted to laugh my head off but I couldn't. I was with the Director, in *his* living room. *Caught in the Act!* Jesus!' Fassett laughed again, putting Tanner more at ease than the news director thought possible.

'Thanks, Fassett.'

Tanner put down the telephone and crushed

out his cigarette. Fassett was a thorough professional, he thought. And Fassett was right. No one could get near Ali and the kids. For all he knew, the CIA had snipers strapped to the trees. What was left for him to do was precisely what Fassett said: nothing. Just go about business as usual. No break from routine, no deviation from the norm. He felt he could play the role now. The protection was everything Fassett said it would be.

However, one thought bothered him, and the more he considered it, the more it disturbed him.

It was nearly four o'clock in the afternoon. The Tremaynes, the Cardones and the Ostermans had all been contacted by now. The harassment had begun. Yet none had seen fit to call the police. Or even to call *him*.

Was it really possible that six people who had been his friends for years were not what they seemed to be?

10

Tuesday – 9:40 A.M. *California Time*

The Karmann Ghia swung off Wilshire Boulevard onto Beverly Drive. Osterman knew he was exceeding the Los Angeles speed limit; it seemed completely unimportant. He couldn't think about anything except the warning he had just received. He had to get home to Leila. They had to talk seriously now. They had to decide what to do.

Why had they been singled out?

Who was warning them? And about what?

Leila was probably right. Tanner was their friend, as good a friend as they'd ever known. But he was also a man who valued reserve in friendship. There were areas one never touched. There was always the slight quality of distance, a thin glass wall that came between Tanner and any other human being. Except, of course, Ali.

And Tanner now possessed information that touched them somehow, meant something to him and Leila. And Zurich was part of it. But, Christ! *How?*

Osterman reached the foot of the Mulholland hill and drove rapidly to the top, past the huge, early-pastiche mansions that were peopled by those near, or once near, the top of the Hollywood spectrum. A few of the houses were going to seed, decaying relics of past extravagance. The speed limit in the Mulholland section was thirty. Osterman's speedometer read fifty-one. He pressed down on the accelerator. He had decided what to do. He would pick up Leila and head for Malibu. The two of them would find a phone booth on the highway and call Tremayne and Cardone.

The mournful wail of the siren, growing louder, jarred him. It was a sound effect in this town of devices. It wasn't real, nothing here was real. It couldn't be for him.

But, of course, it was.

'Officer, I'm a resident here. Osterman. Bernard Osterman. 260 Caliente. Surely you know my house.' It was a statement made positively. Caliente was impressive acreage.

'Sorry, Mr Osterman. Your license and registration, please.'

'Now, look. I had a call at the studio that my wife wasn't feeling well. I think it's understandable I'm in a hurry.'

'Not at the expense of pedestrians. Your license and registration.'

Osterman gave them to him and stared straight ahead, controlling his anger. The police officer wrote lethargically on the long rectangular traffic summons and when he finished, he stapled Bernie's license to it.

At the sound of the snap, Osterman looked up. 'Do you have to mutilate the license?'

The policeman sighed wearily, holding onto the summons. 'You could have lost it for thirty days, mister. I lessened the speed; send in ten bucks like a parking ticket.' He handed the summons to Bernie. 'I hope your wife feels better.'

The officer returned to the police car. He spoke once more through the open window. 'Don't forget to put your license back in your wallet.'

The police car sped off.

Osterman threw down the summons and turned his ignition key. The Karmann Ghia started down the Mulholland slope. Half in disgust, Bernie looked at the summons on the seat next to him.

Then he looked again.

There was something wrong with it. The shape was right, the unreadable print was crowded in the inadequate space as usual, but the paper rang false. It seemed too shiny, too blurred even for a summons from the Motor Vehicle Department of the City of Los Angeles.

Osterman stopped. He picked up the summons and looked at it closely. The violations had been marked carelessly, inaccurately, by the police officer. They hadn't really been marked at all.

And then Osterman realized that the face of the card was only a thin photostat attached to a thicker sheet of paper.

He turned it over and saw that there was a message written in red pencil, partially covered by his stapled license. He ripped the license off and read:

Word received that Tanner's neighbors may have co-operated with him. This is a potentially dangerous situation made worse because our information is incomplete. Use extreme caution and find out what you can. It is vital we know – you know – extent of their involvement. Repeat. Use extreme caution.

Zurich

Osterman stared at the red letters and his fear produced a sudden ache at his temples.

The Tremaynes and the Cardones too!

11

Tuesday – 4:50 P.M.

Dick Tremayne wasn't on the four-fifty local to Saddle Valley. Cardone, sitting inside his Cadillac, swore out loud. He had tried to reach Tremayne at his office but was told that the lawyer had gone out for an early lunch. There was no point in having Tremayne call him back. Joe had decided to return to Saddle Valley and meet all the trains from three-thirty on.

Cardone left the station, turned left at the intersection of Saddle Road, and headed west toward the open country. He had thirty-five minutes until the next train was due. Perhaps the drive would help relax him. He couldn't just wait at the station. If anyone was watching him it would look suspicious.

Tremayne would have some answers. Dick was a damned good lawyer, and he'd know the legal alternatives, if there were any.

On the outskirts of Saddle Valley Joe reached a stretch of road bordered by fields. A Silver Cloud Rolls-Royce passed him on his left, and Cardone noted that the huge automobile was traveling extremely fast, much too fast for the narrow country road. He kept driving for several miles, vaguely aware that he was traveling through open country now. He would probably have to turn around in some farmer's driveway. But ahead of him was a long winding curve which, he remembered, had wide shoulders. He'd turn around there. It was time to head back to the station.

He reached the curve and slowed down, prepared to swing hard to his right onto the wide shoulder.

He couldn't.

The Silver Cloud was parked off the road under the trees, blocking him.

Annoyed, Cardone gunned the engine and proceeded several hundred yards ahead where, since there were no other cars in sight, he made the cramped turn.

Back at the station, Cardone looked at his watch. Five-nineteen, almost five-twenty. He could see the entire length of the platform. He'd spot Tremayne if he got off. He hoped the lawyer would be on the five-twenty-five. The waiting was intolerable.

A car pulled up behind his Cadillac, and Cardone looked up.

It was the Silver Cloud. Cardone began to sweat.

A massive man, well over six feet tall, got out of the car and walked slowly toward Cardone's open window. He was dressed in a chauffeur's uniform.

'Mr Cardione?'

'The name's Cardone.' The man's hands, which gripped the base of Joe's window, were immense. Much larger and thicker than his own.

'Okay. Whatever you like . . .'

'You passed me a little while ago, didn't you? On Saddle Road.'

'Yes, sir, I did. I haven't been far from you all day.'

Cardone involuntarily swallowed and shifted his weight. 'I find that a remarkable statement. Needless to say, very disturbing.'

'I'm sorry . . .'

'I'm not interested in apologies, I want to know why. Why are you following me? I don't know you. I don't like being followed.'

'No one does. I'm only doing what I'm told to do.'

'What is it? What do you want?'

The chauffeur moved his hands, just slightly, as if to call attention to their size and great strength. 'I've been instructed to bring you a message, and then I'll leave. I've a long drive. My employer lives in Maryland.'

'What message? Who from?'

'Mr Da Vinci, sir.'

'Da Vinci?'

'Yes sir. I believe he got in touch with you this morning.'

'I don't know your Mr Da Vinci . . . What message?'

'That you should not confide in Mr Tremayne.'

'What are you talking about?'

'Only what Mr Da Vinci told me, Mr Cardione.'

Cardone stared into the huge man's eyes. There was intelligence behind the blank façade. 'Why did you wait until now? You've been following me all day. You could have stopped me hours ago.'

'I wasn't instructed to. There's a radio-phone in the car. I was told to make contact just a few minutes ago.'

'*Who* told you?'

'Mr Da Vinci, sir . . .'

'That's not his name! Now, who is he?' Cardone fought his anger. He took a deep breath before speaking. 'You tell me who Da Vinci is.'

'There's more to the message,' said the chauffeur, disregarding Cardone's question. 'Mr Da Vinci says you should know that Tremayne may have talked to Mr Tanner. No one's sure yet, but that's what it looks like.'

'He *what*? Talked to him about *what*?'

'I don't know, sir. It's not my job to know. I'm hired to drive a car and deliver messages.'

'Your message isn't *clear*! I don't understand it! What good is a message if it isn't clear!' Cardone strained to keep in control.

'Perhaps the last part will help you, sir. Mr Da Vinci feels it would be a good idea if you tried to find out the extent of Mr Tremayne's involvement with Tanner. But you must be careful. Very, very careful. As you must be careful with your friends from California. That's important.'

The chauffeur backed away from the Cadillac and slapped two fingers against his cap's visor.

'Wait a minute!' Cardone reached for the door handle, but the huge man in uniform swiftly clamped his hands on the window ledge and held the door shut.

'No, Mr Cardione. You stay inside there. You shouldn't call attention to yourself. The train's coming in.'

'No, please! *Please* . . . I want to talk to Da Vinci! We've got to talk! Where can I reach him?'

'No way, sir.' The chauffeur held the door effortlessly.

'You prick!' Cardone pulled the handle and shoved his whole weight against the door. It gave just a bit and then slammed shut again under the chauffeur's hands. 'I'll break you in half!'

The train pulled to a stop in front of the platform. Several men got off and the shriek of two whistle blasts pierced the air.

The chauffeur spoke calmly. 'He's not on the train, Mr Cardione. He *drove* into town this morning. We know that, too.'

The train slowly started up and rolled down the tracks. Joe stared at the immense human being holding the car door shut. His anger was nearly beyond control but he was realistic enough to know it would do him no good. The chauffeur stepped back, gave Cardone a second informal salute and walked rapidly toward the Rolls-Royce. Cardone pushed the car door open and stepped out onto the hot pavement.

'Hello there, Joe!' The caller was Amos Needham, of the second contingent of Saddle Valley commuters. A vice-president of Manufacturers Hanover Trust and the chairman of the special events committee for the Saddle Valley Country Club. 'You market boys have it easy. When it gets rough you stay home and wait for the calm to set in, eh?'

'Sure, sure, Amos.' Cardone kept his eye on the chauffeur of the Rolls, who had climbed into the driver's seat and started the engine.

'I tell you,' continued Amos, 'I don't know where you young fellas are taking us! . . . Did you see the quotes for DuPont? Everybody else takes a bath and it zooms up! Told my trust committee to consult the Ouija board. To hell with you upstart brokers.' Needham chuckled and then suddenly waved his small arm, flagging down a Lincoln Continental approaching the depot. 'There's Ralph. Can I give you a lift, Joe? . . . But, of course not. You just stepped out of your car.'

The Lincoln pulled up to the platform, and Amos Needham's chauffeur started to get out.

'No need, Ralph. I can manipulate a door handle. By the way, Joe . . . that Rolls you're looking at reminds me of a friend of mine. Couldn't be, though. He lived in Maryland.'

Cardone snapped his head around and looked at the innocuous banker. 'Maryland? *Who* in Maryland?'

Amos Needham held the car door open and returned Cardone's stare with unconcerned good humor. 'Oh, I don't think you'd know him. He's been dead for years . . . Funny name. Used to kid him a lot . . . His name was Caesar.'

Amos Needham stepped into his Lincoln and closed the door. At the top of Station Parkway the Rolls-Royce turned right and roared off toward the main arteries leading to Manhattan. Cardone stood on the tarred surface of the Saddle Valley railroad station and he was afraid.

Tremayne!

Tremayne was with Tanner!

Osterman was with Tanner!

Da Vinci . . . Caesar!

The architects of war!

And he, Giuseppe Ambruzzio Cardione, was alone!

Oh, Christ! Christ! Son of God! Blessed Mary! Blessed Mary, Mother of Christ! Wash my hands with his blood! The blood of the lamb! Jesus! Jesus! Forgive me my sins! . . . Mary and Jesus! Christ Incarnate! God all holy! What have I done?

12

Tuesday – 5:00 P.M.

Tremayne walked aimlessly for hours; up and down the familiar streets of the East Side. Yet if anyone had stopped him and asked him where he was, he could not have answered.

He was consumed. Frightened. Blackstone had said everything and clarified nothing.

And Cardone had lied. To somebody. His wife or his office, it didn't matter. What mattered was that Cardone couldn't be reached. Tremayne knew that the panic wouldn't stop until he and Cardone figured out between them what Osterman had done.

Had Osterman betrayed them?

Was that really it? Was it *possible*?

He crossed Vanderbilt Avenue, realizing he had walked to the Biltmore Hotel without thinking about a destination.

It was understandable, he thought. The Biltmore brought back memories of the carefree times.

He walked through the lobby almost expecting to see some forgotten friend from his teens – and suddenly he was staring at a man he hadn't seen in over twenty-five years. He knew the face, changed terribly with the years – bloated, it seemed to Tremayne, lined – but he couldn't remember the name. The man went back to prep-school days.

Awkwardly the two men approached each other.

'Dick . . . Dick Tremayne! It *is* Dick Tremayne, isn't it?'

'Yes. And you're . . . Jim?'

'Jack! Jack Townsend! How are you, Dick?' The men shook hands, Townsend far more enthusiastic. 'It must be twenty-five, thirty years! You look great! How the hell do you keep the weight down? Gave up myself.'

'You look fine. Really, you look swell. I didn't know you were in New York.'

'I'm not. Based in Toledo. Just in for a couple of days . . . I swear to God, I had a crazy thought coming in on the plane. I canceled the Hilton and thought I'd grab a room here just to see if any of the old crowd ever came in. Insane, huh? . . . And look what I run into!'

'That's funny. Really funny. I was thinking the same sort of thing a few seconds ago.'

'Let's get a drink.'

Townsend kept spouting opinions that were formed in the traditions of corporate thought. He was being very boring.

Tremayne kept thinking about Cardone. As he drank his third drink he looked around for the bar telephone booth he remembered from his youth. It was hidden near the kitchen entrance, and only Biltmore habitués-in-good-standing knew of its existence.

It wasn't there any more. And Jack Townsend kept talking, talking, remembering the unmemorable out loud.

There were two Negroes in leather jackets, beads around their necks, standing several feet away from them.

They wouldn't have been there in other days.

The pleasant days.

Tremayne drank his fourth drink in one assault; Townsend *wouldn't* stop talking.

He *had* to call Joe! The panic was starting again. Maybe Joe would, in a single sentence, unravel the puzzle of Osterman.

'What's the matter with you, Dick? You look all upset.'

'S'help me God, this is the first time I've been in here in years.' Tremayne slurred his words and he knew it. 'Have to make a phone call. Excuse me.'

Townsend put his arm on Tremayne's arm. He spoke quietly.

'Are you going to call Cardone?'

'What?'

'I asked if you were going to call Cardone.'

'Who are you? . . . Who the hell are you?'

'A friend of Blackstone. Don't call Cardone. Don't do that under any circumstances. You put a nail in your own casket if you do. Can you understand that?'

'I don't understand *anything*! Who *are* you?

Who's Blackstone?' Tremayne tried to whisper, but his voice carried throughout the room.

'Let's put it this way. Cardone may be dangerous. We don't trust him. We're not sure of him. Any more than we are of the Ostermans.'

'What are you saying?'

'They may have gotten together. You may be flying solo now. Play it cool and see what you can find out. We'll be in touch . . . but Mr Blackstone told you that already, didn't he?'

Then Townsend did a strange thing. He removed a bill from his wallet and placed it in front of Richard Tremayne. He said only two words as he turned and walked through the glass doors.

'Take it.'

It was a one-hundred-dollar bill.

What had it bought?

It didn't buy anything, thought Tremayne. It was merely a symbol.

A price. Any price.

When Fassett walked into the hotel room, two men were already bent over a card table, studying various papers and maps. One was Grover. The other man was named Cole. Fassett removed his Panama hat and sunglasses, putting them on the bureau top.

'Everything okay?' asked Grover.

'On schedule. If Tremayne doesn't get too drunk at the Biltmore.'

'If he does,' said Cole, his attention on a New

Jersey road map, 'a friendly, bribable cop will correct the situation. He'll get home.'

'Have you got men on both sides of the bridge?'

'And the tunnels. He sometimes takes the Lincoln Tunnel and drives up the Parkway. All in radio contact.' Cole was making marks on a piece of tracing paper placed over the map.

The telephone rang. Grover crossed to the bedside table to pick it up.

'Grover here . . . Oh? Yes, we'll double check but I'm sure we would've heard if he had . . . Don't worry about it. All right. Keep in touch.' Grover replaced the receiver and stood by the telephone.

'What's the matter?' Fassett removed his white Palm Beach jacket and began rolling up his sleeves.

'That was Los Angeles logistics. Between the time Osterman left the studio and was picked up on Mulholland, they lost him for about twenty minutes. They're concerned that he may have reached Cardone or Tremayne.'

Cole looked up from the table. 'Around one o'clock our time – ten in California?'

'Yes.'

'Negative. Cardone was in his car and Tremayne on the streets. Neither could be reached . . .'

'I see what they mean, though,' interrupted Fassett. 'Tremayne didn't waste any time this noon trying to get to Cardone.'

'We calculated that, Larry,' said Cole. 'We

would have intercepted both of them if a meeting had been scheduled.'

'Yes, I know. Risky though.'

Cole laughed as he picked up the tracing paper. 'You plan – we'll control. Here's every back road link to "Leather".'

'We've got them.'

'George forgot to bring up a copy, and the others are with the men. A command post should always have a map of the field.'

'*Mea culpa.* I was in briefing until two this morning and had to get the shuttle at six-thirty. I also forgot my razor and toothbrush and God knows what else.'

The telephone rang once again and Grover reached down for it.

'. . . I see . . . wait a minute.' He held the phone away from his ear and looked over at Laurence Fassett. 'Our second chauffeur had a run-in with Cardone . . .'

'Oh, Christ! Nothing rough, I hope.'

'No, no. The hot-tempered All-American tried to get out of the car and start a fight. Nothing happened.'

'Tell him to head back to Washington. Get out of the area.'

'Go back to DC, Jim . . . Sure, you might as well. Okay. See you at camp.' Grover replaced the receiver and walked back to the card table.

'What's Jim going to do "just as well"?' asked Fassett.

'Drop off the Rolls in Maryland. He thinks Cardone got the license number.'

'Good. And the Caesar family?'

'Primed beautifully,' interrupted Cole. 'They can't wait to hear from Giuseppe Ambruzzio Cardione. Like father, unlike son.'

'What's that mean?' Grover held his lighter under his cigarette.

'Old man Caesar made a dozen fortunes out of the rackets. His oldest son is with the Attorney General's office and an absolute fanatic about the Mafia.'

'Washing away family sins?'

'Something like that.'

Fassett walked over to the window and looked down at the long expanse of Central Park South. When he spoke he did so quietly, but the satisfaction in his voice made his companions smile.

'It's all there now. Each one is jolted. They're all confused and frightened. None of them know what to do or whom to talk to. Now we sit and watch. We'll give them a rest for twenty-four hours. A blackout . . . And Omega has no choice. Omega has to make its move.'

13

Wednesday – 10:15 A.M.

It was ten-fifteen before Tanner reached his office. He had found it nearly impossible to leave home, but he knew Fassett was right. He sat down and glanced perfunctorily at his mail and messages. Everyone wanted a conference. No one wanted to make a single decision without his say-so.

Corporate musical chairs. The network sub-brass band.

He picked up the phone and dialed New Jersey.

'Hello Ali?'

'Hi, hon. Did you forget something?'

'No . . . No. Just felt lonely. What are you doing?'

Inside 22 Orchard Place, Saddle Valley, New Jersey, Alice Tanner smiled and felt warm. 'What am I doing? . . . Well, as per the great Khan's orders, I'm overseeing your son's cleaning out the basement. And as the great Khan also instructed, his daughter is spending a hot July morning on her remedial reading. How else could she get into Berkeley by the time she's twelve?'

Tanner caught the complaint. When she was a young girl, his wife's summers were lonely and terrifying. Ali wanted them to be perfect for Janet.

'Well, don't overdo it. Have some kids over.'

'I might at that. But Nancy Loomis phoned and asked if Janet could go there for lunch . . .'

'Ali . . .' Tanner switched the phone to his left hand. 'I'd rather cool it with the Loomises for a few days . . .'

'What do you mean?'

John remembered Jim Loomis from the daily eight-twenty express. 'Jim's trying to boilerplate some market stuff. He's got a lot of fellows on the train to go along with him. If I can avoid him till next week I'm off the hook.'

'What does Joe say?'

'He doesn't know about it. Loomis doesn't want Joe to know. Rival houses, I guess.'

'I don't see that Janet's going to lunch has anything . . .'

'Just saves embarrassment. We don't have the kind of money he's looking for.'

'Amen to that!'

'And . . . do me a favor. Stay near the phone today.'

Alice Tanner's eyes shifted to the telephone in her hand. 'Why?'

'I can't go into it, but I may have an important call . . . What we're always talking about . . .'

Alice Tanner immediately, unconsciously lowered her voice as she smiled. 'Someone's offered you something!'

'Could be. They're going to call at home to set up a lunch.'

'Oh, John. That's exciting!'

'It . . . could be interesting.' He suddenly found it painful to talk to her. 'Speak to you later.'

'Sounds marvelous, darling. I'll turn up the bell. It'll be heard in New York.'

'I'll call you later.'

'Tell me the details then.'

Tanner placed the receiver slowly in its cradle. The lies had begun . . . but his family would stay home.

He knew he had to turn his mind to Standard Mutual problems. Fassett had warned him. There could be no break in his normal pattern, and normalcy for any network news director was a condition close to hypertension. Tanner's mark at Standard was his control of potential difficulties. If there was ever a time in his professional life to avoid chaos, it was now.

He picked up his telephone. 'Norma. I'll read out the list of those I'll see this morning, and you call them. Tell everyone I want the meetings quick and don't let anyone run over fifteen minutes unless I say otherwise. It would help if all problems and proposals were reduced to written half-pages. Pass the word. I've got a lot to catch up on.'

He wasn't free again until 12:30. Then he closed his office door and called his wife.

There was no answer.

He let the phone ring for nearly two minutes, until the spaces between the rings seemed to grow longer and longer.

No answer. No answer at the telephone – the

telephone whose bell was turned up so loud it would be heard in New York.

It was twelve-thirty-five. Ali would figure no one would call between noon and one-thirty. And she probably needed something from the supermarket. Or she might have decided to take the children over to the Club for hamburgers. Or she couldn't refuse Nancy Loomis and had taken Janet over for lunch. Or she had gone to the library – Ali was an inveterate poolside reader during the summer.

Tanner tried to picture Ali doing all these things. That she was doing one, or some, or all, had to be the case.

He dialed again, and again there was no answer. He called the Club.

'I'm sorry, Mr Tanner. We've paged outside. Mrs Tanner isn't here.'

The Loomises. Of course, she went to the Loomises.

'Golly, John, Alice said Janet had a bad tummy. Maybe she took her to the doctor.'

By eight minutes after one, John Tanner had dialed his home twice more. The last time he had let the phone ring for nearly five minutes. Picturing Ali coming through the door breathlessly, always allowing that one last ring, expecting her to answer.

But it did not happen.

He told himself over and over again that he was acting foolishly. He himself had seen the patrol car following them when Ali drove him to the station. Fassett had convinced him yesterday that his watchdogs were thorough.

Fassett.

He picked up the phone and dialed the emergency number Fassett had given him. It was a Manhattan exchange.

'Grover . . .'

Who? thought Tanner.

'Hello? Hello? . . . George Grover speaking.'

'My name is John Tanner. I'm trying to find Laurence Fassett.'

'Oh, hello, Mr Tanner. Is something the matter? Fassett's out. Can I help you?'

'Are you an associate of Fassett's?'

'I am, sir.'

'I can't reach my wife. I've tried calling a number of times. She doesn't answer.'

'She may have stepped out. I wouldn't worry. She's under surveillance.'

'Are you positive?'

'Of course.'

'I asked her to stay by the phone. She thought I was expecting an important call . . .'

'I'll contact our men and call you right back. It'll set your mind at ease.'

Tanner hung up feeling slightly embarrassed. Yet five minutes went by and the expected ring did not come. He dialed Fassett's number but it was busy. He quickly replaced the phone wondering if his impetuous dialing caused Grover to find his line busy. Was Grover trying to reach him? He had to be. He'd try again right away.

Yet the phone did not ring.

Tanner picked it up and slowly, carefully dialed, making sure every digit was correct.

'Grover.'

'This is Tanner. I thought you were going to call right back!'

'I'm sorry, Mr Tanner. We've been having a little difficulty. Nothing to be concerned about.'

'What do you mean, difficulty?'

'Making contact with our men in the field. It's not unusual. We can't expect them to be next to a radio-phone every second. We'll reach them shortly and call you back.'

'That's not good enough!' John Tanner slammed the telephone down and got out of his chair. Yesterday afternoon Fassett had detailed every move made by all of them – even to the precise actions at the moment of his phone call. And now this Grover couldn't reach any of the men supposedly watching his family. What had Fassett said?

'We have thirteen agents in Saddle Valley . . .'

And Grover couldn't reach any of them.

Thirteen men and none could be contacted!

He crossed to the office door. 'Something's come up, Norma. Listen for my phone, please. If it's a man named Grover, tell him I've left for home.'

SADDLE VALLEY
VILLAGE INCORPORATED 1862
Welcome

'Where to now, Mister?'

'Go straight. I'll show you.'

The cab reached Orchard Drive, two blocks from his home; Tanner's pulse was hammering. He kept picturing the station wagon in the driveway. As soon as they made one more turn he'd be able to see it – if it was there. And if it was, everything would be all right. Oh, Christ! Let everything be all right!

The station wagon was not in the driveway.

Tanner looked at his watch.

Two-forty-five. A quarter to three! And Ali wasn't there!

'On the left. The wood-shingled house.'

'Nice place, mister. A real nice place.'

'Hurry!'

The cab pulled up to the flagstone path. Tanner paid and pulled open the door. He didn't wait for the driver's thanks.

'Ali! Ali!' Tanner raced through the laundry room to check the garage.

Nothing. The small Triumph stood there.

Quiet.

Yet there was something. An odor. A faint, sickening odor that Tanner couldn't place.

'Ali! Ali!' He ran back to the kitchen and saw his pool through the window. Oh, God! He stared at the surface of the water and hurried to the patio door. The lock was stuck and so he slammed against it, breaking the latch, and ran out.

Thank God! There was nothing in the water!

His small Welsh terrier dog stirred from its sleep. The animal was attached to a wire run and immediately started barking in its sharp, hysterical yap.

He sped back into the house, to the cellar door.

'Ray! Janet! Ali!'

Quiet. Except for the incessant barking of the dog outside.

He left the cellar door open and ran to the staircase.

Upstairs!

He leapt up the stairs; the doors to the children's rooms and the guest room were open. The door to his and Ali's room was shut.

And then he heard it. The soft playing of a radio. Ali's clock radio with the automatic timer which shut the radio off at any given time up to an hour. He and Ali always used that timer when they played the radio. Never the ON button. It was a habit. And Ali had been gone over two and a half hours. Someone else had turned on the radio.

He opened the door.

No one.

He was about to turn and search the rest of the house when he saw it. A note written in red pencil next to the clock radio.

He crossed to the bedside table.

'Your wife and children went for an unexpected drive. You'll find them by an old railroad depot on Lassiter Road.'

In his panic, Tanner remembered the abandoned depot. It sat deep in the woods on a rarely used back road.

What had he done? What in Christ's name had

he done? He'd killed them! If that was so, he'd kill Fassett! Kill Grover! Kill all those who should have been watching!

He raced out of the bedroom, down the staircase, into the garage. The door was open and he jumped into the seat of the Triumph and started the engine.

Tanner swung the small sports car to the right out of the driveway and sped around the long Orchard Drive curve, trying to remember the quickest way to Lassiter Road. He reached a pond he recognized as Lassiter Lake, used by the Saddle Valley residents for ice skating in winter. Lassiter Road was on the other side and seemed to disappear into a stretch of undisciplined woods.

He kept the accelerator flat against the Triumph's floor. He started talking to himself, then screaming at himself.

Ali! Ali! Janet! Ray!

The road was winding. Blind spots, curves, sun rays coming through the crowded trees. There were no other automobiles, no other signs of life.

The old abandoned depot suddenly appeared. And there was his station wagon – half off the overgrown parking area, into the tall grass. Tanner stamped on his brakes beside the wagon. There was no one in sight.

He jumped out of the Triumph and raced to the car.

In an instant his mind went out of control. The horror was real. The unbelievable had happened.

On the floor of the front seat was his wife. Slumped, motionless. In the back were little Janet and his son. Heads down. Bodies sprawled off the red seats.

Oh, Christ! Christ! It had happened! His eyes filled with tears. His body shook.

He pulled the door open, screaming in terror. And suddenly a wave of odor washed over him. The sickish odor he had smelled in his garage. He grabbed Ali's head and pulled her up, frightened beyond feeling.

'Ali! Ali! My God! *Please! Ali!*'

His wife opened her eyes slowly. Blinking. Conscious but not conscious. She moved her arms.

'Where . . . where? The *children*!' She drew out the word hysterically. The sound of her scream brought Tanner back to his senses. He leapt up and reached over the seat for his son and daughter.

They moved. They were alive! They *all* were *alive*!

Ali climbed out of the station wagon and stumbled to the ground. Her husband lifted his daughter out of the back seat and held her as she started to cry.

'What *happened*? What *happened*?' Alice Tanner pulled herself up.

'Don't talk, Ali. Breathe. As deeply as you can. Here!' He walked to her and handed her the sobbing Janet. 'I'll get Ray.'

'What *happened*? Don't tell me *not* to . . .'

'Be quiet! Just breathe. Breathe hard!'

He helped his son out of the back seat. The boy was sick and started to vomit. Tanner cupped his son's forehead with his hand, holding him around the waist with his left arm.

'John, you simply can't . . .'

'Walk around. Try to get Janet to walk! Do as I *say*!'

Obediently, dazedly, Alice Tanner did what her husband commanded. The boy began to shake his head in Tanner's hand.

'Feeling better, son?'

'Wow! . . . Wow! Where are we?' The boy was suddenly frightened.

'It's all right. It's all right . . . You're all . . . all right.'

Tanner looked over at his wife. She had put Janet's feet on the ground, holding her in her arms. The child was crying loudly now, and Tanner watched, filled with hatred and fear.

He walked to the station wagon to see if the keys were in the ignition.

They weren't. It didn't make sense.

He looked under the seats, in the glove compartment, in the back. Then he saw them. Wrapped in a piece of white paper, an elastic band holding the paper around the case. The packet was wedged between the collapsible seats, pushed far down, nearly out of sight.

His daughter was screaming now, and Alice Tanner picked the child up, trying to comfort her, repeating over and over again that everything was all right.

Making sure his wife could not see him, Tanner held the small package below the back seat, snapped the elastic band and opened the paper.

It was blank.

He crumpled the paper and stuffed it into his pocket. He would tell Ali what had happened now. They'd go away. Far away. But he would *not* tell her in front of the children.

'Get in the wagon.' Tanner spoke to his son softly and went to his wife, taking the hysterical child from her. 'Get the keys out of the Triumph, Ali. We're going home.'

His wife stood in front of him, her eyes wide with fright, the tears streaming down her face. She tried to control herself, tried with all her strength not to scream. 'What happened? What *happened* to us?'

The roar of an engine prevented Tanner from answering. In his anger, he was grateful. The Saddle Valley patrol car sped into the depot and came to a stop less than ten yards from them.

Jenkins and McDermott leapt out of the automobile. Jenkins had his revolver drawn.

'Is everything all right?' He ran up to Tanner. McDermott went rapidly to the station wagon and spoke quietly to the boy in the back seat.

'We found the note in your bedroom. Incidentally, we think we've recovered most of your property.'

'Our what?' Alice Tanner stared at the police officer.

'What property?'

'Two television sets, Mrs Tanner's jewelry, a box of silver, place settings, some cash. There's a list down at the station. We don't know if we've got everything. The car was abandoned several blocks from your house. They may have taken other things. You'll have to check.'

Tanner handed his daughter to Ali.

'What the hell are you talking about?'

'You were robbed. Your wife must have come back while they were in the process. She and the children were gassed in the garage . . . They were professionals, no doubt about it. Real professional methods . . .'

'You're a liar,' said Tanner softly. 'There was nothing . . .'

'Please!' interrupted Jenkins. 'The main thing now is your wife and children.'

As if on signal, McDermott called from inside the station wagon. 'I want to get this kid to the hospital! *Now!*'

'Oh, my God!' Alice Tanner ran to the automobile, carrying her daughter in her arms.

'Let McDermott take them,' said Jenkins.

'How can I trust you? You lied to me. There was nothing missing in my house. No television sets were gone, no signs of any robbery! Why did you lie?'

'There isn't time. I'm sending your wife and children with McDermott.' Jenkins spoke rapidly.

'They're going with *me*!'

'No they're not.' Jenkins raised his pistol slightly.

'I'll kill you, Jenkins.'

'Then what stands between you and Omega?' said Jenkins calmly. 'Be reasonable. Fassett's on his way out. He wants to see you.'

* * *

'I'm sorry. Truly, abjectly sorry. It won't, it *can't* happen again.'

'What *did* happen? Where was your infallible protection?'

'A logistical error on a surveillance schedule that hadn't been cross-checked. That's the truth. There's no point in lying to you. I'm the one responsible.'

'You weren't out here.'

'I'm still responsible. The Leather team's my responsibility. Omega saw that a post wasn't covered – for less than fifteen minutes, incidentally – and they moved in.'

'I can't tolerate that. You risked the lives of my wife and children!'

'I told you, there's no possibility of recurrence. Also – and in an inverted way, this should be comforting – this afternoon confirms the fact that Omega won't kill. Terror, yes. Murder, no.'

'Why? Because you say so? I don't buy it. The CIA track record reads like a disaster file. You're not making any more decisions for *me*, let's get that clear.'

'Oh? You are then?'

'Yes.'

'Don't be a fool. If not for yourself, for your family.'

Tanner got out of the chair. He saw through the Venetian blinds that two men were standing guard outside the motel window.

'I'm taking them away.'

'Where will you go?'

'I don't know. I just know I'm not staying here.'

'You think Omega won't follow you?'

'Why should it . . . they? I'm no part of you.'

'They won't believe that.'

'Then I'll make it clear!'

'Are you going to take out an ad in *The Times*?'

'No!' Tanner swung around and pointed a finger at the CIA man. 'You will! However you want to do it. Because if you don't, I'll tell the story of this operation and your inept, malicious handling of it on every network newscast in the country. You won't survive that.'

'Neither will you because you'll be dead. Your wife dead. Your son, your daughter . . . dead.'

'You can't threaten me . . .'

'For God's sake, look at history! Look at what's *really happened*!' Fassett exploded. Then suddenly he lowered his voice and raised his hand to his chest, speaking slowly. 'Take me . . . My wife was killed in East Berlin. They murdered her for no earthly reason except that she was married to me. I was being . . . taught a lesson. And to teach me that lesson they took my wife. Don't make pronouncements to me. I've been there. You've been safe. Well, you're not safe now.'

Tanner was stunned. 'What are you trying to say?'

'I'm telling you that you'll do exactly what we've planned. We're too close now. I want Omega.'

'You can't force me and you know it!'

'Yes, I can . . . Because if you turn, if you run,

I withdraw every agent in Saddle Valley. You'll be alone . . . and I don't think you can cope with the situation by yourself.'

'I'm taking my family away . . .'

'Don't be crazy! Omega raced in on a simple logistical error. That means they, whoever they are, are alert. Extremely alert, fast and thorough. What chance do you think you'll have? What chance do you give your family? We've admitted a mistake. We won't make any others.'

Tanner knew Fassett was right. If he was abandoned now, he didn't have the resources for control.

'You don't fool around, do you?'

'Did you ever – in a mine field?'

'I guess not . . . This afternoon. What was it?'

'Terror tactics. Without identification. That's in case you're clean. We realized what had happened and put out a counter-explanation. We'll withhold some of your property – small stuff, like jewelry, until it's over. More authentic.'

'Which means you expect me to go along with the "robbery".'

'Of course. It's safest.'

'Yes . . . Of course.' Tanner reached into his pocket for cigarettes. The telephone rang and Fassett picked it up.

He spoke quietly, then turned to the news director. 'Your family's back home. They're okay. Still scared, but okay. Some of our men are straightening up the place. It's a mess. They're trying to lift fingerprints. Naturally, it'll be found the thieves wore gloves. We've told your wife that you're still at headquarters making a statement.'

'I see.'

'You want us to drive you back?'

'No . . . No, I don't. I presume I'll be followed anyway.'

'Safety surveillance is the proper term.'

Tanner entered the Village Pub, Saddle Valley's one fashionable bar, and called the Tremaynes.

'Ginny, this is John. I'd like to talk to Dick. Is he there?'

'John *Tanner*?' Why did she say that? His name. She knew his voice.

'Yes. Is Dick there?'

'No . . . Of course not. He's at the office. What is it?'

'Nothing important.'

'Can't you tell me?'

'I just need a little legal advice. I'll try him at the office. Good-bye.' Tanner knew he had done it badly. He had been awkward.

But then, so had Virginia Tremayne.

Tanner dialed New York.

'I'm sorry, Mr Tanner. Mr Tremayne's out on Long Island. In conference.'

'It's urgent. What's the number?'

Tremayne's secretary gave it to him reluctantly. He dialed it.

'I'm sorry, Mr Tremayne isn't here.'

'His office said he was in conference out there.'

'He called this morning and canceled. I'm sorry, sir.'

Tanner hung up the phone, then dialed the Cardones.

'Daddy and Mommy are out for the day, Uncle John. They said they'd be back after dinner. Do you want them to call you?'

'No . . . no, that's not necessary . . .'

There was an empty feeling in his stomach. He dialed the operator, gave her the information, including his credit card number, and three thousand four hundred miles away a telephone rang in Beverly Hills.

'Osterman residence.'

'Is Mr Osterman there?'

'No, he's not. May I ask who's calling, please?'

'Is Mrs Osterman there?'

'No.'

'When do you expect them back?'

'Next week. Who's calling, please?'

'The name's Cardone. Joseph Cardone.'

'C-A-R-D-O-N-E . . .'

'That's right. When did they go?'

'They left for New York last night. The ten o'clock flight, I believe.'

John Tanner hung up the receiver. The Ostermans were in New York! They'd gotten in by six o'clock that morning!

The Tremaynes, the Cardones, the Ostermans.

All there. None accounted for.

Any or all.

Omega!

14

Thursday – 3:00 A.M.

Fassett had set a convincing scene. By the time Tanner returned home the rooms had been 'straightened up', but there was still disarray. Chairs were not in their proper places, rugs off center, lamps in different positions; the woman of the house hadn't yet put things to rights.

Ali told him how the police had helped her; if she suspected collusion she didn't let on.

But then Alice McCall had lived with violence as a child. The sight of policemen in her home was not unfamiliar to her. She was conditioned to react with a minimum of hysteria.

Her husband, on the other hand, was not conditioned at all for the role he had to play. For the second night, sleep was fitful, ultimately impossible. He looked at the dial on the clock radio. It was nearly three in the morning and his mind still raced, his eyes refused to stay shut.

It was no use. He had to get up, he had to walk around; perhaps eat something, read something, smoke.

Anything that would help him stop thinking.

He and Ali had had a number of brandies before going to bed – too many drinks for Ali;

she was deep in sleep, as much from the alcohol as from exhaustion.

Tanner got out of bed and went downstairs. He wandered aimlessly around; he finished the remains of a cantaloupe in the kitchen, read the junk mail in the hallway, flipped through some magazines in the living room. Finally he went out to the garage. There was still the faint – ever so faint now – odor of the gas which had been used on his wife and children. He returned to the living room, forgetting to turn off the lights in the garage.

Extinguishing his last cigarette, he looked around for another pack; more for the security of knowing there was one than from any immediate need. There was a carton in the study. As he opened the top drawer of his desk, a noise made him look up.

There was a tapping on his study window and the beam of a flashlight waving in small circles against the pane.

'It's Jenkins, Mr Tanner,' said the muffled voice. 'Come to your back door.'

Tanner, relieved, nodded to the dark figure on the other side of the glass.

'This screen-door latch was broken,' said Jenkins softly as Tanner opened the kitchen door. 'We don't know how it happened.'

'I did it. What are you doing out there?'

'Making sure there's no repetition of this afternoon. There are four of us. We wondered what *you* were doing. The lights are on all over downstairs. Even in the garage. Is anything the matter? Has anyone phoned you?'

'Wouldn't you know if they had?'

Jenkins smiled as he stepped through the door. 'We're supposed to, I guess you know that. But there's no accounting for mechanical failures.'

'I suppose not. Care for a cup of coffee?'

'Only if you'd make enough for three other guys. They can't leave their posts.'

'Sure.' Tanner filled the hot water kettle. 'Instant be all right?'

'Be great. Thanks.' Jenkins sat down at the kitchen table, moving his large police holster so it hung free from the seat. He watched Tanner closely and then looked around the room.

'I'm glad you're outside. I appreciate it, really. I know it's a job, but still . . .'

'Not just a job. We're concerned.'

'That's nice to hear. You have a wife and kids?'

'No sir, I don't.'

'I thought you were married.'

'That's my partner, McDermott.'

'Oh, I see . . . You've been on the force here, let's see . . . a couple of years now, isn't it?'

'Just about.'

Tanner turned from the stove and looked at Jenkins. 'Are you one of them?'

'I beg your pardon?'

'I asked if you were one of them. This afternoon you used the name Omega. That means you're one of Fassett's men.'

'I was instructed what to tell you. I've met Mr Fassett, of course.'

'But you're not a small-town policeman, are you?'

Jenkins did not have time to answer. There was a cry from the grounds outside. Both men in the kitchen had heard that sound before, Tanner in France, Jenkins near the Yalu River. It was a scream in the instant of death.

Jenkins bolted to the screen door and raced outside, Tanner following at his heels. Two other men came out of the darkness.

'It's Ferguson! Ferguson!' They spoke harshly, but they did not yell. Jenkins rounded the pool and ran toward the woods beyond Tanner's property. The news editor stumbled and tried to keep up with him.

The mutilated body lay in a clump of weeds. The head was severed; its eyes were wide, as if the lids had been pierced and held with nails.

'Get back, Mr Tanner! Stay back! Don't look! Don't raise your voice!' Jenkins held the petrified news director by the shoulders, pushing him away from the corpse. The two other men ran into the woods, pistols drawn.

Tanner sank to the ground feeling sick, frightened beyond any fear he'd known.

'Listen to me,' whispered Jenkins, kneeling over the trembling man. 'That body in there wasn't meant for you to see. It has nothing to do with *you*! There are certain rules, certain signs we all know about. That man was killed for Fassett. It was meant for *him*.'

The body was wrapped in canvas and two men lifted it up to carry it away. Their moves were silent, efficient.

'Your wife's still sleeping,' said Fassett quietly. 'That's good . . . The boy got up and came downstairs. McDermott told him you were making coffee for the men.'

Tanner sat on the grass on the far side of the pool, trying to make sense out of the last hour. Fassett and Jenkins stood above him.

'For God's sake, how did it happen?' He watched the men carrying the body and his words could hardly be heard. Fassett knelt down.

'He was taken from behind.'

'From behind?'

'Someone who knew the woods behind your house.' Fassett's eyes bored into Tanner's and the news director understood the unspoken accusation.

'It's my fault, isn't it?'

'Possibly. Jenkins left his post. His position was adjacent . . . Why were you downstairs? Why were all the first-floor lights on?'

'I couldn't sleep. I got up.'

'The lights were on in the garage. Why were you in the garage?'

'I . . . I don't understand. I guess I was thinking about this afternoon.'

'You left the garage lights on . . . I can understand a man who's nervous getting up, going downstairs – having a cigarette, a drink. I can understand that. But I don't understand a man going into his garage and leaving the lights on . . . Were you going somewhere, Mr Tanner?'

'Going somewhere? . . . No. No, of course not. Where would I go?'

Fassett looked up at Jenkins, who was watching Tanner's face in the dim reflection of the light coming from the house.

'Are you sure?'

'My God . . . You thought I was running away. You thought I was running away and you came in to stop me!'

'Keep your voice down, please.' Fassett rose to his feet.

'Do you think I'd *do* that? Do you think for one minute I'd leave my family?'

'You could be taking your family with you,' answered Jenkins.

'Oh, Christ! That's why you came to the window. That's why you left your . . .' Tanner couldn't finish the sentence. He felt sick and wondered if he threw up where he could do it. He looked up at the two government men. 'Oh, Christ!'

'Chances are it would have happened anyway.' Fassett spoke calmly. 'It wasn't . . . wasn't part of any original plan. But you've *got* to understand. You behaved *abnormally*. It wasn't *normal* for you to do what you did. You've got to watch every move you make, everything you do or say. You can't forget that. *Ever*.'

Tanner awkwardly, unsteadily, got up. 'You're not going on with this? You've got to call it off.'

'Call it off? One of my men was just killed. We call it off now and you're also dead. So's the rest of your family.'

Tanner saw the sadness in the agent's eyes.

One didn't argue with such men. They told the truth.

'Have you checked on the others?'

'Yes, we have.'

'Where are they?'

'The Cardones are at home. Tremayne stayed in New York; his wife's out here.'

'What about the Ostermans?'

'I'll go into that later. You'd better get back inside. We've doubled the patrol.'

'No you don't. What about the Ostermans? Aren't they in California?'

'You know they're not. You placed a call to them on your credit card at four-forty-six this afternoon.'

'Then where are they?'

Fassett looked at the news director and replied simply. 'They obviously made reservations under another name. We know they're in the New York area. We'll find them.'

'Then it could have been Osterman.'

'It could have been. You'd better get back. And don't worry. We've got an army out here.'

Tanner looked over at the woods where Fassett's man had been murdered. His whole body involuntarily shook for a moment. The proximity of such a brutal death appalled him. He nodded to the government men and started toward his house feeling only a sickening emptiness.

'Is it true about Tremayne?' asked Jenkins softly. 'He's in the city?'

'Yes. He had a fair amount to drink and took a room at the Biltmore.'

'Anyone check the room tonight?'

Fassett turned his attention from the figure of Tanner disappearing into the house. He looked at Jenkins. 'Earlier, yes. Our man reported that he went – probably staggered – to his room a little after midnight. We told him to pull out and pick Tremayne up again at seven. What's bothering you?'

'I'm not sure yet. It'll be clearer when we confirm Cardone's situation.'

'We did confirm it. He's at home.'

'We assume he's at home because we haven't had any reason to think otherwise up to now.'

'You'd better explain that.'

'The Cardones had dinner guests. Three couples. They all came together in a car with New York plates. Surveillance said they left in a hurry at twelve-thirty . . . I'm wondering now if Cardone was in that car. It was dark. He could have been.'

'Let's check it out. With both. The Biltmore'll be no problem. With Cardone we'll have Da Vinci make another phone call.'

Eighteen minutes later the two government men sat in the front seat of an automobile several hundred yards down the road from the Tanner house. The radio came in clearly.

'Information in, Mr Fassett. The Da Vinci call got us nowhere. Mrs Cardone said her husband wasn't feeling well; he was sleeping in a guest room and she didn't want to disturb him. Incidentally, she hung up on us. The Biltmore confirmed.

There's no one in room ten-twenty-one. Tremayne didn't even sleep in his bed.'

'Thank you', New York,' said Laurence Fassett as he flipped the channel button to OFF. He looked over at Jenkins. 'Can you imagine a man like Cardone refusing a telephone call at four-thirty in the morning? From Da Vinci?'

'He's not there.'

'Neither's Tremayne.'

15

Thursday – 6:40 A.M.

Fassett told him he could stay home on Thursday. Not that he had to be given permission; nothing could have dragged him away. Fassett also said that he'd contact him in the morning. The final plans for the total protection of the Tanner family would be made clear.

The news director put on a pair of khaki trousers and carried his sneakers and a sportshirt downstairs. He looked at the kitchen clock: twenty minutes to seven. The children wouldn't be up for at least an hour and a half. Ali, with luck, would sleep until nine-thirty or ten.

Tanner wondered how many men were outside. Fassett had said there was an army, but what good would an army be if Omega wanted him dead? What good had an army been for the government man in the woods at three-thirty in the morning? There were too many possibilities. Too many opportunities. Fassett had to understand that now. It had gone too far. If the preposterous were real, if the Ostermans, the Cardones or the Tremaynes really were a part of Omega, he couldn't simply greet them at his door as if nothing had happened. It was absurd!

He went to the kitchen door and quietly let

himself out. He'd go toward the woods until he saw someone. He'd reach Fassett.

'Good morning.' It was Jenkins, dark circles of weariness under his eyes. He was sitting on the ground just beyond the edge of the woods. He couldn't be seen from the house or even the pool.

'Hello. Aren't you going to get any sleep?'

'I'm relieved at eight. I don't mind. What about you? You're exhausted.'

'Look, I want to see Fassett. I've got to see him before he makes any more plans.'

The patrolman looked at his wristwatch. 'He was going to call you after we gave him the word you were up. I don't think he expected it'd be so early. That may be good though. Wait a sec.' Jenkins walked a few feet into the woods and returned with a canvas-pack radio. 'Let's go. We'll drive over.'

'Why can't he come here?'

'Relax. Nobody could get near your house. Come on. You'll see.'

Jenkins picked up the radio by its shoulder strap and led Tanner through a newly created path in the woods surrounding his property. Every thirty to forty feet were men, kneeling, sitting, lying on their stomachs facing the house, unseen but seeing. As Jenkins and Tanner approached each man, weapons were drawn. Jenkins gave the radio to the patrol on the east flank.

'Call Fassett. Tell him we're on our way over,' he said.

* * *

'That agent was killed last night because the killer knew he'd been recognized. One part of Omega was identified and that was unacceptable.' Fassett sipped coffee, facing Tanner. 'It was also another sort of warning, but that doesn't concern you.'

'He was murdered fifty yards from my house, from my family! *Everything* concerns me!'

'All right! . . . Try to understand. We can assume the information on you has been returned; remember, you're just Tanner the newsman, nothing else. They're circling like hawks now, wary of each other. None knowing whether the others have accomplices, scouts of their own . . . The killer – *one* tentacle of Omega – ran a private surveillance. He collided with the agent; he had no choice but to kill. He didn't know him, he'd never seen him before. The only thing he *could* be sure of was that whoever posted the man would become concerned when he didn't report. Whoever was responsible for that man in the woods would come and find him. That was the warning; his death.'

'You can't be sure of that.'

'We're not dealing with amateurs. The killer knew the body would be removed before daylight. I told you in Washington, Omega's fanatic. A decapitated body fifty yards from your house is the kind of mistake that would call for an NKVD execution. *If* Omega was responsible. If not . . .'

'How do you know they're not working together? If the Ostermans or the Cardones or the Tremaynes are any part of it, they could have planned it together.'

'Impossible. They haven't been in contact since the harassment began. We've fed them all – each of them – contradictory stories, illogical suppositions, half truths. We've had cables routed through Zurich, telephone calls from Lisbon, messages delivered by strangers in dead-end streets. Each couple is in the dark. None know what the others are doing.'

The agent named Cole looked up at Fassett from the chair by the motel window. He knew that Fassett could not be absolutely sure of his last statement. They'd lost the Ostermans for nearly twelve hours. There was a surveillance lapse of three and three-and-a-half hours, respectively, with Tremayne and Cardone. Still, thought Cole, Fassett was right to say what he did.

'Where are the Ostermans? You said last night – this morning – that you didn't know where they were.'

'We found them. In a New York hotel. From what we've learned, it's doubtful Osterman was in the area last night.'

'But, again, you're not sure.'

'I said doubtful. Not beyond doubt.'

'And you're convinced it had to be one of them?'

'We think so. The killer was male almost certainly. It . . . took enormous strength . . . He knew the grounds around your property better than we did. And you should know we've studied your place for weeks.'

'For God's sake then, *stop* them! Confront them! You can't let it go on!'

'Which one?' Fassett asked quietly.

'*All* of them! A man was *killed*!'

Fassett put his coffee cup down. 'If we do as you suggest, which, I admit, is tempting – it was my man who was killed, remember – we not only wash out any chance we have to expose Omega, but we also take a risk with you and your family that I can't justify.'

'We couldn't be taking any greater risk and you know it.'

'You're in no danger. Not as long as you continue to act in a normal manner. If we walk in now we're admitting the weekend is a trap. That trap couldn't have been set without your assistance . . . We'd be signing your death warrants.'

'I don't understand that.'

'Then take my word for it,' said Fassett sharply. 'Omega *must* come to *us*. There's no other way.'

Tanner paused, watching Fassett carefully. 'That's not entirely true, is it? What you're saying is . . . it's too late.'

'You're very perceptive.'

Fassett picked up his cup and went to the table where there was a Thermos of coffee. 'There's only one more day. At the most two. Some part of Omega will break by then. All we need is one. One defection and it's over.'

'And one stick of dynamite in my house blows us to hell.'

'There'll be nothing like that. No violence. Not directed at you. Put simply, you're not important. Not any longer. They'll only be concerned about each other.'

'What about yesterday afternoon?'

'We've put out a police-blotter story. A robbery. Bizarre to be sure, but a robbery nevertheless. Just what your wife thinks happened, the way she thinks it happened. You don't have to deny anything.'

'They'll know it's a lie. They'll call it.'

Fassett looked calmly up from the Thermos. 'Then we'll have Omega, won't we? We'll know which one it is.'

'What am I supposed to do? Pick up a telephone and call you? They may have other ideas . . .'

'We'll hear every word said in your house starting with your first guest tomorrow afternoon. Later this morning two television repairmen will come to fix the sets damaged in the robbery. While tracing antenna wiring they'll also install miniaturized pick-ups throughout your home. Starting with the first arrival tomorrow, they'll be activated.'

'Are you trying to tell me you won't activate them until then?'

Cole interrupted. 'No, we won't. We're not interested in your privacy, only your safety.'

'You'd better get back,' said Fassett. 'Jenkins will drop you off at the south end of your property. You couldn't sleep so you went for a walk.'

Tanner crossed slowly to the door. He stopped and looked back at Fassett. 'It's just like it was in Washington, isn't it? You don't give me any alternative.'

Fassett turned away. 'We'll be in touch. If I were you I'd relax, go to the Club. Play tennis, swim. Get your mind off things. You'll feel better.'

Tanner looked at Fassett's back in disbelief. He was being dismissed, as a less-than-respected subordinate is dismissed before a high policy conference.

'Come on,' said Cole, standing up, 'I'll see you to the car.' As they walked, he added, 'I think you should know that that man's death last night complicates Fassett's job more than you'll ever realize. That killing was directed at him. It was *his* warning.'

The news director looked at Cole closely. 'What do you mean?'

'There are signs between old-line professionals and this is one of them. You're insignificant now . . . Fassett's brilliant. He's set the forces in motion and nothing can stop them. The people who conceived Omega realize what's happened. And they're beginning to see that they may be helpless. They want the man responsible to know they'll be back. Sometime. A severed head means a massacre, Mr Tanner. They took his wife. Now he's got three kids to worry about.'

Tanner felt the sickness coming upon him again.

'What kind of a world do you people live in?'

'The same one you do.'

16

Thursday – 10:15 A.M.

When Alice awoke at ten-fifteen Thursday morning her immediate reaction was to remain in bed forever. She could hear the children arguing downstairs and the indistinguishable but patient words from her husband settling the dispute. She thought about his remarkable sense of small kindnesses that added up to major concern. That wasn't bad after so many years of marriage.

Perhaps her husband wasn't as quick or dramatic as Dick Tremayne, or as sheerly powerful as Joe Cardone, or as witty or bright as Bernie Osterman, but she wouldn't exchange places with Ginny, Betty, or Leila for anything in the world. Even if everything started all over again, she would wait for John Tanner, or *a* John Tanner. He was that rare man. He wanted to share, *had* to share. *Everything.* None of the others did. Not even Bernie, although he was the most like John. Even Bernie had quiet secrets, according to Leila.

In the beginning, Alice had wondered if her husband's need to share was merely the result of his pity for her. Because she was to be pitied, she realized without any sense of self-indulgence. Most of her life before she met John Tanner had been spent in flight or in pursuit of sanctuary.

Her father, a self-professed rectifier of the world's ills, was never able to stay too long in one place. A contemporary John Brown.

The newspapers eventually labeled him . . . lunatic.

The Los Angeles police eventually killed him.

She remembered the words.

Los Angeles, February 10, 1945. Jason McCall, whom authorities believe to have been in the pay of the Communists, was shot down today outside his canyon headquarters when he emerged brandishing what appeared to be a weapon. The Los Angeles police and agents of the Federal Bureau of Investigation unearthed McCall's whereabouts after an extensive search . . .

The Los Angeles police and the agents of the Federal Bureau of Investigation, however, had not bothered to determine that Jason McCall's weapon was a bent piece of metal he called his 'plowshare'.

Mercifully, Alice had been with an aunt in Pasadena when the killing took place. She'd met the young journalism student, John Tanner, at the public inquest after her father's death. The Los Angeles authorities wanted the inquest public. There was no room for a martyr. They wanted it clear that under no circumstances was McCall's death a murder.

Which, of course, it was.

The young journalist – returned from the war – knew it and labeled it as such. And although his story did nothing for the McCall family, it did bring him closer to the sad and bewildered girl who became his wife.

Alice stopped thinking and rolled over on her stomach. It was all past. She was where she wanted to be.

Several minutes later she heard strange male voices downstairs in the hallway. She started to sit up when the door opened and her husband came in. He smiled and bent down, kissing her lightly on the forehead, but in spite of his casualness, there was something strained about him.

'Who's downstairs?' she asked.

'The TV men. They're rehooking the sets, but the outside antenna system's loused up. They have to locate the trouble.'

'Which means I get up.'

'It does. I'm not taking chances with you in bed in front of two well-proportioned men in overalls.'

'You once wore overalls. Remember? In your senior year you had that job at the gas station.'

'And when I got home I also remember they came off with alarming ease. Now, up you go.'

He *was* tense, she thought; he was imposing control on the situation, on himself. He announced that in spite of the pressures which descended on him on Thursdays, on this particular Thursday he was staying at home.

His explanation was simple. After yesterday afternoon, regardless of the continuing police investigation, he wasn't about to leave his family. Not until everything was cleared up.

He took them to the Club, where he and Ali

played doubles with their neighbors, Dorothy and Tom Scanlan. Tom was reputed to be so rich he hadn't gone to work in a decade.

What struck Ali was her husband's determination to win. She was embarrassed when he accused Tom of miscalling a line shot and mortified when he made an unusually violent overhead, narrowly missing Dorothy's face.

They won the set, and the Scanlans turned down another. So they went to the pool, where John demanded what amounted to extraordinary service from the waiters. Late in the afternoon he spotted McDermott and insisted he join them for a drink. McDermott had come to the Club – so John told his wife – to tell a member that his car was long overdue at a parking meter in town.

And always, always, Tanner kept going to the telephone inside the Club. He could have had one brought to the poolside table but he wouldn't do so. He claimed that the Woodward conferences were getting heated and he'd rather not talk in public.

Alice didn't believe it. Her husband had many talents and perhaps the most finely honed was his ability to remain calm, even cold, under acute pressure. Yet today he was obviously close to panic.

They returned to Orchard Drive at eight o'clock. Tanner ordered the children to bed; Alice revolted.

'I've had it!' she said firmly. She pulled her husband into the living room and held his arm. 'You're being unreasonable, darling. I know how you felt. I felt it, too, but you've been barking orders all day long. Do this! Do that! It's not like you.'

Tanner remembered Fassett. He had to remain calm, normal. Even with Ali.

'I'm sorry. It's a delayed reaction, I guess. But you're right. Forgive me.'

'It's over and done with,' she added, not really accepting his quick apology. 'It was frightening, but everything's all right now. It's *over.*'

Oh Christ, thought Tanner. He wished to God it were that simple. 'It's over and I've behaved childishly and I want my wife to say she loves me so we can have a couple of drinks and go to bed together.' He kissed her lightly on the lips. 'And that, madam, is the best idea I've had all day.'

'You took a long time arriving at it,' she said as she smiled up at him. 'It'll take me a few minutes. I promised Janet I'd read her a story.'

'What are you going to read her?'

'"Beauty and the Beast". Ponder it.' She disengaged herself from his arms, touching his face with her fingers. 'Give me ten, fifteen minutes.'

Tanner watched her go back into the hall to the staircase. She'd been through so much, and now this. Now, Omega.

He looked at his watch. It was eight-twenty and Ali would be upstairs for at least ten minutes, probably twice as long. He decided to call Fassett at the motel.

It wasn't going to be the usual conversation with Fassett. No more condescending instructions, no more sermons. It was now the end of the third day; three days of harassment against the suspects of Omega.

John Tanner wanted specifics. He was entitled to them.

Fassett was alarmed, annoyed, at the news director's precise questions.

'I can't take time to phone you whenever someone crosses the street.'

'I need answers. The weekend starts tomorrow, and if you want me to go on with this, you'll tell me what's happened. Where are they now? What have their reactions been? I've *got* to know.'

For a few seconds there was silence. When Fassett spoke, his voice was resigned. 'Very well . . . Tremayne stayed in New York last night. I told you that, remember? While at the Biltmore he met a man named Townsend. Townsend's a known stock manipulator out of Zurich. Cardone and his wife went to Philadelphia this afternoon. She visited her family in Chestnut Hill and he went out to Bala Cynwyd to meet with a man we know is a high capo in the Mafia. They got back to Saddle Valley an hour ago. The Ostermans are at The Plaza. They're having dinner later tonight with a couple named Bronson. The Bronsons are friends from years ago. They're also on the Attorney General's subversive list.'

Fassett stopped and waited for Tanner to speak.

'And none of them have met? They haven't even called each other? They've made no plans? I want the truth!'

'If they've talked it hasn't been on any telephone we can control, which would mean they'd have to be at pay phones at simultaneous times, which they haven't. We know they haven't met – simple surveillance. If any of them has plans, they're individual, not coordinated . . . We're counting on that as I've told you. That's all there is.'

'There doesn't seem to be any relationship. With any of them?'

'That's right. That's what we've concluded.'

'But not what you expected. You said they'd panic. Omega would be in panic by now.'

'I think they are. Every one of them. Separately. Our projections are positive.'

'What the hell does that mean?'

'Think. One couple races to a powerful Mafioso. Another meets with a husband and wife who are as fanatic as anyone in the Presidium. And the lawyer has a sudden conference with an international securities thief out of Zurich. That's panic. The NKVD has many tentacles. Every one of them is on the brink. All we do is sit and wait.'

'Beginning tomorrow, sitting and waiting's not going to be so easy.'

'Be natural. You'll find yourself functioning on two levels really quite comfortably. It's always like that. There's no danger if you even *half* carry it off. They're too concerned with each other now. Remember, you don't have to hide yesterday afternoon. Talk about it. Be expansive. Do and say what comes naturally about it.'

'And you think they'll believe me?'

'They haven't got a choice! Don't you understand that? You made your reputation as an investigative reporter. Do I have to remind you that investigation ends when the subjects collide? That's the age-old wrap-up.'

'And I'm the innocent catalyst?'

'You better believe it. The more innocent, the better the wrap-up.'

Tanner lit a cigarette. He couldn't deny the government man any longer. His logic was too sound. And the safety, the security, the all-holy well-being of Ali and the children was in this cold professional's hands.

'All right. I greet them all at the door as long-lost brothers and sisters.'

'That's the way. And if you feel like it, call them all in the morning, make sure they're coming over. Except the Ostermans, of course. Whatever you'd normally do . . . And remember, we're right there. The most sophisticated equipment the biggest corporation on earth owns is at work for you. Not even the smallest weapon could get through your front door.'

'Is that true?'

'We'd know it if a three-inch blade was in someone's pocket. A four-inch revolver would have you all out of there in sixty seconds.'

Tanner replaced the receiver and drew heavily on his cigarette. As he took his hand off the telephone he had the feeling – the physical feeling – of *leaving, jumping, going away*.

It was a strange sensation, an awesome sense of loneliness.

And then he realized what it was, and it disturbed him greatly.

His sanity was now dependent on a man named Fassett. He was utterly in his control.

PART THREE
The Weekend

17

The taxi drew up to the front of the Tanner house. John's dog, the stringy Welsh terrier, ran up and down the driveway, yapping with each advance and retreat, waiting for someone to acknowledge that the visitors were welcome. Janet raced across the front lawn. The taxi door opened; the Ostermans stepped out. Each carried gift-wrapped boxes. The driver brought out a single large suitcase.

From inside the house, Tanner looked at them both: Bernie, in an expensively cut Palm Beach jacket and light-blue slacks; Leila, in a white suit with a gold chain around her waist, the skirt well above her knees, and a wide-brimmed soft hat covering the left side of her face. They were the picture of California success. Yet somehow there was a trace of artifice with Bernie and Leila; they had moved into the real money barely nine years ago.

Or was their success itself a façade, wondered Tanner as he watched the couple bending down to embrace his daughter. Had they, instead, for years and years been inhabitants of a world where scripts and shooting schedules were only secondary – good *covers*, as Fassett might say?

Tanner looked at his watch. It was two minutes past five. The Ostermans were early – according to their original schedule. Perhaps it was their first mistake. Or perhaps they didn't expect him to be there. He always left the Woodward studio early when the Ostermans came, but not always in time to be home before five-thirty. Leila's letter had said plainly their flight from Los Angeles was due at Kennedy around five. A plane being late was understandable, normal. A flight that got in ahead of schedule was improbable.

They'd have to have an explanation. Would they bother?

'Johnny! For heaven's sake! I thought I heard the pup barking. It's Bernie and Leila. What are you standing there for?' Ali had come out of the kitchen.

'Oh, sorry . . . I just wanted to let Janet have her moment with them.'

'Go on out, silly. I'll just set the timer.' His wife walked back toward the kitchen as Tanner approached the front door. He stared at the brass knob and felt as he thought an actor might feel before making his first entrance in a difficult part. Unsure – totally unsure – of his reception.

He wet his lips and drew the back of his hand across his forehead. Deliberately he twisted the knob and pulled the door back swiftly. With his other hand he unlatched the aluminum screened panel and stepped outside.

The Osterman weekend had begun.

'Welcome, Schreibers!' he shouted with a wide grin. It was his usual greeting; Bernie considered it the most honorific.

'Johnny!'

'Hi, darling!'

Thirty yards away, they shouted back and smiled broad smiles. Yet even thirty yards away John Tanner could see their unsmiling eyes. Their eyes searched his – briefly, but unmistakably. For a split second Bernie even stopped smiling, stopped any motion whatsoever.

It was over in a moment. And there seemed to be a tacit agreement between them not to pursue the unspoken thoughts.

'Johnny, it's so awfully good to see you!' Leila ran across the lawn.

John Tanner accepted Leila's embrace and found himself responding with more overt affection than he thought he could muster. He knew why. He had passed the first test, the opening seconds of the Osterman weekend. He began to realize that Laurence Fassett could be right, after all. Perhaps he *could* carry it off.

Do as you normally do; behave as you'd normally behave. Don't think about anything else.

'John, you look great, just great, man!'

'Where's Ali, sweetie?' asked Leila, who stepped aside so Bernie could throw his long thin arms around Tanner.

'Inside. Casserole-doing-time. Come on in! Here, I'll grab the bag . . . No, Janet, honey, you can't lift Uncle Bernie's suitcase.'

'I don't know why not,' laughed Bernie. 'All it's filled with is towels from The Plaza.'

'The Plaza?' Tanner couldn't help himself. 'I thought your plane just got in.'

Osterman glanced at him. 'Uh uh. We flew in a couple of days ago. I'll tell you about it . . .'

In a strange way it was like old times, and Tanner was astonished that he found himself accepting the fact. There was still the sense of relief at physically seeing each other again, knowing that time and distance were meaningless to their friendship. There was still the feeling that they could take up conversations, continue anecdotes, finish stories begun months previously. And there was still Bernie; gentle, reflective Bernie with his quiet, devastating comments about the palm-lined drug store. Devastating but somehow never condescending; Bernie laughed at himself as well as his professional world, for it *was* his world.

Tanner remembered Fassett's words.

'. . . *you'll find yourself functioning on two levels quite comfortably. It's always like that.*'

Again, Fassett was right . . . In and out; in and out.

It struck Tanner as he watched Bernie that Leila kept shifting her eyes away from her husband to him. Once he returned her look; she lowered her eyes as a child might after a reprimand.

The telephone rang in the study. The sound was jarring to everyone but Alice. There was an extension phone on the table behind the sofa, but John ignored it as he crossed in front of the Ostermans toward the study door.

'I'll take it out here. It's probably the studio.'

As he entered the study he heard Leila speak to Ali, her voice lowered.

'Sweetie, Johnny seems tense. Is anything the matter? The way Bernie drawls on no one can get a word in.'

'Tense is understating it! You should have seen him yesterday!'

The telephone rang again; Tanner knew it wouldn't be normal to let it ring further. Yet he wanted so much to hear the Ostermans' reaction to Ali's story of the Wednesday terror.

He compromised. He picked the phone out of the cradle, held it to his side and listened for several seconds to the conversation.

Something caught his ear. Bernie and Leila reacted to Ali's words too quickly, with too much anticipation. They were asking questions before she finished sentences! They *did* know something.

'Hello? Hello! Hello, hello?' The anxious voice on the other end of the line belonged to Joe Cardone.

'Hello, Joe? Sorry, I dropped the phone . . .'

'I didn't hear it drop.'

'Very soft, very expensive carpets.'

'Where? In that study of yours with the parquet floor?'

'Hey, come on, Joe.'

'Sorry . . . The city was rotten hot today and the market's going to hell.'

'That's better. Now you sound like the cheerful fellow we're waiting for.'

'You mean everybody's there?'

'No. Just Bernie and Leila.'

'They're early. I thought the plane got in at five.'

'They flew in a couple of days ago.'

Cardone started to speak and then abruptly stopped. He seemed to catch his breath. 'Funny they didn't call. I mean, they didn't get in touch with me. Did they with you?'

'No, I guess they had business.'

'Sure, but you'd think . . .' Again Cardone stopped in the middle of a sentence. Tanner wondered whether this hesitation was meant for him; to convince him of the fact that Bernie and Joe hadn't met, hadn't spoken with each other.

'Bernie'll probably tell us all about it.'

'Yeah,' said Cardone, not really listening. 'Well, I just wanted to let you know we'd be late. I'll grab a quick shower; be there soon.'

'See you.' Tanner hung up the phone, surprised at his own calm. It occurred to him that he had controlled the conversation. *Controlled* it. He had to. Cardone was a nervous man and he hadn't called to say he'd be late. To begin with, he wasn't late.

Cardone had phoned to see if the others had come. Or if they were coming.

Tanner returned to the living room and sat down.

'Darling! Ali just told us! How dreadful! How simply terrifying!'

'My God, John! What an awful experience! The police said it was robbery?'

'So did *The New York Times*. Guess that makes it official.'

'I didn't see anything in *The Times*,' stated Bernie firmly.

'It was only a few lines near the back. We'll get better coverage in the local paper next week.'

'I've never heard of any robbery like that,' said Leila. 'I wouldn't settle for that, I really wouldn't.'

Bernie looked at her. 'I don't know. It's actually pretty smart. No identification, no harm to anyone.'

'What I don't understand is why they didn't just leave us in the garage.' Ali turned to her husband. It was a question he hadn't answered satisfactorily.

'Did the police say why?' asked Bernie.

'They said the gas was a low-yield variety. The thieves didn't want Ali or the kids to come to and see them. Very professional.'

'Very scary,' Leila said. 'How did the kids take it?'

'Ray's a neighborhood hero, of course,' said Ali. 'Janet's still not sure what happened.'

'Where *is* Ray?' Bernie pointed to a package in the hall. 'I hope he hasn't outgrown model airplanes. That's one of those remote-control things.'

'He'll love it,' said Ali. 'He's in the basement, I think. John's turning it over to him . . .'

'No, he's outside. In the pool.' Tanner realized that his interruption, his sharp correction of Ali, caused Bernie to look at him. Even Ali was startled by the abruptness of his statement.

So be it, thought Tanner. Let them all know the father was aware, every second, of the whereabouts of his own.

The dog began barking in front of the house;

the sound of a car could be heard in the driveway. Alice walked to the window.

'It's Dick and Ginny. And Ray's *not* in the pool,' she added, smiling at John. 'He's in front saying hello.'

'He must have heard the car,' said Leila for no apparent reason.

Tanner wondered why she made the remark; it was as if she were defending him. He went to the front door and opened it. 'Come on in, son. Some other friends of yours are here.'

When he saw the Ostermans, the boy's eyes lit up. The Ostermans never arrived empty-handed. 'Hello, Aunt Leila. Uncle Bernie!' Raymond Tanner, age twelve, walked into the arms of Leila and then shook hands manfully, shyly, with Bernie.

'We brought you a little something. Actually your buddy Merv suggested it.' Bernie crossed to the hall and picked up the package. 'Hope you like it.'

'Thank you very much.' The boy took the gift and went into the dining room to unwrap it.

Virginia Tremayne came in, the picture of cool sensuality. She was dressed in a man-styled shirt with multicolored stripes and a tight knit skirt which accentuated the movements of her body. There were women in Saddle Valley who resented Ginny's appearance, but they weren't in these rooms. Ginny was a good friend.

'I told Dick you called Wednesday,' she said to Tanner, 'but he says you never reached him. The poor lamb's been holed up in a conference suite with some awful merger people from Cincinnatti or Cleveland or somewhere . . . Leila, darling! Bernie, love!' Ginny pecked Tanner's cheek and choreographed herself past him.

Richard Tremayne came in. He was watching Tanner and what he saw obviously pleased him.

Tanner, on the other hand, felt the look and whipped his head around too quickly. Tremayne didn't have time to shift his eyes away. The news director recognized in the lawyer's stare the look of a doctor studying a medical chart.

For a split second both men silently, unwillingly, acknowledged the tension. And then it passed, as it had passed with the Ostermans. Neither man dared sustain it.

'Hey, John! Sorry I didn't get your message. Ginny mentioned something legal.'

'I thought you might have read about it.'

'What, for God's sake?'

'We didn't get much coverage in the New York papers, but wait'll you read next Monday's weekly. We'll be celebrities.'

'What the hell are you talking about?'

'We were robbed Wednesday. Robbed and kidnapped and chloroformed and God knows what else!'

'You're joking!'

'The hell he is!' Osterman walked into the hallway. 'How are you, Dick?'

'Bernie! How are you, buddy?' The men grasped hands, but Tremayne could not seem to take his attention from John Tanner.

'Did you hear what he said? Did you hear that?

What happened, for Christ's sake? I've been in town since Tuesday. Didn't even have time to get home.'

'We'll tell you all about it. Later. Let me get your drinks.' Tanner walked away rapidly. He couldn't fault Tremayne's reaction. The lawyer was not only shocked by what he'd heard, he was frightened. So much so that he had to make clear he had been gone since Tuesday.

Tanner made drinks for the Tremaynes and then went into the kitchen and looked out past his pool to the edge of the woods. Although there was no one in sight, he knew the men were there. With binoculars, with radios, probably with tiny speakers which magnified conversations taking place in any section of his house.

'Hey, John, I wasn't kidding!' It was Tremayne walking into the kitchen. 'Honest to God, I didn't know anything about it. About Wednesday, I mean. Why the hell didn't you reach me?'

'I tried. I even called a number on Long Island. Oyster Bay, I think.'

'Oh, shit! You know what I mean! You or Ali should have told Ginny. I'd have left the conference, you know that!'

'It's over with. Here's your drink.' Tremayne lifted the glass to his lips. He could drink any of them under the table.

'You can't leave it like that. Why did you call me in the first place?'

Tanner, stupidly, wasn't prepared for the question.

'I . . . I didn't like the way the police handled it.'

'The police? Fat-cap MacAuliff?'

'I never talked to Captain MacAuliff.'

'Didn't you give a statement?'

'Yes . . . yes, I did. To Jenkins and McDermott.'

'Where the hell was old law'n'order himself?'

'I don't know. He wasn't there.'

'Okay, Mac wasn't there. You say Jenkins and McDermott handled it. Ali told me they were the ones who found you . . .'

'Yes. Yes, that's what I was pissed-off about.'

'What?'

'I just didn't like the way they handled it. At least I didn't at the time. I've cooled it now. It was hot then, that's why I tried to reach you.'

'What are you figuring? Police negligence? Abridged rights? What?'

'I don't know, Dick! I just panicked, that's all. When you panic you want a lawyer.'

'I don't. I want a drink.' Tremayne held Tanner's eyes. Tanner blinked – as a small boy defeated in a game of stare.

'It's over with. Let's go back inside.'

'Maybe we ought to talk later. Maybe you have some kind of case and I don't see it.'

Tanner shrugged, knowing that Dick didn't really want to talk later at all. The lawyer was frightened, and his fear arrested his professional instinct to probe. As he walked away, Tanner had the feeling that Tremayne was telling the truth about one aspect of Wednesday afternoon. He hadn't been there himself.

But did he know who had been?

By six, the Cardones still hadn't arrived. No one asked why; the hour passed quickly and if anyone was concerned he hid it well. At ten minutes past, Tanner's eyes were drawn to a car driving slowly past his house. It was the Saddle Valley taxi, the sun causing intermittent, sharp flashes off the black enamel. In the rear window of the automobile he saw Joe Cardone's face for a moment. Joe was making sure all the guests had arrived. Or were still there, perhaps.

Forty-five minutes later the Cardones' Cadillac pulled into the driveway. When they entered the house it was obvious that Joe had had several drinks. Obvious because Joe was not a drinker, he didn't really approve of alcohol, and his voice was just a degree louder than it might have been.

'Bernie! Leila! Welcome to the heart of the eastern establishment!'

Betty Cardone, prim, stoutish, Anglican Betty, properly added to her husband's enthusiasm and the four of them exchanged embraces.

'Betty, you look adorable,' said Leila. 'Joe, my God, Joe! How can a man look so healthy? . . . Bernie built a gym and look what *I* got!'

'Don't you knock my Bernie!' said Joe, his arm around Osterman's shoulder.

'You tell her, Joe.' Bernie moved toward Cardone's wife and asked about the children.

Tanner started toward the kitchen, meeting

Ali in the hallway. She carried a plate of hors d'oeuvres.

'Everything's ready. We can eat whenever we want, so I'll sit down for a while . . . Get me a drink, will you, dear?'

'Sure. Joe and Betty are here.'

Ali laughed. 'I gathered that . . . What's the matter, darling? You look funny.'

'No, nothing. I was just thinking I'd better call the studio.'

Ali looked at her husband. 'Please. Everybody's here now. Our best friends. Let's have fun. Forget about Wednesday, *please*, Johnny.'

Tanner leaned over the tray of hors d'oeuvres and kissed her. 'You're dramatizing,' he said, remembering Fassett's admonition. 'I really do have to call the studio.'

In the kitchen, Tanner walked again to the window. It was a little after seven o'clock and the sun had gone down behind the tall trees in the woods. Shadows lay across the backyard lawn and the pool. And beyond the shadows were Fassett's men.

That was the important thing.

As Ali had said, they were all there now. The best of friends.

The buffet of curry, with a dozen side dishes, was Ali's usual triumph. The wives asked the usual questions and Ali slightly embossed the culinary answers – as usual. The men fell into the normal arguments about the relative merits of the various baseball teams and, in between, Bernie revealed further the humorous – and extraordinary – working methods of Hollywood television.

While the women cleared out the dining room, Tremayne took the opportunity to press Tanner on the robbery. 'What the hell was it last Wednesday? Level with us. I don't buy the burglary story.'

'Why not?' asked Tanner.

'It doesn't make sense.'

'Nobody uses gas on anybody,' added Cardone. 'Blackjacks, blindfolds, a shot in the head, maybe. Not gas.'

'Advanced thinking, perhaps. I'd rather it was a harmless gas than a blackjack.'

'Johnny.' Osterman lowered his voice and looked toward the dining room. Betty came out the kitchen door and began removing several dishes and smiled. He smiled back. 'Are you working on something that might make you enemies?'

'I imagine I always am in one way or another.'

'I mean something like the San Diego thing.'

Joe Cardone watched Osterman carefully, wondering if he might elaborate. San Diego had been a Mafia operation.

'Not that I know of. I've got men digging in a lot of areas, but nothing like that. At least I don't think so. Most of my best people have a free rein . . . Are you trying to tie in Wednesday with something at work?'

'It hadn't struck you?' asked Tremayne.

'Hell, no! I'm a professional newsman. Do you get worried if you're working on a sticky case?'

'Sometimes.'

'I read about that show of yours last Sunday.' Cardone sat down on the couch next to Tremayne. 'Ralph Ashton has friends in high places.'

'That's crazy.'

'Not necessarily.' Cardone had trouble with 'necessarily'. 'I've met him. He's a vindictive man.'

'He's not crazy,' interjected Osterman. 'No, it wouldn't be anything like that.'

'Why should it be anything, period? Anything but a robbery?' Tanner lit a cigarette and tried to watch the faces of the three men.

'Because, Goddamn it, it's not a natural way to get robbed,' exclaimed Cardone.

'Oh?' Tremayne looked at Cardone, sitting next to him on the sofa. 'Are you an expert on robbery?'

'No more than you are, counselor,' said Joe.

18

There was something artificial about the start of the weekend; Ali felt it. Perhaps it was that the voices were louder than usual, the laughter more pronounced.

Usually, when Bernie and Leila arrived, they all began calmly, catching up with each family's affairs. Conversations about this or that child, this or that career decision – these always occupied the first few hours. Her husband called it the Osterman syndrome. Bernie and Leila brought out the best in all of them. Made them talk, really *talk* with one another.

Yet no one had volunteered a single important personal experience. No one had brought up a single vital part of their recent lives – except, of course, the horrible thing on Wednesday afternoon.

On the other hand, Ali realized, she was still concerned about her husband – concerned about his staying home from the office, his short temper, his erratic behavior since Wednesday afternoon. Maybe she was imagining things about everybody else.

The other women had rejoined their husbands; Alice had put away the left-overs. The children were in bed now. And she wouldn't listen to any more talk from Betty or Ginny about maids. She *could* afford a maid! *They* could afford a maid! But she wouldn't *have* one!

Her father had had maids. 'Disciples' he called them. 'Disciples' who cleaned and swept and brought-in and . . .

Her mother had called them 'maids'.

Ali stopped thinking and wondered if she'd had a drink she couldn't handle. She turned on the faucet and dabbed her face with cold water. Joe Cardone walked through the kitchen door.

'The boss-man told me if I wanted a drink, I pour it myself. Don't tell me where, I've been here before.'

'Go right ahead, Joe. Do you see everything you need?'

'Sure do. Lovely gin; beautiful tonic . . . Hey, what's the matter? You been crying?'

'Why should I be? I just splashed water on my face.'

'Your cheeks are all wet.'

'Water on the face does that.'

Joe put down the bottle of tonic and approached her. 'Are you and Johnny in any trouble? . . . This Wednesday afternoon . . . okay, it was a crazy type of robbery, Johnny told me . . . but if it was anything else, you'd let me know, wouldn't you? I mean, if he's playing around with sharks you wouldn't keep it a secret from me, would you?'

'Sharks?'

'Loan-sharks. I've got clients at Standard Mutual. Even a little stock. I know the company . . . You and Johnny live very well, but sixty thousand dollars after taxes isn't that much any more.'

Alice Tanner caught her breath. 'John does very well!'

'That's relative. In my opinion, John's in that big middle mess. He can't take over and he won't let go of his little kingdom to try for anything better. That's his business, and yours. But I want you to tell him for me . . . I'm his friend. His good friend. And I'm clean. Absolutely *clean.* If he needs anything, you tell him to call me, all right?'

'Joe, I'm touched. I really am. But I don't think it's necessary. I don't, really.'

'But you'll tell him?'

'Tell him yourself. John and I have an unspoken pact. We don't discuss his salary any more. Frankly because I agree with you.'

'Then you've got problems.'

'You're not being fair. Problems to you may not be problems for us.'

'I hope you're right. Tell him that, too.' Cardone walked rapidly back to the bar and picked up his glass. Before Ali could speak he walked through the door back into the living room.

Joe was telling her something and she didn't understand.

'Nobody appointed you or any other member of *any* news media to set yourselves up as infallible guardians of the truth! I'm sick and tired of it! I live with it every day.' Tremayne stood in front of the fireplace, his anger obvious to everyone.

'Not infallible, of course not,' answered Tanner. 'But no one gave the courts the right to stop us from looking for information as objectively as we can.'

'When that information is prejudicial to a client *or* his opponent you have no right to make it public. If it's factual, it'll be heard in court. Wait'll the verdict's rendered.'

'That's impossible and you know it.'

Tremayne paused, smiled thinly, and sighed. 'I know I do. Realistically, there's no solution.'

'Are you sure you want to find one?' asked Tanner.

'Of course.'

'Why? The advantage is yours. You win the verdict, fine. If you lose, you claim the court was corrupted by a biased press. You appeal.'

'It's the rare case that's won on appeal,' said Bernard Osterman, sitting on the floor in front of the sofa. 'Even I know that. They get the publicity, but they're rare.'

'Appeals cost money,' added Tremayne with a shrug. 'Most of the time for nothing. Especially corporate appeals.'

'Then force the press to restrain itself when there's a lot of heat. It's simple.' Joe finished his drink and looked pointedly at Tanner.

'It's not simple,' said Leila, sitting in an armchair opposite the sofa. 'It becomes judgment. Who defines restraint? That's what Dick means. There's no clear-cut definition.'

'At the risk of offending my husband, God forbid,' Virginia laughed as she spoke, 'I think an informed public is just as important as an unbiased courtroom. Perhaps they're even connected. I'm on your side, John.'

'Judgment, again,' said her husband. 'It's opinion. What's factual information and what's interpreted information?'

'One's truth,' said Betty off-handedly. She was watching her husband. He was drinking too much.

'Whose truth? Which truth? . . . Let's create a hypothetical situation. Between John and myself. Say I've been working for six months on a complicated merger. As an ethical attorney I'm dealing with men whose cause I believe in; by putting together a number of companies thousands of jobs are saved, firms which are going bankrupt suddenly have new lives. Then along come several people who are getting hurt – because of their own ineptness – and start shouting for injunctions. Suppose they reach John and start yelling "Foul!" Because they seem – seem, mind you – like underdogs, John gives their cause one *minute*, just one *minute* of network time across the country. Instantly my case is prejudiced. And don't let anyone tell you the courts aren't subject to media pressure. One *minute* as opposed to *six months*.'

'Do you think I'd allow that? Do you think any of us would?'

'You need copy. You always need copy! There are times when you don't understand!' Tremayne's voice grew louder.

Virginia stood up. 'Our John wouldn't do that, darling . . . I'm for another cup of coffee.'

'I'll get it,' said Alice, rising from the sofa.

She'd been watching Tremayne, startled by his sudden vehemence.

'Don't be silly,' answered Ginny, going into the hallway.

'I'd like a drink.' Cardone held out his glass, expecting someone to take it.

'Sure, Joe.' Tanner took his glass. 'Gin and tonic?'

'That's what I've been drinking.'

'Too much of,' added his wife.

Tanner walked into the ktichen and began making Cardone's drink. Ginny was at the stove.

'I'm heating the Chemex; the candle burned out.'

'Thanks.'

'I always have the same problem. The damn candles go out and the coffee's cold.'

Tanner chuckled and poured the tonic. Then he realized that Ginny was making a comment, a rather unattractive comment. 'I told Ali to get an electric pot, but she refuses.'

'John?'

'Yes?'

'It's a beautiful night. Why don't we all take a swim?'

'Sure. Good idea. I'll backwash the filter. Let me get this to Joe.' Tanner returned to the living room in time to hear the opening bars of 'Tangerine'. Ali had put on an album called 'Hits of Yesterday'.

There were the proper responses, the laughs of recognition.

'Here you are, Joe. Anyone else for anything?'

There was a chorus of no-thanks. Betty had gotten up and was facing Dick Tremayne by the mantel. Tanner thought they looked as though they'd been arguing. Ali was at the stereo showing Bernie the back of the album cover; Leila Osterman sat opposite Cardone, watching him drink his gin and tonic, seemingly annoyed that he drank so quickly.

'Ginny and I are going to backwash the pool. We'll take a swim, okay? You've all got suits here; if not, there're a dozen extras in the garage.'

Dick looked at Tanner. It was a curious look, thought the news editor. 'Don't teach Ginny too much about that damned filter. I'm holding firm. No pool.'

'Why not?' asked Cardone.

'Too many kids around.'

'Build a fence,' said Joe with a degree of disdain.

Tanner started out toward the kitchen and the back door. He heard a sudden burst of laughter behind him, but it wasn't the laughter of people enjoying themselves. It was forced, somehow unkind.

Was Fassett right? Was Omega showing the signs? Were the hostilities slowly coming to the surface?

Outside he walked to the edge of the pool, to the filter box. 'Ginny?'

'I'm over here, by Ali's tomato plants. This stake fell down and I can't retie the vine.'

'Okay.' He turned and walked over to her. 'Which one? I can't see it.'

'Here,' said Ginny, pointing.

Tanner knelt down and saw the stake. It hadn't fallen over, it had been snapped. 'One of the kids must have run through here.' He pulled up the thin broken dowel and placed the tomato vine carefully on the ground. 'I'll fix it tomorrow.'

He got up. Ginny stood very close to him and put her hand on his arm. He realized they couldn't be seen from the house.

'I broke it,' Ginny said.

'Why?'

'I wanted to talk to you. Alone.'

She had undone several buttons of her blouse below the neckline. He could see the swell of her breasts. Tanner wondered if Ginny was drunk. But Ginny never got drunk, or if she did, no one ever knew it.

'What do you want to talk about?'

'Dick, for one thing. I apologize for him. He can become gross . . . rude, when he's upset.'

'Was he rude? Upset? I didn't notice.'

'Of course you did. I was watching you.'

'You were wrong.'

'I don't think so.'

'Let's get the pool done.'

'Wait a minute.' Ginny laughed softly. 'I don't frighten you, do I?'

'My friends don't frighten me,' Tanner said, smiling.

'We know a great deal about each other.'

Tanner watched Ginny's face closely, her eyes, the slight pinching of her lips. He wondered if this was the moment the unbelievable was about to be revealed to him. If it was, he'd help her say it. 'I suppose we always think we know our friends. I sometimes wonder if we ever do.'

'I'm very attracted . . . physically attracted to you. Did you know that?'

'No, I didn't,' said Tanner, surprised.

'It shouldn't bother you. I wouldn't hurt Ali for the world. I don't think physical attraction necessarily means a commitment, do you?'

'Everyone has fantasies.'

'You're sidestepping.'

'I certainly am.'

'I told you, I wouldn't harm your commitments.'

'I'm human. They'd be harmed.'

'I'm human, too. May I kiss you? At least I deserve a kiss.'

Ginny put her arms around the startled Tanner's neck and pressed her lips against his, opening her mouth. Tanner knew she was doing her best to arouse him. He couldn't understand it. If she meant what she was doing, there was nowhere to complete the act.

Then he did understand. She was promising.

She meant that.

'Oh, Johnny! Oh, God, Johnny!'

'All right, Ginny. All right. Don't . . .' Perhaps she really was drunk, thought Tanner. She'd feel like a fool tomorrow. 'We'll talk later.'

Ginny pulled slightly back. Her lips to the side of his. 'Of course, we'll talk later . . . Johnny? . . . Who is Blackstone?'

'Blackstone?'

'Please! I've got to know! Nothing will change, I promise you that! *Who is Blackstone?*'

Tanner held her shoulders, forcing her face in front of his own.

She was crying.

'I don't know any Blackstone.'

'Don't do this!' she whispered. 'Please, for God's sake, don't do this! Tell Blackstone to *stop it*!'

'Did Dick send you out here?'

'He'd kill me,' she said softly.

'Let me get it straight. You're offering me . . .'

'Anything you want! Just leave him *alone* . . . My husband's a good man. A very, very decent man. He's been a good friend to you! Please, don't hurt him!'

'You love him.'

'More than my life. So please, don't hurt him. And tell Blackstone to stop!'

She rushed off into the garage.

He wanted to go after her and be kind, but the specter of Omega prevented him. He kept wondering whether Ginny, who was capable of offering herself as a whore, was also capable of things far more dangerous.

But Ginny wasn't a whore. Careless, perhaps, even provocative in a humorous, harmless way, but it had never occurred to Tanner or anybody Tanner knew that she would share her bed with anyone but Dick. She wasn't like that.

Unless she was Omega's whore.

There was the forced laughter again from inside

the house. Tanner heard the opening clarinet strains of 'Amapola'. He knelt down and picked the thermometer out of the water.

Suddenly he was aware that he wasn't alone. Leila Osterman was standing several feet behind him on the grass. She'd come outside silently; or perhaps he was too preoccupied to hear the kitchen door or the sound of her footsteps.

'Oh, hi! You startled me.'

'I thought Ginny was helping you.'

'She . . . spilled filter powder on her skirt . . . Look, the temperature's eighty-three. Joe'll say it's too warm.'

'If he can tell.'

'I see what you mean,' said Tanner, getting to his feet, smiling. 'Joe's no drinker.'

'He's trying.'

'Leila, how come you and Bernie got in a couple days ago?'

'He hasn't told you?' Leila was hesitant, seemingly annoyed that the explanation was left to her.

'No. Obviously.'

'He's looking around. He had conferences, lunches.'

'What's he looking for?'

'Oh, projects. You know Bernie; he goes through phases. He never forgets that *The New York Times* once called him exciting . . . or incisive, I never remember which. Unfortunately, he's acquired expensive tastes.'

'You've lost me.'

'He'd like to find a class series; you know, the

old Omnibus type. There's a lot of talk around the agencies about upgrading.'

'Is there? I hadn't heard it.'

'You're in news, not programming.'

Tanner took out a pack of cigarettes and offered one to Leila. As he lit it he could see the concern, the strain, in her eyes. 'Bernie has a lot going for him. You and he have made the agencies a great deal of money. He won't have any trouble; he's persuasive as hell.'

'It takes more than persuasion, I'm afraid,' Leila said. 'Unless you want to work for a percentage of nonprofit culture . . . No, it takes influence. Enormous influence; enough to make the money people change their minds.' Leila drew heavily on her cigarette, avoiding Tanner's stare.

'Can he do that?'

'He might be able to. Bernie's word carries more weight than any other writer's on the coast. He has "clout", as they say . . . It extends to New York, take my word for it.'

Tanner found himself not wanting to talk. It hurt too much. Leila had all but told him, he thought. All but proclaimed the power of Omega. Of course Bernie was going to do what he wanted to do. Bernie was perfectly capable of making people change their minds, reverse decisions. Or Omega was, and he was part of it – part of them.

'Yes,' he said softly. 'I'll take your word for it. Bernie's a big man.'

They stood quietly for a moment, then Leila spoke sharply. 'Are you satisfied?'

'What?'

'I asked if you were satisfied. You've just questioned me like a cop. I can even furnish you with a list of his appointments, if you'd like. And there are hairdressers, department stores, shops – I'm sure they'd confirm my having been there.'

'What the hell are you talking about?'

'You know perfectly well! That's not a very nice party in there, in case you haven't noticed. We're all behaving as if we'd never met before, as if we really didn't like our new acquaintances.'

'That has nothing to do with me. Maybe you should look to yourselves.'

'Why?' Leila stepped back. Tanner thought she looked bewildered, but he didn't trust his appraisal. 'Why should we? What *is* it, John?'

'Can't *you* tell *me*?'

'Good Lord, you *are* after him, aren't you? You're after *Bernie*.'

'No, I'm not. I'm not after anyone.'

'You listen to me, John! Bernie would give his life for you! Don't you know that?'

Leila Osterman threw the cigarette on the ground and walked away.

As Tanner was about to carry the chlorine bucket to the garage, Ali came outside with Bernie Osterman. For a moment he wondered whether Leila had said anything. Obviously she hadn't. His wife and Bernie simply wanted to know where he kept the club soda and to tell him that everyone was getting into suits.

Tremayne stood in the kitchen doorway, glass

in hand, watching the three of them talking. To Tanner he seemed nervous, uneasy.

Tanner walked into the garage and placed the plastic bucket in the corner next to the garage toilet. It was the coolest place. The kitchen door opened and Tremayne walked down the steps.

'I want to see you a minute.'

'Sure.'

Tremayne turned sideways and slid past the Triumph. 'I never see you driving this.'

'I hate it. Getting in and out of it's murder.'

'You're a big guy.'

'It's a small car.'

'I . . . I wanted to say I'm sorry about that bullshit I was peddling before. I have no argument with you. I got burned on a case several weeks ago by a reporter on *The Wall Street Journal*. Can you imagine? *The Journal!* My firm decided not to go ahead on the strength of it.'

'Free press or fair trial. A damned valid argument. I didn't take it personally.'

Tremayne leaned against the Triumph. He spoke cautiously. 'A couple of hours ago, Bernie asked you – he was talking about last Wednesday – if you were working on anything like that San Diego story. I never knew much about that except that it's still referred to in the newspapers . . .'

'It's been exaggerated out of proportion. A series of waterfront payoffs. Indigenous to the industry, I think.'

'Don't be so modest.'

'I'm not. It was a hell of a job and I damned

near got the Pulitzer. It's been responsible for my whole career.'

'All right . . . Fine, good . . . Now, I'm going to stop playing games. Are you digging around something that affects me?'

'Not that I know of . . . It's what I said to Bernie; I've a staff of seventy-odd directly involved with news gathering. I don't ask for daily reports.'

'Are you telling me you don't know what they're doing?'

'I'm better than that,' said Tanner with a short laugh. 'I approve expenditures; nothing is aired without my clearing it.'

Tremayne pushed himself away from the Triumph. 'All right, let's level . . . Ginny came back inside fifteen minutes ago. I've lived with that girl for sixteen years. I know her . . . She'd been crying. She was outside with you and she came back crying. I want to know why.'

'I can't answer you.'

'I think you'd better try! . . . You resent the money I make, don't you?'

'That's not true.'

'Of course it is! You think I haven't heard Ali on your back! And now you subtly, off-handedly drop that nothing is *aired* without your *clearing* it! Is that what you told my wife? Am I supposed to hear the details from *her*? A wife can't testify; are you *protecting* us? What do you *want*?'

'Get hold of yourself! Are you into something so rotten you're getting paranoid? Is that it? You want to tell me about it?'

'No. No! Why was she *crying*?'

'Ask her yourself!'

Tremayne turned away and John Tanner could see the lawyer's body begin to shake as he passed his hands on the hood of the small sports car.

'We've known each other a long time; but you've never understood me at all . . . Don't make judgments unless you understand the men you're judging.'

So this was it, thought Tanner. Tremayne was admitting it. He was part of Omega.

And then Tremayne spoke again and the conclusion was destroyed. He turned around and the look on his face was pathetic.

'I may not be beyond reproach, I know that, but I'm within the law. That's the system. I may not like it all the time, but I respect that *system*!'

Tanner wondered if Fassett's men had placed one of their electronic pick-ups in the garage. If they had heard the words, spoken in such sorrow, with such a ring of truth. He looked at the broken man in front of him.

'Let's go into the kitchen. You need a drink and so do I.'

19

Alice flipped the switch under the living-room windowsill so the music would be heard on the patio speakers. They were all outside now on the pool deck. Even her husband and Dick Tremayne had finally gotten up from the kitchen table; they'd been sitting there for twenty minutes and Ali thought it strange they'd hardly spoken.

'Hello, gracious lady!' The voice was Joe's, and Alice felt herself grow tense. He walked from the hallway into view; he was in swimming trunks. There was something ugly about Joe's body; it dwarfed objects around it. 'You're out of ice, so I made a phone call to get some.'

'At this hour?'

'It's easier than one of us driving.'

'Who'd you call?'

'Rudy at the liquor store.'

'It's closed.'

Cardone walked toward her, weaving a bit. 'I got him at home; he wasn't in bed . . . He does little favors for me. I told him to leave a couple of bags on the front porch and charge it to me.'

'That wasn't necessary. I mean the charging.'

'Every little bit helps.'

'Please.' She walked toward the sofa if for no other reason than to get away from Cardone's gin-laden breath. He followed her.

'Did you think over what I told you?'

'You're very generous, but we don't need any help.'

'Is that what John said?'

'It's what he *would* say.'

'Then you haven't talked to him?'

'No.'

Cardone took her hand gently. She instinctively tried to pull it away, but he held it – firmly, with no trace of hostility, only warmth; but he held it nevertheless. 'I may be a little loaded but I want you to take me seriously . . . I've been a lucky man; it hasn't been hard at all, not really . . . Frankly, I even feel a little guilty, you know what I mean? I admire Johnny. I think the world of him because he *contributes* . . . I don't contribute much; I just take. I don't hurt anybody, but I take . . . You'd make me feel better if you'd let me *give* . . . for a change.'

He let her hand go and because she didn't expect it, her forearm snapped back against her waist. She was momentarily embarrassed. And perplexed. 'Why are you so determined to give us something? What brought it up?'

Cardone sat down heavily on the arm of the couch. 'You hear things. Rumors, gossip, maybe.'

'About us? About us and money?'

'Sort of.'

'Well, it's not true. It's simply not true.'

'Then let's put it another way. Three years ago when Dick and Ginny and Bernie and Leila went skiing with us at Gstaad, you and Johnny didn't want to go. Isn't that right?'

Alice blinked, trying to follow Joe's logic. 'Yes, I remember. We thought we'd rather take the children to Nassau.'

'But now John's very interested in Switzerland, isn't that right?' Joe's body was swaying slightly.

'Not that I know of. He hasn't told me about it.'

'Then if it's not Switzerland, maybe it's Italy. Maybe he's interested in Sicily; it's a very interesting place.'

'I simply don't understand you.'

Cardone got off the arm of the couch and steadied himself. 'You and I aren't so very different, are we? I mean, what credentials we have weren't exactly handed to us, were they? . . . We've earned them, after our own Goddamn fashion . . .'

'I think that's insulting.'

'I'm sorry, I don't mean to be insulting . . . I just want to be honest, and honesty starts with where you are . . . where you were.'

'You're drunk.'

'I certainly am. I'm drunk and I'm nervous. Lousy combination . . . You talk to John. You tell him to see me tomorrow or the next day. You tell him not to worry about Switzerland or Italy, all right? You tell him, no matter what, that I'm clean and I like people who contribute but don't hurt other people . . . That I'll pay.'

Cardone took two steps toward Ali and grabbed her left hand. Gently but insistently, he brought it to his lips, eyes closed, and kissed her palm. Ali had seen that type of kiss before; in her childhood she'd seen her father's fanatical adherents do the same. Then Joe turned and staggered into the hallway.

At the window a shifting of light, a reflection, a change of brightness caught Ali's eye. She turned her head. What she saw caused her to freeze. Outside on the lawn, no more than six feet from the glass, stood Betty Cardone in a white bathing suit, washed in the blue-green light of the swimming pool.

Betty had seen what had happened between Alice and her husband. Her eyes told Ali that.

Joe's wife stared through the window and her look was cruel.

The full tones of the young Sinatra filled the warm summer night as the four couples sat around the pool. Individually – it seemed never by twos to John Tanner – one or another would slip into the water and paddle lazily back and forth.

The women talked of schools and children while the men, on the opposite side of the deck, spoke less quietly of the market, politics, an inscrutable economy.

Tanner sat on the base of the diving board near Joe. He'd never seen him so drunk, and he bore watching. If any or all around the deck were part of Omega, Joe was the weakest link. He'd be the first to break.

Small arguments flared up, quickly subsiding. At one point, Joe's voice was loud and Betty reacted swiftly but quietly.

'You're drunk, husband-mine. Watch out.'

'Joe's all right, Betty,' said Bernie, clapping Cardone's knee. 'It was rotten-hot in New York today, remember?'

'You were in New York, too, Bernie,' answered Ginny Tremayne, stretching her legs over the side of the pool. 'Was it really that rotten-hot?'

'Rotten-hot, sweetheart.' It was Dick who spoke across the water to his wife.

Tanner saw Osterman and Tremayne exchange glances. Their unspoken communication referred to Cardone but it was not meant that he, Tanner, should understand or even notice. Then Dick got up and asked who'd like refills.

Only Joe answered yes.

'I'll get it,' said Tanner.

'Hell, no,' replied Dick. 'You watch the ball-player. I want to call the kid anyway. We told her to be back by one; it's damn near two. These days you have to check.'

'You're a mean father,' said Leila.

'So long as I'm not a grandfather.' Tremayne walked across the grass to the kitchen door.

There was silence for several seconds, then the girls took up their relaxed conversation and Bernie lowered himself over the side into the pool.

Joe Cardone and Tanner did not speak.

Several minutes later, Dick came out of the kitchen door carrying two glasses. 'Hey, Ginny! Peg was teed off that I woke her up. What do you think of that?'

'I think she was bored with her date.'

Tremayne approached Cardone and handed him his glass. 'There you are, fullback.'

'I was a Goddamn halfback. I ran circles around your Goddamn Levi Jackson at the Yale Bowl!'

'Sure. But I talked to Levi. He said they could always get you. All they had to do was yell "tomato sauce" and you went for the sidelines!'

'Pretty Goddamn funny! I murdered that black son of a bitch!'

'He speaks well of you, too,' said Bernie, smiling over the side of the pool.

'And I speak well of *you*, Bernie! And big Dick, here!' Cardone clumsily got to his feet. 'I speak well of *all* of you!'

'Hey, Joe . . .' Tanner got off the board.

'Really, Joe, just sit down,' ordered Betty. 'You'll fall over.'

'Da Vinci!'

It was only a name but Cardone shouted it out. And then he shouted it again.

'*Da Vinci . . .*' He drew out the sound, making the dialect sharply Italian.

'What does *that* mean?' asked Tremayne.

'You tell me!' roared Cardone through the tense stillness around the pool.

'He's crazy,' said Leila.

'He's positively drunk, if nobody minds my saying so,' added Ginny.

'Since we can't – at least I can't – tell you what a Da Vinci is, maybe you'll explain.' Bernie spoke lightly.

'Cut it out! Just *cut it out*!' Cardone clenched and reclenched his fists.

Osterman climbed out of the water and approached Joe. His hands hung loosely at his sides. 'Cool it, Joe. Please . . . Cool it.'

'*Zurichchchch!*' The scream from Joe Cardone could be heard for miles, thought Tanner. It was happening! He'd said it!

'What do you mean, Joe?' Tremayne took a halting step toward Cardone.

'*Zurich!* That's what I mean!'

'It's a city in Switzerland! So what the hell else?' Osterman stood facing Cardone; he wasn't about to give quarter. 'You say what you mean!'

'No!' Tremayne took Osterman by the shoulder.

'Don't talk to me,' yelled Cardone. 'You're the one who . . .'

'*Stop it! All of you!*' Betty stood on the concrete deck at the end of the pool. Tanner would never have believed such strength could come from Cardone's wife.

But there it was. The three men parted from one another, as chastised dogs. The women looked up at Betty, and then Leila and Ginny walked away while Ali stood immobile, uncomprehending.

Betty continued, reverting now to the soft, suburban housewife she seemed to be. 'You're all behaving childishly and I know it's time for Joe to go home.'

'I . . . I think we can all have a nightcap, Betty,' said Tanner. 'How about it?'

'Make Joe's light,' answered Betty with a smile.

'No other way,' said Bernie.

'I'll get them.' Tanner started back toward the door. 'Everyone in?'

'Wait a minute, Johnny!' It was Cardone, a wide grin on his face. 'I'm the naughty boy so let me help. Also, I gotta go to the bathroom.'

Tanner went into the kitchen ahead of Cardone. He was confused, bewildered. He had expected that when Joe screamed the name 'Zurich' it would all be over. Zurich was the key that should have triggered the collapse. Yet it did not happen.

Instead, the opposite occurred.

A control was imposed; imposed by the most unlikely source imaginable, Betty Cardone.

Suddenly, from behind him came a crash. Tremayne was standing in the doorway, looking at the fallen Cardone.

'Well. A mountain of Princeton muscle just passed out! . . . Let's get him into my car. I'm chauffeur tonight.'

Passed out? Tanner didn't believe it. Cardone was drunk, yes. But he was nowhere near collapsing.

20

The three men dressed quickly and manhandled the lurching, incoherent Cardone into the front seat of Tremayne's car. Betty and Ginny were in the back. Tanner kept watching Joe's face, especially the eyes, for any signs of pretense. He could see none. And yet there was something false, he thought; there was too much precision in Cardone's exaggerated movements. Was Joe using silence to test the others, he wondered?

Or were his own observations being warped by the progressive tension?

'Damn it!' exclaimed Tremayne. 'I left my jacket inside.'

'I'll bring it to the Club in the morning,' said John. 'We're scheduled for eleven.'

'No, I'd better get it. I left some notes in the pocket; I may need them . . . Wait here with Bernie. I'll be back in a second.'

Dick ran inside and he grabbed his jacket from a hallway chair. He looked at Leila Osterman, who was polishing the top of a table in the living room.

'If I get these rings now maybe the Tanners'll have some furniture left,' she said.

'Where's Ali?'

'In the kitchen.' Leila continued rubbing the table top.

As Tremayne entered the kitchen, Alice was filling the dishwasher.

'Ali?'

'Oh! . . . Dick. Joe all right?'

'Joe's fine . . . How's John?'

'Isn't he out there with you?'

'I'm in here.'

'It's late; I'm too tired for jokes.'

'I couldn't feel less like joking . . . We've been good friends, Ali. You and Johnny mean a lot to us, to Ginny and me.'

'We feel the same; you know that.'

'I thought I did. I really believed it . . . Listen to me . . .' Tremayne's face was flushed; he swallowed repeatedly, unable to control the pronounced twitch over his left eye. 'Don't make judgments. Don't let John make . . . editorial judgments that hurt people unless he understands why they do what they do.'

'I don't understand what you're – '

'That's very important,' interrupted Tremayne. 'He should try to understand. That's one mistake I never commit in court. I always try to understand.'

Alice recognized the threat. 'I suggest that you say whatever it is you're saying to him.'

'I did and he wouldn't answer me. That's why I'm saying it to you . . . Remember, Ali. No one's ever completely what he seems. Only some of us are more resourceful. Remember that!'

Tremayne turned and left; a second later Ali heard the front door close. As she looked at the empty doorway, she was aware of someone else nearby. There was the unmistakable sound of a quiet footstep. Someone had walked through the dining room and was standing in her pantry, around the corner, out of sight. She walked slowly, silently to the arch. As she turned into the small narrow room she saw Leila standing motionless against the wall, staring straight ahead.

Leila had been listening to the conversation in the kitchen. She gasped when she saw Ali, then laughed with no trace of humor. She knew she'd been caught.

'I came for another cloth.' She held up a dustrag and went back inside the dining room without speaking further.

Alice stood in the center of the pantry wondering what dreadful thing was happening to all of them. Something was affecting the lives of everyone in the house.

They lay in bed; Ali on her back, John on his left side away from her. The Ostermans were across the hall in the guest room. It was the first time they'd been alone together all night.

Alice knew her husband was exhausted but she couldn't postpone the question – or was it a statement – any longer.

'There's some trouble between you and Dick and Joe, isn't there?'

Tanner rolled over; he looked up at the ceiling, almost relieved. He knew the question was coming and he had rehearsed his answer. It was another lie; he was getting used to the lies.

But there was so little time left – Fassett had guaranteed that. He began slowly, trying to speak off-handedly.

'You're too damned smart.'

'I am?' She shifted to her side and looked at her husband.

'It's nasty, but it'll pass. You remember my telling you about that stock business Jim Loomis was peddling on the train?'

'Yes. You didn't want Janet to go over for lunch . . . to the Loomis', I mean.'

'That's right . . . Well, Joe and Dick jumped in with Loomis. I told them not to.'

'Why?'

'I checked on it.'

'What?'

'I checked on it . . . We've got a few thousand lying around drawing five percent. I figured why not? So I called Andy Harrison – he's head of Legal at Standard, you met him last Easter. He made inquiries.'

'What did he find out?'

'The whole thing smells. It's a boilerplate operation. It's rotten.'

'Is it illegal?'

'Probably will be by next week . . . Harrison suggested we do a feature on it. Make a hell of a show. I told that to Joe and Dick.'

'Oh, my God! That you'd do a program on it?'

'Don't worry. We're booked for months. There's no priority here. And even if we did, I'd tell them. They could get out in time.'

Ali heard Cardone and Tremayne again: '*Did you speak to him? What did he say?*' '*Don't let Johnny make judgments. . . .*' They had been panicked and now she understood why. 'Joe and Dick are worried sick, you know that, don't you?'

'Yeah. I gathered it.'

'You *gathered* it? For heaven's sake, these are your friends! . . . They're frightened! They're scared to death!'

'Okay. Okay. Tomorrow at the Club, I'll tell them to relax . . . The San Diego vulture isn't vulturing these days.'

'Really, that was cruel! No wonder they're all so upset! They think you're doing something terrible.' Ali recalled Leila's silent figure pressed against the pantry wall, listening to Tremayne alternately pleading and threatening in the kitchen. 'They've told the Ostermans.'

'Are you sure? How?'

'Never mind, it's not important. They must think you're a horror . . . Tomorrow morning, for heaven's sake, tell them not to worry.'

'I said I would.'

'It explains so much. That silly yelling at the pool, the arguments . . . I'm really very angry with you.' But Alice Tanner wasn't angry; the unknown was known to her. She could cope with it. She lay back, still concerned, still worried, but with a degree of calm she hadn't felt for several hours.

Tanner shut his eyes tight, and let his breath out. The lie had gone well. Better than he had thought it would. It was easier for him now, easier to alter the facts.

Fassett had been right, he could manage them all.

Even Ali.

21

He stood by the bedroom window. There was no moon in the sky, just clouds barely moving. He looked below at the side lawn and the woods beyond, and wondered suddenly if his eyes were playing tricks on him. There was the glow of a cigarette, distinctly seen. Someone was walking and smoking a cigarette in full view! Good Christ! he thought; did whoever it was realize that he was giving away the patrol?

And then he looked more closely. The figure was in a bathrobe. It was Osterman.

Had Bernie seen something? Heard something?

Tanner silently, rapidly went to the bedroom door and let himself out.

'I thought you might be up and around,' said Bernie sitting on a deck chair, looking at the water in the pool. 'This evening was a disaster.'

'I'm not so sure about that.'

'Then I assume you've given up your senses of sight and sound. It was a wet night at Malibu. If we all had had knives that pool would be deep red by now.'

'Your Hollywood mentality's working overtime.' Tanner sat down at the edge of the water.

'I'm a writer. I observe and distill.'

'I think you're wrong,' Tanner said. 'Dick was

uptight about business; he told me. Joe got drunk. So what?'

Osterman swung his leg over the deck chair and sat forward. 'You're wondering what I'm doing here . . . It was a hunch, an instinct. I thought you might come down yourself. You didn't look like you could sleep any more than I could.'

'You intrigue me.'

'No jokes. It's time we talk.'

'About what?'

Osterman got up and stood above Tanner. He lit a fresh cigarette with the stub of his first. 'What do you want most? I mean for yourself and your family?'

Tanner couldn't believe he'd heard correctly. Osterman had begun with the tritest introduction imaginable. Still, he answered as though he took the question seriously.

'Peace, I guess. Peace, food, shelter, creature comforts. Are those the key words?'

'You've got all that. For your current purposes, anyway.'

'Then I *really* don't understand you.'

'Has it ever occurred to you that you have no right to select anything any more? Your whole life is programmed to fulfill a predetermined *function*; do you realize that?'

'It's universal, I imagine. I don't argue with it.'

'You can't argue. The system won't permit it. You're trained for something; you gain experience – that's what you do for the rest of your life. No arguments.'

'I'd be a rotten nuclear physicist; you'd be less than desirable in brain surgery . . .' Tanner said.

'Of course everything's relative; I'm not talking fantasy. I'm saying that we're controlled by forces we can't control any longer. We've reached the age of specialization, and that's the death knell. We live and work within our given circles; we're not allowed to cross the lines, even to look around. You more than me, I'm afraid. At least I have a degree of choice as to which piece of crap I'll handle. But crap, nevertheless . . . We're stifled.'

'I hold my own; I'm not complaining. Also, my risks are pretty well advertised.'

'But you have no back-ups! Nothing! You can't afford to stand up and say *this is me*! Not on the money-line, you can't! Not with *this* to pay for!' Osterman swung his arm to include Tanner's house and grounds.

'Perhaps I can't . . . on the money-line. But who can?'

Osterman drew up the chair and sat down. He held Tanner's eyes with his own and spoke softly. 'There's a way. And I'm willing to help.' He paused for a moment, as if searching for words, then started to speak again. 'Johnny . . .' Osterman stopped once more. Tanner was afraid he wouldn't continue, wouldn't find the courage.

'Go on.'

'I've got to have certain . . . assurances; that's very important!' Osterman spoke rapidly, the words tumbling forth on top of each other.

Suddenly both men's attention was drawn to

the house. The light in Janet Tanner's bedroom had gone on.

'What's that?' asked Bernie, not bothering to disguise his apprehension.

'Just Janet. That's her room. We finally got it through her head that when she goes to the bathroom she should turn on the lights. Otherwise she bumps into everything and we're all up for twenty minutes.'

And then it pierced the air. Terrifyingly, with ear-shattering horror. A child's scream.

Tanner raced around the pool and in the kitchen door. The screams continued and lights went on in the other three bedrooms. Bernie Osterman nearly ran up Tanner's back as the two men raced to the little girl's room. Their speed had been such that Ali and Leila were just then coming out of their rooms.

John rushed against the door, not bothering about the doorknob. The door flew open and the four of them ran inside.

The child stood in the center of the room over the body of the Tanners' Welsh terrier. She could not stop screaming.

The dog lay in a pool of blood.

Its head had been severed from its body.

John Tanner picked up his daughter and ran back into the hallway. His mind stopped functioning. There was only the terrifying picture of the body in the woods alternating with the sight of the small dog. And the horrible words of the man in the parking lot at the Howard Johnson's motel.

'A severed head means a massacre.'

He had to get control, he *had* to.

He saw Ali whispering in Janet's ear, rocking her back and forth. He was aware of his son crying several feet away and the outline of Bernie Osterman comforting him.

And then he heard the words from Leila.

'I'll take Janet, Ali. Go to Johnny.'

Tanner leapt to his feet in fury. 'You touch her, I'll *kill* you! Do you hear me, I'll *kill* you!'

'*John!*' Ali yelled at him in disbelief. 'What are you *saying*?'

'*She* was across the hall! Can't you see that? She was *across the hall*!'

Osterman rushed toward Tanner, pushing him back, pinning his shoulders against the wall. Then he slapped him hard across the face.

'That dog's been dead for hours! Now, cut it out!'

For hours. It couldn't be for hours. It had just happened. The lights went on and the head was severed. The little dog's head was cut off . . . And Leila was across the hall. She and Bernie. Omega! A massacre!

Bernie cradled his head. 'I had to hit you. You went a little nuts . . . Come on, now. Pull yourself together. It's terrible, just terrible, I know. I got a daughter.'

Tanner tried to focus. First his eyes, then his thoughts. They were all looking at him, even Raymond, still sobbing by the door of his room.

'Isn't anybody here?' Tanner couldn't help himself. Where were Fassett's men? Where in God's name *were* they?

'Who, darling?' Ali put her arm around his waist in case he fell again.

'Nobody here.' It was a statement said softly.

'*We're* here. And we're calling the police. Right now!' Bernie put Tanner's hand on the staircase railing and walked him downstairs.

Tanner looked at the thin, strong man helping him down the steps. *Didn't Bernie understand? He was Omega. His wife was Omega! He couldn't phone the police!*

'The police? You want the police?'

'I certainly do. If that was a joke, it's the sickest I've ever seen. You're damned right I want them. Don't you?'

'Yes. Of course.'

They reached the living room; Osterman took command.

'Ali, you call the police! If you don't know the number, dial the operator!' And then he went into the kitchen.

Where were Fassett's men?

Alice crossed to the beige telephone behind the sofa. In an instant it was clear she didn't have to dial.

The beam of a searchlight darted back and forth through the front windows and danced against the wall of the living room. Fassett's men had arrived at last.

At the sound of the front door chimes, Tanner wrenched himself off the couch and into the hallway.

'We heard some yelling and saw the light on. Is

everything all right?' It was Jenkins and he barely hid his anxiety.

'You're a little late!' Tanner said quietly. 'You'd better come on in! Omega's been here.'

'Take it easy.' Jenkins walked into the hallway, followed by McDermott.

Osterman came out of the kitchen.

'Jesus! You people are fast!'

'Twelve-to-eight shift, sir,' said Jenkins. 'Saw the lights on and people running around. That's unusual at this hour.'

'You're very alert and we're grateful . . .'

'Yes, sir,' Jenkins interrupted and walked into the living room. 'Is anything the matter, Mr Tanner? Can you tell us or would you rather speak privately?'

'There's nothing private here, officer.' Osterman followed the policemen and spoke before Tanner could answer. 'There's a dog upstairs in the first bedroom on the right. It's dead.'

'Oh?' Jenkins was confused. He turned back to Tanner.

'Its head was cut off. Severed. We don't know who did it.'

Jenkins spoke calmly. 'I see . . . We'll take care of it.' He looked over at his partner in the hallway. 'Get the casualty blanket, Mac.'

'Right.' McDermott went back outside.

'May I use your phone?'

'Of course.'

'Captain MacAuliff should be informed. I'll have to call him at home.'

Tanner didn't understand. This wasn't a police

matter. It was Omega! What was Jenkins doing? Why was he calling MacAuliff? He should be reaching *Fassett*! MacAuliff was a local police officer; acceptable, perhaps, but fundamentally a political appointment. MacAuliff was responsible to the Saddle Valley town council, not to the United States government. 'Do you think that's necessary? At this hour? I mean, is Captain . . .'

Jenkins cut Tanner off abruptly. 'Captain MacAuliff is the Chief of Police. He'd consider it very abnormal if I didn't report this directly to him.'

In an instant Tanner understood. Jenkins had given him the key.

Whatever happened, whenever it happened, however it happened – there could be no deviation from the norm.

This was the Chasm of Leather.

And it struck Tanner further that Jenkins was making his phone call for the benefit of Bernard and Leila Osterman.

Captain Albert MacAuliff entered the Tanner house and immediately made his authority clear. Tanner watched him deliver his instructions to the police officers, in a low, commanding voice. He was a tall, obese man, with a thick neck which made his shirt collar bulge. His hands were thick, too, but strangely immobile, hanging at his sides as he walked – the mark of a man who'd spent years patrolling a beat on foot, shifting his heavy club from one hand to the other.

MacAuliff had been recruited from the New

York police and he was a living example of the right man for the right job. Years ago the town council had gone on record that it wanted a no-nonsense man, someone who'd keep Saddle Valley clear of undesirable elements. And the best defense in these days of permissiveness was offense.

Saddle Valley had wanted a mercenary.

It had hired a bigot.

'All right, Mr Tanner, I'd like a statement. What happened here tonight?'

'We . . . we had a small party for friends.'

'How many?'

'Four couples. Eight people.'

'Any hired help?'

'No . . . No, no help.'

MacAuliff looked at Tanner, putting his note-book at his side. 'No maid?'

'No.'

'Did Mrs Tanner have anyone in during the afternoon? To help out?'

'No.'

'You're sure?'

'Ask her yourself.' Ali was in the study where they'd made makeshift beds for the children.

'It could be important. While you were at work she might have had some coloreds or PR's here.'

Tanner saw Bernie recoil. 'I was home all day.'

'Okay.'

'Captain.' Osterman stepped forward from Leila's side. 'Somebody broke into this house and slit that dog's throat. Isn't it possible that it was a thief? Mr and Mrs Tanner were robbed last Wednesday. Shouldn't we check . . .'

It was as far as he got. MacAuliff looked at the writer and scarcely disguised his contempt. 'I'll handle this, Mr . . .' The Police Chief glanced at his notebook. 'Mr Osterman. I'd like Mr Tanner to explain what happened here tonight. I'd appreciate it if you'd let *him* answer. We'll get to you in good time.'

Tanner kept trying to get Jenkins' attention, but the policeman avoided his eyes. The news director didn't know what to say – or what specifically *not* to say.

'Now then, Mr Tanner.' MacAuliff sat down and returned to his notebook, pencil poised. 'Let's start at the beginning. And don't forget things like deliveries.'

Tanner was about to speak when McDermott's voice could be heard from the second floor.

'Captain! Can I see you a minute? The guest room.'

Without saying anything, Bernie started up the stairs in front of MacAuliff, Leila following.

Instantly, Jenkins approached Tanner's chair and bent over. 'I've only got time to say this once. Listen and commit! Don't bring up any Omega business. None of it. Nothing! I couldn't say it before, the Ostermans were hovering over you.'

'Why not? For Christ's sake, this *is* Omega business! . . . What am I supposed to say? Why shouldn't I?'

'MacAuliff's not one of us. He's not cleared for

anything. . . . Just tell me the truth about your party. That's *all*!'

'You mean he doesn't *know*?'

'He doesn't. I told you, he's not cleared.'

'What about the men outside, the patrols in the woods?'

'They're not his men . . . If you bring it up he'll think you're crazy. And the Ostermans will know. If you point at me I'll deny everything you say. You'll look like a psycho.'

'Do you people think that MacAuliff . . .'

'No. He's a good cop. He's also a small-time Napoleon so we can't use him. Not openly. But he's conscientious, he can help us. Get him to find where the Tremaynes and the Cardones went.'

'Cardone was drunk. Tremayne drove them all home.'

'Find out if they *went* straight home. MacAuliff loves interrogations; he'll nail them if they're lying.'

'How can I . . .'

'You're worried about them. That's good enough. And remember, it's nearly over.'

MacAuliff returned. McDermott had 'mistaken' the lateral catch in the guest room window as a possible sign of a break-in.

'All right, Mr Tanner. Let's start with when your guests arrived.'

And so John Tanner, functioning on two levels, related the blurred events of the evening. Bernie and Leila Osterman came downstairs and added very little of consequence. Ali came out of the study and contributed nothing.

'Very well, ladies and gentlemen.' MacAuliff got out of the chair.

'Aren't you going to question the others?' Tanner also rose and faced the police captain.

'I was going to ask you if we could use your telephone. We have procedures.'

'Certainly.'

'Jenkins, call the Cardones. We'll see them first.'

'Yes, sir.'

'What about the Tremaynes?'

'Procedures, Mr Tanner. After we speak to the Cardones we'll call the Tremaynes and *then* see them.'

'That way no one checks with anyone else, right?'

'That's right, Mr Osterman. You familiar with police work?'

'I write your guidelines every week.'

'My husband's a television writer,' said Leila.

'Captain.' Patrolman Jenkins spoke from the telephone. 'The Cardones aren't home. I've got the maid on the line.'

'Call the Tremaynes.'

The group remained silent while Jenkins dialed. After a brief conversation Jenkins put down the telephone.

'Same story, Captain. The daughter says they're not home either.'

22

Tanner sat up with his wife in the living room. The Ostermans had gone upstairs; the police departed in search of the missing couples. Neither John nor Ali was comfortable. Ali because she had decided in her own mind who had killed the dog, John because he couldn't get out of his mind the implications of the dog's death.

'It was Dick, wasn't it?' Alice asked.

'Dick?'

'He threatened me. He came into the kitchen and threatened me.'

'*Threatened* you?' If that was so, thought Tanner, why hadn't Fassett's men come sooner. 'When? How?'

'When they were leaving . . . I don't mean he threatened me personally. Just generally, all of us.'

'What did he say?' Tanner hoped Fassett's men were listening now. It would be a point he'd bring up later.

'He said you shouldn't make judgments. Editorial judgments.'

'What else?'

'That some . . . some people were more resourceful. That's what he said. That I should remember that people weren't always what they seemed . . . That some were more resourceful than others.'

'He could have meant several things.'

'It must be an awful lot of money.'

'What's a lot of money?'

'Whatever he and Joe are doing with Jim Loomis. The thing you had looked into.'

Oh, God, thought Tanner. The real and the unreal. He'd almost forgotten his lie.

'It's a lot of money,' he said softly, realizing he was on dangerous ground. It would occur to Ali that money itself was insufficient. He tried to anticipate her. 'More than just money, I think. Their reputations could go down the drain.'

Alice stared at the single lighted table lamp. 'Upstairs you . . . you thought Leila had done it, didn't you?'

'I was wrong.'

'She *was* across the hall . . .'

'That wouldn't make any difference; we went over that with MacAuliff. He agreed. A lot of the blood had dried, congealed. The pup was killed hours ago.'

'I guess you're right.' Ali kept picturing Leila with her back pressed against the wall, staring straight ahead, listening to the conversation in the kitchen.

The clock on the mantel read five-twenty. They had agreed they would sleep in the living room, in front of the study, next to their children.

At five-thirty the telephone rang. MacAuliff had not found the Tremaynes or the Cardones.

He told Tanner that he had decided to put out a missing persons bulletin.

'They may have decided to go into town, into New York,' said Tanner quickly. A missing persons bulletin might drive Omega underground, prolong the nightmare. 'Some of those Village spots stay open. Give them more time. They're friends, for heaven's sake!'

'Can't agree. No place stays open after four.'

'They may have decided to go to a hotel.'

'We'll know soon enough. Hotels and hospitals are the first places MPB's go to.'

Tanner's mind raced. 'You've searched the surrounding towns? I know a few private clubs . . .'

'So do we. Checked out.'

Tanner knew he had to think of something. Anything that would give Fassett enough time to control the situation. Fassett's men were listening on the line, there was no question about that; they'd see the danger instantly.

'Have you searched the area around the old depot? The one on Lassiter Road?'

'Who the hell would go out there? What for?'

'I found my wife and children there on Wednesday. Just a thought.'

The hint worked. 'Call you back,' MacAuliff said. 'I'll check that out.'

As he hung up the telephone, Ali spoke. 'No sign?'

'No . . . Honey, try to get some rest. I know of a couple of places – clubs – the police may not know about. I'll try them. I'll use the kitchen phone. I don't want to wake the kids.'

Fassett answered the phone quickly.

'It's Tanner. Do you know what's happened?'

'Yes. That was damned good thinking. You're hired.'

'That's the last thing I want. What are you going to do? You can't have an interstate search.'

'We know. Cole and Jenkins are in touch. We'll intercept.'

'And then what?'

'There are several alternate moves. I don't have time to explain. Also, I need this line. Thanks, again.' Fassett hung up.

'Tried two places,' said Tanner, coming back into the living room. 'No luck . . . Let's try to get some sleep. They probably found a party and dropped in. Lord knows we've done that.'

'Not in years,' said Ali.

Both of them pretended to sleep. The tick of the clock was like a metronome, hypnotic, exasperating. Finally, Tanner realized his wife was asleep. He closed his eyes, feeling the heavy weight of his lids, aware of the complete blackness in front of his mind. But his hearing would not rest. At six-forty he heard the sound of a car. It came from in front of his house. Tanner got out of the chair and went quickly to the window. MacAuliff walked up the path, and he was alone. Tanner went out to meet him.

'My wife's asleep. I don't want to wake her.'

'Doesn't matter,' said MacAuliff ominously. 'My business is with you.'

'What?'

'The Cardones and the Tremaynes were rendered unconscious by a massive dose of ether. They were left in their car off the road by the Lassiter depot. Now I want to know why you sent us there. How did you know?'

Tanner could only stare at MacAuliff in silence.

'Your answer?'

'So help me, I didn't know! I didn't know *anything* . . . I'll never forget Wednesday afternoon as long as I live. Neither would you if you were me. The depot just came to mind, I *swear* it!'

'It's one hell of a coincidence, isn't it?'

'Look, if I *had* known I would have told you hours ago! I wouldn't put my wife through this. For Christ's sake, be reasonable!'

MacAuliff looked at him questioningly. Tanner pressed on. 'How did it happen? What did they say? Where are they?'

'They're down at the Ridge Park Hospital. They won't be released until tomorrow morning at the earliest.'

'You must have talked with them.'

According to Tremayne, MacAuliff said, the four of them had driven down Orchard Drive less than half a mile when they saw a red flare in the road and an automobile parked on the shoulder. A man waved them down; a well-dressed man who looked like any resident of Saddle Valley. Only he wasn't. He'd been visiting friends and was on his way back to Westchester. His car had suddenly developed engine trouble and he was stuck. Tremayne offered to drive the man back to his friends' house. The man accepted.

That was the last Tremayne and the two wives remembered. Apparently Cardone had been unconscious throughout the incident.

At the deserted depot the police found an unmarked aerosol can on the floor of Tremayne's car. It would be examined in the morning, but MacAuliff had no doubt it was ether.

'There must be a connection with last Wednesday,' said Tanner.

'It's the obvious conclusion. Still, anyone who knows this neck of the woods knows that the old depot area is deserted. Especially anyone who read the papers or heard about Wednesday afternoon.'

'I suppose so. Were they robbed . . . too?'

'Not of money, or wallets or jewelry. Tremayne said he was missing some papers from his coat. He was very upset.'

'Papers?' Tanner remembered the lawyer saying he had left some notes in his jacket. Notes that he might need. 'Did he say which papers?'

'Not directly. He was hysterical – didn't make too much sense. He kept repeating the name "Zurich".'

John held his breath and, as he had learned to do, tensed the muscles of his stomach, trying with all his strength to suppress his surprise. It was so like Tremayne to arrive with written-down, pertinent data concerning the Zurich accounts. If there *had* been a confrontation, he was armed with the facts.

MacAuliff caught Tanner's reaction. 'Does Zurich mean something to you?'

'No, why should it?'

'You always answer a question with a question?'

'At the risk of offending you again, am I being officially questioned?'

'You certainly are.'

'Then, no. The name Zurich means nothing to me. I can't imagine why he'd say it. Of course, his law firm is international.'

MacAuliff made no attempt to conceal his anger. 'I don't know what's going on, but I'll tell you this much. I'm an experienced police officer and I've had some of the toughest beats a man can have. When I took this job I gave my word I'd keep this town clean. I meant that.'

Tanner was tired of him. 'I'm sure you did, Captain. I'm sure you always mean what you say.' He turned his back and started for the house.

It was MacAuliff's turn to be stunned. The suspect was walking away and there was nothing Saddle Valley's Police Chief could do about it.

Tanner stood on his front porch and watched MacAuliff drive off. The sky was brighter but there'd be no sun. The clouds were low, the rain would come, but not for a while.

No matter. Nothing mattered. It was over for him.

The covenant was broken now. The contract between John Tanner and Laurence Fassett was void.

For Fassett's guarantee had proven false. Omega did not stop with the Tremaynes, the

Cardones and the Ostermans. It went beyond the constituency of the weekend.

He was willing to play – *had* to play – under Fassett's rules as long as the other players were the men and women he knew.

Not now.

There was someone else now – someone who could stop a car on a dark road in the early morning hours and create terror.

Someone he didn't know. He couldn't accept that.

Tanner waited until noon before heading toward the woods. The Ostermans had decided to take a nap around eleven-thirty and it was a good time to suggest the same to Ali. They were all exhausted. The children were in the study watching the Saturday morning cartoons.

He walked casually around the pool, holding a six iron, pretending to practice his swing, but actually observing the windows on the rear of the house: the two children's rooms and the upstairs bathroom.

He approached the edge of the woods and lit a cigarette.

No one acknowledged his presence. There was no sign, nothing but silence from the small forest. Tanner spoke softly.

'I'd like to reach Fassett. Please answer. It's an emergency.'

He swung his golf club as he said the words.

'I repeat! It's urgent I talk with Fassett! Someone say where you are!'

Still no answer.

Tanner turned, made an improvised gesture toward nothing, and entered the woods. Once in the tall foliage he used his elbows and arms to push deeper into the small forest, toward the tree where Jenkins had gone for the portable radio.

No one!

He walked north; kicking, slashing, searching. Finally he reached the road.

There was no one there! No one was guarding his house! No one was watching the island!

No one!

Fassett's men were gone!

He raced from the road, skirting the edge of the woods, watching the windows fifty yards away on the front of his house.

Fassett's men were gone!

He ran across the back lawn, rounded the pool and let himself into the kitchen. Once inside he stopped at the sink for breath and turned on the cold water. He splashed it in his face and then stood up and arched his back, trying to find a moment of sanity.

No one! No one was guarding his house. No one guarding his wife and his children!

He turned off the water and then decided to let it run slowly, covering whatever footsteps he made. He walked through the kitchen door, hearing the laughter of his children from the study. Going upstairs, he silently turned the knob of his bedroom door. Ali was lying on top of their bed, her bathrobe fallen away, her nightgown rumpled. She was breathing deeply, steadily, asleep.

He closed the door and listened for any sound from the guest room. There was none.

He went back down into the kitchen, closed the door and walked through the archway into the small pantry to make sure that, too, was shut.

He returned to the telephone on the kitchen wall, lifting the receiver. He did not dial.

'Fassett! If you or any of your men are on this line, cut in and acknowledge! And I mean *now*!'

The dial tone continued; Tanner listened for the slightest break in the circuit.

There was none.

He dialed the motel. 'Room twenty-two, please.'

'I'm sorry, sir. Room twenty-two is not occupied.'

'Not occupied? You're wrong! I spoke to the party at five o'clock this morning!'

'I'm sorry, sir. They checked out.'

Tanner replaced the receiver, staring at it in disbelief.

The New York number! The emergency number!

He picked up the telephone, trying to keep his hand from trembling.

The beep of a recording preceded the flat-toned voice.

'The number you have reached is not in service. Please check the directory for the correct number. This is a recording. The number you have reached . . .'

John Tanner closed his eyes. It was inconceivable! Fassett couldn't be reached! Fassett's men had disappeared!

He was alone!

He tried to think. He *had* to think. Fassett had to be found! Some gargantuan error had taken place. The cold, professional government man with his myriad ruses and artifices had made some horrible mistake.

Yet Fassett's men were gone. Perhaps there was no mistake at all.

Tanner suddenly remembered that he, too, had resources. There existed for Standard Mutual Network necessary links to certain government agencies. He dialed Connecticut information and got the Greenwich number of Andrew Harrison, head of Standard's legal department.

'Hello, Andy? . . . John Tanner.' He tried to sound as composed as possible. 'Sorry as hell to bother you at home but the Asian Bureau just called. There's a story out of Hong Kong I want to clear . . . I'd rather not go into it now, I'll tell you Monday morning. It may be nothing, but I'd rather check . . . I guess CIA would be best. It's that kind of thing. They've cooperated with us before . . . Okay, I'll hold on.' The news editor cupped the telephone under his chin and lit a cigarette. Harrison came back with a number and Tanner wrote it down. 'That's Virginia, isn't it? . . . Thanks very much, Andy. I'll see you Monday morning.'

Once more he dialed.

'Central Intelligence. Mr Andrews' office.' It was a male voice.

'My name is Tanner. John Tanner. Director of News for Standard Mutual in New York.'

'Yes, Mr Tanner? Are you calling Mr Andrews?'

'Yes. Yes, I guess I am.'

'I'm sorry, he's not in today. May I help you?'

'Actually, I'm trying to locate Laurence Fassett.'

'Who?'

'Fassett. Laurence Fassett. He's with your agency. It's urgent I speak with him. I believe he's in the New York area.'

'Is he connected with this department?'

'I don't know. I only know he's with the Central Intelligence Agency. I told you, it's urgent! An emergency, to be exact!' Tanner was beginning to perspire. This was no time to be talking to a clerk.

'All right, Mr Tanner. I'll check our directory and locate him. Be right back.'

It was a full two minutes before he returned. The voice was hesitant but very precise.

'Are you sure you have the right name?'

'Of course I am.'

'I'm sorry, but there's no Laurence Fassett listed with the switchboard or in any index.'

'That's impossible! . . . Look, I've been working with Fassett! . . . Let me talk with your superior.' Tanner remembered how Fassett, even Jenkins, kept referring to those who had been 'cleared' for Omega.

'I don't think you understand, Mr Tanner. This is a priority office. You called for my associate . . . my subordinate, if you like. My name is

Dwight. Mr Andrews refers decisions of this office to me.'

'I don't care who you are! I'm telling you this is an emergency! I think you'd better reach someone in much higher authority than yourself, Mr Dwight. I can't put it plainer. That's *all*! Do it *now*! I'll hold on!'

'Very well. It may take a few minutes . . .'

'I'll hold.'

It took seven minutes, an eternity of strain for Tanner, before Dwight returned to the line.

'Mr Tanner, I took the liberty of checking your own position so I assume you're responsible. However, I can assure you you've been misled. There's no Laurence Fassett with the Central Intelligence Agency. There never has been.'

23

Tanner hung up the telephone and supported himself on the edge of the sink. He pushed himself off and walked mindlessly out the kitchen door onto the backyard patio. The sky was dark. A breeze rustled the trees and caused ripples on the surface of the pool. There was going to be a storm, thought Tanner, as he looked up at the clouds. A July thunderstorm was closing in.

Omega was closing in.

With or without Fassett, Omega was real, that much was clear to Tanner. It was real because he had seen and sensed its power, the force it generated, capable of removing a Laurence Fassett, of manipulating the decisions and the personnel of the country's prime intelligence agency.

Tanner knew there was no point trying to reach Jenkins. What had Jenkins said in the living room during the early morning hours? . . . 'If you point at me, I'll deny everything . . .' If Omega could silence Fassett, silencing Jenkins would be like breaking a toy.

There had to be a starting point, a springboard that could propel him backward through the lies. He didn't care any longer; it just had to end, his family kept safe. It wasn't his war any more. His only concern was Ali and the children.

Tanner saw the figure of Osterman through the kitchen window.

That was it! Osterman was his point of departure, his break with Omega! He walked quickly back inside.

Leila sat at the table while Bernie stood by the stove boiling water for coffee.

'We're leaving,' Bernie said. 'Our bag's packed; I'll call for a taxi.'

'Why?'

'Something's terribly wrong,' said Leila, 'and it's none of our business. We're not involved and we don't care to be.'

'That's what I want to talk to you about. Both of you.'

Bernie and Leila exchanged looks.

'Go ahead,' said Bernie.

'Not here. Outside.'

'Why outside?'

'I don't want Ali to hear.'

'She's asleep.'

'It's got to be outside.'

The three of them walked past the pool to the rear of the lawn. Tanner turned and faced them.

'You don't have to lie any more. Either of you. I just want my part over with. I've stopped caring.' He paused for a moment. 'I know about Omega.'

'About what?' asked Leila.

'Omega . . . Omega!' Tanner's voice – his whisper – was pained. 'I don't *care*! So help me *God*, I *don't care*!'

'What are you talking about?' Bernie watched

the news director, taking a step toward him. Tanner backed away. 'What's the matter?'

'For God's sake, don't do this!'

'Don't do what?'

'I told you! It doesn't make any difference to me! Just please! *Please!* Leave Ali and the kids alone. Do whatever you want with me! . . . Just leave *them alone*!'

Leila reached out and put her hand on Tanner's arm. 'You're hysterical, Johnny. I don't know what you're talking about.'

Tanner looked down at Leila's hand and blinked back his tears. 'How can you do this? Please! Don't lie any longer. I don't think I could stand that.'

'Lie about what?'

'You never heard about any bank accounts in Switzerland? In Zurich?'

Leila withdrew her hand and the Ostermans stood motionless. Finally, Bernie spoke quietly. 'Yes, I've heard of bank accounts in Zurich. We've got a couple.'

Leila looked at her husband.

'Where did you get the money?'

'We make a great deal of money,' answered Bernie cautiously. 'You know that. If it would ease whatever's troubling you, why don't you call our accountant. You've met Ed Marcum. There's no one better . . . or cleaner . . . in California.'

Tanner was confused. The simplicity of Osterman's reply puzzled him; it was so natural. 'The Cardones, the Tremaynes. They've got Zurich accounts, too?'

'I guess they have. So do fifty percent of the people I know on the coast.'

'Where did they get the money?'

'Why don't you ask them?' Osterman kept his voice quiet.

'*You* know!'

'You're being foolish,' said Leila. 'Both Dick and Joe are very successful men. Joe probably more than any of us.'

'But why *Zurich*? *What's in Zurich?*'

'A degree of freedom,' answered Bernie softly.

'That's it! That's what you were selling last night! "What do you want most?", you said. Those were your words!'

'There's a great deal of money to be made in Zurich, I won't deny that.'

'*With Omega!* That's how you make it, *isn't it? Isn't it?*'

'I don't know what that means,' said Bernie, now apprehensive himself.

'*Dick* and *Joe*! They're with *Omega*! So are *you*! The "Chasm of Leather"! Information for Zurich! *Money for information!*'

Leila grabbed her husband's hand. 'The phone calls, Bernie! The messages.'

'Leila, please . . . Listen, Johnny. I swear to you I don't know what you're talking about. Last night I offered to help you and I meant it. There are investments being made; I was offering you money for investments. That's all.'

'Not for information? Not for Omega?'

Leila clutched her husband's hand; Bernie

responded by looking at her, silently commanding her to calm herself. He turned back to Tanner. 'I can't imagine any information you might have that I could want. I don't know any Omega. I don't know what it is.'

'Joe knows! Dick knows! They both came to Ali and me! They threatened us.'

'Then I'm no part of them. *We're* no part.'

'Oh, God, Bernie, something happened . . .' Leila couldn't help herself. Bernie reached over and took her in his arms.

'Whatever it is, it hasn't anything to do with us . . . Perhaps you'd better tell us what it's all about. Maybe we can help.'

Tanner watched them, holding each other gently. He wanted to believe them. He wanted friends; he desperately needed allies. And Fassett had said it; not *all* were Omega. 'You *really* don't know, do you? You *don't* know what Omega is. Or what "Chasm of Leather" means.'

'No,' said Leila simply.

Tanner believed them. He had to believe them, for it meant he wasn't alone any more. And so he told them.

Everything.

When he had finished the two writers stood staring at him, saying nothing. It had begun to drizzle lightly but none of them felt the rain. Finally, Bernie spoke.

'And you thought I was talking about . . . *we* had something to do with *this*?' Bernie narrowed his eyes in disbelief. 'My God! It's insane!'

'No, it's not. It's real. I've seen it.'

'You say Ali doesn't know?' asked Leila.

'I was told not to tell her, that's what they *told* me!'

'Who? Someone you can't even reach on the phone? A man Washington doesn't acknowledge? Someone who pumped you full of lies about us?'

'A man was *killed*! My family could have been killed last Wednesday! The Cardones and the Tremaynes were gassed last night!'

Osterman looked at his wife and then back at Tanner.

'*If* they really were gassed,' he said softly.

'You've got to tell Alice.' Leila was emphatic. 'You can't keep it from her any longer.'

'I know. I will.'

'And then we've got to get out of here,' said Osterman.

'Where to?'

'Washington. There are one or two Senators, a couple of Congressmen. They're friends of ours.'

'Bernie's right. We've got friends in Washington.'

The drizzle was beginning to turn into hard rain. 'Let's go inside,' said Leila, touching Tanner's shoulder gently.

'Wait! We can't talk in there. We can't say anything inside the house. It's wired.'

Bernie and Leila Osterman reacted as though they'd been slapped. 'Everywhere?' asked Bernie.

'I'm not sure . . . I'm not sure of anything any more.'

'Then we don't talk inside the house; or if we do we put on a radio loud and whisper.'

Tanner looked at his friends. Thank God! Thank *God*! It was the beginning of his journey back to sanity.

24

In less than an hour the July storm was upon them. The radio reports projected gale force winds; medium-craft warnings were up from Hatteras to Rhode Island, and the Village of Saddle Valley was neither so isolated nor inviolate as to escape the inundation.

Ali awoke with the first thunder and John told her – whispered to her – through the sound of the loud radios, that they were to be prepared to leave with Bernie and Leila. He held her close to him and begged her not to ask questions, to trust him.

The children were brought into the living room; a television set moved in front of the fireplace. Ali packed two suitcases and placed them beside the garage entrance. Leila boiled eggs and wrapped celery and carrot sticks.

Bernie had said they might not stop driving for an hour or two.

Tanner watched the preparations and his mind went back a quarter of a century.

Evacuation!

The phone rang at two-thirty. It was a suppressed, hysterical Tremayne who – falsely, thought Tanner – recounted the events of the Lassiter depot and made it clear that he and Ginny were too shaken to come over for dinner.

The Saturday evening dinner of an Osterman weekend.

'You've got to tell me what's going on!' Alice Tanner spoke to her husband in the pantry. There was a transistor radio at full volume and she tried to turn it down. He held her hand, preventing her, and pulled her to him.

'Trust me. Please *trust* me,' he whispered. 'I'll explain in the car.'

'In the car?' Ali's eyes widened in fright as she brought her hand to her mouth. 'Oh, my God! What you're saying is . . . you *can't* talk.'

'Trust me.' Tanner walked into the kitchen and spoke, gestured really, to Bernie. 'Let's load.' They went for the suitcases.

When Tanner and Osterman returned from the garage, Leila was at the kitchen window looking out on the backyard. 'It's becoming a regular gale out there.'

The phone rang and Tanner answered it.

Cardone was an angry man. He swore and swore again that he'd rip apart and rip apart once more the son of a bitch who'd gassed them. He was also confused, completely bewildered. His watch was worth eight hundred dollars and it wasn't taken. He'd had a couple of hundred in his wallet and it was left intact.

'The police said Dick had some papers stolen. Something about Zurich, Switzerland.'

There was a sharp intake of breath from Cardone and then silence. When Joe spoke he could hardly be heard. 'That's got nothing to do with *me*!' And then he rapidly told Tanner without much conviction that a call from Philadelphia had warned him that his father might be extremely ill. He and Betty would stay around home. Perhaps they'd see them all on Sunday. Tanner hung up the phone.

'Hey!' Leila was watching something out on the lawn. 'Look at those umbrellas. They're practically blowing away.'

Tanner looked out the window above the sink. The two large table umbrellas were bending under the force of the wind. The cloth of each was straining against the thin metal ribs. Soon they'd rip or invert themselves. Tanner knew it would appear strange if he didn't take care of them. It wouldn't be normal.

'I'll get them down. Take two minutes.'

'Want some help?'

'No sense both of us getting wet.'

'Your raincoat's in the hall closet.'

The wind was strong, the rain came down in torrents. He shielded his face with his hands and fought his way to the farthest table. He reached up under the flapping cloth and felt his fingers on the metal hasp. He started to push it in.

There was a shattering sound on the top of the wrought iron table. Pieces of metal flew up, searing his arm. Another report. Fragments of cement at his feet bounced off the base of the table. And then another shot, now on his other side.

Tanner flung himself under the metal table, crouching to the far side, away from the direction of the bullets.

Shots came in rapid succession, all around him, kicking up particles of metal and stone.

He started to crawl backwards onto the grass but the small eruptions of wet dirt paralysed him. He grabbed for a chair and held it, clutched it in front of him as though it were the last threads of a disintegrating rope and he were high above a chasm. He froze in panic, awaiting his death.

'Let go! Goddamn it! Let go!'

Osterman was pulling at him, slapping him in the face and wrenching his arms from the chair. They scrambled back toward the house; bullets thumped into the wooden shingles.

'Stay away! Stay away from the door!' Bernie screamed. But he wasn't in time, or his wife would not heed the command. Leila opened the door and Bernie Osterman threw Tanner inside, jumping on top of him as he did so. Leila crouched below the window and slammed the door shut.

The firing stopped.

Ali rushed to her husband and turned him over, cradling his head, wincing at the blood on his bare arms.

'Are you hit?' yelled Bernie.

'No . . . no, I'm all right.'

'You're not all right! Oh, God! Look at his arms!' Ali tried to wipe the blood away with her hand.

'Leila! Find some alcohol! Iodine! Ali, you got iodine?'

Tears were streaming down her cheeks, Alice could not answer the question. Leila grabbed her shoulders and spoke harshly.

'Stop it, Ali! *Stop* it! Where are some bandages, some antiseptic? Johnny needs help!'

'Some spray stuff . . . in the pantry. Cotton, too.' She would not let go of her husband. Leila crept toward the pantry.

Bernie examined Tanner's arms. 'This isn't bad. Just a bunch of scratches. I don't think anything's embedded . . .'

John looked up at Bernie, despising himself. 'You saved my life . . . I don't know what to say.'

'Kiss me on my next birthday . . . Good girl, Leila. Give me that stuff.' Osterman took a medicine can and held the spray steady on Tanner's arms. 'Ali, phone the police! Stay away from the window but get hold of that fat butcher you call a police captain!'

Alice reluctantly let her husband go and crawled past the kitchen sink. She reached up the side of the wall and removed the receiver.

'It's dead.'

Leila gasped. Bernie leapt toward Ali, grabbing the phone from her hand.

'She's right.'

John Tanner turned himself over and pressed his arms against the kitchen tile. He was all right. He could move.

'Let's find out where we stand,' he said slowly.

'What do you mean?' asked Bernie.

'You girls stay down on the floor . . . Bernie, the light switch is next to the telephone. Reach up and turn it on when I count to three.'

'What are you going to do?'

'Just do as I say.'

Tanner crept to the kitchen door, by the bar, and stood up out of sight of the window. The rain, the wind, the intermittent rumble of thunder were the only sounds.

'Ready? I'm going to start counting.'

'What's he going to do?' Ali started up, but Osterman grabbed her and held her to the floor.

'You've been here before, Bernie,' John said. 'Infantry Manual. Heading: Night Patrols. Nothing to worry about. The odds are a thousand to one on my side.'

'Not in any book I know.'

'Shut up! . . . One, two, *three*!'

Osterman flipped the switch and the overhead kitchen light went on. Tanner leapt toward the pantry.

It came. The signal. The sign that the enemy was there.

The shot was heard, the glass shattered, and the bullet smashed into the wall, sending pieces of plaster flying. Osterman turned off the light.

On the floor, John Tanner closed his eyes and spoke quietly. 'So, that's where we stand. The microphones were a lie . . . Everything, a lie.'

'*No! Stay back! Get back!*' screamed Leila before any of them knew what she meant. She lunged, followed by Alice, across the kitchen toward the doorway.

Tanner's children had not heard the shots outside; the sounds of the rain, the thunder, and the television set had covered them. But they'd heard the shot fired into the kitchen. Both women fell on them now, pulling them to the floor, shielding them with their bodies.

'Ali, get them into the dining room! Stay on the floor!' commanded Tanner. 'Bernie, you don't have a gun, do you?'

'Sorry, never owned one.'

'Me neither. Isn't it funny! I've always disapproved of anyone buying a gun. So Goddamned primitive.'

'What are we going to do?' Leila was trying to remain calm.

'We're going to get out of here,' answered Tanner. 'The shots are from the woods. Whoever is firing doesn't know whether we have weapons or not. He's not going to shoot from the front . . . at least I don't think so. Cars pass on Orchard pretty frequently . . . We'll pile into the wagon and get the hell out.'

'I'll open the door,' said Osterman.

'You've been hero enough for one afternoon. It's my turn . . . If we time it right, there's no problem. The door goes up fast.'

They crept into the garage.

The children lay in the back section of the wagon between the suitcases, cramped but protected. Leila and Ali crouched on the floor behind the front seat. Osterman was at the wheel and Tanner stood by the garage door, prepared to pull it up.

'Go ahead. Start it!' He would wait until the engine was full throttle then open the door and jump into the wagon. There were no obstructions. The station wagon would clear the small Triumph and swing around easily for the spurt forward down the driveway.

'Go ahead, Bernie! For Christ's sake, start it!'

Instead, Osterman opened his door and got out. He looked at Tanner.

'It's dead.'

Tanner turned the ignition key on the Triumph. The motor did not respond. Osterman opened the hood of the wagon and beckoned John over. The two men looked at the motor, Tanner holding a match.

Every wire had been cut.

'Does that door open from the outside?' asked Bernie.

'Yes. Unless it's locked.'

'Was it?'

'No.'

'Wouldn't we have heard it open?'

'Probably not with this rain.'

'Then it's possible someone's in here.'

The two men looked over at the small bathroom door. It was closed. The only hiding place in the garage. 'Let's get them out of here,' whispered Tanner.

Ali, Leila, and the two children went back into the house. Bernie and John looked around the walls of the garage for any objects which might serve as weapons. Tanner took a rusty axe; Osterman, a garden fork. Both men approached the closed door.

Tanner signaled Bernie to pull it open. Tanner

rushed in, thrusting the blade of the axe in front of him.

It was empty. But on the wall, splotched in black spray paint, was the Greek letter *Ω*.

25

Tanner ordered them all into the basement. Ali and Leila took the children down the stairs, trying feebly to make a game of it. Tanner stopped Osterman at the staircase door.

'Let's put up a few obstacles, okay?'

'You think it's going to come to that?'

'I just don't want to take chances.'

The two men crept below the sight-lines of the windows and pushed three heavy armchairs, one on top of another, the third on its side, against the front door. Then they crawled to each window, standing out of sight, to make sure the locks were secure.

Tanner, in the kitchen, took a flashlight and put it in his pocket. Together they moved the vinyl table against the outside door. Tanner shoved the aluminum chairs to Osterman, who packed them under the table, one chair rim braced under the doorknob.

'This is no good,' Bernie said. 'You're sealing us up. We should be figuring out how to get away!'

'Have *you* figured that out?'

In the dim light Osterman could see only the outline of Tanner's body. Yet he could sense the desperation in his voice.

'No. No, I haven't. But we've got to *try*!'

'I know. In the meantime we should take every precaution . . . We don't know what's out there. How many or where they are.'

'Let's finish it, then.'

The two men crawled to the far end of the kitchen, beyond the pantry to the garage entrance. The outside garage door had been locked, but for additional security they propped the last kitchen chair under the knob and crept back into the hallway. They picked up their primitive weapons – the axe and the garden fork – and went down into the basement.

The sound of the heavy rain could be heard pounding on the small, rectangular windows, level with the ground outside the cellar. Intermittent flashes of lightning lit up the cinderblock walls.

Tanner spoke. 'It's dry in here. We're safe. Whoever's out there is soaked to the skin, he can't stay there all night . . . It's Saturday. You know how the police cars patrol the roads on weekends. They'll see there are no lights on and come investigate.'

'Why should they?' asked Ali. 'They'll simply think we went out to dinner . . .'

'Not after last night. MacAuliff made it clear he'd keep an eye on the house. His patrol cars can't see through to the back lawn but they'll notice the front. They're bound to . . . Look.' Tanner took his wife's elbow and led her to the single front window just above ground level to the side of the flagstone steps. The rain made rivulets on the panes of glass; it was hard to see. Even the street lamp on Orchard Drive was not always visible. Tanner took the flashlight out of his pocket and motioned Osterman over. 'I was telling Ali, MacAuliff said this morning that he'd have the house watched. He will, too. He doesn't want any more trouble . . . We'll take turns at this window. That way no one's eyes will get tired or start playing tricks. As soon as one of us sees the patrol car, we'll signal up and down with the flashlight. They'll see it. They'll stop.'

'That's good,' said Bernie. 'That's very good! I wish to hell you'd said that upstairs.'

'I wasn't sure. Funny, but I couldn't remember if you could see the street from this window. I've cleaned this basement a hundred times, but I couldn't remember for sure.' He smiled at them.

'I feel better,' said Leila, trying her best to instill John's confidence into the others.

'Ali, you take the first shift. Fifteen minutes apiece. Bernie, you and I will keep moving between the other windows. Leila, sort of stay with Janet, will you?'

'What can I do, Dad?' Raymond asked.

Tanner looked at his son, proud of him.

'Stay at the front window with your mother. You'll be permanent there. Keep watching for the police car.'

Tanner and Osterman paced between the two windows at the rear of the house and the one at the side. In fifteen minutes, Leila relieved Ali at the front window. Ali found an old blanket which she made into a small mattress so Janet could lie down. The boy remained at the window with Leila, peering out, intermittently rubbing his hand on the glass as if the action might wipe away the water outside.

No one spoke; the pounding rain and blasts of wind seemed to increase. It was Bernie's turn at the front. As he took the flashlight from his wife he held her close for several seconds.

Tanner's turn came and went, and Ali once again took her place. None of them said it out loud but they were losing hope. If MacAuliff was patrolling the area, with concentration on the Tanner property, it seemed illogical that a police car hadn't passed in over an hour.

'There it is! There it is, Dad! See the red light?'

Tanner, Bernie and Leila rushed to the window beside Alice and the boy. Ali had turned on the flashlight and was waving it back and forth. The patrol car had slowed down. It was barely moving, yet it did not stop.

'Give me the light!'

Tanner held the beam steady until he could see, dimly but surely, the blurred reflection of the white car through the downpour. Then he moved the beam vertically, rapidly.

Whoever was driving had to be aware of the light. The path of the beam had to cross the driver's window, hit the driver's eyes.

But the patrol car did not stop. It reached the line of the driveway and slowly drove away.

Tanner shut off the flashlight, not wanting to turn around, not wanting to see the faces of the others.

Bernie spoke softly. 'I don't like this.'

'He had to see it. He *had* to!' Ali was holding her son, who was still peering out the window.

'Not necessarily,' lied John Tanner. 'It's a mess out there. His windows are probably just as clouded as ours. Maybe more so. Car windows fog up. He'll be around again. Next time we'll make sure. Next time, I'll run out.'

'How?' asked Bernie. 'You'd never make it in time. We piled furniture in front of the door.'

'I'll get through this window.' Tanner mentally measured the space. It was far too small. How easily the lies came.

'I can crawl out of there, Dad!' The boy was right. It might be necessary to send him.

But he knew he wouldn't. He couldn't.

Whoever was in the patrol car had seen the beam of light and hadn't stopped.

'Let's get back to the windows. Leila, you take over here. Ali, check Janet. I think she's fallen asleep.'

Tanner knew he had to keep them doing something, even if the action meant nothing. Each would have his private thoughts, his private panic.

There was a shattering crack of thunder. A flash of lightning lit up the basement.

'Johnny!' Osterman's face was against the left rear window. 'Come here.'

Tanner ran to Osterman's side and looked out. Through the whipping patterns of the downpour he saw a short, vertical beam of light rising from the ground. It was moving from far back on the lawn, beyond the pool, near the woods. The beam swayed slowly, jerkily. Then a flash of lightning revealed the figure holding the flashlight. Someone was coming toward the house.

'Someone's worried he's going to fall into the pool,' whispered Bernie.

'What is it?' Ali's intense voice came from the makeshift mattress where she sat with her daughter.

'There's somebody out there,' answered Tanner. 'Everybody stay absolutely still . . . It could be . . . all right. It might be the police.'

'Or the person who shot at us! Oh, God!'

'Ssh! Be quiet.'

Leila left the front window and went over to Alice.

'Get your face away from the glass, Bernie.'

'He's getting nearer. He's going around the pool.'

The two men moved back and stood at the side of the window. The man in the downpour wore a large poncho, his head sheltered by a rain hat. He extinguished the light as he approached the house.

Above them, the prisoners could hear the kitchen door rattling, then the sound of a body crashing against the wood. Soon the banging stopped and except for the storm there was silence. The figure left the area of the kitchen door, and Tanner could see from his side of the window the beam of light darting up and down. And then it disappeared around the far end of the house by the garage.

'Bernie!' Leila stood up beside Alice and the child. 'Look! Over there!'

Through her side window came the intermittent shafts of another beam of light. Although it was quite far away, the beam was bright; it danced closer. Whoever was carrying that light was racing toward the house.

Suddenly it went out and again there was only the rain and the lightning. Tanner and Osterman went to the side window, one on each side, and cautiously looked out. They could see no one, no figure, nothing but rain, forced into diagonal sheets by the wind.

There was a loud crash from upstairs. And then another, this one sharper, wood slamming against wood. Tanner went toward the stairs. He had locked the cellar door, but it was thin; a good kick would break it from its hinges. He held the axe level, prepared to swing at anything descending those stairs.

Silence.

There were no more sounds from the house.

Suddenly, Alice Tanner screamed. A large hand was rubbing the pane of glass in the front window. The beam of a powerful flashlight pierced the darkness. Someone was squatting behind the light, the face hidden under a rain hood.

Tanner rushed to his wife and daughter, picking up the child from the blanket.

'Get back! Get back against the wall!'

The glass shattered and flew in all directions under the force of the outsider's boot. The kicking continued. Mud and glass and fragments of wood came flying into the basement. Rain swept through the broken window. The six prisoners huddled by the front wall as the beam of light flashed about the floor, the opposite wall and the stairs.

What followed paralysed them.

The barrel of a rifle appeared at the edge of the window frame and a volley of ear-shattering shots struck the floor and rear wall. Silence. Cinderblock dust whirled about the basement; in the glare of the powerful flashlight it looked like swirling clouds of stone mist. The firing began again, wildly, indiscriminately. The infantryman in Tanner told him what was happening. A second magazine had been inserted into the loading clip of an automatic rifle.

And then another rifle butt smashed the glass of the left rear window directly opposite them. A wide beam of light scanned the row of human beings against the wall. Tanner saw his wife clutching their daughter, shielding the small body with her own, and his mind cracked with fury.

He raced to the window, swinging the axe toward the shattered glass and the crouching figure behind it. The form jumped back; shots pounded into the ceiling above Tanner's head. The shaft of light from the front window caught him now. It's over, Tanner thought. It was going to be over for him. Instead, Bernie was swinging the garden fork at the rifle barrel, deflecting shots away from Tanner. The news director crawled back to his wife and children.

'Get over here!' he yelled, pushing them to the

far wall, the garage side of the basement. Janet could not stop screaming.

Bernie grabbed his wife's wrist and pulled her toward the basement corner. The beams of light crisscrossed each other. More shots were fired; dust filled the air; it became impossible to breathe.

The light from the rear window suddenly disappeared; the one from the front continued its awkward search. The second rifle was changing its position. And then from the far side window came another crash and the sound of breaking glass. The wide beam of light shone through again, now blinding them. Tanner shoved his wife and son toward the rear corner next to the stairs. Shots poured in; Tanner could feel the vibration as the bullets spiraled into the wall above and around him.

Crossfire!

He held the axe tightly, then he lunged forward, through the fire, fully understanding that any one bullet might end his life. But none could end it until he reached his target. Nothing could prevent that!

He reached the side window and swung the axe diagonally into it. An anguished scream followed; blood gushed through the opening. Tanner's face and arms were covered with blood.

The rifle in the front window tried to aim in Tanner's direction, but it was impossible. The bullets hit the floor.

Osterman rushed toward the remaining rifle, holding the garden fork at his shoulder. At the last instant he flung it through the outline of the broken glass as if it were a javelin. A cry of pain; the firing stopped.

Tanner supported himself against the wall under the window. In the flashes of lightning he could see the blood rolling down over the cinderblock.

He was alive, and that was remarkable.

He turned and went back toward his wife and children. Ali held the still screaming Janet. The boy had turned his face into the wall and was weeping uncontrollably.

'Leila! Jesus, God! *Leila!*' Bernie's hysterical roar portended the worst. '*Leila, where are you?*'

'I'm here,' Leila said quietly. 'I'm all right, darling.'

Tanner found Leila against the front wall. She had not followed his command to move.

And then Tanner saw something which struck his exhausted mind. Leila wore a large greenish brooch – he hadn't noticed it before. He saw it clearly now, for it shone in the dark. It was iridescent, one of those mod creations sold in fashionable boutiques. It was impossible to miss in the darkness.

A dim flash of lightning lit up the wall around her. Tanner wasn't sure but he was close to being sure: there were no bullet markings near her.

Tanner held his wife and daughter with one arm and cradled his son's head with the other. Bernie ran to Leila and embraced her. The wail of a siren was heard through the sounds of the outside storm, carried by the blasts of wind through the smashed windows.

They remained motionless, spent beyond human endurance. Several minutes later they heard the voices and the knocking upstairs.

'Tanner! Tanner! Open the door!'

He released his wife and son and walked to the broken front window.

'We're here. We're here, you Goddamned filthy pricks.'

26

Tanner had seen these two patrolmen numerous times in the Village, directing traffic and cruising in radio cars, but he didn't know their names. They had been recruited less than a year ago and were younger than Jenkins and McDermott.

Now he attacked. He pushed the first policeman violently against the hallway wall. The blood on his hands was smudged over the officer's raincoat. The second patrolman had dashed down the basement stairs for the others.

'For Christ's sake, let go!'

'You dirty *bastard*! You *fucking punk*! We could have been . . . *would* have been *killed* down there! All of us! My wife! My children! *Why did you do that?* You give me an answer and give it to me quick!'

'Goddamn it, let go! Do *what*? *What* answer, for God's sake?'

'You passed this house a half hour ago! You saw the Goddamn flashlight and you beat it! You raced out of here!'

'You're crazy! Me and Ronnie been in the north end! We got a transmission to get over here not five minutes ago. People named Scanlan reported shots . . .'

'Who's in the other car? I want to know who's in the other *car*!'

'If you'll take your Goddamned hands off me I'll go out and bring in the route sheet. I forget who – but I know *where* they are. They're over on Apple Drive. There was a robbery.'

'The Cardones live on Apple Drive!'

'It wasn't the Cardones' house. I know that one. It was Needham. An old couple.'

Ali came into the hall from the stairs, holding Janet in her arms. The child was retching, gasping for air. Ali was crying softly, rocking her daughter back and forth in her arms.

Their son followed, his face filthy from the dust, smudged with his tears. The Ostermans were next. Bernie held on to Leila's waist, supporting her up the stairs. He held on to her as though he would never let her go.

The second patrolman came slowly through the doorway. His expression startled the other officer.

'Holy Mary Mother of God,' he said softly. 'It's a human slaughterhouse down there . . . I swear to Christ I don't see how any of 'em are alive.'

'Call MacAuliff, Get him over here.'

'The line's dead,' said Tanner, gently leading Ali to the couch in the living room.

'I'll go radio in.' The patrolman named Ronnie went to the front door. 'He won't believe this,' he said quietly.

The remaining patrolman got an armchair for Leila. She collapsed into it and for the first time started to weep. Bernie leaned over behind his wife and caressed her hair. Raymond crouched beside his father, in front of his mother and sister.

He was so terrified he could do nothing but stare into his father's face.

The policeman wandered toward the basement stairs. It was obvious he wanted to go down, not only out of curiosity, but because the scene in the living room was somehow so private.

The door opened and the second patrolman leaned in. 'I told Mac. He picked up the radio call on his car frequency. Jesus, you should have heard him. He's on his way.'

'How long will it be?' asked Tanner from the couch.

'Not long, sir. He lives about eight miles out and the roads are rotten. But the way he sounded he'll be here faster than anyone else could.'

'I've stationed a dozen deputies around the grounds and two men in the house. One will stay downstairs, the other in the upper hallway. I don't know what else I can do.' MacAuliff was in the basement with Tanner. The others were upstairs. Tanner wanted the police captain to himself.

'Listen to me! Someone, one of *your* men, passed this house and refused to stop! I know damned well he saw the flashlight! He saw it and drove away!'

'I don't believe that. I checked. Nobody in the cars spotted anything around here. You saw the route sheet. This place is marked for extra concentration.'

'I *saw* the patrol car *leave*! . . . Where's Jenkins? McDermott?'

'It's their day off. I'm thinking of calling them back on duty.'

'It's funny they're off on weekends, isn't it?'

'I alternate my men on weekends. The weekends are very well covered. Just like the council ordered.'

Tanner caught the tone of self-justification in MacAuliff's voice.

'You've got to do one other thing.'

MacAuliff wasn't paying attention. He was inspecting the walls of the cinderback cage. He stooped his immense frame down and picked up several lead slugs from the floor.

'I want every piece of evidence picked up here and sent down for analysis. I'll use the FBI if Newark can't do it . . . What did you say?'

'I said you've got to do one more thing. It's imperative, but you've got to do it with me alone. Nobody else.'

'What's that?'

'You and I are going to find a phone, and you're going to get on it and make two calls.'

'Who to?' MacAuliff asked the question because Tanner had taken several steps toward the cellar staircase to make sure no one was there.

'The Cardones and the Tremaynes. I want to know where they are. Where they *were*.'

'What the hell . . .'

'Just do as I say!'

'You think . . .'

'I don't think *anything*! I just want to know where they are . . . Let's say I'm still worried about them.' Tanner started for the stairs, but

MacAuliff stood motionless in the center of the room.

'Wait a minute! You want me to make the calls and then follow up with verification. Okay, I'll do it . . . Now, it's my turn. You give me a pain. You aggravate my ulcer. What the hell's going on? There's too much crap here to suit me! If you and your friends are in some kind of trouble, come clean and tell me. I can't do a thing if I don't know who to go after. And I'll tell you this,' MacAuliff lowered his voice and pointed his finger at the news director, his other hand on his ulcerated stomach, 'I'm not going to have my record loused up because you play games. I'm not going to have mass homicide on my beat because you don't tell me what I should know so I can prevent it!'

Tanner stood where he was, one foot on the bottom step. He looked and wondered. He could tell in a minute, he thought.

'All right . . . Omega . . . You've heard of Omega?' Tanner stared into MacAuliff's eyes, watching for the slightest betrayal.

'I forgot. You're not cleared for Omega, are you?'

'What the hell are you talking about?'

'Ask Jenkins. Maybe he'll tell you . . . Come on, let's go.'

Three telephone calls were made from MacAuliff's police car. The information received was clear, precise. The Tremaynes and the Cardones were neither at home nor in the vicinity.

The Cardones were in Rockland County, across the New York line. Dining out, the maid said; and if the police officer reached them would he be so kind as to ask them to call home. There was an urgent message from Philadelphia.

The Tremaynes, Virginia sick again, had returned to their doctor in Ridge Park.

The doctor confirmed the Tremaynes' visit to his office. He was quite sure they'd gone into New York City. As a matter of fact, he had prescribed dinner and a show. Mrs Tremayne's relapse was primarily psychological. She had to get her mind on things other than the Lassiter depot.

It was all so specific, thought Tanner. So well established through second and third parties.

Yet neither couple was really accounted for.

For as Tanner reconstructed the events in the basement, he realized that one of the figures intent on killing them could have been a woman.

Fassett had said Omega was killers and fanatics. Men *and* women.

'There's your answer.' MacAuliff's words intruded on Tanner's thoughts. 'We'll check them out when they return. Easy enough to verify whatever they tell us . . . as you know.'

'Yes . . . Yes, of course. You'll call me after you talk to them.'

'I won't promise that. I will if I think you should know.'

The mechanic arrived to repair the automobiles. Tanner took him through the kitchen into the garage and watched the expression on his face as he inspected the severed wires.

'You were right, Mr Tanner. Every lead. I'll splice in temporary connections and we'll make them permanent down at the shop. Somebody played you a rotten joke.'

Back in the kitchen Tanner rejoined his wife and the Ostermans. The children were upstairs in Raymond's room where one of MacAuliff's policemen had volunteered to stay with them, play whatever games they liked, try to keep them calm while the adults talked.

Osterman was adamant. They *had* to get out of Saddle Valley, they had to get to Washington. Once the station wagon was repaired they'd leave, but instead of driving they'd go to Kennedy Airport and take a plane. They'd trust no taxis, no limousines. They'd give MacAuliff no explanations; they'd simply get in the car and go. MacAuliff had no legal right to hold them.

Tanner sat next to Ali, across from the Ostermans, and held her hand. Twice Bernie and Leila had tried to force him to explain everything to his wife and both times Tanner had said he would do so privately.

The Ostermans thought they understood.

Ali didn't and so he held her hand.

And each time Leila spoke Tanner remembered her shining brooch in the darkness of the basement – and the unmarked wall behind her.

The front door chimed and Tanner went to answer it. He came back smiling.

'Sounds from reality. The telephone repair

crew.' Tanner did not return to his seat. The blurred outlines of a plan were slowly coming into focus. He'd need Ali.

His wife turned and looked at him, reading his thoughts. 'I'm going up to see the children.'

She left and Tanner walked to the table. He reached down for his pack of cigarettes and put them in his shirt pocket.

'You're going to tell her now?' asked Leila.

'Yes.'

'Tell her everything. Maybe she'll make some sense out of this . . . Omega.' Bernie still looked unbelieving. 'Christ knows, I can't.'

'You saw the mark on the wall.'

Bernie looked strangely at Tanner. 'I saw a mark on the wall.'

'Excuse me, Mr Tanner.' It was the downstairs policeman at the kitchen door. 'The telephone men want to see you. They're in your study.'

'Okay. Be right out.' He turned back to Bernie Osterman. 'To refresh your memory, the mark you saw was the Greek letter Omega.'

He walked rapidly out the kitchen door and went to the study. Outside the windows, the storm clouds hovered, the rain, though letting up, was still strong. It was dark in the room; only the desk lamp was on.

'Mr Tanner.' The voice came from behind and he swung around. There was the man named Cole, dressed in the blue jacket of the telephone company, looking at him intently. Another man stood next to him. 'Please don't raise your voice.'

Tanner's shock was such that he lost control of

himself. He lunged at the agent. 'You son of a bitch . . .'

He was stopped by both men. They held his arms tightly behind him, pressed against the small of his back. Cole gripped his shoulders and spoke rapidly, with great intensity.

'Please! We know what you've been through! We can't change that, but we can tell you it's over! It's *over*, Mr Tanner. Omega's cracked!'

'Don't you tell me anything! You bastards! You filthy bastards! You don't exist! They never heard of Fassett! Your phones are disconnected! Your . . .'

'We had to get out fast!' interrupted the agent. 'We had to abandon both posts. It was mandatory. It will all be explained to you.'

'I don't believe a thing you say!'

'Just listen! Make up your mind later, but *listen*. Fassett's not two miles from here putting the last pieces together. He and Washington are closing in. We'll have Omega by morning.'

'What Omega? What Fassett? I called Washington! I talked to McLean, Virginia!'

'You spoke with a man named Dwight. In title, he's Andrews' superior, but not in fact. Dwight was never cleared for Omega. He checked with Clandestine Services, and the call came to the Director. There was no alternative but to deny, Mr Tanner. In these cases we always deny. We *have* to.'

'Where are the guards outside? What happened to all your Goddamned taps? Your shock troops who wouldn't let us be touched?'

'It will all be explained to you . . . I won't lie. Mistakes are made. One massive error, if you like. We can never make up for them, we know that. But we've never been faced with an Omega before. The main point is – the objective is right in front of us. We're on target now!'

'That's horseshit! The *main point* is my wife and children were almost killed!'

'Look. Look at this.' Cole took a small metal disk from his pocket. His colleague let go of Tanner's arms. 'Go on, take it. Look at it closely.'

Tanner took the object in his hand, and turned it to catch the light. He saw that the tiny object was corroded, pockmarked.

'So?'

'That's one of the miniaturized pick-ups. The corrosion is acid. Acid dropped on it, to ruin it. The pick-ups have been messed up in every room. We're not getting any transmissions.'

'How could anyone find them?'

'It's easy enough with the proper equipment. There's no evidence on any of these, no finger-prints. That's Omega, Mr Tanner.'

'Who is it?'

'Even I don't know that. Only Fassett does. He's got everything under control. He's the best man in three continents. If you won't take my word ask the Secretary of State. The President, if you like. Nothing more will happen in this house.'

John Tanner took several deep breaths and looked at the agent. 'You realize you haven't explained anything.'

'I told you. Later.'

'That's not good enough!'

Cole returned Tanner's questioning look. 'What choice have you got?'

'Call that policeman in here and start yelling.'

'What good would that do you? Buy you a couple of hours of peace. How long would it last?'

Tanner would ask him one further question. Whatever the answer, it would make no difference. The plan in John Tanner's mind was crystallizing. But Cole would never know it.

'What's left for me to do?'

'Do nothing. Absolutely nothing.'

'Whenever you people say that, the mortars start pounding the beach.'

'No mortars now. That's over with.'

'I see. It's over with . . . All right. I . . . do . . . nothing. May I go back to my wife now?'

'Of course.'

'Incidentally, is the telephone really fixed?'

'Yes, it is.'

The news editor turned, his arms aching, and walked slowly into the hallway.

No one could be trusted any longer.

He would force Omega's hand himself.

27

Ali sat on the edge of the bed and listened to her husband's story. There were moments when she wondered if he were sane. She knew that men like her husband, men who functioned a great deal of the time under pressure, were subject to breakdowns. She could understand maniacs in the night, lawyers and stockbrokers in the panic of impending destruction, even John's compelling drive to reform the unreformable. Yet what he was telling her now was beyond her comprehension.

'Why did you agree?' she asked him.

'It sounds crazy, but I was trapped. I didn't have a choice. I had to go through with it.'

'You volunteered!' said Ali.

'Not really. Once I agreed to let Fassett reveal the names, I signed an affidavit which made me indictable under the National Security Act. Once I knew who they were I was hung. Fassett knew I would be. It was impossible to continue normal relationships with them. And if I didn't, I might step over the line and be prosecuted.'

'How awful,' said Ali softly.

'Filthy is more to the point.'

He told her about the succeeding episodes with Ginny and Leila outside by the pool. And how Dick Tremayne had followed him into the garage.

Finally how Bernie had started to tell him something just before Janet's screams had wakened the household.

'He never told you what it was?'

'He said he was only offering me money for investments. I accused them both of being part of Omega . . . Then he saved my life.'

'No. Wait a minute.' Ali sat forward. 'When you went out for the umbrellas and we all watched you in the rain . . . and then the shots started and we all panicked . . . I tried to go out and Leila and Bernie stopped me. So I screamed and tried to break away. Leila – not Bernie – held me against the wall. Suddenly she looked at Bernie and said, "You can go, Bernie! It's all right, Bernie!" . . . I didn't understand, but she ordered him.'

'A woman doesn't send her husband in front of a firing squad.'

'That's what I wondered about. I wondered if I'd have the courage to send you out . . . for Bernie.'

And so Tanner told his wife about the brooch; and the wall with no bullet marks.

'But they were *in* the basement, darling. They weren't *outside*. They weren't the ones who shot at us.' Ali stopped. The memory of the horror was too much. She couldn't bring herself to speak further of it. Instead, she told him about Joe's hysterics in the living room and the fact that Betty Cardone had watched them through the window.

'So here we are,' he said when she had finished. 'And I'm not sure where that is.'

'But the man downstairs said it would be over. He told you that.'

'They've told me a lot of things . . . But which one is it? Or is it all three?'

'Who?' she asked.

'Omega. It has to be in couples. They have to operate in couples . . . But the Tremaynes and the Cardones were gassed in the car. They *were* left on Lassiter . . . Or were they?'

Tanner put his hands in his pockets and paced the floor. He went to the window and leaned against the sill, looking out on the front lawn.

'There are a lot of cops outside. They're bored to death. I bet they haven't seen the basement. I wonder – '

The glass shattered. Tanner spun around and blood spurted out of his shirt. Ali screamed, running to her husband as he fell to the floor.

More shots were fired but none came through the window. They were outside.

The patrolman in the hallway crashed through the door and raced to the fallen Tanner. No more than three seconds later the downstairs guard rushed into the room, his pistol drawn. Voices were heard yelling outside on the grounds. Leila entered, gasped, and ran to Ali and her fallen husband.

'Bernie! For God's sake, *Bernie*!'

But Osterman did not appear.

'Get him on the bed!' roared the patrolman from the upstairs hallway. 'Please, ma'am, let go! Let me get him on the bed!'

Osterman could be heard yelling on the staircase. 'What the hell happened?' He came into the room. 'Oh, *Jesus*! Oh, Jesus *Christ*!'

Tanner regained consciousness and looked around. MacAuliff stood next to the doctor; Ali sat on the bed. Bernie and Leila were at the footrail, trying to smile at him reassuringly.

'You're going to be fine. Very superficial,' said the doctor. 'Painful, but not serious. Shoulder cartilage, that's what it is.'

'I was shot?'

'You were shot.' MacAuliff agreed.

'Who shot me?'

'We don't know that.' MacAuliff tried to conceal his anger, but it surfaced. The captain was obviously convinced he was being ignored; that vital information was being withheld from him. 'But I tell you this, I intend to question each one of you if it takes all night to find out what's happening here. You're all being damned fools and I won't permit it!'

'The wound is dressed,' said the doctor, putting on his jacket. 'You can get up and around as soon as you feel like it, only take it easy, Mr Tanner. Not much more than a deep cut. Very little loss of blood.' The doctor smiled and left rapidly. He had no reason to remain.

The moment the door was closed, MacAuliff made his abrupt statement. 'Would you all wait downstairs, please? I want to be left alone with Mr Tanner.'

'Captain, he was just shot,' said Bernie firmly. 'You can't question him now; I won't let you.'

'I'm a police officer on official business; I don't need your permission. You heard the doctor. He's not seriously hurt.'

'He's been through enough!' Ali stared at MacAuliff.

'I'm sorry, Mrs Tanner. This is necessary. Now will you all please . . .'

'No, we will *not*!' Osterman left his wife's side and approached the police chief. 'He's not the one who should be questioned. *You* are. Your whole Goddamn police force should be put on the carpet . . . I'd like to know why that patrol car didn't stop, Captain! I heard your explanation and I don't accept it!'

'You continue this, Mr Osterman, I'll call in an officer and have you locked up!'

'I wouldn't try that . . .'

'Don't tempt me! I've dealt with your kind before! I *worked* New York, sheenie!'

Osterman had grown very still. 'What did you say?'

'Don't provoke me. You're provoking me!'

'Forget it!' said Tanner from the bed. 'I don't mind, really.'

Alone with MacAuliff, Tanner sat up. His shoulder hurt, but he could move it freely.

MacAuliff walked to the end of the bed and held the footrail with both hands. He spoke calmly. 'You talk now. You tell me what you know or I'll book you for withholding information in attempted murder.'

'They were trying to kill *me*.'

'That's still murder. M-u-r-d-e-r. It doesn't make any difference whether it's yours or that big Jew bastard's!'

'Why are you so hostile?' Tanner asked. 'Tell me. You should be begging at my feet. I'm a taxpayer and you haven't protected my house.'

MacAuliff made several attempts to speak but he was choking on his own anger. Finally he controlled himself.

'Okay. I know a lot of you don't like the way I run things. You bastards want to put me out and get some fucking hippie from a half-assed law school! Well, the only way you can do that is if I louse up. And I'm not *gonna* louse up! My record stays clean! This town stays clean! So you tell me what's going on and if I need help, I'll call it in! I can't do that without something to go on!'

Tanner rose from the bed, at first unsteadily, and then, to his surprise, firmly.

'I believe you. You're too frantic to lie . . . And you're right. A lot of us *don't* like you. But that may be chemical, so let's let it go . . . Still, I'm not answering questions. Instead, I'm giving you an order. You'll keep this house guarded night and day until I tell you to stop! Do you understand that?'

'I don't *take* orders!'

'You'll take them from me. If you don't, I'll plaster you across sixty million television screens as the typical example of the outdated, uneducated, unenlightened threat to real law enforcement! You're obsolete. Get that pension and run.'

'You couldn't do that . . .'

'Couldn't I? Check around.'

MacAuliff stood facing Tanner. The veins in his neck were so apparent the news director thought they would burst. 'I hate you bastards!' he said coldly. 'I hate your guts.'

'As I do yours . . . I've seen you in action . . . But that doesn't matter now. Sit down.'

Ten minutes later MacAuliff rushed out of the house into the diminishing July storm. He slammed the front door behind him and gave cursory orders to several police deputies on the lawn. The men acknowledged with feeble salutes, and MacAuliff climbed into his car.

Tanner took a shirt from his bureau drawer and awkwardly put it on. He went out of the bedroom and started down the stairs.

Ali was in the hallway talking to the police officer and saw him. She rushed up to meet him on the staircase landing.

'There are police crawling all over the place. I wish it were an army . . . Oh, Lord! I'm trying to be calm. I really am! But I can't!' She embraced him, conscious of the bandage beneath his shirt. 'What are we going to do? Who are we going to *turn* to?'

'Everything's going to be all right . . . We just have to wait a little longer.'

'What for?'

'MacAuliff is getting me information.'

'What information?'

Tanner moved Ali against the wall. He spoke

quietly, making sure the policeman wasn't watching them. 'Whoever was outside those basement windows is hurt. One I know is badly wounded – in the leg. The other we can't be sure of, but Bernie thinks he hit him in the shoulder or the chest. MacAuliff's going out to see the Cardones and the Tremaynes. He'll phone me then. It may take quite a while, but he'll get back to me.'

'Did you tell him what to look for?'

'No. Nothing. I simply asked him to follow up their stories about where they were. That's all. I don't want MacAuliff making decisions. That's for Fassett.'

But it wasn't for Fassett, thought Tanner. It wasn't for anyone but him any longer. He'd tell Ali when he had to. At the last minute. So he smiled at her and put his arm around her waist and wished he could be free to love her again.

The telephone rang at ten-forty-seven.

'John? It's Dick. MacAuliff was over to see me.' Tremayne was breathing hard into the telephone, but was keeping his voice reasonably calm. His control was stretched very thin, however.

'. . . I have no idea what you're involved with – intended murder, for God's sake! – and I don't *want* to know, but it's more than I can take! I'm sorry, John, but I'm getting the family out of here. I've got reservations on Pan Am at ten in the morning.'

'Where are you going?'

Tremayne did not reply. Tanner spoke again. 'I asked you where you were going.'

'Sorry, John . . . this may sound rotten, but I don't want to tell you.'

'I think I understand . . . Do us a favor, though. Drop by on the way to the airport.'

'I can't promise that. Good-bye.'

Tanner held his finger down on the phone and then released it. He dialed the Saddle Valley police station.

'Police headquarters. Sergeant Dale.'

'Captain MacAuliff, please. John Tanner calling.'

'He's not here, Mr Tanner.'

'Can you reach him? It's urgent.'

'I can try on the car radio; do you want to hold?'

'No, just have him call me as soon as possible.' Tanner gave his telephone number and hung up. MacAuliff was probably on his way to the Cardones. He should have arrived by now. He'd call soon. Tanner returned to the living room. He wanted to unnerve the Ostermans.

It was part of his plan.

'Who called?' asked Bernie.

'Dick. He heard what happened . . . He's taking the family and leaving.'

The Ostermans exchanged looks.

'Where?'

'He didn't say. They've got a flight in the morning.'

'He didn't say where he was going?' Bernie stood up casually but couldn't hide his anxiety.

'I told you. He wouldn't tell me.'

'That's not what you said.' Osterman looked at

Tanner. 'You said "didn't say". That's different from not telling you.'

'I suppose it is . . . You still think we should head down to Washington?'

'What?' Osterman was looking at his wife. He hadn't heard Tanner's question.

'Do you still think we should go to Washington?'

'Yes.' Bernie stared at Tanner. 'Now more than ever. You need protection. Real protection . . . They're trying to kill you, John.'

'I wonder. I wonder if it's me they're trying to kill.'

'What do you mean?' Leila stood up, facing Tanner.

The telephone rang.

Tanner returned quickly to the study and picked up the receiver. It was MacAuliff.

'Listen,' said Tanner quietly. 'I want you to describe exactly – *exactly* – where Tremayne was during your interrogation.'

'In his study.'

'*Where* in his study?'

'At his desk. Why?'

'Did he get up? Did he walk around? To shake your hand, for instance?'

'No . . . No, I don't think so. No, he didn't.'

'What about his wife? She let you in?'

'No. The maid. Tremayne's wife was upstairs. She was sick. We verified that; called the doctor, remember?'

'All right. Now tell me about the Cardones. Where did you find them?'

'Spoke first with his wife. One of the kids let me in. She was lying on the sofa, her husband was in the garage.'

'Where did you talk with him?'

'I just told you. In the garage. I didn't get there too soon either. He's on his way to Philadelphia. His father's sick. They gave him the last rites.'

'Philadelphia? . . . Where exactly was he?'

'In the *garage*, I said! His bags were packed. He was in the car. He told me to be quick. He wanted to take off.'

'He was *in* the car?'

'That's right.'

'Didn't that seem strange to you?'

'Why should it? For Christ's sake, his father's dying! He wanted to get the hell to Philadelphia. I'll check it out.'

Tanner hung up the phone.

Neither couple was seen by MacAuliff under normal conditions. None stood, none walked. Both had reasons not to be at his house on Sunday.

Tremayne behind a desk, frightened, immobile.

Cardone seated in an automobile, anxious only to drive away.

One or both *wounded*.

One or both, perhaps, Omega.

The time had come. Outside the rain had stopped; his traveling would be easier now, although the woods would still be wet.

In the kitchen, he changed into the clothes he'd carried down from the bedroom: black trousers, a black long-sleeved sweater, and sneakers. He put money in his pocket, making sure that his change included at least six dimes. Finally, he clipped a pencil-light to the top of his sweater.

Then he went to the hallway door and called Ali into the kitchen. He dreaded this moment far more than anything which lay before him. Yet there was no other way. He knew he had to tell her.

'What are you doing? Why – '

Tanner held his fingers to his lips and drew her close to him. They had walked to the far end of the kitchen by the garage door, the furthest point from the hallway. He whispered calmly to her.

'Remember I asked you to trust me?'

Ali nodded her head slowly.

'I'm going out for a while; just for a little while. I'm meeting a couple of men who can help us. MacAuliff made contact.'

'Why can't they come here? I don't want you to go outside. You can't go outside!'

'There's no other practical way. It's been arranged,' he lied, knowing she suspected the lie. 'I'll phone you in a little while. You'll know everything's all right then. But until I do, I want you to tell the Ostermans I went for a walk . . . I'm upset, anything you like. It's important they think *you* believe I went for a walk. That I'll be back any minute. Maybe I'm talking to some of the men outside.'

'Who *are* you going to meet? You've got to tell me.'

'Fassett's men.'

She held his gaze. The lie was established between them now and she searched his eyes. 'You have to do this?' she asked quietly.

'Yes.' He embraced her roughly, anxious to leave, and walked rapidly to the kitchen door.

Outside he strolled about his property, establishing his presence with the police deputies in front and back of his house, to the point where he guessed he was no longer really watched. And then, when he felt no one was looking at him, he disappeared into the woods.

He made a wide circle toward the west, using the tiny beam of the pencil light to avoid obstacles. The wetness, the softness of the earth, made the going difficult, but eventually he saw the backyard lights of his neighbors the Scanlans, three hundred feet from his property line. He was soaked as he approached the Scanlans' back porch and rang the bell.

Fifteen minutes later – again longer than Tanner had anticipated – he climbed into Scanlan's Mercedes coupé and started the engine. Scanlan's Smith & Wesson magazine-clip pistol was in his belt, three extra clips of ammunition in his pocket.

Tanner swung left down Orchard Drive toward the center of the Village. It was past midnight; he was behind the schedule he had set.

He took momentary stock of himself and his actions. He had never considered himself an exceptionally brave man. Whatever courage he had ever displayed was always born of the moment. And he wasn't feeling courageous now. He was desperate.

It was strange. His fear – the profound, deeply felt terror he had lived with for days – now created its own balance, gave birth to its own anger. Anger at being manipulated. He could accept it no longer.

Saddle Valley was quiet, the main street softly lit by replicas of gas lamps, the storefronts in keeping with the town's image of quiet wealth. No neons, no floodlights, everything subdued.

Tanner drove past The Village Pub and the taxi stand, made a U-turn, and parked. The public telephone was directly across from the Mercedes. He wanted the car positioned far enough away so he could see the whole area. He walked across the street and made his first call.

'It's Tanner, Tremayne. Be quiet and listen to me . . . Omega's finished. It's being disbanded. I'm calling it off. Zurich's calling it off. We've put you through the final test and you've failed. The stupidity displayed by everyone is beyond belief! I'm issuing the phase-out orders tonight. Be at the Lassiter depot at two-thirty. And don't try to call my home. I'm phoning from the Village. I'll take a taxi to the area. My house is being watched, thanks to *all* of you! Be at the depot at two-thirty and bring Virginia. Omega's collapsed! If you want to get out alive, be there . . . Two-thirty!'

Tanner pressed down the receiver. The Cardones next.

'Betty? It's Tanner. Listen closely. You get

hold of Joe and tell him Omega is finished. I don't care how you do it, but get him back here. That's an order from Zurich. Tell him that! . . . Omega's collapsed. You've all been damn fools. Disabling my cars was stupid. I'm issuing phase-out orders tonight at the Lassiter depot at two-thirty. You and Joe be there! Zurich expects you. And *don't* try to phone me back. I'm calling from the Village. My house is watched. I'll take a taxi. Remember. The Lassiter depot – tell Joe.'

Once more Tanner pressed the receiver down. His third call was to his own home.

'Ali? Everything's fine, darling. There's nothing to worry about. Now, don't talk! Put Bernie on the phone right away . . . Ali, not *now*! Put Bernie on the *phone*! . . . Bernie, it's John. I'm sorry I took off but I had to. I know who Omega is but I need your help. I'm calling from the Village. I'll need a car later . . . not now; later. I don't want mine seen in the Village. I'll use a taxi. Meet me out at the Lassiter depot at two-thirty. Turn right out of the driveway and go east on Orchard – it curves north – for about a mile. You'll see a large pond, there's a white fence around it. On the other side is Lassiter Road. Go down Lassiter a couple of miles and you'll see the depot . . . It's over, Bernie. I'll have Omega at the depot at two-thirty. For Christ's sake *don't, don't blow it*! Trust me! *Don't* call anybody or *do* anything! Just *be* there!'

Tanner hung up the telephone, opened the door and ran toward the Mercedes coupé.

28

He stood in the darkened doorway of a toy store. It occurred to him that Scanlan's Mercedes was a familiar car in the Village and the Tremaynes, the Cardones, and perhaps even the Ostermans knew Scanlan was his nearest neighbor. That might be to his advantage, he considered. If the assumption were made that he'd borrowed the automobile, it would be further assumed that he remained in the area. The hunt, then, would be thorough. There was nothing to do but wait now. Wait until a little after two o'clock before driving out to the Lassiter depot.

Wait in the center of the Village to see who came after him; who tried to stop him from making the rendezvous. Which couple? Or would it be all three? For Omega had to be frightened now. The unutterable had been said; the mystery brought out into the open.

Omega would have to try to stop him now. If anything Fassett had said was true, that was their only course of action. To intercept him before he reached the depot.

He counted on it. They wouldn't stop him – he'd make sure of that, but he wanted to know in advance who the enemy was.

He looked up and down the street. There were only four people visible. A couple walking a

Dalmatian, a man emerging from the Pub, and the driver asleep in the front seat of his taxi.

From the east end of town Tanner saw the headlights of a car approaching slowly. Soon he saw it was his own station wagon. He pressed back into the recessed, unlit doorway.

The driver was Leila Osterman. Alone.

Tanner's pulse quickened. What had he done? It had never occurred to him that any of the couples would separate in a crisis! Yet Leila was alone! And there was nothing to prevent Osterman from holding his family as hostages! Osterman was one of those being protected, not one of the hunted. He could move about freely, leave the premises if he wished. Force Ali and the children to go with him if he thought it necessary!

Leila parked the station wagon in front of the Pub, got out, and walked rapidly over to the taxi driver, shaking him awake. They talked quietly for a moment; Tanner couldn't hear the voices. Eventually Leila turned back to the Pub and went in. Tanner remained in the doorway, fingering the dimes in his pocket, waiting for her to come out. The waiting was agony. He had to get to the phone. He had to get through to the police! He had to make sure his family was safe!

Finally she appeared, got in the wagon, and drove off. Five or six blocks west she turned right; the car disappeared.

Tanner raced across the street to the telephone booth. He dropped in a dime and dialed.

'Hello?'

Thank God! It was Ali!

'It's me.'

'Where are you . . .'

'Never mind that now. Everything's fine . . . Are you all right?' He listened carefully for any false note.

'Of course, I am. We're worried sick about you. What are you doing?'

She sounded natural. It was all right.

'I don't have time. I want . . .'

She interrupted him. 'Leila went out looking for you. You've made an awful mistake . . . We've talked. You and I were wrong, darling. Very *wrong*. Bernie got so worried he thought . . .'

He cut her off. He didn't have the seconds to waste; not on the Ostermans, not now. 'I've got to get off the phone. Stay with the guards. Do as I say. Don't let them out of your sight!'

He hung up before she could speak. He had to reach the police. Every moment counted now.

'Headquarters. Jenkins speaking.'

So the one man on the Saddle Valley police force cleared for Omega was back. MacAuliff had recalled him.

'Headquarters,' repeated the patrolman testily.

'This is John Tanner . . .'

'Jesus Christ, where have you been? We've been looking all over for you!'

'You won't find me. Not until I want you to . . . Now, listen to me! The two policemen in the house – I want them to stay with my wife. She's never to be left alone! The children either! Never! None of them can be alone with Osterman!'

'Of course! We know that! Now, where are you? Don't be a damned fool!'

'I'll phone you later. Don't bother to trace this call. I'll be gone.'

He slammed down the receiver and opened the door, looking for a better vantage point than the storefront. He couldn't run unobserved from the doorway. He started back across the street. The taxi driver was asleep again.

Suddenly, without warning, Tanner heard the roar of an engine. The blurred outline of a car without headlights sped toward him. It came out of nowhere at enormous speed; he was its target. He raced toward the opposite sidewalk only feet ahead of the rushing car. He threw himself toward the curb, twisting his body away from the automobile.

At the same instant he felt a great blow on his left leg. There was a piercing sound of tires braking on asphalt. Tanner fell, rolling with his plunge, and saw the black car narrowly miss the Mercedes, then speed away down Valley Road.

The pain in his leg was excruciating; his shoulder was throbbing. He hoped to Christ he could walk! He had to be able to *walk*!

The cab driver was running toward him.

'Jesus! What happened?'

'Help me up, will you, please?'

'Sure! Sure! You okay? . . . That guy must've had a load on! Jesus! You could've been killed. You want me to get a doctor?'

'No. No. I don't think so.'

'I got a telephone right over there! I'll call the cops! They'll have a doctor here in no time!'

'No! No, don't! I'm all right . . . Just help me walk around a bit.' It was painful for him, but Tanner found he could move. That was the important fact. The pain didn't matter now. Nothing mattered but Omega. And Omega was out in the open!

'I better call the police anyway,' said the driver, holding on to Tanner's arm. 'That clown should get yanked off the road.'

'No . . . I mean, I didn't get the license. I didn't even see what kind of car. It wouldn't do any good.'

'I guess not. Serve the bastard right, though, if he plows himself into a tree.'

'Yeah. That's right.' Tanner was walking by himself now. He'd be all right.

The telephone at the taxi stand rang across the street.

'There goes my phone . . . You okay?'

'Sure. Thanks.'

'Saturday night. Probably the only call I'll get on the whole shift. Only keep one cab on duty Saturday night. That's one too many.' The driver moved away. 'Good luck, buddy. You sure you don't want a doctor?'

'No, really. Thanks.'

He watched the driver take down an address, then heard his voice as he repeated it.

'Tremayne. Sixteen Peachtree. Be there in five minutes, ma'am.' He hung up and saw Tanner watching him. 'How d'you like that? She wants to go to a motel at Kennedy. Who do you suppose she's shacking up with out there?'

Tanner was bewildered. The Tremaynes had two cars of their own . . . Had Tremayne intended to ignore the command to meet at the Lassiter depot? Or, by making sure the single Saturday night taxi was away, was Tremayne hoping to isolate him in the Village?

Either was possible.

Tanner hobbled toward an alley running alongside of the Pub, used primarily for deliveries. From there, since it led to a municipal parking lot, he could escape undetected if it were necessary. He stood in the alley and massaged his leg. He'd have a huge welt in an hour or so. He looked at his watch. It was twelve-forty-nine. Another hour before he would drive to the depot. Perhaps the black car would return. Perhaps others would come.

He wanted a cigarette, but did not want to strike a match near the street. He could cup the glow of a cigarette, not the flame of a match. He walked ten yards into the alley and lit up. He heard something. Footsteps?

He inched his way back toward the Valley Road entrance. The Village was deserted. The only sounds were muted, coming from the Pub. Then the Pub's door opened and three people came out. Jim and Nancy Loomis with a man he didn't recognize. He laughed sadly to himself.

Here he was, John Tanner, the respected Director of News for Standard Mutual, hiding in a darkened alley – filthy, soaked, a bullet crease in his shoulder and a welling bruise on his leg from a driver intent on murder – silently watching Jim and Nancy come out of the Pub. Jim Loomis. He had been touched by Omega and he'd never know it.

From the west end of Valley Road – the direction of Route Five – came an automobile travelling quietly at no more than ten miles an hour. The driver seemed to be looking for someone or something on Valley Road.

It was Joe.

He hadn't gone to Philadelphia. There was no dying father in Philadelphia. The Cardones had lied.

It was no surprise to Tanner.

He pressed his back against the alley wall and made himself as inconspicuous as he could, but he was a large man. For no other reason than that it gave him security, Tanner withdrew the pistol from his belt. He'd kill Cardone if he had to.

When the car was within forty feet of him, two short blasts from a second automobile, coming from the other direction, made Cardone stop.

The second car approached rapidly.

It was Tremayne. As he passed the alley, Tanner could see the look of panic on his face.

The lawyer pulled up beside Cardone and the two men spoke quickly, softly. Tanner couldn't make out the words, but he could tell they were spoken rapidly and with great agitation. Tremayne made a U-turn, and the automobiles raced off in the same direction.

Tanner relaxed and stretched his pained body. All were accounted for now. All he knew about and one more he didn't. Omega plus one, he considered. Who was in the black automobile? Who had tried to run him down?

There was no point in putting it off any longer. He'd seen what he had to see. He'd drive to within a few hundred yards of the Lassiter depot and wait for Omega to declare themselves.

He walked out of the alley and started for the car. And then he stopped.

There was something wrong with the car. In the subdued light of the gas lamps he could see that the automobile's rear end had settled down to the surface of the street. The chrome bumper was inches above the pavement.

He ran to the car and unclipped his pencil light. Both back tires were flat, the metal rims supporting the weight of the automobile. He crouched down and saw two knives protruding from the deflated rubber.

How? When? He was within twenty yards every second! The street was deserted! No one! No one could have crept behind the Mercedes without being seen!

Except, perhaps, those few moments in the alley. Those moments when he lit a cigarette and crouched by the wall watching Tremayne and Cardone. Those seconds when he'd thought he'd heard footsteps.

The tires had been slashed not five minutes ago!

Oh Christ! thought Tanner. The manipulation

hadn't stopped at all! Omega was at his heels. Knowing. Knowing every move he made. Every second!

What had Ali started to say on the phone? Bernie had . . . what? He started toward the booth, taking the last dime out of his pocket. He pulled the pistol out of his belt and looked around as he crossed the street. Whoever punctured the tires might be waiting, watching.

'Ali?'

'Darling, for God's sake come home!'

'In a little while, hon. Honest, no problems. No problems at all . . . I just want to ask you a question. It's important.'

'It's just as important that you get *home*!'

'You said before that Bernie had decided something. What was it?'

'Oh . . . when you called the first time. Leila went out after you; Bernie didn't want to leave us alone. But he was worried that you might not listen to her and since the police were here, he decided to go find you himself.'

'Did he take the Triumph?'

'No. He borrowed a car from one of the police.'

'Oh, Christ!' Tanner didn't mean to explode into the phone but he couldn't help it. The black automobile out of nowhere! The *plus-one* was really part of the three! 'Is he back?'

'No. Leila is, though. She thinks he may have gotten lost.'

'I'll call you.' Tanner hung up. Of course Bernie was 'lost'. There hadn't been time for him to get back. Not since Tanner had been in the alley, not since the tires were slashed.

And now he realized that somehow he had to reach the Lassiter depot. Reach it and position himself before any part of Omega could stop him, or know where he was.

Lassiter Road was diagonally northwest, about three miles from the center of the Village. The depot perhaps another mile or two beyond. He'd walk it. It was all he could do.

He started as quickly as he could, his limp diminishing with movement, then ducked into a doorway. No one followed him.

He kept up a zigzag pattern northwest until he reached the outskirts of town – where there were no sidewalks, only large expanses of lawn. Lassiter wasn't far away now. Twice he lay on the ground while automobiles raced past him, drivers oblivious to anything but the road in front of them.

Finally, through a back stretch of woods behind a well-trimmed lawn, neither unlike his own, he reached Lassiter Road.

On the rough tarred surface he turned left and started the final part of his journey. It wasn't any farther than a mile or a mile and a half by his calculations. He could reach the deserted depot in fifteen minutes if his leg held out. If it didn't, he'd simply slow down, but he'd get there. His watch read one-forty-one. There was time.

Omega wouldn't arrive early. It couldn't afford to. It – or they – didn't know what was waiting for them.

Tanner limped along the road and found he felt better – more secure – holding Scanlan's pistol in his hand. He saw a flicker of light behind him. Headlights, three or four hundred yards away. He crossed into the woods bordering on the road and lay flat on the muddy ground.

The car passed him traveling slowly. It was the same black car that had run him down on Valley Road. He couldn't see the driver; the absence of street lights made any identification impossible.

When it was out of sight, Tanner went back to the road. He had considered walking in the woods but it wasn't feasible. He could make better time on the cleared surface. He went on, hobbling now, wondering whether the black automobile belonged to a policeman currently stationed at 22 Orchard Drive. Whether the driver was a writer named Osterman.

He had gone nearly half a mile when the lights appeared again, only now in front of him. He drove into the brush, hoping to God he hadn't been seen, unlatching the safety of his pistol as he lay there.

The automobile approached at incredible speed. Whoever was driving was racing back to find someone.

Was it to find him?

Or Leila Osterman?

Or was it to reach Cardone, who had *no* dying father in Philadelphia. Or Tremayne, who *wasn't* on his way to the motel at Kennedy Airport.

Tanner got up and kept going, his leg about to

collapse under him, the pistol gripped tightly in his hand.

He rounded a bend in the road and there it was. A single sagging street lamp lit the crumbling station house. The old stucco depot was boarded up, giant weed drooping ominously from the cracks in the rotted wood. Small ugly leaves grew out of the foundation.

There was no wind, no rain, no sound but the rhythmic drip of water from thousands of branches and leaves – the last exhausted effects of the storm.

He stood on the outskirts of the decayed, overgrown parking area trying to decide where to position himself. It was nearly two o'clock and a secluded place had to be found. The station house itself! Perhaps he could get inside. He started across the gravel and weeds.

A blinding light flashed in his eyes; his reflexes lurched him forward. He rolled over on his wounded shoulder, yet felt no pain. A powerful searchlight had pierced the dimness of the depot grounds, and gunshots echoed throughout the deserted area. Bullets thumped into the earth around him and whistled over his head. He kept rolling, over and over, knowing that one of the bullets had hit his left arm.

He reached the edge of the sunken gravel and raised his pistol toward the blinding light. He fired rapidly in the direction of the enemy. The searchlight exploded; a scream followed. Tanner kept pulling the trigger until the clip was empty. He tried to reach into his pocket with his left hand for a second clip and found he couldn't move his arm.

There was silence again. He put down the pistol and awkwardly extracted another clip with his right hand. He twisted the pistol on its back and with his teeth holding the hot barrel, pushed the fresh clip into the chamber, burning his lips as he did so.

He waited for his enemy to move. To make any sound at all. Nothing stirred.

Slowly he rose, his left arm now completely immobile. He held the pistol in front of him, ready to pull the trigger at the slightest movement in the grass.

None came.

Tanner backed his way toward the door of the depot, holding his weapon up, probing the ground carefully with his feet so that no unexpected obstacle would cause him to fall. He reached the boarded-up door, knowing he couldn't possibly break it down if it was nailed shut. Most of his body was inoperative. He had little strength left.

Still, he pushed his back against the door and the heavy wood gave slightly, creaking loudly as it did so. Tanner turned his head just enough to see that the opening was no more than three or four inches. The ancient hinges were caked with rust. He slammed his right shoulder against the edge of the door and it gave way, plunging Tanner into the darkness, onto the rotted floor of the station.

He lay where he was for several seconds. The station house door was three-quarters open, the upper section snapped away from its hinges. The street lamp fifty yards away provided a dull wash of illumination. Broken and missing boards from the roof were a second, inadequate source of light.

Suddenly Tanner heard a creaking behind him. The unmistakable sound of a footstep on the rotted floor. He tried to turn around, tried to rise. He was too late. Something crashed into the base of his skull. He felt himself grow dizzy, but he saw the foot. A foot encased in bandages.

As he collapsed on the rotted floor, blackness sweeping over him, he looked upward into a face.

Tanner knew he had found Omega.

It was Laurence Fassett.

29

He couldn't know how long he'd been unconscious. Five minutes? An hour? There was no way to tell. He couldn't see his watch, he couldn't move his left arm. His face was against the rough splintered floor of the crumbling station house. He could feel the blood slowly trickling from his wounded arm; his head ached.

Fassett!

The manipulator.

Omega.

As he lay there, isolated fragments of past conversations raced through his mind.

'. . . we should get together . . . our wives should get together . . .'

But Laurence Fassett's wife had been killed in East Berlin. Murdered in East Berlin. That fact had been his most moving entreaty.

And there was something else. Something to do with a Woodward broadcast . . . The broadcast about the CIA a year ago.

'. . . I was in the States then. I saw that one.'

But he wasn't 'in the States' then. In Washington Fassett had said he'd been on the Albanian border a year ago. '. . . forty-five days of haggling.' In the field. It was why he'd contacted John Tanner, the solid, clean news director of

Standard Mutual, a resident of the target, Chasm of Leather.

There were other contradictions – none as obvious, but they were there. They wouldn't do him any good now. His life was about to end in the ruins of the Lassiter depot.

He moved his head and saw Fassett standing above him.

'We've got a great deal to thank you for. If you are as good a shot as I think you are you've created the perfect martyr out there. A dead hero. If he's only wounded, he'll soon be dead at any rate . . . Oh, he's the other part of us, but even he'd recognize the perfect contribution of his sacrifice . . . You see, I didn't lie to you. We are fanatics. We have to be.'

'What now?'

'We wait for the others. One or two are bound to show up. Then it'll be over. Their lives and yours, I'm afraid. And Washington will have its Omega. Then, perhaps, a field agent named Fassett will be given another commendation. If they're not careful, they'll make me Director of Operations one day.'

'You're a traitor.' Tanner found something in the dark shadows by his right hand. It was a loose piece of flooring about two feet long, an inch or so wide. He awkwardly, painfully, sat up, pulling the plank to his side.

'Not by my lights. A defector, perhaps. Not a traitor. Let's not go into that. You wouldn't understand or appreciate the viewpoint. Let's just say in my opinion you're the traitor. *All* of you. Look around you . . .'

Tanner lashed out with the piece of wood and crashed it with all his might across the bandaged foot in front of him. Blood erupted instantly, spreading through the gauze. Tanner flung himself upward into Fassett's groin, trying desperately to reach the hand with the gun. Fassett screamed in anguish. Tanner found the agent's wrist with his right hand, his left arm immobile, serving only as a limp tentacle. He drove Fassett back against the wall and ground his heel into Fassett's wounded foot, stamping it over and over again.

Tanner wrenched the gun free and it fell to the floor, sliding toward the open door and the dim shaft of light. Fassett's screams shattered the stillness of the station house as he slumped against the wall.

John lunged for the pistol, picked it up and held it tightly in his hand. He got up, every part of his body in pain, the blood flowing now out of his arm.

Fassett was barely conscious, gasping in agony. Tanner wanted this man alive, wanted Omega alive. But he thought of the basement, of Ali and the children, and so he took careful aim and fired twice, once into the mass of blood and flesh which was Fassett's wound, once into the knee cap of the leg.

He lurched back toward the doorway, supporting himself in the frame. Painfully, he looked at his watch: two-thirty-seven. Seven minutes after Omega's appointed time.

No one else would come now. Half of Omega lay in agony in the station house; the rest in the tall, wet grass beyond the parking lot.

He wondered who it was.

Tremayne?

Cardone?

Osterman?

Tanner tore off part of his sleeve and tried to wrap it around the wound in his arm. If only he could stop the bleeding, even a bit. If he could do that perhaps he could make it across the old parking area to-where the searchlight was.

But he couldn't, and, off balance, fell backwards to the floor. He was no better off than Fassett. Both their lives would ebb away right there. Inside the ancient depot.

A wailing began; Tanner wasn't sure if it was a trick of his brain or if it was real. Real! It was growing louder.

Sirens, then the roar of engines. Then the screeching of brakes against the loose gravel and wet dirt.

Tanner rose to his elbow. He tried with all his strength to get up – only to his knees, that would be good enough. That would be sufficient to crawl. Crawl to the doorway.

The beams of searchlights filtered through the loose boards and cracked stucco, one light remaining on the entrance. Then a voice, amplified by a bull horn.

'This is the police! We are accompanied by federal authorities! If you have weapons, throw them out and follow with your hands up! . . . If you are holding Tanner hostage, release him! You are surrounded. There's no way for you to escape!'

Tanner tried to speak as he crawled toward the door. The voice sounded once again.

'We repeat. Throw out your weapons . . .'

Tanner could hear another voice yelling, this one not on a horn.

'Over here! Throw a light over here! By this automobile! Over here in the grass!'

Someone had found the rest of Omega.

'Tanner! John Tanner! Are you inside!?'

Tanner reached the entrance and pulled himself up by the edge of the door into the spill of light.

'There he is! Jesus, *look* at him!'

Tanner fell forward. Jenkins raced to his side.

'There you are, Mr Tanner. We've tied you up as best we can. It'll hold till the ambulance gets here. See if you can walk.' Jenkins braced Tanner around the waist and pulled him to his feet. Two other policemen were carrying out Fassett.

'That's him . . . That's Omega.'

'We know. You're a very impressive fellow. You did what no one else was able to do in five years of trying. You got Omega for us.'

'There's someone else. Over there . . . Fassett said he was the other part of them.'

'We found him. He's dead. He's still there. You want to go over and see who it is? Tell your grandchildren some day.'

Tanner looked at Jenkins and replied haltingly. 'Yes. Yes, I would. I guess I'd better know.'

The two men walked over into the grass. Tanner was both fascinated and repelled by the moment that approached, the moment when he would see for himself the second face of Omega. He sensed that Jenkins understood. The revelation had to be of his own observation, not second hand. He had to bear witness to the most terrible part of Omega.

The betrayal of love.

Dick. Joe. Bernie.

Several men were examining the black automobile with the ruined searchlight. The body lay face down by the sedan's door. In the dark, Tanner could see it was a large man.

Jenkins turned on his flashlight and kicked the body over. The beam of light shone into his face.

Tanner froze.

The riddled body in the grass was Captain Albert MacAuliff.

A police officer approached and spoke to Jenkins from the edge of the parking area.

'They want to come over.'

'Why not? It goes with their territories. The beach is secured.' Jenkins spoke with more than a trace of contempt.

'Come on!' yelled McDermott to some men in the shadows on the other side of the parking lot.

Tanner could see the three tall figures walking across the gravel, walking slowly, reluctantly.

Bernie Osterman, Joe Cardone. Dick Tremayne.

He limped with Jenkins' help out of the grass,

away from Omega. The four friends faced each other; none knew what to say.

'Let's go,' said Tanner to Jenkins.

'Pardon us, gentlemen.'

PART FOUR
Sunday Afternoon

30

Sunday afternoon in the Village of Saddle Valley, New Jersey. The two patrol cars roamed up and down the streets as usual, but they remained at cruising speeds, lazily turning into the shady roads. The drivers smiled at the children and waved at the residents doing their Sunday chores. Golf bags and tennis rackets could be seen in small foreign convertibles and in gleaming station wagons. The sun was bright; the trees and the lawns glistened, refreshed by the July storm.

Saddle Valley was awake, preparing for a perfect Sunday afternoon. Telephones were dialed, plans made, a number of apologies offered for last evening's behavior. They were laughed off – what the hell, last evening was Saturday night. In Saddle Valley, New Jersey, Saturday nights were quickly forgiven.

A late model dark blue sedan with whitewall tires drove into the Tanner driveway. Inside the house John Tanner got up from the couch and walked painfully to the window. His upper chest and his entire left arm was encased in bandages. So, too, was his left leg, from thigh to ankle.

Tanner looked out the window at the two men walking up the path. One he recognized as Patrolman Jenkins – but only on second glance. Jenkins was not in his police uniform. Now he looked like a Saddle Valley commuter – a banker or an advertising executive. Tanner didn't know the second man. He'd never seen him before.

'They're here,' he called toward the kitchen. Ali came out and stood in the hallway. She was dressed casually in slacks and a shirt, but the look in her eyes wasn't casual at all.

'I suppose we've got to get it over with. The sitter's out with Janet. Ray's at the club . . . I suppose Bernie and Leila are at the airport by now.'

'If they made it in time. There were statements, papers to sign. Dick's acting as everyone's attorney.'

The chimes rang and Ali went to the door. 'Sit down, darling. Just a little at a time, the doctor said.'

'Okay.'

Jenkins and his unfamiliar partner came in. Alice brought coffee and the four of them sat across from each other, the Tanners on the couch, Jenkins and the man he introduced as Grover in the armchairs.

'You're the one I talked to in New York, aren't you?' John asked.

'Yes, I am. I'm with the Agency. Incidentally, so is Jenkins. He's been assigned here for the past year and a half.'

'You were a very convincing policeman, Mr Jenkins,' said Ali.

'It wasn't difficult. It's a pleasant place, nice people.'

'I thought it was the Chasm of Leather.'

Tanner's hostility was apparent. It was time for explanations. He had demanded them.

'That, too, of course,' added Jenkins softly.

'Then we'd better talk about it.'

'Very well,' said Grover. 'I'll summarize in a few words. "Divide and kill". That was Fassett's premise. Omega's premise.'

'Then there really was a Fassett. That was his name, I mean.'

'There certainly was. For ten years Laurence Fassett was one of the finest operatives in the Agency. Excellent record, dedicated. And then things happened to him.'

'He sold out.'

'It's never that simple,' said Jenkins. 'Let's say his commitments changed. They altered drastically. He became the enemy.'

'And you didn't know it?'

Grover hesitated before replying. He seemed to be searching for the least painful words. His head nodded, imperceptibly. 'We knew . . . We found out gradually, over a period of years. Defectors of Fassett's caliber are never revealed overnight. It's a slow process; a series of assignments with conflicting objectives. Sooner or later a pattern emerges. When it does, you make the most of it . . . Which is exactly what we did.'

'That seems to me awfully dangerous, complicated.'

'A degree of danger, perhaps; not complicated, really. Fassett was maneuvered, just as he maneuvered you and your friends. He was brought into the Omega operation because his credentials warranted it. He was brilliant and this was an explosive situation . . . Certain laws of espionage are fundamental. We correctly assumed that the enemy would give Fassett the responsibility of keeping Omega *intact*, not *allowing* its destruction. He was at once the defending general and the attacking force. The strategy was well thought out, take my word for it. Do you begin to see?'

'Yes.' Tanner was barely audible.

'"Divide and kill". Omega existed. Chasm of Leather *was* Saddle Valley. The checks on residents *did* uncover the Swiss accounts of the Cardones and the Tremaynes. When Osterman appeared, he, too, was found to have an account in Zurich. The circumstances were perfect for Fassett. He had found three couples allied with each other in an illegal or at least highly questionable financial venture in Switzerland.'

'Zurich. That's why the name Zurich made them all nervous. Cardone was petrified.'

'He had every reason to be. He and Tremayne. One the partner in a highly speculative brokerage house with a lot of Mafia financing; and the other an attorney with a firm engaged in unethical mergers – Tremayne, the specialist. They could have been ruined. Osterman had the least to lose, but, nevertheless, as part of the public media, an indictment might have had disastrous effects. As you know better than we do, networks are sensitive.'

'Yes,' said Tanner again without feeling.

'If, during the weekend, Fassett could so intensify mistrust between the three couples that they began hurling accusations at each other – the next step would be violence. Once *that possibility* was established, the real Omega intended to murder at least two of the couples, and Fassett could then present us with a substitute Omega. Who could refuse him? The subjects would be dead. It . . . was brilliant.'

Tanner rose painfully from the couch and limped to the fireplace. He gripped the mantel angrily.

'I'm glad you can sit there and make professional judgments.' He turned on the government men. 'You had no right, *no* right! My *wife,* my *children* were damn near *killed*! Where were your men outside on the grounds? What happened to all that protective equipment from the biggest corporation in the world? Who listened on those electronic . . . *things* which were supposedly installed all over the house? *Where was everybody? We were left in that cellar to die!*'

Grover and Jenkins let the moment subside. They accepted Tanner's hostility calmly, with understanding. They'd been through such moments before. Grover spoke quietly, in counterpoint to Tanner's anger.

'In operations such as these, we anticipate that errors – I'll be honest, generally one massive error – occur. It's unavoidable when you consider the logistics.'

'*What error?*'

Jenkins spoke. 'I'd like to answer that . . .

The error was mine. I was the senior officer at "Leather" and the only one who knew about Fassett's defection. The only one. Saturday afternoon McDermott told me that Cole had unearthed extraordinary information and had to see me right away. I didn't check it out with Washington, I didn't confirm it. I just accepted it and drove into the city as fast as I could . . . I thought that Cole, or someone here at "Leather", had discovered who Fassett really was. If that had been the case a whole new set of instructions would have to come from Washington . . .'

'We were prepared,' interrupted Grover. 'Alternate plans were ready to be implemented.'

'I got into New York, went up to the hotel suite . . . and Cole wasn't there. I know it sounds incredible, but he was out to dinner. He was simply *out to dinner.* He left the name of the restaurant, so I went there. This all took time. Taxis, traffic. I couldn't use the phone; all conversations were recorded. Fassett might have been tipped. Finally I got to Cole. He didn't know what I was talking about. He'd sent no message.'

Jenkins stopped, the telling of the story angered and embarrassed him.

'That was the error?' asked Ali.

'Yes. It gave Fassett the time he needed. *I* gave him the time.'

'Wasn't Fassett risking too much? Trapping himself? Cole denied the message.'

'He calculated the risk. Timed it. Since Cole was constantly in touch with "Leather", a single message, especially second hand, could be garbled. The fact that I fell for the ruse also told him something. Put simply, I was to be killed.'

'That doesn't explain the guards outside. Your going to New York doesn't explain their not being there?'

'We said Fassett was brilliant,' continued Glover. 'When we tell you why they weren't there, why there wasn't a single patrol within miles, you'll understand just how brilliant he was . . . He systematically withdrew all the men from your property on the grounds that *you were Omega.* The man they were guarding with their lives was, in reality, the enemy.'

'*What?*'

'Think about it. Once you were dead, who could disprove it?'

'Why would they believe it?'

'The electronic pick-ups. They'd stopped functioning throughout your house. One by one they stopped transmitting. You were the only one here who knew they existed. Therefore, *you* were eliminating them.'

'But I wasn't! I didn't know where they were! I still don't!'

'It wouldn't make any difference if you did.' It was Jenkins who spoke. 'Those transmitters had operating capacities of anywhere from thirty-six to forty-eight hours only. No more. I showed you one last night. It was treated with acid. They all were. The acid gradually ate through the miniature plates and shorted out the transmissions . . . But all the men in the field knew was that they weren't functioning. Fassett then announced that he'd made the error. *You* were Omega and he hadn't realized it. I'm told he did it very effectively. There's something awesome about a man like Fassett admitting a major mistake. He withdrew the patrols and then he and MacAuliff moved in for the kill. They were able to do it because I wasn't there to stop them. He'd removed me from the scene.'

'Did you know about MacAuliff?'

'No,' answered Jenkins. 'He wasn't even a suspect. His cover was pure genius. A bigoted small-town cop, veteran of the New York police, and a right-winger to boot. Frankly, the first hint we had of his involvement was when you said the police car didn't stop when you signaled from the basment. Neither patrol car was in the vicinity at the time; MacAuliff made sure of that. However, he carries a red signal light in his trunk. Simple clamp device that can be mounted on top. He was circling your house, trying to draw you out . . . When he finally got here, two things struck us. The first was that he'd been reached by car radio. Not at home. The second was a general description supplied by those on duty. That MacAuliff kept holding his stomach, claimed to be having a severe ulcer attack. MacAuliff had no history of ulcers. It was possible that he'd been wounded. It turned out to be correct. His "ulcer" was a gash in his stomach. Courtesy of Mr Osterman.'

Tanner reached for a cigarette. Ali lit it for him.

'Who killed the man in the woods?'

'MacAuliff. And don't hold yourself responsible. He would have killed him whether you got up and turned on the light or not. He also gassed your family last Wednesday. He used the police riot supply.'

'What about our dog? In my daughter's bedroom.'

'Fassett,' said Grover. 'You had ice cubes delivered at one-forty-five; they were left on the front porch. Fassett saw the chance to create further panic and so he simply took them in. You were all at the pool. Once he got inside, he could maneuver; he's a pro. He was just a man delivering ice cubes. Even if you saw him, he could have told you it was extra precaution on his part. You certainly couldn't have argued. And Fassett obviously was the man on the road who gassed the Cardones and the Tremaynes.'

'Everything was calculated to keep us *all* in a constant state of panic. With no let up. Force my husband to think it was each of them.' Ali stared at Tanner and spoke quietly. 'What have we done? What did we say to them?'

'At one time or another I was convinced each person had given himself . . . or herself . . . away. I was positive.'

'You were looking for that desperately. The relationships in this house, during the weekend, were intensely personal. Fassett knew that.' Grover looked over at Jenkins. 'Of course, you must realize that they were all frightened. They had good reason to be. Regardless of their own personal, professional guilts, they shared a major one.'

'Zurich?'

'Precisely. It accounted for their final actions. Cardone wasn't going to a dying father in Philadelphia last night. He'd called his partner Bennett to come out. He didn't want to talk on the phone and he thought his house might be watched. Yet he wasn't about to go far away from his family. They met at a diner on Route Five . . . Cardone told Bennett about the Zurich manipulation and offered his resignation for a settlement. His idea was to turn state's evidence for the Justice Department in return for immunity.'

'Tremayne said he was leaving this morning . . .'

'Lufthansa. Straight through to Zurich. He's a good attorney, very agile in these sorts of negotiations. He was getting out with what he could salvage.'

'Then they both – separately – were leaving Bernie with the mess.'

'Mr and Mrs Osterman had their own plans. A syndicate in Paris was prepared to assume their investment. All it would have taken was a cablegram to the French attorneys.'

Tanner rose from the couch and limped toward the windows overlooking his backyard. He wasn't sure he wanted to hear any more. The sickness was everywhere. It left no one, it seemed, untouched. Fassett had said it.

It's a spiral, Mr Tanner. No one lives in a deep freeze any more.

He turned slowly back to the government men. 'There are still questions.'

'We'll never be able to give you all the answers,' said Jenkins. 'No matter what we tell you now, the questions will be around for a long time. You'll find inconsistencies, seeming contradictions, and they'll turn into doubts. The questions will become real again . . . That's the difficult part. Everything was too subjective for you. Too personal. You operated for five days in a state of exhaustion, with little or no sleep. Fassett counted on that too.'

'I don't mean that. I mean physical things . . . Leila wore a brooch that could be seen in the dark. There were no bullet marks in the wall around her . . . Her husband wasn't here when I was in the Village last night. Someone slashed the tires then and tried to run me down . . . The rendezvous at the Lassiter depot was *my* idea. How could Fassett have known if one of them hadn't told him? . . . How can you be so sure? You didn't know about MacAuliff. How do you know they aren't . . .' John Tanner stopped as he realized what he was about to say. He looked at Jenkins, who was staring at him.

Jenkins had spoken the truth. The questions were real again, the deceptions too personal.

Grover leaned forward in his chair. 'In time everything will be answered. Those questions aren't difficult. Fassett and MacAuliff worked as a team. Fassett had the telephone taps moved to his new location once he left the motel. He easily could have radioed MacAuliff in the Village to kill you and then gone out to the depot when MacAuliff told him he'd failed. Obtaining other automobiles is no problem, slashing tires no feat . . . Mrs Osterman's brooch? An accident of dress. The unmarked wall? Its location, as I understand it, makes direct fire almost impossible.'

'"Almost", "could have" . . . oh, God.' Tanner walked back to the sofa and awkwardly sat down. He took Ali's hand. 'Wait a minute.' He spoke haltingly. 'Something happened in the kitchen yesterday afternoon . . .'

'We know,' interrupted Jenkins gently. 'Your wife told us.'

Ali looked at John and nodded. Her eyes were sad.

'Your friends, the Ostermans, are remarkable people,' continued Jenkins. 'Mrs Osterman saw that her husband wanted to, *had* to go out and help you. He couldn't stand by and watch you killed . . . They're very close to each other. She was giving him permission to risk his life for you.'

John Tanner closed his eyes.

'Don't dwell on it,' said Jenkins.

Tanner looked at Jenkins and understood.

Grover got out of his chair. It was a signal for Jenkins, who did the same.

'We'll go now. We don't want to tire you out. There'll be plenty of time later. We owe you that . . . Oh, by the way. This belongs to you.' Grover reached into his pocket and withdrew an envelope.

'What is it?'

'The affidavit you signed for Fassett. Your agreement with Omega. You'll have to take my word that the recording is buried in the archives. Lost for a millennium that way. For the sake of both countries.'

'I understand . . . One last thing.' Tanner paused, afraid of his question.

'What is it?'

'Which of them called you? Which of them told you about the Lassiter depot?'

'They did it together. They all met back here and decided to phone the police.'

'Just like that?'

'That's the irony, Mr Tanner,' said Jenkins. 'If they had done what they should have done earlier, none of this would have happened. But it was only last night that they got together and told each other the truth.'

Saddle Valley was filled with whispers. In the dimly lit Village Pub men gathered in small groups and talked quietly. At the Club, couples sat around the pool and spoke softly of the strange rumors circulated – the Cardones had taken a long vacation, no one knew where; there was trouble in his firm, some said. Richard Tremayne was drinking more than usual, and his usual was too much. There were other stories about the Tremaynes, too. The maid was no longer there, the house a far cry from what it had been. Virginia's garden was going to seed.

But soon the stories stopped. Saddle Valley was nothing if not resilient. People forgot to ask about the Cardones and the Tremaynes after a while. They never fitted in, really. Their friends were hardly the kind a person wanted at the Club. There simply wasn't the time for much concern. There was so much to do. Saddle Valley, in summer, was glorious. Why shouldn't it be?

Isolated, secure, inviolate.

And John Tanner knew there'd never be another Osterman weekend.

Divide and kill.

Omega had won, after all.